Where Preda...

by

Meg Newhouse

Published

by

Sable Publishing House
PO Box 107, Wellington, Somerset TA21 1BD
United Kingdom

www.Sable-Publishing-House.com

Where Predators Roam

Copyright © 2007   Meg Newhouse

All rights reserved. No part of this publication may be reproduced, stored in a retrieval system or transmitted in any form, or by any means electronic, mechanical, photocopying, recording or otherwise, without the prior permission of the Publisher, Sable Publishing House and copyright holder, Meg Newhouse who has asserted the moral right to be identified as the author of this work.

Cover design © 2007 Sable Publishing House
Published by Sable Publishing House, June 2007.

About The Author

Meg Newhouse was born and educated in Lancashire where she now lives. She spent most of her working life in Rhodesia (now Zimbabwe) and became fascinated with the history of Southern Africa, an interest that gave rise to this, her first novel.

* * * * * * *

I have seen the sun rise on the Zambezi
and marvelled at the midnight rainbow
hanging in the swirling spray of moonlit clouds
over the mighty Victoria Falls.
I have watched vast herds of elephant, zebra, buffalo
thunder across the endless veld
raising red dust in the setting sun.
I have smelled the earth's sweet scent
when the first rain falls
and heard the soulful cry of the fish eagle
scoring the empty places with its need.
And there, forever in memory,
I tasted freedom.

Meg Newhouse
May 2007.

* * * * * * *

Dedication

For my family

John, Diane, Edgar, Douglas,
Mark, James and Philippa

Foreword

In the politically correct atmosphere of the 21st century, the word colonialism is frowned upon. With our new found knowledge and more enlightened attitudes it is easy to be critical of the men and women who set out to spread British ideas of civilization along with the Christian faith. But, like us, their beliefs were bound to the age they lived in. 'Where Predators Roam' reflects the opinions and religious faith of the Victorians as it tells the interesting story of a family travelling sixteen hundred miles in an ox wagon. Whilst the background is authentic, the charming story revolves around the heroine, 9 year old Jane Hargreaves, who has to deal with her own emotional issues whilst coping as a 'little mother'. The adventures, escapades and real life family scenes are realistic and captivating.

I make no apology for writing about Matabeleland and Southern Africa as it was in the middle of the nineteenth century. Whilst it is currently politically correct to be ashamed of the colonial era and even to apologize for it, the Victorians themselves were proud of their achievements, their country, their faith and their Queen. Rightly or wrongly they had no qualms about spreading their ideas around the globe. Their legacy lives on world wide and not only in place names such as Victoria.

We too are bound by the customs, beliefs and mores of our age, but our modern lives are easy by comparison.

The journey from Bulawayo to Cape Town now takes a few hours by air and probably less than two days by car or train, travelling in comfort. In 1865 travelling at the pace of the oxen, which was three miles an hour, the journey took several months depending on the weather, the condition of the oxen and any unforeseen events.

The land between the Limpopo and Zambezi Rivers was occupied by the San people for centuries until the arrival of the Bantu who settled there. The Matabele themselves crossed the Limpopo River from the south and took the land by force from the previous inhabitants a brief twenty years before the arrival of the European missionaries.

'Where Predators Roam' is the story of a missionary family making the epic journey of sixteen hundred miles and experiencing hardships, deprivation, fear and frustration; though there are moments of joy and delight. Who will not sympathise with nine year old Jane Hargreaves as she tries to cope with the care of three younger siblings and her own emotions? Whilst the adventures and escapades of young Harry are captivating, the story itself is enthralling.

For people who know only modern Africa the interest may lie in understanding the feelings and conflicts of the past, but the story is written chiefly for pleasure.

CHAPTER 1

1865

"Why did baby Joshua have to go and live with Jesus?"
The question was not unexpected, but it wasn't an easy one for nine year old Jane to answer. She held her little sister close and stifled her own questions and tears as she sought to answer her six-year-old sister. She knew she must comfort and console Isabelle as she had done for as long as she could remember.
They were both shivering in bed on this cold evening in early May, clinging together for warmth and comfort under the two thin woollen blankets.
Jane sighed and took a deep breath. "Joshua came too soon so he was too small to stay with us. He has gone to be a little angel in heaven," she explained carefully.
"So why did our mother have to go with him to heaven? When is she coming back to us?" persisted Isabelle.
Jane was old enough to know that their mother was dead too and that she would never come back to them, but she didn't know how to explain it to her little sister. They had not been allowed to go to the graveyard near the church where their mother and stillborn brother had been buried that morning, but she had seen the grave being dug the day before, next to the one where Mrs Thomas and her baby had been buried.
It was nearly three years since Mrs Thomas had died and Isabelle had been very small then, but Jane had been six years old and she remembered how sad all the grown-ups had been. Mother had tried then to explain how people became sick with the fever and that they died and went to live in heaven.
Two days ago, father had told all the children that their mother was very sick with fever and that she might have to go to heaven with Joshua. He had then taken them into the bedroom to say goodbye to her.
Jane gulped back her tears, "Joshua was too small to go by himself," she explained, "he needed someone to go with him. Our mother isn't coming back to us. She has to stay in heaven with Joshua. Jesus loves little children. I think Joshua will be happy there." As an afterthought she added, "I expect our mother will be happy too."
There was silence for a time as Isabelle thought about what her sister had said. Jane had said that baby Joshua needed mother to look after him, but what about herself and the two little boys, Harry and James? They needed her too.
Isabelle put her thoughts into words, "Who will look after Harry and James

and all of us now?"
This question had worried Jane for days ever since their mother had lain in bed with the fever. The two little boys had been taken to stay with the Reverend John Moffat and his wife, but the Moffats were both sick now and finding it too hard to cope with the Hargreaves boys as well as their own four little ones. Yesterday she had heard that the Moffats were going to leave Inyati as soon as they were well enough to travel and go to stay with the Reverend John's parents at Kuruman where they would be properly cared for by the Reverend Robert Moffat and his wife. When they left, Jane would have not only Isabelle, but also her two little brothers to look after and she worried that she might not be able to manage. She was quite used to caring for Isabelle and helping mother with the two boys because there was no one else to help apart from a little Matabele girl not much older than herself who really wasn't much help, but she wasn't sure that she could manage everything by herself.
She knew how to cook most meals and had been able to bake the bread by herself for more than a year now, but there were so many other things to do. Besides the cooking, baking, mending, washing, cleaning and sewing, mother had also made all their soap and candles as well as helping the missionaries with the Sunday School.
"You'll look after me won't you?" Isabelle's trembling voice interrupted Jane's thoughts. She was obviously close to tears and needing reassurance from her elder sister. "You won't leave me will you?"
Jane hugged her sister, "No of course I won't leave you. I'll look after you until you're big enough to look after yourself. Let's say our prayers now and then we can go to sleep."
Shivering, they climbed out of bed and knelt on the rug mother had made for them only a few months ago. They took it in turns to say a favourite prayer and after they had said the Lord's Prayer together Jane asked God to take care of their mother and baby brother.
Together, their teeth chattering now, they settled once more in the bed father had made for them when they first arrived at Inyati five years ago. It was made of wood and the legs rested in tins filled with water so that the white ants wouldn't eat the wood. White ants were very destructive and anything made from wood soon disappeared; fence posts and wooden buildings collapsed regularly and had to be replaced, which was an added burden for all the missionaries.
Now it was the beginning of the cold dry season and the two girls were glad to be able to snuggle together to keep warm.
"I'm not sleepy yet," stated Isabelle in a clear wide-awake voice. "Tell me

about our real mother and how you all came from England before I was born. If our real mother is in heaven she can talk to our second mother can't she?"
Jane wasn't quite sure what heaven was like. She thought it was a beautiful place with a bright shining sun, lovely music, gentle animals and angels everywhere, but whether they spoke to each other or not she couldn't decide and if they did she wondered if they spoke in English or Sindebele. It would have to be English she thought because the Matabele didn't know about heaven yet and if they didn't know about it they couldn't go there could they? Jane couldn't really remember her own mother very well, but she had told Isabelle this story so often that it had begun to seem quite real to her and she repeated it now.
"I was only little, not much older than James is now and we lived in England with grandmother and grandfather, but our father wanted to come to Africa to teach the people here about God and Jesus. He said the poor people here had never heard about God and that it was God's will that he should come to teach the heathens."
"What are heathens?" interrupted Isabelle.
"You've asked me that before and I told you. Heathens are people who don't know about God. Now don't interrupt again or I shan't have time to finish. We packed up all our clothes and we left grandfather's house in a carriage. Then we travelled in a train. Do you remember the pictures father used to draw for us when he told us stories about England? They reminded me that I was frightened of the engine at first. It was like a great big monster, a huge green dragon spitting sparks and smoke into the air. When we climbed inside the carriage it was better but it was still noisy and we swayed about from side to side going da-da-da-dum. Our mother sang it with me. We looked out of the windows at fields with sheep and horses and cattle. Sometimes we could see houses and people and carriages. Once the train gave a loud whistle and I screamed because we went into a tunnel and it was very dark. After a long time we arrived in a big town where there were many people and we went in a carriage to the seaside where there were big ships. We had to climb a steep ladder to get on the ship and we lived on the ship for a long time. Many weeks, I think. Mother didn't like it at first because it made her very sick and she had to stay in bed. I thought it was fun going up and down on the water. Our mother was pretty, with long dark hair and eyes just like yours. She used to tell me stories and play with me. She sang songs, too, and was always laughing. Grandmother has a photograph of her on her wedding day and you can see it if we ever go to England, but you've seen the photographs of our two sets of grandparents and our aunts and uncles

haven't you? Our mother is on one of them, you must remember looking at it, but she looks like a girl, not a mother.

Then we arrived in Africa at a place called Cape Town. It was funny being on land again and everyone had difficulty in walking straight. We kept expecting the ground to go up and down. It was so funny. Cape Town was busy all the time with many, many people and carts and wagons and carriages and shops. The people were all different colours, not like people in England. I was frightened when I first saw black faces.

We stayed in Cape Town for many days so that we could recover from the sea journey and buy all the food and other things we would need at Inyati. The grown-ups had a lot to do to prepare for the journey to Matabeleland, but mother and the friends who looked after us took me to play on the sand nearly every day, so it was fun for me. At last the ox-wagon was ready. You know the wagon that father sometimes uses when he has to travel to villages far away in Matabeleland that was our home until we reached Inyati. We travelled away from Cape Town along a long dusty road all the way to Kuruman where you were born and our mother died when you were about two days old. The people at Kuruman were kind to us and we stayed there for a long time whilst our father went back to Cape Town to bring us our second mother. I don't know how long he was away, you were just beginning to crawl I think and this strange man came one day and wanted to take us away. We both cried, but our new mother was kind and gentle so we soon became happy again."

"She wasn't always kind and gentle with me," interposed Isabelle. "She often got cross and shouted at me. She liked Harry and James better than me." Isabelle was feeling sorry for herself, and began to sob.

Jane was momentarily at a loss. It was true that the little boys received more attention than either Isabelle or Jane, but Jane thought that was only natural because they were younger and James was still a baby really. Besides, Isabelle could be very naughty at times. She liked to be the centre of attention and often went out of her way to get it. She was untidy with her few belongings and usually tried to shirk her chores, complaining that washing the clothes made her hands sore and abandoning her tasks, leaving Jane to do them on her own. Many times Jane had covered up for her little sister to save her from a scolding or worse. Still, there was no point in remonstrating with her now when she was already upset. Jane waited for the sobs to subside and then continued with her story. "We had another long ride in the ox wagon and sometimes we were happy, but sometimes it was hot and dry. There was dust everywhere and dust in the wind so that our eyes were sore and we cried because we were thirsty. The grown-ups were sad when the oxen died. It was very hard for everybody and our new mother thought we might never reach Inyati."

Isabelle had fallen asleep and Jane moved her arm gently away so as not to disturb her. Jane had pins and needles in her hand and she rubbed it fiercely to reduce the pain. Then she lay still, her eyes wide open looking up at the thatch. She spotted a movement on the rafter and wondered if there was a rat there tonight, possibly the same one that had fallen on her last night. There were rats everywhere and she didn't like them at all, in fact she hated the feel of their tiny feet whenever they ran over her body, but she wasn't frightened of them any more. When she first saw one in the house she had screamed and run to her father for protection. He had explained that all creatures had been created by God and that they all had a place in the world, but he also said that rats and other animals should not be inside houses, so he would try to keep them out if he could. Sometimes the rats bit people at night when they were sleeping. Jane had seen nasty sores on people's fingers and toes caused by rat bites. Rats also chewed at books, paper and clothes, as well as ruining the family food in the larder and that was why Jane disliked them.

The rats came from the town where Mzilikazi (the king of the Matabele people) had lived and from the bush all around. Now Mzilikazi had moved his town, as the Matabele did every few years, but the rats had stayed and infested every one of the missionaries' houses and their food stores. Mother and father had desperately tried to keep them out, but they still appeared everywhere. Jane didn't know which she disliked more, the rats or the snakes. The snakes ate the rats and that was a good thing, but she was still afraid of snakes. Father had told her that not all snakes were dangerous to people and she had tried to learn to identify the harmless ones. Unfortunately, the Matabeles hated snakes and killed them on sight, leaving crumpled, mangled bodies that were impossible to identify. Soon all snakes would hide away because of the cold weather, but the trouble was that they loved to hide in the thatch or holes in the walls of the house, where they were safe and warm.

Jane thought it was very strange that all the missionaries said every living creature was made by God and should receive love and care, but they went out into the bush and shot birds and animals. She knew that they all needed meat to eat, but the feathers, skins and tusks were used for trading. It was strange and she really didn't understand it.

She fell asleep thinking about the animals that were around them in the bush. Jane felt considerably more cheerful next morning when her father called her to carry a letter to Reverend John Moffat. She had already been working for several hours by then for she rose at first light to let the hens out of their small brick house. They were kept locked in so that their eggs would not be stolen or the hens themselves eaten by predators and the minute the door was open they would rush out to begin scratching in the dust for insects. Jane loved to watch them and she had a name for each hen, but she had no time to linger today. Hurriedly she collected the eggs and walked back to the kitchen hut, the hens scrambling behind her, for they were given the scrapings from the porridge pot each day. In the kitchen hut a little Matabele girl stood at the stove stirring mealie meal porridge.

Nomalanga was an outcast from her Matabele village on account of the fact that she was a dwarf. Once this was realised her family and the other villagers had chased her into the bush as an outcast. She had come to the mission for help and the king had said she might stay and be a helper. At first mother had thought it would mean just another mouth to feed although she felt sorry for the poor mite, however Nomalanga had been willing to learn the strange ways and habits of these funny people and now she could manage several tasks by herself.

Whilst the porridge was bubbling, Jane had mixed the dough for the bread and set it to rise in the warmest spot. She had then fed Isabelle and put father's breakfast on the table. She had found time to eat a little porridge herself and was planning the day's chores, pleased that the butter and cheese had been made the day before, when she heard father calling her name. She knew that she could safely leave the washing up and sweeping to Nomalanga, so she hurried out of the kitchen and across the dusty path into the house.

The Reverend Henry Hargreaves stood beside the table in the tiny room he was pleased to call his study. The door was open, but Jane stood and tapped gently on it, waiting for the summons to enter this room that was so private she must never enter without express permission.

"Ah Jane, there you are. Come in child. Now I've just written a letter to Reverend John to tell him that we will travel with him to Kuruman," he told her. "I've decided that the boys must go and stay with their grandparents in Cape Town. I cannot possibly look after them and do my work here and however good and kind you are, Jane, I know you would find it difficult to be mother to all three little ones. You and Isabelle will go to school in England. It is an appropriate time for you to be with people who are like us and to learn how English girls should behave. Perhaps you should have gone before; you are already nine years old and a little old for starting school, still it can't be helped, there never seemed to be a good opportunity before. I expect I shall travel to England with you, but I haven't made up my mind about that yet though I really need to see the Directors of the Missionary Society. There are many things to discuss. They don't seem to understand what things are like here and keep sending letters asking about the number of new converts to Christianity. That appears to be their sole concern and since we haven't yet confirmed a single Matabele it is hard to describe exactly what we are doing here in terms that would be acceptable to people who are ignorant of life in Africa. We had first to learn the language of the natives in order to converse with them and try to discover what their beliefs actually were. Then we had to know the language well enough so that we could teach Christian fundamentals. It's like trying to teach them about the sea or railways because they haven't seen them and cannot comprehend what they are. They don't even have names or words for the many things we want to describe and discuss with them and this vast void between us makes all our work slow and laborious.

We have spent hours, day and night, translating hymns and the Bible into Sindebele, but until we can teach the people to read it will all be in vain. There is no written language here and the people had never seen books before so they regarded them as a special type of magic and thought that we could give them magic to read the books. Then they resented the fact that we couldn't just do that and only came to lessons when the king expressly told them to do so. Now they don't come at all. Perhaps I can talk to the Directors myself and try to get them to understand the difficulties and that the lack of positive results is not a reflection on our labours. Perhaps I can give some lectures and earn some money for the mission. We are always so short of trade goods and have no money to buy food from the traders who make the arduous journey here. I need to tell people just how deprived we all are and how God's work here depends on their generosity."

Henry shook his head in dismay. He realised suddenly that what had begun as an explanation of future plans for the family had become a diatribe against the state of affairs in the mission and in any case it was not his custom to discuss affairs with his eldest child. Had his wife been here it would have been different. He would have been able to talk it over with her. As she wasn't, he had talked on rather thoughtlessly. He took a deep breath and pulled himself up to his full height of well over six feet. Stroking his full brown beard, he coughed to hide his embarrassment and looked into the eager brown eyes so like his own. Normally he was rather aloof with his children, though he regarded Jane as an apt pupil and enjoyed teaching her. This elder daughter of his might never be the beauty her younger sister was obviously destined to be, but if the over-wide brow and pale oval face framed by straight dark brown hair didn't attract suitors, her gentle bearing, kindness and above all her obedience surely must. Every man required a woman who was obedient, knew her place in the world and who would cater to all his needs. 'Yes,' he thought, 'she had been well trained in domestic chores and understood the value a man placed on his creature comforts.' Henry became aware that he was still clutching the letter and that his daughter was still looking at him, waiting for his instructions.

"Yes, well, here's the letter. Off you go" he ordered.

Jane couldn't contain her surprise. "Are we really going to England?" she blurted out before she could stop herself. Then more soberly she added hopefully, "May I go and tell the Sykes and Thomas families the news?" It was such a good opportunity to be outside the house and to talk to someone else that she momentarily forgot that father frowned upon impulsive behaviour. She herself visited all the families on the mission station, even though many of them didn't speak to each other, not that she ever had much time for visiting, but occasionally mother had wanted peace and quiet in the house and had asked Jane to take the younger children for a walk. Looking at her father now she saw his face darken and his eyebrows lift at her temerity.

"I thought I had told you that this family was to stay out of the squabbles of the people here. I hope you haven't been disobeying me." Jane looked at the floor and refrained from speaking. Her father let the heavy silence hang for a moment to indicate his displeasure, then went on. "In answer to your question, no, certainly not. The Reverend John must inform them because they will have to manage on their own for many months, possibly a year. It is not our place to tell them."

Chastened, Jane gave a little curtsey and hurried out through the door and into the bedroom she shared with the other children. She found her little sister sitting on the bed playing with her rag doll, and the blankets she had pulled up so neatly were in a tangle.

"Oh Isabelle," she admonished her little sister, "it's bad enough that you don't do much to help, but when you mess up the work I have already done you make life much harder for me." She was about to give the little girl a gentle slap to indicate her frustration, but Isabelle opened her hazel eyes wide and gave her sister a warm impulsive hug. "Sorry Jane, I didn't mean to wrinkle the blankets. It just happened." It was the usual excuse, but Jane felt her disappointment evaporating as she contemplated the news her father had divulged only a short time before.

"Alright, just be more careful next time. Now come on, we're going out for a walk and I have some exciting news to tell you."

Jane helped Isabelle to put on her boots and laced them up for her. She put on her bonnet and tied the ribbons gently but firmly under her chin, then gave her a shawl to put over her shoulders. Her own bonnet and shawl were soon put on and the two of them left the house.

Isabelle, holding tightly to Jane's hand, was watching her with surprise at the contained excitement in her elder sister. Gone was the serious and tearful expression of the past weeks and in its place there was a secret smile.

Looking through the tiny window of his study the Reverend Henry Hargreaves watched his daughters walk along the path. Jane with her straight back and sedate walk, as her parents had taught her, Isabelle bouncing along beside her, her dark curls rising and falling with each springy step that threatened to dislodge her bonnet. The dark curls came from his side of the family, as did Jane's brown eyes, but Isabelle had her mother's hazel eyes and happy disposition. He thought of his first wife with a pang of regret, she who had suffered many miscarriages denying him the joy of sons when he had longed for them, and who had then died so suddenly at Kuruman after Isabelle's birth leaving him distraught and alone in a country where it was essential for a man to have a woman at his side.

His second wife had given him little Henry (named for his father but called Harry to distinguish between them) and James. Now she too had left him, and again with the burden of small children. There was nothing to be done about it here in this wilderness. He would have to seek a third wife, either in Cape Town or back in his native Yorkshire. He must make sure that he picked a girl who was sturdy and healthy enough to face the rigours of this heathen country and who was capable of bearing him more children. Four children were hardly enough for a healthy young man in his prime and who believed in the biblical teachings: Genesis Chapter 1 v28: 'and God said unto them, 'Be fruitful and multiply' and again in Chapter 3 v16: 'in sorrow thou shalt bring forth children'.

A man needed daughters to comfort him and bring comfort to him in his old age. Sons he needed aplenty to bear his name into the future and if necessary to support him for the rest of his life. Who knew how many children would survive into adulthood anyway? God took the young and the old indiscriminately.

In addition to following the injunctions of the Bible, from a purely practical point of view his four young children needed a mother to care for their needs. Henry was averse to admitting man's baser needs, his own in particular. He couldn't altogether ignore the demands of his loins, but strict prayer and strong personal discipline helped. He refused to be like some of the traders and hunters who eased their needs with the native women. Henry couldn't understand how any man of education and breeding could behave like an animal of the field just to relieve the demands of his own body. It was beyond his comprehension. The hunters of the Transvaal were sensible, practical men, who brought their wives and families with them in their wagons for the six or seven months of the hunting season. Family life for them never altered or faltered, only the location changed. Well, he, Henry Hargreaves would have to wait many months, perhaps even a year, before he could remarry and resume a normal life again, and it was a daunting thought. With difficulty Henry brought his thoughts back to the immediate future. He had made the decision to leave Inyati immediately after his wife's death when he had stopped to consider his changed circumstances and what it meant to his family, now he needed to sit down and make a list of the things that had to be done before he could depart.

The very first thing would be to obtain the king's permission to cross the Limpopo. No one might enter or leave Matabeleland without Mzilikazi's permission. The king (with his army) had conquered the inhabitants of this land less than thirty years ago, killing most of the residents. He then held the remainder in thrall, guarding the land he had taken with fierce and determined pride. Like any conqueror, he regarded the land he had stolen as his by right and there was no one strong enough to deny him. The Reverend John Moffat would be able to arrange an audience with the king, as he had more influence. Henry would talk to him about it. The family would need two wagons, one as a home, the other to carry their trade goods and other chattels. Henry already had a suitable fully tented wagon, it was the one he had bought in the Cape when he had first arrived there in 1859 and he also had a baggage wagon, but he had only one span of trained oxen. It was essential that he obtain at least another sixteen trained beasts, preferably one or two more even, as untrained oxen were a danger and went wild when they were in-spanned for the first time. They could easily destroy a wagon. Henry remembered the chaos in Cape Town at the very beginning of the missionary venture when untrained oxen were yoked to the Moffats' wagon. They were lucky to avoid a very nasty disaster. As it was, the family was considerably shaken and some of their goods destroyed. Henry wondered where he might buy trained oxen. He might be able to buy some from Mzilikazi or one of the traders at the king's town. He would ask Thomas' advice.

The Reverend Thomas Morgan Thomas was a taciturn man who was frequently at loggerheads with the other missionaries, but he and Henry managed to get along quite well. Thomas was a practical man from a poor background and with little education until he had reached manhood. Then, by his own determined efforts, he had taught himself, and even taken a medical course. This stood him in good stead in the wilds of Africa, making him a favourite with the king, whom he had managed to cure of illness on a number of occasions.

Henry continued with his list. He would need to make some spare yokes and carry at least one spare disselboom and probably a replacement wheel. He thought he had better write a note to Thomas immediately, but, changing his mind, he decided to go and talk to him instead, risking John's wrath as he would have to disclose his intention to depart to Thomas and before John himself had been able to inform his colleagues.

Henry set off to the forge where he knew Thomas was working this morning, still ruminating about the necessities he must arrange for the journey he was contemplating. The problems seemed endless, but talking them over with Thomas would help.

CHAPTER 2

Jane and Isabelle walked along the path towards the Moffats' house. They waved to the young Matabeles who were herding the cattle and the even younger children who were herding the goats towards the stream from the thorn-fenced kraal where they had been kept all night. They called out greetings to them in the formal way of the people. Both Jane and Isabelle spoke Sindebele almost as well as English, though with a different vocabulary. Many common English words such as fork, glass and book didn't exist in Sindebele, because these items were unknown to the Matabele people.

Every week Jane and Isabelle went with the family to the Sunday services in the church the missionaries had built. They also attended the Sunday school their mother had started. They had soon picked up simple words and phrases in Sindebele and once they had made friends with the native children their vocabularies had increased by leaps and bounds. By the time she was seven Jane had begun to tell stories about Jesus to the smaller children in the Sunday school by looking at her own book written in English and immediately translating the words into Sindebele. In her light, clear voice she had also helped her father to teach some of the hymns he had translated.

Jane had always been interested in the lives of the Matabele children whose customs were so different from her own. She loved the little black babies with their soft skin and large brown eyes. She once longed to have a baby strapped to her back just like the young Matabele girls did whilst their mothers were working in the crops. She had asked mother if she could carry James on her back like the natives and mother had been horrified.

The Matabele people were fascinated by the shape of the missionaries' houses and couldn't understand how they could have windows to look through, but not climb through, as windows and glass were new conceptions to them. They called the windows 'seeing, seeing,' and loved to peer through them. The houses the natives lived in had no windows, they were round and low and dark and smoky inside.

Since the king had left, because his chief town was moved to a different location, the new native settlement at Inyati was much smaller. Almost all of the people had followed the king to make a new town many miles away to the southwest. Father had explained to her that the land round a native town soon became poor and over-used. It was also dirty and pest ridden. In addition, there was no longer enough grazing for the cattle and goats, so after a few years the king would order his people to move to a new site chosen near a river many miles away.

The old houses were destroyed and nature could take over once again. At Inyati the soldiers of the Inyati regiment with their families had stayed behind, but they had built a new village on the other side of the mission.

Jane didn't like going inside the village huts, they frightened her with their low doorways and flickering shadows, but Isabelle loved going in them and Jane often had to overcome her fear and go inside to find her when she disappeared just as she was supposed to be helping with the washing.

Nomalanga sometimes took the boys to the village for a walk. Harry and James became familiar with the eating habits of the Matabele and were quite happy to sit and dip their fingers into the communal mealie porridge pot, then scoop up the pumpkin or bean relish and eat it with evident appreciation. Mother had been absolutely horrified when they had tried to follow the custom at home instead of using their spoons and forks. Fortunately she hadn't told father, who had been away from home at that time or both boys would have been spanked and Jane had since been able to keep them out of trouble by carefully supervising them at meals.

Thinking of food reminded Jane that she would have to make the bread and prepare lunch before too long. There was some meat left over from the funeral meal, so if she had enough vegetables she could make a stew. Finding enough food was a constant worry even with the dam and the fine vegetable garden started by the Reverend Robert Moffat five years ago and she remembered mother being in tears about the shortage of food, especially after visits from the king and his followers. The Matabele had enormous appetites and although meat was their favourite food they became addicted to sugary tea and coffee served with all the newly baked bread, cakes and pies prepared by the missionary wives. No one could refuse the king's demands and he had a habit of appearing on baking days when he and the people with him would consume the family's weekly supplies at one sitting. These hearty appetites condemned the missionary families to real hunger at times and they would be forced to watch in anguish as their supplies were demolished.

Jane's thoughts about lunch and food were forgotten when the gate of the Moffats' garden was reached. Jane and Isabelle saw their young brothers playing in the dust by the door alongside the Moffat children, Livingstone, Mary, and Bruce, who were being watched over by a nursemaid not much older than Jane.

"Harry, James," shouted Isabelle happily as she rushed towards them. Jane walked more slowly and decorously, as she had been taught. Decorum was a word that had been instilled in her from an early age and she knew that young ladies did not rush about madly.

Isabelle would have to learn to contain her impulsive nature thought Jane, and she would have to be the one to teach her. Nevertheless her heart was full of love and warmth as she swung James up into her arms and put a hand on Harry's shoulder as he flung his arms around her, his boisterous welcome almost sweeping her off her feet.

"Steady there," she said through her laughter, "you'll knock me over and then who will pick me up?"

"We will, of course," stated Harry stoutly. "I'm strong enough to pick you up and Livingstone will help me won't you?"

Livingstone, the eldest of the Moffat children grinned at Jane, who smiled back at him. Then she looked at Harry and smiled fondly at him, "I expect you are, Harry. You are both big and strong." She put James back on his feet. "Just wait a minute now. I have a letter to give to the Reverend John, then I can come out and play with you all for a short time before I go home."

Once Henry's decision to leave had been accepted and made official, the following days went by in a whirl of excitement for Jane. Her imagination, usually kept in tight check, was now allowed full rein. She really couldn't remember what England was like and she had absolutely no recollection of the hardships of the lengthy journey from the south, but leaving a house that was sad and gloomy without mother's presence, especially in the bleak winter weather, was like one of her fairy tales. She had been facing endless days of drudgery trying to be mother to a young family, facing food problems daily and trying to cope with the washing and ironing. Suddenly the future prospect was completely changed. They would all be living in a wagon and on the move every day and it was true they would still need to eat, but she knew that the servants going with them would help and somehow it was all so exciting the thoughts of daily duties no longer weighed so heavily. When she arrived in England she would go to school and that too would be exciting. She knew she would be sad to leave the two little boys behind in Cape Town but as that farewell was many weeks away she refused to even think of it just now.

They had very few clothes or other goods to take with them and packing would occupy only a few hours once the departure date had been set, so Jane's days followed the same routine as previously. The animals still needed care, food had to be cooked and the house kept clean. She was very strict with Isabelle and made sure that she did her share of the work, reminding her constantly of what mother would have wanted and how mother did things.

Both girls wept for their mother when they had time to think of her and longed for her to be there to help them. It was hard for them to realise that she had gone out of their lives forever.

Little Harry and James went to stay at the Thomas' house as Mrs Moffat was still not very well and the adults decided that Jane shouldn't have the extra burden just yet. The missionaries were waiting for the king's permission to leave and John and Henry had to make arrangements for their duties to be either shelved for the time being or undertaken by the two families who were remaining. In addition, the wagons had to be fully serviced and sufficient trained oxen acquired.

Two houses were to be left empty, but visiting hunting parties and even travellers wanting to visit the magnificent Victoria Falls discovered by David Livingstone almost ten years previously would appreciate such accommodation, poor though it was. It was better to keep the houses aired and in use as much as possible, as they would soon deteriorate.

All the books, clothes, curtains, furniture and rugs would have to be removed and items that couldn't be fitted into the wagons would be given to the remaining families on the understanding that if anything survived the year it would be returned. Rats, dormice, cockroaches, wasps and white ants would destroy anything other than metal and stone and they were a constant menace to the four households.

When at last the king's permission was received, packing began in earnest. The larder was emptied and any food not required for the journey was shared out between the two families staying behind. There was precious little anyway as tinned and dried goods would be needed on the trek, but the pumpkin, bean and onion harvest had been a good one that year so some of these could be happily distributed. Most of the livestock had to be left, too.

In return, the Thomas and Sykes families offered practical help. They also took this opportunity to write letters to family and friends far away. Small gifts were hastily wrapped, as this was one of the few occasions when such items could be sent. Mail arrived at Inyati infrequently, usually once every six months and suitable mail carriers were welcomed with feelings of joy by the news-starved missionaries. On this occasion post for Kuruman was given to the Moffats and mail for Cape Town or overseas was handed to Henry, since he could take it all the way himself.

At last the day of departure dawned and everyone was astir early. The Reverend Thomas, with his new wife, Caroline, brought Harry and James across to the Hargreaves' house.

The two boys had not been home since before their mother's death and they raced around calling for her. Over and over their pitiful cries echoed through the four empty rooms. "Mama, mama, we are home. Where are you?" Isabelle was in floods of tears as the grown-ups tried to catch the boys and explain to them that their mother was in heaven. Harry evaded capture and James scuttled behind his brother, sobbing for mama with every breath he took.

Jane finally managed to hold onto Harry long enough to say, "Mama isn't here, Harry. She is in heaven now."

"You told us that before," shouted Harry angrily. "That was when we were away, but now we are here. Where can we find her? She must come back for us now." His fear, frustration and anger filled his whole body and he was almost hysterical. James too was infected by his brother's tantrum and sobbed inconsolably, "I want mama!" Isabelle's cries only added to the chaotic scene and Jane felt utterly powerless. Soothingly she spoke to her little brothers, holding them close, knowing that father would soon lose his temper at having to endure such a display.

Caroline Thomas led Isabelle outside, telling her gently but firmly that she must try to be brave and not upset the little ones any more.

Gradually Isabelle controlled her sobs and when prompted to find some toys for Harry and James she produced two clay oxen she and her friends had made only the day before. The models were handed over and slowly the boys calmed down as Jane gently wiped their faces, speaking comfortingly all the while.

Jane led the boys outside and showed them that the oxen were about to be in-spanned, an activity she knew would divert them and with Nomalanga to watch them she would be able to complete the packing. She had wasted enough time already. Caroline would willingly have helped but she was expecting a child shortly and had been warned not to exert herself too much.

The children were soon enthralled by the sights and sounds of oxen being in-spanned with shouting, whistling, bellowing, calling, the rattling of chains and cracking of whips and other noises and the general hustle and bustle involved in trying to push and pull sixteen huge beasts into position. Each ox had its own place and partner in the span and would refuse to be anywhere else, so it was important for everyone to know each beast and where it had to be yoked. Nomalanga had the greatest difficulty in keeping the children out of danger.

Harry, his tears and questions momentarily forgotten, constantly leapt up and down, waving his model ox in the air as each ox was put into place. Unaware that he was doing so, he moved closer and closer to the scene of action.

For reasons known only to herself, Isabelle chose this moment to reclaim her model ox from him and a tussle ensued. In fury, Harry dragged his precious toy out of his sister's reach and raced round the back of the wagon, Isabelle chasing after him. He looked back to see if she was catching up with him and tripped up, falling under the back wheel. Fortunately the brakes had been applied, but the whole wagon moved backwards just enough to pin his sleeve to the ground and pinching the flesh of his arm. He screamed in terror and pain. The grown-ups came running at the sound of the screams and Henry, who was the first one to arrive, grabbed his son from the ground to yank him out of harm's way.

Partly because he had received a shock and partly because he was having a frustrating morning, Henry was furious with his son and he took out his anger on Jane too, blaming her for allowing the accident to happen. In vain she tried to explain that she had been carrying the family blankets to make up the beds in the wagon. Her explanations fell on deaf ears as her harassed father strode off back to the wagon carrying the trade goods. Jane bit back the tears of frustration and anger that her father hadn't even bothered to listen to her explanation, whilst Caroline led a sobbing Harry back out of harm's way. He still clutched his clay ox and looked furiously at Isabelle who was frightened at what had occurred and, knowing that Harry could have been seriously hurt, she ran inside the house and hid.

No one knew she had gone until her absence was noticed much later when Caroline went in search of her. There were few hiding places in a small empty house so Isabelle had hidden behind the door to her father's study. Caroline soon spotted her and, talking kindly to her, persuaded her to come outside.

"It's alright, Isabelle. Harry is fine now. He had a nasty fright and he will have a bruise on his arm, but there are no bones broken. You must come and say you're sorry though and you must also apologise to your father and Jane, as they both had a shock. Indeed we all had a fright, but it's all over. Come."

Reluctantly, Isabelle took Caroline's hand and was led outside to make her apologies. Henry looked stern and told her gruffly that she had better learn how to behave like a young lady in future adding, "If you give someone a present you cannot and must not try to take it back. Remember that, young lady. I never want to see such behaviour again."

Crestfallen and close to tears, Isabelle said she was sorry to Harry and Jane. She was relieved when Jane took her hand and gently kissed her cheek. All was now ready, the four wagons fully laden and the oxen waiting for the command to start. Gravely the children said goodbye to Mrs Thomas and to the Reverend William Sykes, who had arrived with his wife to wish them god-speed. The four missionary families gathered together for prayers and blessing not only for the journey ahead, but also for the wellbeing of the families left behind.

The children had asked if they could walk for the first half-hour and permission was given as long as they stayed well away from the wagons. Only baby Ruth with her nursemaid would be riding in the Moffat wagon as they set off on the great adventure. The three men mounted their horses and John Moffat gave the order to start. The long whips, expertly wielded by the drivers, cracked in the air above the leading oxen and the bulky, unwieldy vehicles creaked and groaned forward one after the other.

Behind the four wagons bulging with family belongings there were two spare horses, extra oxen, a milch cow and some goats to provide milk for the children or meat at a later date. Some of the hens and two piglets were confined in cages at the back of the family wagon and these too would provide food on days when the men failed to shoot game on the journey.

So at last the Hargreaves and Moffat families, eleven people in all, waved goodbye to those left behind in this lonely wilderness, for that brief moment forgetting the daily disputes and animosity that had marred their lives, as tears and sadness filled their hearts.

CHAPTER 3

Jane, Isabelle and Livingstone, who was only eleven months younger than Isabelle, could keep pace with the oxen quite easily. Harry and James with Bruce and Mary Moffat also marched sturdily along for the first half hour, but as the younger ones kept playing chasing games they were soon exhausted and Harry was delighted when he was lifted into the saddle in front of his father. He emitted gleeful shouts at the others until admonished by his father. Nomalanga had to carry James for a time as he had begun to lag and Bruce and Mary too had to be carried by their nursemaids. Within the hour they reached a deep gully with no easy way around and the leader had to find a suitable crossing place. He finally chose to cross at a place where the banks were less steep. Even so, such obstacles were dangerous, as wagons could easily overturn or the disselboom might break and wheels crack. The foot passengers stayed well away as the wagons lurched their way through, but followed on before the animals were driven across.

All the children decided to ride on the wagons now even though the rough ground made the ride very uncomfortable. The three men took it in turns to ride in front of the little convoy for a time before changing to ride behind or alongside. The man in front had to look out for the best road through the trees and assist the leader to avoid unnecessary obstacles as well as choosing the smoothest route. The man at the back often rode in a cloud of dust stirred up by the moving wagons and animals in front of him, all the while making sure that there were no stragglers. The man on the flank kept an eye on the full length of the cavalcade as far as he was able and watched the children if they were walking to make sure they came to no harm.

No danger was expected on this first part of the journey as hunters and the local people had killed many of the wild animals and, although there were predators about at night, they were unlikely to attack a large noisy party travelling in daylight. The missionaries were also safe from any ill-intentioned Matabele soldiers because they were specially protected by the king's orders. This didn't mean that their goods wouldn't be stolen and every effort had been made to ensure that all belongings were secured as tightly as possible. The sail of the tented wagon and the tarpaulin over the wagon were fixed as tight as was humanly possible to prevent wandering hands from removing precious belongings or equally precious food.

The Matabele were well known for helping themselves to anything that took their fancy and very clever they were too at acquiring other people's property. Several men (missionaries, hunters, traders and travellers alike) had lost hats from their heads or blankets from their beds whilst being distracted by a group of wily young Matabele who would crow in delight at their own cleverness and success. Bandages and medicines had been known to 'disappear' from medical cases. Often other goods such as clothes might be missed by their legitimate owners after a visit by a crowd of natives, an annoying and frustrating experience. It was one of the difficulties the newcomers to the country had had to face and endeavoured to prevent. The missionaries had laboured to instil the Ten Commandments in their flock, but they had to admit complete and utter failure.

By mid-morning, after more than three hours' trek, John Moffat, who was riding point at that stage, called a halt. They had arrived at a stream where pools of water were clearly visible at intervals in the otherwise sandy riverbed. Henry, who had been riding far behind, came galloping forward to discover the reason for the stoppage.

"Hello there, Thomas. What's happened? Why have we stopped?" he called out as he came abreast his colleague who was riding parallel to the wagons.

"We've reached water and this is a good place to give the animals a drink and a rest. We've not had any stoppages this morning so we've covered a good few miles," explained Thomas.

"Well, I fully agree that the animals must be in need of water and a rest, I could do with something myself, I'm absolutely parched after riding in the dust you all create, but I think we should cross over the stream before we outspan, then we can make a straightforward move this evening."

"That certainly makes fair sense. We don't want to tire out the beasts at the beginning of the evening trek and they are pulling well still so they can manage these banks easily now. Let's go and consult with John, before he off-saddles and the men start to unyoke the oxen."

Thomas and Henry galloped forward through the bush calling to the drivers to remain in their seats as they were to cross the stream immediately. They found John already dismounted and leading his horse into the shade. He stopped abruptly as the two others skidded to a halt in a whirl of dust and Thomas shouted to the driver of the Moffat wagon to climb back into his seat. John wasn't pleased to have his two colleagues interfering with his orders and was about to countermand Thomas' direction when Henry held up his hand pleadingly.

He spoke urgently, but quietly, "Let's just discuss this privately, if you will John. It's not going to help any of us if we start arguing in front of the servants."

John looked questioningly at Henry, who now dismounted so that he could talk to his colleague on the same level and appear less threatening.

"Look, it was my idea. I thought it would be advantageous if we took the wagons across the drift now. The beasts are still in good condition and it won't take us too long, then we can all have a decent rest. When we in-span again this evening we shall all be refreshed and can make an immediate start without having to face this obstacle. Later in the day it could be dark by the time we are all on the other side or if we got stuck we might have to spend the night here."

Thomas, unusually for him and very sensibly on this occasion, said nothing, but nodded his head in agreement. He realized that any comment he might make could exacerbate an already delicate situation, resulting in a fiery argument with John digging in his heels and insisting upon an immediate out-span. John stared hard at Henry for a full minute, then, obviously reaching the conclusion that his colleague was not questioning his leadership, but was making an honest and fairly sound proposal, he nodded curtly. Mounting his horse once more, he indicated that they should examine the stream banks to find the best place to cross.

They had gone no more than thirty yards northwards through the bush when they came to a place where it was obvious that other wagons had made a crossing at some time in the past. There had been an attempt to cut the banks into a gentler slope and the men could see that the bed of the river here was of smooth rock. It was ideal.

They rode quickly back to where they had left the wagons. The Moffat wagon was too close to the stream to turn easily so Henry took his wagons through first. The passengers, meanwhile, had prudently dismounted to avoid the unnerving tilting of the wagon as it went from the top of the riverbank to the bed of the river several feet below. The loose animals came hurrying after the Hargreaves wagon as they smelt the water and it was with the greatest difficulty that the drovers kept them to one small pool.

Emily Moffat and her little family had to wait for some time for their wagon to arrive. Turning a wagon and sixteen oxen in the bush was no mean feat and a huge turning circle was required before the Moffat wagons could turn northwards towards the crossing place.

By midday the oxen had been unyoked and taken in relays to the pool. It took the full strength of every man present to maintain any order as the huge beasts became uncontrollable when they scented water.

Water for travellers and servants alike had been collected from a pool further downstream, as the animals trampled in the water and soon made a mud bath instead of a pool. The hens and piglets had also been released to join in the fun and the children watched in fascination as almost a hundred animals churned the water into thick black mud. The two piglets were a joy to watch as they rolled over and over, squealing with delight and somehow managing to evade the thumping hooves and flashing horns in the melee around them.

Two of the servants had collected a pile of wood and immediately set about making a fire to boil the water for coffee. Jane was particularly delighted that this would no longer be her chore, in fact she might only have to be responsible for looking after the children for the next few months and supervising their meals, a possibility she contemplated with quiet delight. Nomalanga was there to help her at least as far as Kuruman and would do the washing in addition to washing up the cooking pots which was such a chore because the pots were heavy and black with soot.

Emily had suggested that all the midday meals should be cold ones with bread and butter when they had it with cold meat or cheese and possibly bread with jam or biscuits afterwards with a cup of milk for the children and coffee for the adults. The families had agreed that this was a good plan as they all preferred to eat a hot meal in the morning and another at night when the weather was colder than at midday.

Whilst the children were engaged in watching the animals and were supervised by the nursemaids, Emily and Jane set the table for the grown-ups and buttered the bread. They made sandwiches with thin slices of meat or cheese and put these on plates for the little ones.

When all was ready, the children were brought to wash their hands and faces in a bowl of water before saying a prayer. They were then seated on a kaross with their plates of food beside them. The mugs of milk were given out after the food had been eaten and had to be carefully held to avoid spillage on the kaross.

Everyone was happy to enjoy a picnic atmosphere with all the fun of eating outside and being allowed to sit on the ground. Jane felt she was rather too grown up to be forced to eat with the little children, but she realized that she would not be allowed to eat with the grown-ups and listen to their conversation so she accepted her place and tried to feel happy, too.

At home, the whole family sat round the table and Jane had been able to talk to mother and father sometimes when they had permitted conversation.

The children had completed their meal, though the adults had barely begun theirs, when to everyone's surprise a crowd of villagers appeared. They surrounded the little encampment and stood staring at the missionary families whilst calling and shouting to each other in loud voices.

White people had lived in Matabeleland for nearly five years now and white hunters had travelled widely throughout the countryside, but most Matabele people had never seen a white person before and practically none had seen a white woman or white children, so these rarities excited great interest. Egging each other on and with a boldness that surprised the families the villagers pushed closer and closer. The smell of smoke and hot bodies was overwhelming in the confined area round the wagons.

Emily put her arms protectively round Bruce and Mary as they ran to her in fear, and drew them to her whilst John called to the servants, who were seated under the trees close by roasting and eating their meat, and told them to go and sit on the wagons to guard them. Henry followed suit, but realised that it was probably an empty gesture as most of the servants were Bechuanas who had come from Kuruman and were despised by the warlike Matabele. Luckily, just then Thomas spotted a man he had seen before and called out to him in Sindebele, "Greetings, friend. Are these people from your village?"

At the sound of their own language the general hubbub of the crowd ceased as everyone stopped talking to listen to what the stranger might say. They all looked at the man Thomas had addressed and waited for his reply.

"I am the headman of the village. These are my people," the fellow stated with obvious pride, then he patted his cheek insolently and continued, "I know you, Thomasi. You pulled out my bad tooth and never gave me a present." This statement was made in a highly aggrieved tone of voice.

For reasons unknown to the white people, the natives expected gifts continuously and for the most obscure reasons, but would give nothing in return, not even their labour if they could avoid it.

Thomas now remembered this man, who had arrived at the mission with a badly swollen face and suffering excruciating torment from an abscess under a rotten tooth. He had been able to pull out the tooth and had treated the infected gum for several days until it had healed, and the man was delighted. However, instead of offering payment for his successful treatment and showing gratitude for the alleviation of his pain, he had demanded a present. The missionaries themselves were desperate for food and clothing and frequently did without things themselves in order to minister to the people they had come to help, so it wasn't possible to keep handing out gifts.

Despite being informed that there was nothing to give him, this man had stayed at Inyati, pestering Thomas continually for a gift of calico, beads, powder or shot and refusing to leave until he was paid. Eventually he was given some meat a hunter had brought in as a gift for the missionaries and with very bad grace he accepted a large portion. When he finally departed, grumbling as he did so, he was heard to threaten the lives of those who had dared to deprive him of what he considered his by right.

Remembering all this Thomas realised that the fellow would be no help to them at all. Far from assisting the missionaries to cope with the crowd and perhaps persuade them to depart peacefully he was more likely to consider this an opportune moment to gain as many goods for himself as he possibly could.

Thomas related his experiences with this headman to John and Henry and they all agreed that it would be useless to appeal to him for assistance in persuading the villagers to disperse. The crowd had little to interest them in daily village life, especially in winter when there were no crops to tend, so the arrival of the missionary party was considered to be a wonderful diversion, with much to fascinate them. There was the language to listen to and the clothes to be felt, there were actions and customs to observe as well as wagons, tables, chairs and cutlery to discuss. Those who could reach the white people wanted to touch their skin and their hair as well as their clothes, which was annoying for all concerned.

Emily, especially, was disinclined to bear any more of this sort of attention and asked John to escort her with the two children to their wagon, where the baby was asleep. It was with the greatest difficulty that they managed to force their way through the crowd and then prevent people from climbing up into the wagon after them. With Emily safely inside, John fastened the opening tightly then asked the driver to be on guard, giving him strict instructions not to let anyone mount the wagon. The driver agreed, on the promise of a small gift, and swung his whip menacingly to show that he was in charge.

Returning to his colleagues, John initiated a discussion on the best course of action. Their meal still lay unfinished on the table and was in danger of disappearing should they move away at all, in fact they were lucky that it was still there, but none of them felt inclined to try to eat it in the present situation.

Suddenly Thomas nodded at Henry and reached out to remove the four mugs from the table. Deftly Henry lifted the tablecloth with the plates, cutlery and food inside and lifted the whole feast into the air just as several hands reached forwards to grab it and the three men were rudely jostled. Maintaining his balance with difficulty, Henry placed the cloth and its contents in his own wagon where one of his servants was already seated on the driver's box. He handed the man the driver's whip and told him to protect the wagon and its goods from thieves.

"My!" ejaculated John, with admiration in his voice. "That was better than the theatre. It looked a bit like a magic trick I once saw. You must have had a lot of practise. What made you both act just then?"

Henry and Thomas looked at each other and Henry spoke for them both. "We both heard a whisper and sensed that that little group of young men was going to act together immediately. I'm surprised it took them so long. They're not usually so slow. We were lucky not to lose everything."

CHAPTER 4

Whilst the men were discussing ways and means of persuading the crowd to depart, the children were all happily playing. Jane knelt on the kaross with James and showed him how to draw pictures in the sand with a twig. Isabelle, Harry and Livingstone had collected sticks, stones and small seedpods and were engrossed in their own game.

Normally all the children had a rest on their beds after lunch, but as they had all spent quite some time in the wagons that morning it was decided that they would be better playing in the fresh air for a time and Jane was asked to supervise them as the nursemaids and Nomalanga were still eating. Harry had wanted to play hide-and-seek, but Jane had vetoed that as she wanted to be able to keep her eye on them all and wasn't at all keen to have to search the bush for them. Harry was annoyed by that decision and it was obvious that he was about to make a strong protest, when Livingstone had brought out two miniature wagons beautifully carved out of wood.

"Let's play with these," he said holding them up for the others to see.

"We can make roads with sticks," suggested Isabelle.

"Yes and these seed pods can be the oxen," added Livingstone.

"I'll make the roads," stated Harry boldly. He held a strong stout stick in one hand, sitting astride it like a cockhorse. Clicking his tongue, he trotted around, making furrows in the dry surface of the soil.

The villagers were fascinated as they stared at these strange children in their odd clothes and talking their unknown language. The Matabele were practically naked, wearing only small aprons fore and aft hanging from a string around the waist. A few of the older women also had skin cloaks over their shoulders to protect them from the winter chill. It was a novel sight for them to see people, especially children, not only clothed from head to foot, but also to have coverings for their feet. Imperceptibly, they crept closer, hoping to touch one of these little strangers, to feel their clothes and their skin.

The children, who could all understand Sindebele and had spent their whole lives with the Matabele people, were oblivious to the crowd around them and ignored the loud remarks as being commonplace.

"Ah, look! See how white is their skin!" called one.

"Those girls are covered all over. They look as if they are hiding," shouted another. Everyone laughed.

"They don't want us to see them," a man replied. There was more laughter.

"Why do they cover their feet like that?" asked a child.

"Perhaps their feet are not like ours," came a reply.

"Aieee, look at their hair, it is long like the lion's hair," observed an old man.

"Yes that boy's hair is like the grass in winter," agreed the man next to him.

"Have you seen his eyes? They are like the sky," cried a young girl.

With his long fair hair and bright blue eyes, Harry had once been ashamed of looking so different from his native playmates and had desperately longed to have dark brown eyes and a shiny brown skin so that he could be like them. More recently however he had become proud of his looks and his likeness to his parents.

As he grew tall and strong for his age, with a natural flair for leadership and a bold sense of adventure, his goatherd companions began to treat him like a young god who persistently led them into a variety of escapades from which he always escaped unscathed. Now he stood and looked straight at the crowd, preening himself like a young cockerel, flinging his head from side to side, causing his silken locks to ripple in the sunlight. The women in the group ululated and laughed in delight, clapping their hands and urging him on.

Henry caught a glimpse of what was going on out of the corner of his eye and turned to see exactly what Harry was doing. He was not at all pleased to see his son acting in such a brazen fashion and called out sharply, "Harry. That is quite enough. Stop it at once. Go back and play with Isabelle and Livingstone this minute."

Harry knew better than to defy his father and, giving his audience a pert grin, sheepishly returned to his game. As he passed Jane she gave him a slap on his bottom, "You're always up to mischief and you know father will blame me if you don't behave yourself." She admonished him, but her slap was more like a gentle pat and left him totally unworried.

The children continued with their game of in-spanning and out-spanning their 'oxen' from the wagons and were unaware of the crowd drawing ever closer.

Jane, though, was beginning to feel shut in and was about to speak out, when, in a flurry of movement, a youth leapt forward and grabbed up the wagon Harry had been purposefully propelling forward along his road.

His concentration shattered, Harry let out a roar of fury and, jumping up, he grasped hold of the stick he had used to make the roads. His shouts of annoyance, spoken automatically in Sindebele, were followed by a stream of language he had obviously learned from the goatherds. Then in one fluid movement he flung his stick like a spear and caught the fleeing thief full in the back of his neck. The youth fell sprawling and moaning to the ground.

With amazing speed Isabelle jumped to her feet and reclaimed the wagon that had fallen to the earth undamaged. She handed it to Livingstone who thanked her and hurried over to his father, feeling relieved to have both his toys safe. Isabelle looked at the prostrate youth and smiled in triumph. She remained staunchly at her brother's side and added her insults as Harry paused to draw breath.

Henry had been involved in a serious discussion with Thomas and John, but had deliberately positioned himself so that he could keep an eye on the children. He had watched in amazement as the drama had unfolded much too quickly for him to prevent any of it. The snatching of the toy and Harry's volatile reaction could perhaps have been foreseen, but the fluent invective that followed filled Henry with deep shame and annoyance. Henry was uncertain of the meaning of many of the words Harry was aiming at the youth as his own knowledge of Sindebele was limited to his translations of hymns, the Bible or to the domestic scene, but the gist was unmistakable. He was stunned not only by his son's diatribe, but also by the fact that he had felled one of the villagers. When he realised that his pretty little daughter was aiding and abetting her brother, Henry was completely scandalised. What a great embarrassment this was with his two colleagues as interested spectators.

Not only was Henry appalled by the events he and everyone else had just witnessed, but there was also an underlying fear that the crowd might seek retribution. Automatically he stepped forward, intending to take part in the scene either as a peacemaker, protector or to censure his son, whichever proved more appropriate. He wondered if presents would be demanded to pay for the attack and following insults.

To his surprise Thomas laid a restraining hand on his shoulder and held him back. "Wait. Just wait and see what happens," he urged.

Astonishingly, far from being angry at the fracas, the villagers had been utterly diverted and thoroughly delighted. They began to laugh and jeer at the young man who had attempted to steal the toy and failed, as he staggered to his feet looking discomfited and rubbing his neck ruefully, though entirely unhurt. He might have a slight bruising at the back of his neck, but it was the shock and the proximity of his fellows that had caused his over-reaction to the feeling of humiliation as he had actually tripped up just as the stick had hit him. He felt even more mortified by the taunts from the crowd not because he had tried to steal from the children but because he hadn't succeeded and even worse he had been bested by a child only half his size.

Harry, who was not quite five years old, was tall and well-built for his age and had spent more than a year playing with the goatherds whose chief pastime whilst caring for their charges all day was to throw sticks and stones at different targets. Harry was much stronger than most of his contemporaries and had developed an astonishing accuracy, so that he could hit a moving target without difficulty nine times out of ten. On several occasions he had brought home doves that he had killed and his mother had been grateful to him for providing much needed food for the family.

The villagers now began to clap slowly and stamp their feet rhythmically, at the same time chanting praises for Harry. "Young warrior, destroyer of enemies. Young warrior, leader of men." These lines were repeated over and over as the noise reverberated through the bright afternoon sunshine and dust rose over their heads to dance in the sunbeams slanting through the trees.

Jane had watched the action unfold without any attempt to interfere; now she judged it was time to take her siblings to the wagon before Harry started any more nonsense. Holding James by the hand, she walked over to where Isabelle and Harry were still standing side by side.

"Come Isabelle, and you too, Harry. It's time to wash your hands and faces and have a short rest. You have had a long time to play today, so don't argue, just do as I say."

With a bright, charming smile for the villagers, Jane led the way back to the wagon, followed slowly and reluctantly by Harry and Isabelle. Quickly they rinsed their hands and faces in a bowl of water and with James they clambered up into the wagon, over their father's bed onto their own.

They were both aware of their father's stern disapproval and hoped to avoid any retribution by creeping quietly past him and refraining from any remarks as they lay down without a sound. Jane sat on father's bed and began to read. She knew that father was extremely angry with them.

Henry was in a quandary since his son's actions had received such vociferous approval he could hardly show his own disapproval in this public place. He wasn't about to let the incident be forgotten or remain unpunished, but that would have to wait for an opportune moment. Of one thing he was very sure, his children were in need of strict discipline and he couldn't understand how he had failed to notice it before.

Meanwhile, there were more pressing matters needing his attention. He would deal with the children later, he assured himself.

The adults had been disturbed during their meal and were anxious to finish eating, though reluctant to do so in front of a noisy audience members of which might easily grab the food from the table.

Emily, who had retired discreetly to the Moffat wagon earlier, had been sitting on the wagon seat for some time past and had witnessed the confrontation between Harry and the youth. Now she joined the men to ask if they had decided on any action.

John turned to her with a smile, "Thomas has just been telling us about the headman of this village who came to Inyati once and demanded presents when Thomas saved him a great deal of pain by removing a tooth." Emily smiled in acknowledgement and sympathy as John went on, "We all know that the demand for presents is impossible to avoid and we are equally aware of the persistence of these people aimed at wearing down opposition. They are determined to force us to accede to their demands. They never give up, do they?" John looked at each of them in turn. "Has anyone any idea of how we can be left in peace?"

"Well one thing is certain. We can't give presents to the whole village," stated Thomas forcefully. "It might be possible to bribe the headman with the promise of a gift later if he leads his people away now, but knowing this man he will hang on like a leech, demanding everything we have and once we give in we shall never be free of demands."

Henry was the next to speak up, "I'm not in favour of offering bribes or presents to anyone. We have weeks of travelling ahead of us with insufficient food to see us through without buying provisions at villages on the way. Our trade goods are very limited and we cannot afford to part with lead or powder as we need all we have to shoot for the pot.

Even if we go out hunting every day we cannot guarantee to provide enough meat for the servants as well as our families. Why is it, I wonder, that these people think we have endless stores and goods to give away, when actually we are very poor?"

Emily smiled at him and spoke gently, "Our goods are different from theirs and therefore attractive to them. A coat or dress is highly prized however old and tattered it might be because they have no such items and no means of procuring them. Acquiring beads and baubles makes them richer than the next person. The only thing they aren't interested in is money, as it has no meaning here."

Henry acknowledged her wisdom, "Yes, of course you're right Emily, but we are likely to be besieged and pestered at every stop we make and it will become unbearable. Being surrounded and touched, facing the possibility of losing precious goods and food, being badgered and plagued for gifts and at the same time being insulted and almost manhandled is not to be lightly borne. We shall have to make our position clear right from the start. If we stand firm and tell these people that we are friends of the king going to his town by invitation and that all our goods are the king's then they must respect that. Furthermore we shall tell them that we will report their behaviour to the king."

John nodded, "Harsh words, Henry. We have always turned the other cheek in our dealings with the Matabele and trodden softly to avoid offence or confrontation. Perhaps we are becoming less forgiving. I must say that we have never had quite as much trouble on previous journeys to the south, but that might be because there are different villagers near here now."

"You are right in your supposition," interposed Thomas. "I had forgotten it until now, but this headman used to live in the north-east and if I remember rightly I heard that he had cheated two traders not long ago by reclaiming some cattle he had sold them. They lost their cattle and the goods they had used to pay for them. I hadn't heard that he had moved south so it must have been quite recent. He will certainly see us as a source for his own enrichment. It would be best if you spoke to him, John."

Thomas was planning another hunting and trading trip to the north as soon as he had been given leave by the king and he was keen to avoid any confrontation with the Matabele. This headman already bore him a grudge and he had no intention of aggravating the situation. It was astounding how quickly news travelled around the country and reputations or lives were easily lost.

Henry agreed that as the son of Robert Moffat, the king's beloved 'Mshete', John was the best person to speak to the headman and the crowd and try to persuade them to return to their village as there was no benefit for them in remaining.

Accordingly, John took a commanding position in the middle of the small space still unoccupied and, calling for silence, he introduced himself as the son of Mshete. The crowd fell silent. Everyone in Matabeleland had heard of Mshete, the man who had visited Mzilikazi long ago in the country south of the Limpopo before he had crossed that river and conquered the inhabitants of this country he now called his own. The villagers gazed at the young bearded white man as he proceeded to tell them about the mission at Inyati and the missionaries intention to visit the king. In a country with no newspapers or official messengers of any kind it was amazing how news travelled like a bushfire throughout the land and even if they never went to Inyati or personally saw the missionaries they were familiar with them through oral reports. The Matabele couldn't really understand these strange white men who did not come to trade or to hunt like the other white men, but who talked of a God of kindness and love. It was an alien conception for a warlike race. Even more peculiar was their insistence on only one wife for a man when they all knew that a man needed as many wives as he could afford, hundreds for the king, many tens for the chiefs and up to ten for the successful warrior.

John tailored his speech to suit the Matabele custom of approaching a subject by a roundabout way. "This man is Thomasi who is a special friend of the king. He has cured Mzilikazi many times and made him well again. The king needs to see him now. Thomasi is travelling to see the king. Mzilikazi is our friend who has cared for us for all the years we have known him. He will be angry with anyone who steals our goods or stops us from reaching his town. We shall tell the king that we have seen his people of this village. We shall tell him that you have been friendly to us and helped us."

Every time the king's name was mentioned the people shouted loudly and the string of praise names lengthened with the repetition. The missionaries were all accustomed to this and waited patiently for the shouts to die down and for John to continue. John looked directly at the headman and asked him, "Do you want me to tell the king that you are the best man to be headman of this village? Do you want us to praise you for your help?"

The man was silent. Then in a surly voice he muttered to his followers, "We must obey the king."

It took a long time, but eventually the crowd dispersed, issuing threats as they departed.

"The king should let us wash our spears in their blood so that we can have all their goods."

"We shall destroy them. We should do it now."

Having heard these threats before, the men shook their heads sadly, but Emily was very pale and declared that she would feel better if she could have a strong cup of coffee.

At last, with a sigh of relief they were all able to sit down to the unfinished meal, thankful that they were all safe and that to the best of their knowledge nothing had been stolen.

* * * * * * *

CHAPTER 5

Once the wagons were all on the move and he had time to spare during the early part of the evening trek on that first day of their journey, Henry took Isabelle and Harry to task. Leading them well away from the families and out of sight of the wagons, he chastised them both, after venting his displeasure at their behaviour in no uncertain terms. He left them in no doubt that their conduct had shocked and shamed him. "No respectable person should ever behave in such a fashion and I certainly do not want to witness this wantonness ever again. Your mother would have been deeply ashamed to think that her children had acted like savages."

Henry was almost at a loss for words as he tried to convey his anger without losing control of himself and by mentioning their mother he had in fact caused the children more hurt than his caning had. They hung their heads in shame and tried to subdue their sobs.

Once he had accepted their apologies and promises not to err again he allowed them to rejoin Jane and Nomalanga who with James were keeping pace with the Hargreaves wagon.

They ran up to their big sister and each quietly took hold of one of her hands. Jane could tell by their demeanour that they were both considerably chastened. Isabelle had been caned on her hands and was stifling sobs, but Harry, whose bottom was still stinging from his caning, had wiped away his tears and was pretending that nothing untoward had happened.

Henry, still feeling ruffled, was somewhat mollified by the apologies and assurances of better behaviour in the future, but as he mounted his horse once more he was satisfied that his decision to take his family back to civilization was the correct one. "Not a moment too soon," he muttered to himself. "I hope they have now learned a lesson and will control their tongues in future. I have been too lax with them. I should have seen that they were running wild. Perhaps I should have taken them south before now, although it just never seemed to be the right time and there was always so much to be done. How Sykes and Thomas will manage on their own I don't know, especially as they dislike each other so much.

Still I can't stay to help them, especially now that I'm aware how much these children need to learn how to behave like Christians in a civilized world."

He rode on beside the wagons, lost in his own thoughts, until he remembered that he must keep a sharp lookout for wild animals at this time of day. Casting aside his worries, he cantered in a wide arc, searching the bush ahead and behind the wagons and being extra careful to explore the areas where people were walking. No one had seen lions or wolves in this area for a long time, but it was essential to be wary. He called out to Jane and told her to walk closer to Emily who was just ahead and advised her that if the wagons had to stop for any reason before the evening out-span she was to climb on board with her brothers and sister.

Jane had been well aware that Isabelle and Harry would be chastised. She had seen the stern expression on their father's face when they had both shouted insults at the thief and again when he called them to him as the trek got underway this evening. On another occasion she would have given both of them a warm, sympathetic hug and told them that the soreness would soon wear off, but her sympathies were not with her siblings just now for she realized that she also would receive a reprimand. In vain she tried to think what she could have done to prevent an incident that had happened so quickly whilst she was fully occupied with James that she had been unable to react any quicker than she had done. She had never heard Harry speak like that before and although some of the words were unknown to her she felt sure that they were oaths, the sort of words she shouldn't know.

Only once, when she was quite young, had she let slip a forbidden word that she had heard one of the hunters use and hadn't realized that it was a swear word. The reaction from mother had been instantaneous, a slap on the face and the washing out of her mouth with soapy water. The horrid taste and the shock of incurring such fury was an occurrence Jane had never wished to repeat. Although the incident had taken place several years ago the shame was still with her and since then she had regularly reminded both Isabelle and Harry what would happen if they ever repeated some of the words they heard used by their Matabele friends or by visiting traders and hunters.

Until now Harry had been able to restrain his impulsive tongue in front of his parents, but obviously the sheer impudence of the youth in stealing his toy and the fact that he was speaking in Sindebele had blown all caution out of his mind and he had reacted as he would have done when out in the bush with the goatherds. Jane couldn't find it in her heart to blame him for reacting so quickly to the theft, though she wished he hadn't been quite so vehement and forceful in his actions and his language. Still, Isabelle had managed to rescue Livingstone's model wagon and that was satisfactory. What a day it had been with the rush early in the morning to complete the packing, the distress of the boys when they couldn't find their mother, Harry's accident under the wagon, the long day of travel and the unpleasant altercation after lunch. Jane hoped that the next day might be easier for her as she still had to face father's wrath.

The children had been given a meal of hot soup and bread before the evening trek had begun and needed only milk and a biscuit when the oxen were outspanned for the night. Once Jane had put the younger ones to bed she went to see her beloved cow and the other animals in the thorn fenced kraal beside the baggage wagons. As the eldest, she was always allowed to stay up for almost an hour after family prayers and the time when the younger ones were sent to bed. At home she had spent the time reading by candlelight or listening to her parents discussing their day's work. On this cold evening she preferred to be with the animals rather than crouching by the campfire.

As she walked round the back of their family wagon she whispered soft goodnights to the piglets and hens in their cages and hoped that they wouldn't be too cold as they stayed hidden in their thick straw then she pushed through into the kraal. She could sense the quiet, warm feeling of contented animals and hear their gentle breathing amidst their stirrings and movements. The oxen were dark shapes against the flames of the fires in the background as they lay on the ground, but the horses were tethered to the wagons, each with a blanket over its back to protect it from the cold, as horses were precious and needed to be tended with care.

The goats were huddled together in a group further away nearer the fires, where the servants were still cooking their evening meal. The fires would be kept burning all night, with one of the servants to tend them if they burned low. Wild animals didn't like fire and the light they gave off enabled a watcher to see the eyes of any predator, giving him time to act and rouse the rest of the camp.

Behind her, Jane heard the branches of the thorn fence rustle and crackle as someone pushed through the gap by the wagon where she had entered. She turned quickly with breath indrawn until she recognized her father.

"Jane!" The voice was slightly irritated. "There's no need to be startled. I need to talk to you and this is a good place and time to do so," he stated clearly, but quietly.

It was exactly what Jane had expected and she was relieved that it would soon be over and that she wouldn't have to wait in suspense any longer.

Henry continued quietly but forcefully, "You were a witness to that appalling scene after lunch. You heard what Harry and Isabelle had to say. You saw how Harry attacked the Matabele youth. Do you condone such behaviour?"

Numbly Jane shook her head then realising that her father was waiting for a reply she spoke softly, "No father."

"You did nothing to stop them. You sat there and watched as if it was entertainment for your benefit," he went on accusingly.

Oh how unfair! She had been concentrating on James and had been as surprised as anyone else by the rapid chain of events. She had been totally dismayed by what had happened and too shocked to act immediately. As soon as she had been able to gather her wits together she had taken the children to the wagon, fearing for their safety in case the crowd had reacted angrily. Why had father not acted? He had been standing almost as close as she had been and could have reached Harry probably more quickly than she could.

"Well, I'm waiting for your explanation," Henry prodded.

"I'm sorry father," she whispered. "I was trying to teach James his letters and we were drawing pictures. I wasn't watching the others. They were all playing so happily."

"It was your task to look after all the children, not just one. You are the eldest and your mother relied on you to teach the younger ones how to behave. You should know that language has to be moderate at all times and tempers controlled. Harry's outburst was atrocious and his conduct downright wicked, whilst Isabelle's behaviour was worse because she is older and of the gentler sex and should know how to restrain herself in front of others. How can I introduce children with such outrageous behaviour to our friends in Kuruman and later to our relations in Cape Town?"

Jane could think of no response to this that would in any way calm the situation and remained with bent head, accepting the rebuke, however unfair she deemed it to be. The silence dragged on endlessly before her father spoke again, still furious, though wanting to appear forgiving.

"Well I shan't chastise you this time, but I shall hold you responsible for Harry and Isabelle's behaviour in the future. I expect you to ensure that they act like civilized people at all times and woe betide you or them if they disgrace themselves again." With that parting shot Henry strode off back to the campfire.

Jane watched her father go and gulped back a sob of frustration. She was much too young to understand the total humiliation felt by her father as he heard his two young children express their anger and contempt in such a crude fashion, especially with Thomas and the Moffats as interested spectators.

Henry frequently felt depressed by the complete lack of progress made by the missionaries to instil Christian virtues in the Matabele people. Despite all the sacrifices they made, the deprivations and isolation, the discomforts, hardships, dangers and often near starvation their zealous efforts had fallen on stony ground. It was the bitterest blow to discover that instead of civilising the savages and setting them a good example, his own family had become barbarians. It was the ultimate shame.

As he reached his seat by the fire and nodded to his companions he did acknowledge to himself that the blame didn't lie entirely with Jane. His wife had been too fully occupied with domestic tasks and the evangelical duties she had undertaken. Perhaps some of the blame must lie with her, as she was ultimately responsible for the children's upbringing in an environment that precluded governesses and nursery-maids.

All the children needed to be in a more civilised society, he thought, if they were to learn to become acceptable by that society. Nevertheless he was right to chide Jane. As the eldest she must be in control and teach the younger ones, as their mother would have done. Satisfied, he leaned back in his chair and joined in the evening's discussion.

In despair Jane flung her arms round the cow's neck, "Oh Sandy," she sobbed, "you are my only comfort."

Her tears flowed freely down the warm, soft brown hair under her cheek as, for a time, she was consumed with misery and felt lost in the utter hopelessness of her position.

She loved her sister and little brothers dearly and had thought that this journey, with fewer domestic duties, would give her more freedom to enjoy their company and be herself. Instead she faced bigger responsibilities because father was now with them all day and was fully aware of all their actions. Harry's escapades at home had gone unobserved for the greater part by both their parents who were occupied elsewhere and even Jane was privy to only a few of them which she had discovered quite by chance. His impulsive daredevil nature was exploited by his playmates who incited him to tackle feats they would hesitate to attempt themselves. Of course he had adopted their words and sayings as if they were his own, it was natural when they were out in the bush. Jane understood the differences between behaviour and language at home and the customs to be followed when they were with the Matabele. "Why, oh why, can't Harry be more careful?" she agonized.

Slowly her tears dried and she patted Sandy's shoulder as an acknowledgement of the solace offered by the gentle beast. Often she had milked the cow when Nomalanga or her parents were not available to do so and there was always consolation to be gained when she rested her head against the solid body. It was a pity that Sandy would have to be left behind at the king's town to be returned to Inyati later. "I hope you are still at Inyati when I come back from England. I shall be grown up then. Will you still recognise me, I wonder?" The thought was intriguing and she bade the animals goodnight, feeling less upset and more in control.

Father was right, now that mother had gone she was in charge of the children. Fathers went to work, mothers looked after the house and the children which was hard work too, but wasn't as important as men's work. At least, she thought, I'm better off than the Matabele girls who have to grow all the food and carry all the water as well as look after the house and children.

Calling goodnight to the adults still talking by the fire and shivering in the cold night air, Jane climbed up into the wagon and crawled across her father's bed. Removing her shawl, dress and boots she slipped into the one already occupied by her siblings, glad of the warmth of their bodies. The flimsy canvas tent saved them from wind and rain, but did little to keep out the cold. Despite her shivering, she was so exhausted she soon fell asleep.

*   *   *   *   *   *   *

CHAPTER 6

The children slept through the early morning trek that had begun before dawn the next day, only waking when the Bembesi was reached and they were dragged out of bed, hurriedly dressed, hauled out of the wagons and led staggering sleepily across the sandy river bed.

In the middle of the river bed there was a narrow band of water still flowing but not deep and only a few yards wide and servants were detailed to carry the smaller children across. Emily chose to be lifted into the saddle behind John from where she clung grimly to him as he splashed through the drift.

Henry took up Harry and James as a special treat, but Jane had the indignity of being carried and she was resentful of the fact that father would only let the boys ride; she ignored the fact that Isabelle and the Moffat children were all being carried because she was nine years old and a young lady not a child. For years she had pestered her father to let her learn to ride, pleas that became even more persistent when Harry began his riding lessons at the age of two. Father consistently refused because he didn't have a lady's side-saddle and he said firmly that no young lady would ever be allowed to sit astride a horse. It was all so unfair.

"I wish I was a boy," she thought rebelliously. "They have all the fun and none of the work that we have to do."

Nevertheless, she stood up like a young lady when the river had been traversed, shook her dress into place and, taking Isabelle's hand, led her up the western bank.

The breakfast fires had already been lit on this farther bank and they were all glad to stand near the warmth they afforded as the morning chill seeped through their hastily donned clothes. Breakfast, however, was delayed as the first wagon sank in the deep sand, and it was a full hour before it was dragged up onto the bank and along past where the fires had been lit, allowing room for the following wagons to pass.

The children had gradually awakened properly and like Emily had been interested in the efforts to move the wagon.

All the men and servants, even the nursemaids, were fully employed in heaving and pushing. Levering the wagon up with poles under the back axle then hastily pushing forward with people at the back and the sides and on each of the wheels with others urging on the oxen, a foot would be gained as everyone strove to pull the dragging wheels clear of the sand.

It was with the utmost efforts of all that the vehicle was prevented from slipping back six inches each time and when the water was reached the work was even harder.

The little ones soon became restless as progress was slow and time was passing with no sign of their breakfast arriving. Harry wandered away from the fire and discovered that his breath hung like a white cloud as he puffed out. "Look I'm a dragon," he called out to the others. "I'm coming to eat you up." He ran round and round roaring and puffing and using his hands like claws. The other children screamed in happy delight as they joined in the game and pretended to run away from the dragon.

Emily looked at Jane and smiled, "Young Harry is so full of energy. I hope his grandparents will be able to tame him."

She sounded as if she considered this would be unlikely thought Jane ruefully watching her brother race around through the bush yelling loudly. Perhaps she is right Harry is certainly a handful.

"At least the children will all keep warm by running about, but I wish they would be a little less noisy," sighed Emily, shivering and holding her hands out to feel the warmth of the flames.

Jane felt there was censure in Emily's voice and wondered if she should make her brother come and stand quietly by the fire, but it was cold and there were no chairs where they could sit down. She herself was soon tired of standing still and wished that she too could run about to keep warm. Emily didn't look well and complained of having another headache, which perhaps explained her irritation with the children whose happy shouts had earned her disapproval.

"Shall I ask Nomalanga to fetch some water now?" Jane asked Emily. "The men have stopped for a rest while more oxen are being brought to add to the span."

"Yes dear, do that. If we have boiling water ready, the coffee and the porridge shouldn't take too long to prepare. I shall be ready for a cup of coffee when the wagon finally arrives."

"I could find the coffee and meal in our wagon," Jane offered. "If I bring it across now, we could start cooking right away and the little ones can have their breakfast without having to wait for your wagon."

"That is an excellent, and a very kind, thought," agreed Emily. "It is obviously going to be a long time before I can reach my stores."

On being called and told of her new task Nomalanga was happy to leave the heavy work in the sand and water. With one of the nursemaids she walked back to the Hargreaves wagon that was still stationary on the eastern bank, and collected the water containers. They walked upstream away from the place where the oxen and men were churning up the mud and soon filled all the containers, carrying them on their heads, as was the custom, back to the picnic place. Jane then asked Nomalanga to go back to their family wagon to bring over the supplies of coffee, sugar, milk and meal. She also remembered to ask for the large pot for the porridge and a kettle in which to heat the water for coffee.

Emily was leaning against a tree, looking very pale. Jane asked Nomalanga to make yet another journey to the Hargreaves' wagon to collect cups and plates, two chairs and a blanket.

Emily sank gratefully into one of the chairs and wrapped the blanket round herself as Nomalanga began to make the porridge and Jane put a kettle of water on one of the fires to heat for the coffee.

When the Moffat wagon was finally pulled up onto the bank, Emily roused herself and with her nursemaids to help, she set up the tables ready for breakfast whilst the men went back with the oxen to bring across the baggage wagon.

They had found a place where the ground was firmer just a little way downstream and bringing the next three wagons across, whilst still requiring strenuous effort, was considerably less time consuming.

The children, meanwhile, were called to the tables where, after hand washing and the saying of grace, they were seated on the chairs on piles of pillows so that they could reach the table to eat their porridge and drink their milk. They may be out in the bush and on a journey which undoubtedly would entail hardships of many kinds, but Emily was determined that good manners and civilised behaviour must be maintained. After breakfast they would all go down to one of the pools to wash, once John or one of the other men had declared it free of crocodiles or other dangerous creatures.

It was several hours before everyone had eaten and the animals had been allowed to drink at the river. At last John was able to call for the oxen to be in-spanned again, a task that was becoming easier as everyone was more practised and Henry was greatly relieved when they were on the move without any unwanted visitors appearing, though it was nine o'clock by now. The only village near this place was a military kraal close to the eastern bank of the Bembesi not far from their overnight out-span. It had been almost deserted as the wagons passed by in the early morning light. No doubt the soldiers were away on the king's business and Henry smiled grimly to himself as he thought of what that business might be.

Sometimes the soldiers were sent to destroy a Matabele village by killing every one of the inhabitants and burning the huts, taking away any usable goods they could find. This happened if the headman had incurred the displeasure of the king in some way or had broken the law.

Occasionally it happened if someone in the village had attracted the ill will or jealousy of a member of the king's court. Then the offended man would go to the king with an accusation of witchcraft, demanding retribution.

The soldiers sent to carry out the king's orders did so with delight and cruel efficiency even if the village concerned included some of their own relations. Every person would be brutally murdered from the very old to the newborn babies.

The missionaries had longed to stop this custom, but their own position in the country was far too precarious to risk not only their own lives but also the lives of their wives and children.

Regretfully they could only hope and pray that one day they would carry the message of peace into the heart of government here and persuade Mzilikazi and his councillors to deal more leniently with the people and possibly refuse to believe in witchcraft. Perhaps that was expecting too much, despite God's help.

Henry had been at the king's town once when a triumphant impi had returned from a successful raid on a Mashona kraal. The soldiers, singing a song of victory and jubilation, had been welcomed by the whole population of the town with shouts of joy and acclamation. The warriors, waving their spears and occasionally beating them on their shields, had pushed and herded their stolen cattle, goats and captive prisoners before them. Each slave carried the spoils pillaged from their village. Henry had seen the fear, shame and desperate sorrow in the bent heads and slumped shoulders as the beaten women, youths and children submitted to the blows, jeers and insults of their captors. They were now slaves and would have to obey their new masters. Forced to forget their murdered families, previous lives, language and customs they would become the lowest caste in the Matabele nation with the youths trained to become Matabele warriors.

In this way Mzilikazi's army grew ever larger and his herds increased more rapidly than just by natural increase.

Henry was jerked out of his reverie when his horse stumbled, forcing him to recollect where he was and what he was supposed to be doing.

As all was quiet and he was riding on the flank Henry cantered forward to talk to John, who was a short way in front.

The road, if it could be called a road, was particularly wide at this point. Trekkers tended to make their own road, especially if previous travellers' wagons had made deep ruts or trees had re-grown after being partially chopped down. In parts there were five or six different wagon tracks side by side as visitors had been using this route for more than five years.

John welcomed Henry's company and the two walked their horses along companionably.

"We were fortunate to enjoy our breakfasts in peace and quiet today," remarked Henry. "It was a great relief to me when we set off without being set upon."

"Indeed it was," John agreed, "but I don't suppose we shall be so lucky every time we stop. I'm not sure whether we are regarded as a source of entertainment, relieving the boredom of uneventful lives, or as eternal providers."

"Probably a little of both, and as if the begging and stealing weren't enough, we also have to accept the threats," Henry added with feeling.

"We certainly have made little headway with teaching the Ten Commandments. Christian teaching is so foreign here I wonder sometimes if we will ever convince these people that the only way to live is by God's law."

"We can but hope and pray," said Henry sententiously.

"Yes, of course. We wouldn't be missionaries if we didn't believe in our duty to God and we must accept that it is God's will that we are here, but I shan't be sorry to arrive at Kuruman and leave Matabeleland behind. Still, we should be at the king's town tomorrow and I for one will be relieved. Emily is not at all well and needs to be able to rest quietly. Riding in the wagon isn't restful and the only alternative is to walk, which tires her. We may have to stay at the king's town for a longer period than we had planned."

Henry nodded sympathetically, "I noticed how pale she was yesterday and she was certainly weary after walking across the river bed this morning. The fever is a curse in this country and we all grow weaker each time we suffer the infection."

He sighed deeply, remembering how his wife had suffered, being doubly weakened by childbirth. Determinedly, he cast his gloomy thoughts aside as he remembered what he had thought about earlier.

"I wonder if we ought to arrange a time each day for the children to have lessons," he suggested casually. "It is many weeks before we reach Kuruman and even longer before I arrive at Cape Town. It isn't good for them to miss out on their schooling for so long. What do you think?"

John looked speculatively at Henry and a smile tugged at his mouth. "Worrying about young Harry are you? Think he needs to be kept in check, perhaps?"

Henry felt himself redden. It had occurred to him last night, whilst worrying about Harry's behaviour, that the discipline of lessons might curb Harry's exuberance a little, forcing him to sit still and concentrate on serious matters instead of mischief. It had indeed been the chief reason for his proposal, as he would need the help of both John and Emily when she was recovered fully. The Moffat children would also have to be included in the lessons.

John peered at Henry and shouted with laughter at his colleague's obvious discomfiture.

"Oh Henry, most men would give a fortune to have a son like young Harry. He is clever, robust and is obviously going to be a great sportsman. I for one have on more than one occasion longed to be able to do what Harry did yesterday; stopping and punishing a thief. We as God's workers have to restrain our impulses and turn the other cheek however strong the temptations. Of course we are in a vulnerable position too as we have to maintain peace amongst our flock who suffer restraint only from their king. If we stepped out of line in any way the mission would be imperilled. We might lose our lives along with our families too."

Henry nodded soberly. John was right in his assessment of their position, but his appreciation of Harry's actions had ignored the diatribe spoken in fluent Sindebele.

"It wasn't so much Harry's action that worried me, it was the fluent abuse with which he was obviously familiar. How can a boy not yet five speak like that when he comes from a home where the spoken language never admits oaths? Never, ever, has he heard profane language."

John realized how much this meant to Henry so he did his best to reassure him. "Children learn a great many things from their parents, but they also learn from friends and acquaintances. Possibly they learn most from their peers. Young Harry has spent many hours with the goatherds over the past months so it was inevitable that he would pick up their habits just as he learned to throw and aim so accurately playing games with them.

Now he will go to school in Cape Town and eventually he will forget the unfortunate words he picked up so readily here. Forget it, Henry. Sometimes in this man's world it is a help to know rough language, but it is also useful to know when and where to use it. Harry used it yesterday and it earned him praise from the crowd, if he uses only polite language in polite society he will go far."

"Thank you, John, I'll remember that, and you agree that lessons should start as soon as we reach the king's town tomorrow?"

"As soon as Emily is well, we'll make the arrangements," John agreed.

CHAPTER 7

"I'd better just look around and see that all is well," remarked Henry, feeling considerably cheered by his conversation with John. He trotted off, searching the bush for any signs of danger along the right flank and stopping to talk to his driver who was handling his team of oxen with his usual aplomb. Bokkis was a driver of note and greatly respected amongst the hunters for he too was a hunter of no little skill. He had guided visitors and hunters to the Victoria Falls on numerous occasions and had killed many elephants himself. Henry appreciated how lucky he was to have been able to employ him on this occasion.

Bokkis greeted Henry formally and after the exchange reminded him that there was no meat left for the drivers. Henry listened attentively then promised that he would do what he could to remedy the situation.

"I expect you'd like to join in the hunt too," he suggested. "I'll make sure that you have enough bullets for that gun of yours, but we haven't seen much game so far."

"I have seen guinea fowl and francolin," Bokkis informed him, "and they make good eating if we can collect enough of them. There are still seeds on the ground, so they will be fat and juicy. There are small buck here too, but they are very shy."

Henry laughed at the driver's obvious enthusiasm at the prospect of a hunt and then enjoying a satisfying meal and made a note to have his shotgun ready as well as a rifle to use if they came across buck or even better a buffalo.

Walking his horse now he eventually reached the rear of the procession beyond the loose animals where he came across Thomas looking less than cheerful in the pall of dust. Thomas brightened up when he recognised the approaching horseman as Henry.

"Good. I hope you've come to relieve me. I shall be sick if I breathe in any more of this dust," he muttered resentfully. "I wish I'd just ridden to the king's town on my own instead of offering to help you. Nothing but dust in the air all day and a hard bed under the wagon at night, walking along at less than three miles an hour when I could have galloped there and have been back home on the same day if I'd been on my own."

Henry accepted Thomas' grumbling with equanimity for it was in fact just a statement of the truth, but he also knew that Thomas needed to see the king on his own behalf and that by travelling slowly with the Moffat and Hargreaves families he could justify being away from the mission station for many days, possibly even a week.

At Inyati he would have to liaise with William Sykes as there was no one now to act as intermediary and this would be anathema to him.

"Well we all have to take turns at the back here so we know what it's like and we change every hour, or even less, which isn't too long to bear. I'll be back in about ten minutes to relieve you. I want to talk to John about hunting this evening," Henry clapped Thomas on the shoulder. "Cheer up, we shall be at the king's town by tomorrow morning and you can relax for a few days."

With that parting shot he urged his horse into a gallop and traversed the left flank, only slowing down when he saw the children walking and playing games in front of him. He marvelled afresh at their boundless energy as they skipped and ran around, sometimes tossing sticks or pebbles into the bush away from the wagons. Young James tried valiantly to keep up with his older brother but his little legs were not as strong as Harry's and his dress was a handicap. He was much too young to be breeched yet, but Henry thought that he might be able to arrange for that important ceremony to take place on his return from England.

It would be three months at least before he reached Cape Town, the sea journey was about six weeks each way and allowing time to find a wife and to arrange to see the Board responsible for the missionaries would probably take another six weeks or two months. James would still be under the age of three, Henry calculated, but he might be able to persuade the boys' grandparents to humour him and act before he made the long journey back to Matabeleland.

Jane, Nomalanga and the nursemaids were supervising the children as Emily was resting in her wagon. Henry slowed his horse to a walk, noting with satisfaction that Jane called them all to her and stood protectively by them as the horse approached.

His horse, Oscar, was a fine steady steed and Henry was proud of the way he stood stock still whenever Henry was about to take a shot. It didn't matter whether the shot was from the saddle or from a standing position with Henry leaning across the saddle, Oscar was thoroughly reliable and would remain motionless, but he might easily be spooked if numerous little figures were darting about throwing their arms around and shouting.

"May I ride with you, father?" asked Harry hopefully.

Henry paused for a moment then decided, "When I come back you shall have a ride," he promised.

The girls knew that there was no point in asking if they could have a ride. Henry was unaccustomed to seeing so much of his children. Looking after children was women's work and he was always so busy around the mission station or local villages that he was rarely in his own house. Even when he was there he would be at work in his own study and the children knew better than to disturb him there. It was irritating now to have them round him all the time and he was unsure what to say to them outside the schoolroom, but he had a duty to them and he would do it to the best of his ability until he could find a mother to care for them.

A few minutes later he rejoined John at the head of the trek. John was surprised to see him again. "I thought you were going to send Thomas forward," he queried.

"I will do so shortly. I just wanted to talk to you about going out hunting this afternoon. Bokkis informed me that the servants have no meat left and you know how unhappy they are when there is only meal to eat. Possibly two of us could go out and one stay at the wagons to look after the families. What do you think?"

John agreed fully. "Yes, it is essential to keep everyone well fed and I'm sure we could use some fresh meat too. I would offer to go out hunting, but I'm still feeling the effects of the fever and a hard gallop might be beyond me. It's best if I stay in camp. Besides, Thomas is the Nimrod of our little group and you are no mean shot, so you two are much more likely to be successful."

Henry smiled at the compliment, "No need to be modest, John, I've seen you drop a buffalo with a heart shot at a hundred yards, but I fully understand that you don't want to overtax your strength at this stage and it would be a comfort to Emily if you were with her."

The two men smiled at each other, remembering the hunts they had been able to share, never enough of course, they had to put work first, even before feeding their families sometimes.

Wheeling his horse about, Henry rode off to relieve Thomas, picking up Harry on the way and giving him riding lessons until they outspanned at eleven o'clock. Henry had been disturbed to see that they were being followed by a group of young Matabeles, but there was little he could do about it and he knew that once again they would be surrounded when they stopped.

Once they had been released from the yokes, the animals were taken to graze some distance away as the grass near the road was in poor condition. The pigs and the hens were let out of their cages to enjoy some freedom and get whatever food they could find. Everyone else prepared to eat their mid-day meal, but as Henry had suspected, within a very short time local villagers appeared. First there was a line of women carrying beer pots on their heads, then a second group, carrying pumpkins, pots of grain, maize cobs and baskets of beans or groundnuts. The men of the village and a horde of children all chattering excitedly accompanied them.

John walked towards the group and warned them that if they wished to sell any of their goods they would have to wait until the missionaries had eaten. Speaking sternly, John asked them to sit down where they were and promised to call them as soon as he was ready. Surprisingly the villagers took notice of his words and remained where they were, despite making loud protests.

Emily was delighted to be able to finish her meal, even if it was rather hurried and eating in the presence of other people was disturbing. As soon as she had finished she took her children and retired to the Moffat wagon, leaving the maids to clear away the mugs and plates. Jane, too, ushered her siblings to their own wagon and once they were settled on the bed, with Harry choosing to lie on father's bed, she found her book and sat at the front of the wagon. Isabelle was also reading, but James soon fell asleep.

Harry was playing with his toy snake. One of the visiting traders had given it to him many months before and as it was made from a real snakeskin it looked remarkably genuine. In fact Harry had often taken it around Inyati to frighten people and to show them that he was not afraid of snakes, that indeed he could handle them with impunity. He had been thrilled by the horrified reactions of the recipients of his pranks and kept these escapades very quiet.

Jane had been aware of some of Harry's mischievousness and had tried to curb his excesses, but even she was unaware of the alteration he had made to his toy. Whilst staying with the Thomas family the Reverend Thomas had taken him to the forge for a morning where he had shown young Harry how to shoe a horse. The sights, sounds and smells of the operation had fascinated Harry. Whilst it was in progress he had watched with concentrated delight each step of the heating and hammering into shape, the cutting, the fitting and the final nailing on.

Once the horse had been led away, Harry's attention strayed from the fire and the anvil to the tools and metals hanging from the walls. He had seen them all before as his father too worked in the forge from time to time, but to Harry they were endlessly attractive. Then on the floor he noticed a Y-shaped piece of metal. He picked it up, more out of curiosity than with any purpose in mind, however as he twirled it in his fingers it reminded him of a snake's forked tongue. It occurred to him at that moment that he could use this little piece of metal to complete his toy snake, making it even more realistic. No one would want to use this little thing, it wasn't important, so he put it in his pocket. Later that day when no one was around he fitted the metal into the snake's jaws. It was perfect. The addition also remained Harry's little secret chiefly because events had moved quickly and only a few days had elapsed between his discovery and the beginning of the journey.

Outside, John, Henry and Thomas were bartering for pots of beer. They didn't want many as they themselves drank little. They just wanted to be able to quench their thirsts occasionally. If they bought a few extra pots for the servants it would be as a gesture of goodwill since they had no desire for the servants to become drunk.

They were also examining large baskets of corn and smaller ones containing nuts. The shrill insistent voices continually begging payment whilst thrusting the items forward, interrupted the men's conversation as they discussed the merits of one pot or another. It was like being in a hen-house when the birds were disturbed as the ear-throbbing cackle was interspersed with shouted bids and counter-bids.

They were expecting negotiations to last most of the afternoon, as was the custom. Each transaction could last anywhere up to an hour and the sellers' initial demands were always outrageous. Making ridiculously low counter offers was all part of the ritual with exclamations, raised hands and expressions of disbelief and a running commentary like a comic opera.

During this period, whilst the missionaries were concentrating on the wares and the bargaining, a few of the wily villagers edged away from the scene of operations and towards the various wagons, intent on discovering any treasures that appeared to be unclaimed or lacking an owner or were just temporarily lying around.

Harry became aware of fingers slipping between the sail of the wagon and the wood of the wagon side just by his head. The fingers were followed by a hand as the sail was worked looser despite the tight lacing and the hand began to wander about feeling for any loose object of interest. When the fingers reached his hair Harry decided that it was time to act and he pushed his snake's fangs into the back of the prying hand.

There was a shriek of agony and the hand was hurriedly withdrawn as the sharp metal caused two distinct puncture wounds. Harry followed up his advantage by pushing the snake's head into the gap so that it appeared just in front of his victim's eyes. With another agonised shout the would-be thief rushed towards the crowd, "Nyoka, a nyoka. I have been bitten. I am dying." He threw himself dramatically on the ground and writhed about in apparent agony.

The terror soon affected everyone and picking up the victim the villagers

fled en masse only stopping to pick up the goods they had wanted to sell.
Harry, feeling guilty about the effect his action had caused, slipped the metal fangs into his pocket and feigned sleep. Henry, guessing that it was his son's toy snake at the root of the confusion, since there were no snakes visible at this time of the year, came to see what had happened. Jane explained what had occurred and that the thief had had his hand on Harry's head before Harry had retaliated. As Harry had already dealt with a potential thief and the villagers had all departed to the relief of the travellers, Henry felt that he should say no more.

Jane heaved a sigh of relief as her father turned away without making any criticism of Harry's action.

She had dreaded another reprimand and further blame for her lack of supervision. She knew that father hadn't been deceived by Harry's pretence of sleep any more than she was herself, but she was grateful that he had decided against punishment.

Later in the afternoon, Henry and Thomas, accompanied by Bokkis, who was astride one of the spare horses, rode out of camp with their rifles and shotguns. They headed back towards the river, knowing that the game would seek water as the light began to fade.

When they reached the riverbank they turned upstream, away from the villages they knew. Bokkis rode towards a small patch of woodland where he was certain he would find guinea fowl, leaving the others to seek larger game.

They walked their horses through the bush near the river, searching the area for any signs of movement. There was nothing.

When eventually nearly two hours later they turned for home, they were both despondent, disappointed by the lack of opportunity so they were pleased to hear several shots coming from the direction that Bokkis had taken.

"It sounds as if Bokkis has had some luck," remarked Thomas quietly.

Henry held up a warning hand and pointed towards some thick bush between themselves and the river. Both men reined in their horses and peered at the shadowy form barely discernible in the fading light. It was a buffalo, probably an old bull rejected by the herd.

Both men dismounted, holding their rifles at the ready. Silently they began to approach the animal that was standing and staring malevolently at them.

Henry looked at Thomas and nodded. Thomas would make the first shot and Henry would keep his bullet in reserve. The buffalo was one of the most dangerous animals in Africa and if Thomas' bullet failed to kill this one instantly the nearly two thousand pound beast would kill them. They would have little chance of escaping. A wounded buffalo was lethal.

They were now close enough to see sufficiently clearly and couldn't risk moving closer or waiting any longer which might give the buffalo time to charge. There was no wind. Thomas took aim and fired. Henry waited with his rifle raised to his shoulder, but a second shot wasn't required as the heavy beast fell to the ground.

They approached their prey with great caution and only when they were fully convinced of its death did they relax and Henry was able to congratulate Thomas on his success.

There was a sense of revelry in the camp that night as the smell of roasting meat rose with the smoke into the chill night air. Villagers had come to share in the feast and brought beer as well ensuring that the celebration continued far into the night.

Thomas would keep the horns and skin to trade at a later date, but the others were happily satisfied with the good meal of steak and liver and the present of a large amount of fat to render down. This grease would be used to keep the wagon axles moving easily and prevent excessive wear. It was an essential item and a precious one.

Jane, lying in bed and feeling warm for a change, as the many fires seemed to have dispersed the chill, fell asleep despite the loud sounds of happy revelry all around.

CHAPTER 8

It was very cold, damp and misty as John breakfasted alone early the next morning on some of the meat from the previous evening washed down with hot, sweet, black coffee. He had agreed to be the one to ride ahead of the wagons following the accepted custom of informing the king of their impending arrival.

The missionaries knew that the king was already aware of their movements. His network of spies advised and warned him of every occurrence throughout Matabeleland, and even beyond the borders, as soon as anything happened or was rumoured. Nevertheless they were bound by the rules of Matabele custom.

Henry and Thomas were in no hurry to follow. There was no need for an early morning trek that day as they were already close to the king's town. They hoped that the weather might improve, as indeed it did, enabling the families to enjoy a leisurely breakfast before the oxen were inspanned.

As they approached the king's town they were soon surrounded by a hot, dusty, noisy crowd and however jolly the throng appeared it was annoying for the families, who were hemmed in on all sides.

In expectation of just such an event Thomas had chosen to ride alongside the Moffat wagon whilst Henry stayed close to his own.

The more adventurous and impudent youths were clinging to the sides and backs of the wagons, risking serious injury, but blissfully unaware of the dangers until one fell off right in the path of the following span of oxen. The slow pace of the oxen and the speed of the youth's reaction to his fall averted any injury and provided entertainment for the onlookers, but it was a worry for Henry and Thomas who feared that the mood of the multitude might quickly change into hostility if serious injury befell one of their number: bodies were easily crushed by the iron-clad heavy, wooden wheels and loaded wagons.

Jane sat on a box near the front of the wagon with Isabelle and James between herself and Nomalanga, whilst Harry stood beside Bokkis. He had a toy whip and was pretending to drive.

Unlike the grown-ups the children were unworried by the crowd and in fact found the noise and chatter exciting.

They were looking forward to meeting the king, as only Jane could remember having seen him before. Henry had rarely visited Mzilikazi and had only once taken the children with him on the express order of the king, who had wanted to see the new white child when Harry was born.

Henry was considerably relieved when he saw John approaching. He was accompanied by an induna and several warriors who soon forced the mob aside.

"We can outspan beside the traders' stores," John called out. "In fact Wood has said we can put the wagons inside his fence to keep them safe. The king is delighted to see us and has asked us all to go and speak with him as soon as we have outspanned."

"What about the children?" asked Henry.

"Oh, we've all got to go, but I think Emily and the little ones might be forgiven. I have already explained to the king that she is ill. Quite rightly he was more worried that she might bring sickness into the town, but I reassured him that it was just the fever and that she would soon recover here where the air is better. I think she would find it hard having to walk a mile to the king's kraal. Not only that but then having to cope with all those fierce dogs before getting on hands and knees to crawl through the door into a dark, smoke-filled hut and face up to being offered dishes of hot beef."

Henry agreed wholeheartedly, "It is much more sensible for her to remain in the wagon. His majesty would be deeply offended if she refused to eat his beef. We know it is considered a great honour to eat and drink with the king. I only hope Wood can manage to keep some of these people away from her so that she can rest." An hour later Henry was facing the pack of dogs that haunted the area around the king's hut.

With the aid of the stick with which he had armed himself and the help of some of the many bystanders, he and the children managed to escape injury, though it was an unpleasant ordeal.

They then crawled on their hands and knees through the low door into the king's hut, Henry following the four children to protect them. Thomas, and John with two of his children, were already there sitting with their backs to the wall. By their expressions both suggested commiseration and understanding of his confrontation with the dogs as they had just experienced exactly the same.

His majesty lay on a bed of skins on the floor opposite the door, surrounded by some of his wives and indunas. Henry and the children spoke the customary formal greetings before sitting where the king indicated beside John. Dishes of steaming beef were being brought round by two servants and another was carrying a pot of beer. The visitors were urged to eat and drink. Knowing the customs and that he must in no way offend his host, Henry drew out his knife and, picking out a large chunk of beef from the dish, held it to Harry's mouth. As his son took a bite, Henry cut the piece off, sawing with his knife between the beef and Harry's face, and then offered the chunk to Jane, Isabelle and James who in turn each took a bite which Henry had to cut off so that they had a small piece to eat. They all began to chew happily except for Jane who gagged as she tried to cope with the undercooked meat whilst the blood ran down her chin. She had never enjoyed almost raw meat and especially this piece with no salt and feeling slimy.

"Come here, boy," Mzilikazi ordered, looking straight at Harry.

Unlike Isabelle and James who were completely overawed by this immense black man and clung to Jane, Harry marched forward confidently to stand before the king, who laughed delightedly, "Uhu! Uhu! I see this mighty warrior. You are tiny, no higher than my thigh, but you fight like a man. You will be like the lion; you have a lion's hair on your head. Yes when you are grown you shall come and fight in my army. You will be a big induna for the Matabele." Mzilikazi looked at Henry; "He will be a mighty warrior this son of yours. Guard him well."

Jane was longing for the fresh air and for an opportunity to avoid eating any more of the meat, but her hopes were doomed to disappointment as the king continued to talk to the missionaries about their work and about Inyati.

He also spoke of his beloved friend Mshete, Robert Moffat, who was John's father. Mzilikazi asked John to persuade his father to come to Matabeleland to see him and to cure his illness. John promised to do his best.

The sight of the dishes of beef made Jane feel sick but she was able to avoid this catastrophe by making sure that she chose to eat very small pieces. To her relief she discovered the other chunks of meat had been particularly well cooked and were far from unpleasant. The children were not expected to join in the conversation, nor were they allowed to drink the beer, but had to sit uncomfortably still as the morning wore on.

All the men knew that this was a courtesy visit and that no business would be discussed until a second or even third visit. Even though they had already been given permission to leave the country they wouldn't be allowed to cross the border until the king had given them the road yet again.

However frustrating it might be they had no choice but to await the king's pleasure. Eventually they were given permission to leave the hut on the promise of a visit the following day.

Knowing that they might be held up for a week at least, Henry decided that the pigs should be slaughtered and during the late mid-day meal one of the storekeepers offered to do it the next day in payment of a ham.

Throughout the afternoon, as Jane tried to take a reading lesson with the younger children, they were continuously pestered by the people of the king's town. Sometimes these unwelcome visitors would just stand and stare or laugh and talk loudly about the white people and their funny customs.

Sometimes they would try to touch the children, feel their clothes or snatch their books, and this was most annoying.

Jane was afraid that Harry might lose his temper again and strike out at one of them. She appealed to the storekeeper for help. Joseph Wood came to the wagon and apologised for not being able to close the gate in the fence which he had to keep open for his customers, but he knew of a way to lessen the intrusion.

"Listen, my friends," he called in a voice loud enough to be heard over the babble, "these people are special people in their own country. They are very important and that is why they are friends of the king. They need to be by themselves."

"Ah so they are of the real nation," said one man, nodding his head wisely.

Jane knew that the Matabeles who were pure Zulu were known as the real nation and were regarded as being more important than those who were of mixed tribes and considerably more important than the slaves. She smiled to herself at the thought, but was relieved to see that the storekeeper's words had an immediate effect. It was true that there were still people coming to see them, though with more respect and much less intrusion.

That night Jane awoke suddenly, disturbed by the howling of the wolves all round the town. She lay awake listening. It was a horrible noise and she knew that these beasts were dangerous, but she felt safe enough in the wagon. She could feel the warmth of her brothers and sister and hear their gentle breathing. She could also hear her father's breathing only a few feet away and that was very reassuring. As she lay listening to the sounds inside the wagon and to the animal noises outside she realized that there were lions hunting close by. There had been roars in the distance for some time and they had become gradually closer.

"Please God, look after Sandy and the horses and all our oxen," she whispered into the night. As the howling and the roaring reached a crescendo she hid under the blankets and, still praying for her beloved animals, she drifted into sleep.

The next morning was damp and chilly; the king's town hidden by a misty drizzle.

During the breakfast of hot porridge news came from the king's kraal that lions had killed two of the king's cattle in the hours of darkness and a young girl had been injured by wolves as they tried to drag her from her bed beside a fire.

The king was sending out a party of young warriors almost immediately to seek out and to kill the lion or lions.

Jane was horrified by the news, her heart going out to the young girl who was wounded as she slept and she remembered her prayers in the night. How lucky her family had been to be safe inside a wagon. The other children were in turn excited and frightened by the story, whilst Thomas and Henry, who had both longed to see this type of hunt, leapt to their feet, determined to be present at the confrontation.

"What a bit of luck that was," said Thomas happily as he and Henry hurriedly mounted their horses. The previous day they had obtained permission from the king to go out hunting and their horses were already saddled, so they lost no time in galloping to the royal enclosure. The hunting party of twenty young warriors was on the point of departure and the newcomers were welcomed. Having been warned that they could use their guns only for their own protection and that they were not in any way to interfere with the hunt, they set off. Henry and Thomas remained mounted, knowing full well that they couldn't keep pace with the warriors for any length of time.

Although there were many guns in Matabeleland and a number of warriors had learned how to shoot, the lion hunt was to be conducted on foot by men armed only with assegais. It was a prospect that appealed to Henry and Thomas. With breakfast over, Charles, the older trader whose store was close by, said that he would now honour the promise he had made to Henry the previous day and slaughter the pigs.

Jane hadn't wanted to watch, but as Harry and Isabelle insisted on being present and Jane was responsible for them she had had little choice.

In the event, she had found it all less distressing than she had anticipated. She felt sorry for the little animals, though she had always known that they were kept to provide food, but once the deed was done she took the greatest interest in the proceedings.

The butcher dispatched both animals very quickly with the minimum of fuss and with great skill. The blood was collected in a bucket and the children were fascinated to see what the inside of an animal looked like.

When she was younger Jane had actually thought that her body was an empty shell and that food filled up the space like mother's jam going into a jar.

After the scalding to remove the dirt and bristles the carcasses were opened up. Jane gazed in awe as the heart and lungs were revealed and the mass of intestines spilled out all over the table.

"See now, that's his heart which is like yours and his lungs for breathing. Now I'll put the heart and the kidneys and the liver into this bowl which will be for our meal this evening. We'll have a great fry up. Bokkis and Nomalanga shall have the other innards, your father tells me, and they can share them with some of the others."

The children were given the bladders, which were then blown up and gave them hours of fun as they kicked them or patted them around in the air. The bulk of the meat would be salted so that it could be carried on the journey, but there was sufficient to keep them supplied for the next few days as well.

That evening, as they feasted on fried liver and kidneys served with sweet potatoes and pumpkin, Henry and Thomas described their exciting and successful lion hunt.

"We had to ride about three miles following the trackers," explained Henry.

"They were very quick at the beginning," said Thomas, "and we could ride almost at a gallop."

"Then they lost the tracks for a while on some rocky ground. They all spread out and eventually one spotted the trail, so off we went again," Henry continued.

"When at last they spotted where the animals were lying, they noticed there were two of them and made a circle round them. We had to stay away then so we dismounted, but kept close to our horses just in case the lions came at us."

Thomas was eager to describe the adventure and went on, "Gradually the warriors made the circle smaller as they advanced towards the lions. The lions had been asleep when we first saw them and they were well fed so they hadn't moved much as the Matabele crept up to them, but now they stood up and began to show that they didn't like being disturbed."

"They made growling noises and began to swish their tails about," said Henry, taking over the story. "The warriors watched them all the time and crept closer and closer. Then one of the lions sprang up and the warriors on either side struck it with their assegais, so it turned on them. Every time it turned towards one man, the others struck it, so it didn't know which way to turn."

"Yes," went on Thomas. "Then the second lion joined in the fight, but the warriors were so quick at dodging all round the animals that they were confused. I have never seen such bravery. In the end both lions were killed and their skins taken to Mzilikazi to show him that the killers of his cattle were now dead. The king was delighted and will reward them all for their bravery."

"It was certainly worth seeing," said Henry. "It will be a good story to tell people in England."

CHAPTER 9

They awoke to a day of cold drizzle even worse than it had been the day before, but Joseph Wood had a fire going in his store and invited Thomas and the two families to prepare their breakfast inside.

The children had never been inside a store before and were wide- eyed as they looked around. The floor was earth, covered with cow dung that had been polished after it had been smoothed and hardened, making a surface that was shiny and not as dusty as bare earth. There was a window in one of the walls that were made of sun-dried bricks, but there was no glass in the window only a shutter that could be swung down to keep out the rain or the wild animals at night. Looking up, they could see that it was like their own home at Inyati where the thatching of the roof over the poles and rafters was clearly visible. There was no ceiling. In fact the children had never heard the word ceiling.

As it was a single room and the only shelter he had, it was Joseph's bedroom as well as a living room and store and his bed was along one wall. There was also a fireplace in a corner with a simple chimney to protect the thatch from sparks.

Joseph's store goods were minimal as he was awaiting the arrival of two wagons from the south to replenish his stocks. On the shelves, which were planks fastened to the wall, there were some boxes of matches, a bullet mould, some bars of lead, one or two tins of beef and two jars of pickles. There were two large tins of beads on the floor. Several muskets of German origin hung on nails on one of the walls. On the trestle table in the centre of the room, which served as a counter or a dining table when required, there were bolts of calico and cotton cloth.

A plank balanced on two upturned boxes made a bench and other boxes were used as seats. The chest in the corner behind the door and furthest from the fireplace held boxes of gunpowder.

Nomalanga helped Jane to prepare a big pot of porridge. Then Jane cooked bacon and fried eggs, with bread to dip in the yolks, which made such a wonderful change for everyone that they were all in good spirits and there was a great deal of laughter around the table.

Jane was particularly pleased to be sitting at the table with the grown-ups and had not been banished to the bench with the smaller children.

As she watched the last slice of bread disappear she knew that one task that day would be to bake more. She could make bread in an oven or in a pot on a hot fire, so she asked Mister Wood if he was going to keep the fire going all day.

"I don't have enough wood to keep it hot enough for your baking, young lady, but George Lawson has an oven beside his store, he also has a huge wood pile and I'm sure he'd be delighted for you to use it. Just go along there and ask."

He gave her the direction of the store and she said she would go there later. As there were only four permanent stores here she could hardly get lost. In addition to Joseph Wood and George Lawson there was Charles who had offered to slaughter the pigs, and Franz Greite, a German trader whose wife was about to produce their first child and they were yet to meet him.

"It would be better if you waited until the weather clears up a little," Henry warned her. "You could take some lessons with the little ones until then. It is Sunday tomorrow so you could read them a Bible story first and I don't think they have done any History or Geography for a long time. Harry and Livingstone both need to practise their Latin too and you know enough to be able to help them with that."

Jane nodded her head submissively," Yes father."

In fact she didn't mind teaching the younger children because it tested her memory too. As she was going to go to school in England she wanted to be sure that she wouldn't be the bottom of the class.

She turned to speak to the storekeeper, "Mr Wood, will you allow us to stay here in the store? It has more room for us to sit and it is much warmer than the wagon. Perhaps the Matabele won't disturb us as much here," she added hopefully.

Joseph laughed, "You're more than welcome young miss, but I think there will be as much of a crowd as usual once the weather clears and if you leave your wagon unattended you'd better make sure that all your goods are hidden away and the tent fastened securely."

Henry said he would see to all that as soon as Jane had brought in the books she needed and the ingredients for her bread making. "Could you bring the churn as well please, father? I have saved the cream for three days now so I should be able to make the butter whilst the bread is baking."

Henry agreed that he should carry the churn into the store.

As they were finishing eating, a messenger arrived from Mzilikazi summoning the missionaries to visit the king immediately.

John hadn't been able to face breakfast so Henry went to find him. He was still in his wagon and was looking very pale; he was feeling less than well as recurring fever took its toll. He begged Henry to make his apologies, "I really cannot walk to the king's in this cold, damp weather," he explained.

"You would be wise to stay in bed and try to keep warm. I'll ask Thomas to make up a draught for you and another for Emily," promised Henry. "Do

you think you could manage a bowl of soup or some mulled wine?"
Both John and Emily felt that some warm liquid would be beneficial and Henry promised to send them something with the medicine.
Back at his own wagon Henry found a cloak to cover his shoulders although he was already damp, then hastily hid the family blankets in a box under the bed and made sure that other valuables were put away. He picked up the butter churn before closing the tent and tightening every lace. It was most annoying to feel so vulnerable. On the way out he would find Bokkis and ask him to watch the wagon as he had done the previous day. No doubt he would have to kill another goat so that there would be some meat to offer as a reward.
Thomas agreed to make up some medicine immediately and suggested hot thin porridge, with milk and sugar, to give the patients sustenance.
Jane put what was left of their breakfast porridge into a pot and thinned it with milk, then heated it over the fire whilst Thomas prepared the medicine. By the time they had completed the task and taken the mugs to the Moffat wagon the drizzle had eased somewhat, but the damp cold was still unpleasant.
Thomas and Henry wasted no time after that, walking very briskly indeed, then fought their way through the pack of dogs and the queue of people waiting to see the king before being summoned to enter.
They found it difficult to cope with the offerings of beef and beer so early in the day and it was much too soon after their own meal. However they forced themselves to eat sufficient to avoid offence. They were both thankful that the brisk, chilly walk from the store to the king's had helped to digest their breakfasts a little.
Remembering what father had said, Jane chose to tell the story of David and Goliath first, which was a favourite of the boys and appealed to Isabelle as well, especially as there were pictures to look at in the book of Bible stories. Isabelle made the connection between David's feat and that of her brother when he felled the toy thief and for a time she and Livingstone called Harry 'David', as they teased him. Restoring order, Jane continued with Geography, which entailed reciting the continents and oceans, some rivers and capital cities.
As they were becoming restless, Jane let them play a clap dance next before going on to History and the kings of England. She decided to sing some nursery rhymes then before asking the boys to conjugate the Latin verbs they had already learned. She had her father's book to help her as girls weren't supposed to learn Latin although she had been allowed to stay and listen to the boys' lessons and had learned as much as they.

As the morning was now well advanced Jane suggested that the others should go outside to play for a while so that she could mix the dough for the bread. Nomalanga could look after them now that she had finished the washing up.

Thankfully the little ones took their balloons and hurried out of the store.

"Be careful not to fall on the muddy ground," Jane called after them.

Trying to keep clothes clean and mended was a daily problem and Jane knew that she could not do any work on a Sunday.

By now a crowd had appeared to watch, discuss and touch the strangers and Jane found herself surrounded. She had mixed the ingredients but the dough had to be kneaded and she had to appeal to Joseph for help. Hands were already trying to grab the dough and Jane could scarcely move.

Covering the bowl with a cloth she leaned over it, "Leave me alone," she spoke furiously in Sindebele. "I have work to do and you are in my way."

The crowd hesitated momentarily at her words and Joseph was able to come to her rescue.

"You'll have to wait for your father to come back before you can walk along to George's store. These people won't let you alone for a moment. I'll stand here beside you until he returns, but they know this is food and they'll want to grab it if they can."

Meanwhile Henry and Thomas were preparing to take their leave of the king after more than an hour's discussion. They had given their version of the lion hunt they had witnessed the day before taking it in turn to describe each little act with a great deal of drama and were full of praise for the bravery of the warriors. The king listened intently; he loved a good story and often told stories himself. He asked to hear the story again with emphasis on the actions of each of the warriors. Finally, as the men felt they had exhausted their repertoire and were beginning to despair, the king was pleased to give them the road. They were free to leave whenever they wished and they could now make definite plans.

As they neared the stores, a message was brought to them asking Thomas to go at once to the Greites' store to assist in the birth of the baby. Both men set off to run the last few hundred yards with Henry going straight to his wagon to get his medical box in case it was needed. Thomas was taken straight into the store by a nervous Franz Greite who left him there and then returned to the front of the store to guard the door and prevent anyone else from entering.

Henry retrieved his medical case from under the bed and pausing only to lace up the tent of the wagon again he handed the box over to the father, who was pacing up and down. Henry then went to Woods' store where Joseph and Jane greeted him with enthusiasm.

"We need a little help here, Henry," stated Joseph bluntly. "Jane cannot knead the dough without someone trying to grab a handful. I think the best thing is to clear the store of people altogether."

Speaking loudly in Sindebele, Henry told the people that only those who had come into the store to buy goods were allowed to stay. With Joseph's help he ushered out everyone without goods to barter and shortly the store was empty.

"That was a bright idea of yours Henry, but I expect the crowd will wait outside and trouble you as you walk to George's store."

Henry laughed shortly, "Perhaps you'll come with us then. Between us we should be able to see that Jane manages to reach the oven safely."

Jane kneaded the bread and set it to rise by the fire. She then began to turn the handle of the butter churn. It wasn't hard to turn whilst the cream was still very liquid but it was a lengthy and tiring task, so she was relieved when Joseph offered his help.

As it happened, the crowd had faded away by the time that Jane was ready to take the dough to the oven, which had been fired earlier by Nomalanga whilst Jane was teaching. Once the dough was in the oven Jane was free to play with the little ones who had followed her to George's store. What a joy it was for her to be able to enjoy some fresh air and to be free of domestic duties for a time. To her dismay, she noticed that Isabelle's dress had a very muddy hem and that James had obviously fallen over. His dress had a long muddy smear all down the front. Her momentary anger had to be repressed when she remembered how difficult it was to prevent these accidents.

"Perhaps I can rub off the worst mud when it is dry," she thought hopefully.

"I shall have to find some clean clothes for them both tomorrow before father holds the morning service. Nomalanga isn't a Christian and doesn't come to church with us. I think I shall ask her to wash these clothes tonight when the children are asleep."

Henry went to see to the slaughter of the goat as he had promised half of it to Bokkis. The other half could be roasted in the oven when the bread was taken out and would provide not only their hot evening meal, but also enough cold meat for the meals on Sunday. On the way to talk to the herdsman who would slaughter the goat, Henry called at the Moffat wagon to check on John and Emily and found them both prostrate. It became clear that they would not be fit enough to travel for many days, possibly even longer. Determinedly John urged Henry to travel without them.

Henry wrestled with the problem throughout the rest of the morning. He knew that it would be foolhardy to travel to Kuruman on his own. There were too many risks and he couldn't place his children in such danger. Wagons could easily break down, oxen could die or wild animals could create havoc. All travellers were well aware of the perils and generally preferred to travel in company with others whenever it was possible, but what could he do now since the Moffats were not free to travel?

The lunch of freshly baked bread with butter and cheese was well under way when Thomas joined them with the joyful news of the safe arrival of a baby girl.

"Do you think you could take some food into them?" Thomas asked Jane. "There is no one to help them and neither of them has stopped to think about eating."

Jane hastily collected a plate with thick slices of bread and butter and a chunk of cheese. Henry gave Isabelle a jug filled with watered wine and the two little girls took the food along to the Greites' store.

"Come in. Come in. God bless you." Franz said as he opened the door for them to enter. He took the plate and the jug and placed them on a box that doubled as a table before turning to them and asking, "Would you like to see the baby?"

The girls were led to the other side of the rather dark room where Mrs Greite lay in the bed. In a wooden crib beside her they could see the newborn child with her tuft of dark hair and screwed up red face.

"She is very beautiful," said Jane softly. "I hope she brings you much joy."

Isabelle said nothing but put out a tentative hand to touch the tiny head.

Then she spoke, "We were going to have a baby like this, but he went to live in heaven and our mother went with him, so we didn't see him."

Jane could see that her little sister was close to tears so she smiled bravely at Mrs Greite, "Thank you for letting us see her. We'll come again tomorrow if we may."

"Of course you may. Yes of course and thank you for this good food."

Franz, his face beaming, showed them out, delighted to have food to share with his wife, who was still exhausted after her ordeal.

CHAPTER 10

The first part of Sunday morning had been a great trial for Jane. She had dressed herself in the only dress she had other than her black mourning dress. Her black dress was still wet from the wash the day before and couldn't be worn, but she felt apprehensive about wearing a brown one so soon after mother's death. Both boys needed clean clothes and Jane was trying to find them in the box that was kept under the bed. It was a daunting task in a confined space and tested her strength to the utmost.

Father was busy trying to dress himself, which he always found difficult in the limited space of the wagon tent. The top of the tent was many inches short of six feet so he had to sit on his bed or half-stand with his upper body bent over. Generally he accepted the restrictions with resignation, but when the top button of his waistcoat came off in his hand his frustration was unleashed in a shout of fury.

"Jane. Find your sewing things and sew on this button immediately. Why it has to come off at a time when I am in a hurry to go and talk to Thomas about today's service I don't know. The perversity of human endeavour to cross God's will, no doubt."

Jane had had to abandon her search for the boys' clothes and find the sewing things to attend to father's waistcoat, which was annoying. Isabelle had done nothing to help and in fact she had begun to fight with her brothers, pulling the blankets off James to wrap round herself, for it was still very chilly. Predictably, James started to scream in his anger at the outrage and Harry joined in the tussle.

Father was irritable and the noise from the children didn't improve his temper. He gave each one of them a sharp slap and told them that they would be put outside if he heard another word from them before breakfast.

The ensuing silence was broken only by James muffled sobs as Jane managed to complete her sewing task.

Finding the clothes for the boys at last, she gave James a quick cuddle and told Isabelle to dress herself immediately. Harry needed no further bidding as he noticed his father's steely stare and he hastily pulled on his breeches, his stockings and shoes whilst Jane dressed James.

As soon as Harry had put on his jacket Jane brushed his hair so that he could follow father into the store for breakfast. The other three followed on several minutes later.

Nomalanga had warmed some milk on the fire so the children ate bread and milk whilst the men ate bread and meat with coffee to drink. Jane saw how quickly her baking had almost disappeared and knew that she would have to bake again on Monday.

For the Hargreaves family Sundays always followed a set routine. No cooking was allowed, so the meals were prepared the day before and usually eaten cold, though in winter some food might be re-heated.

All domestic and routine chores were suspended and only essential tasks were allowed. Reading the Bible or gentle walks were acceptable occupations.

There was a religious service in the morning, Sunday school in the afternoon and a service in the evening.

At Inyati in 1860 the services had sometimes been attended by a number of Matabele as the king, in order to please his friend Mshete, had ordered them to be there. Once Mzilikazi had moved away, fewer people came. At first some people had attended in the hope of receiving presents, but over the years they had begun to accept that presents were rarely, if ever, forthcoming, with the resulting drop in attendance.

Both Henry and Thomas had reminded the king yesterday that today was Sunday, God's special day, and he had promised to send some of his people to listen to what the white people had to say.

Accordingly, at half past nine they chose a place just outside Joseph Wood's fence opposite the place where the Moffat wagon was standing inside the fence. This meant that John, Emily and their younger children would be able to hear the service without being troubled by the crowd.

"The word congregation would definitely be a misnomer", Thomas had once remarked to Henry as they had surveyed the chattering and restless group of people ordered to the service by Mzilikazi many years ago, before he had so suddenly departed from Inyati. Arriving at any time but the right one and wandering about aimlessly or greeting friends was commonplace and had long ago been accepted by the missionaries.

Henry was gratified to see that all the storekeepers had decided to attend and they were greeted warmly by Thomas as they stood in a little group just in front of the two missionaries alongside the children.

Jane was holding her mother's very precious hymnbook; 'Hymns Ancient and Modern' and thoughtfully she offered it to Joseph, who held it so that his friends could read the words. Jane and her siblings knew all the words off by heart and rarely needed to use the book, but father had recently given her mother's book and she carried it with great pride. They had decided to sing the first two hymns in English, but to give the sermon and sing the last two hymns in Sindebele.

Accordingly, they began with Henry's favourite, 'Rock of Ages' followed by 'Hark My Soul It Is The Lord.' With six strong male voices and several children's voices the hymn soared through the cool morning air, bringing comfort to the Moffats, who joined in quietly. The ever-increasing multitude, though far from quiet, failed to drown the words. The music of the Matabele was so totally different from the sounds they now heard and their reactions varied from amazement to amusement.

Henry's prayer of thanks for the day, for God's goodness and for the safe arrival of a new soul were spoken in the native language and for a moment there was a cessation of chatter as the Matabele tried to understand just who this God was. Mzilikazi was their God.

Thomas had chosen to read the first chapter of Genesis, but there were frequent interruptions, which made his task an onerous one.

The service ended with the hymns; 'When I survey The Wondrous Cross' and 'O God Our Help In Ages Past.' As these were mother's favourites, both Jane and Isabelle were very close to tears, remembering how she would sing them around the house.

It was during the afternoon when all was quiet around the wagons and stores that a sudden disturbance erupted, shattering the peace. A number of deep thuds were followed by a shout of pain and anger and then surprisingly the sound of a shotgun being fired and a great howl of pain.

Frightened, Jane jumped up from the seat at the front of the wagon where she had been quietly absorbed in her story of "Oliver Twist," by Charles Dickens and climbed down to seek father's help.

Henry and Thomas had been sitting in Wood's store chatting with Joseph, Charles and George whilst Franz had stayed at his own store with his wife and new baby. The five men, each with a gun in his hand, came pouring out of the store and stared around to ascertain the direction and cause of the commotion. Slowly and carefully they walked towards the opening in the fence. Jane stood and watched them.

What they saw amazed them. A Matabele youth was running away from the Greites' store towards the town. There was a thin trickle of blood on one leg where a pellet from a shotgun had obviously struck him and he was heading towards a group of youths, gesticulating and shouting loudly to them. Purposefully, the group began to move towards Greites' store.

"Go back inside the wagon, Jane, and stay there quietly. There is no danger to you. We will go and see if we can help Franz." Henry's words were quiet but forceful and obediently Jane returned to the wagon. She picked up her book and began to read, trying to stop herself from shivering in fear as she always did whenever people fought. It was difficult to concentrate on the words and ignore the sounds from outside.

"Thomas, you and I will go and see what is happening. We had better leave our guns here as none of those youths is armed and we don't want to appear aggressive. The others can stay here, but there is very little we can do if the Matabele decide to wipe out all the white people as they often threaten to do. There are too few of us and too many of them. We shall have to keep them calm and appeal to Mzilikazi if the situation gets out of hand."

The others approved Henry's suggestion and two of them reached out to take the guns from Thomas and Henry.

"Do you think I should go to the king's right away and seek his help?" asked Charles.

Henry shook his head, "We need to know just what is going on. I'm sure that no harm will come to Franz or his family. We know that the traders, like the missionaries, are here with the king's express permission and are under his protection. The Matabele are too afraid of their king to go against his wishes."

With that Henry and Thomas walked confidently towards the store, which stood about fifty yards away. Immediately they could see that the Matabele youths were ransacking the store. Franz stood helplessly watching them remove all his trade goods.

Bearing their trophies, the group marched jauntily back towards their town, jeering at Franz as they passed him and threatening him with worse consequences if ever he attacked one of their number again.

When they reached the store Henry and Thomas could see that Franz was pale and shaking, partly from fear and partly from anger. They strove to reassure him and discover the reasons for this apparent theft.

"Is your family all right?" asked Henry.

Franz looked blank. "My wife? My baby? Yes they're all right. The Matabele didn't take any notice of them, just marched straight into the store and took everything they could find there. Some of them have been waiting for any excuse to obtain a gun and now they've succeeded," he added bitterly.

Life for storekeepers in Matabeleland was extremely hard without an extra unnecessary loss such as this. Most of them barely made a living and lived in appalling conditions with a poor diet and a social life that consisted of drinking (when they could get the drink) or gambling with travellers or hunters who might come their way. Franz had brought his wife from the south to share his lonely life and this had made his store popular with many men who spent weeks and months without seeing a white woman.

"Come," said Thomas briskly, "let's reassure your wife that you are safe and sound and you can tell us what happened. We can always appeal to the king for help if your goods have been stolen without cause. Henry and I will do all we can to help."

The story Franz told was a familiar one. A few weeks ago when his wife could no longer carry buckets of water or help him to lift the boxes, tusks and other heavy goods Franz had considered employing a Matabele youth as a helper. There was one particular young man who had pestered and pestered him for a blanket. As he had nothing to offer in exchange Franz had consistently refused to hand him one. Blankets, like all store goods, had to be bought or offered in exchange for labour. They were rarely free gifts.

This seemed to be a difficult concept for the Matabele, who felt that they could and should have whatever they fancied and their beliefs resulted in persistent begging, or if that failed, stealing.

Over the years some Matabele had learned that they could earn blankets or guns by going with the hunters and travellers as guides or carriers although they were never satisfied when they came to receive the agreed payment and always demanded much more.

Unfortunately at this time of the year the hunters were already scattered throughout Matabeleland hunting in their chosen territory and this youth had not been chosen to accompany any of them, either that or he had elected not to go, but he still wanted a blanket.

After weeks of daily harassment Franz had finally come to an agreement with the youth. He would employ him to help around the store and on any trading trips over an agreed length of time. The payment for these services would be the desired blanket.

Sadly, as Franz had foreseen, the willingness to work was minimal and even worse was the continual disappearance of small articles from the store. With so little in the way of trade goods and personal belongings every item was familiar and soon missed.

Franz was in a quandary, he had agreed to give a blanket and knew that he would be forced to keep his side of the bargain. There was no possibility of backtracking on an agreement of this kind. He could neither alter it nor cancel it. He knew that and accepted it.

He also knew that he would need help when his trade goods arrived from the south very soon and he was expecting some hunters to bring in their trophies of horns, hides and tusks within the week.

On the other hand he didn't need the aggravation of an assistant who arrived when he felt like it and couldn't be relied upon to do any of the tasks expected. Least of all did he want to lose any more of his precious goods. He had tried to devise a routine that kept the youth working outside the store. This succeeded for a time although the youth refused to carry buckets of water and objected strongly to cutting up logs. He was not going to do women's work!

Then this morning Franz had found his remaining sugar and coffee had gone. He lost his temper and told the youth that he was no longer employed and that he must stay away from the store altogether. The youth, predictably, had demanded his blanket. Franz had compromised by offering a length of calico. Since the youth had done very little work and had stolen more than his labour was worth, Franz considered that he was being generous. Throwing the calico onto the ground, the youth had stormed out.

Franz naively thought that that was the end of the incident and that the youth would soon cool down before returning to collect his payment. He was mistaken.

A few hours later stones came flying through the window and the open door of Franz' store. Luckily no one was hit, but one large stone bounced against the baby's crib, awakening her and setting her crying.

Furious at such a cowardly attack and fearing that his family might well be injured if more missiles were thrown, Franz grabbed his shotgun and fired at the shadow he could see beyond the window. He had not aimed deliberately and had certainly not intended to do any harm. It was a reaction intended to frighten away the attacker and defend his family.

Truthfully, he had felt some satisfaction when he heard the howl of anguish outside and had reached the doorway in time to see the youth fleeing towards the town. What he had not bargained for was the immediate revenge. He realized that he had been stupid to react so violently and he regretted his hasty action.

Henry and Thomas could understand fully the whole chain of events. Whilst sympathising with Franz, they agreed that the firing of a weapon at a Matabele and the resultant injury to him was a serious offence. The only recourse was to seek immediate audience with the king and explain the whole story.

"If we all go to the town now and seek the assistance of one of the king's indunas we might be able to see the king this afternoon," suggested Franz hopefully.

"We might be lucky, but it is more likely that we shall have to wait until tomorrow morning," said Henry soothingly.

Thomas frowned, "We'll ask him to arbitrate about the payment to the youth for his work and for the injury. You will probably have to apologise for that assault, I expect. When he has made that decision we can ask him to order the return of the stolen goods."

Franz looked relieved and smiled at his wife, who was sitting beside the bed at the other side of the room listening anxiously to the discussion.

"I'll just tell the others what we plan," Henry explained as he stood up and walked towards the door. "They are waiting ready armed in case there was a serious fight and they needed to protect themselves. They can unload their weapons and put them out of sight now. We'll go up to the king's as soon as I get back."

As Henry had forecast, they were unable to see the king that evening. When they reached the royal enclosure the king was in the cattle kraal and had left strict instructions that he was not to be disturbed. Cattle were extremely important to the king and meant more to him than any human. He visited his cattle kraal morning and evening to see the animals and to check on their welfare, he recognized each one and knew immediately if any were sick.

The vast Matabele herds were spread throughout the country and were left in the care of selected indunas. They were the nation's wealth and all belonged to the king. Only he could order one to be slaughtered and woe betide any induna who lost a beast for whatever reason.

As it was now almost dusk Henry and Thomas had to hurry back to conduct the evening service. Their day had been rudely interrupted and they had been so caught up in the drama that they had almost forgotten that it was indeed Sunday. Franz was left to worry about his fate for the rest of the night, but there was nothing to be done to help him.

CHAPTER 11

Harry hated Sundays. He didn't mind the services too much because he knew the hymns and liked singing and the missionaries often told Bible stories instead of giving long talks. If there were long talks Harry would think about other things, especially about tricks he could play on his friends. There were no chairs to sit on at the services, but all the family were used to sitting on the ground as the Matabeles did, they were just glad when the ground was dry.
After the service Harry could usually persuade mother to let them take a walk with Nomalanga or Jane before lunch and there were always opportunities to talk to people or throw a stick without being scolded too much.
Rest time was always boring unless he was really tired. He could read a little, but it was hard work and he preferred it when he could listen to Jane or Isabelle reading stories.
Sunday school was alright, usually. They were permitted to draw pictures sometimes when they had learned a new hymn or prayer. They were allowed to play with the Noah's Ark on a Sunday, too. He and Isabelle had made up different games and he enjoyed making his lions eat her cattle, or the dogs chase the cats. They always had to keep quiet about these variations, as mother would be angry if she knew.
The afternoon after Sunday school was the worst time if no one felt like going for a walk, especially in the summer when it was very hot. Jane and Isabelle were happy to sit and read, but Harry was restless, hating the quiet and the inactivity.
On this Sunday at the king's town life was considerably more exciting. Harry had wakened from his afternoon rest at the sound of the shot and had seen Jane run to talk to father. When she returned to the wagon she was surprised to see Harry wide awake. "What has happened?" he asked. "I heard a shotgun being fired."
"Yes, I heard it, too," Jane answered him. "I went to ask father about it, but he doesn't know. He and the Reverend Thomas have gone to Mr Greite's store to try to find out. He told me to stay in the wagon and not to be frightened as we were quite safe and no one would hurt us."
"Are you frightened?" Harry asked curiously. It would be strange if she was, he thought, because he considered it was all very exciting and not in the slightest bit frightening.
Jane disliked the idea of being considered a coward, but she was also honest,

"I am a little bit worried, because the shot was fired in Mr Greite's store and he has a new baby there."

That at least was true and it made her sound braver than she actually felt.

Harry thought for a moment, "Isn't it time to get up yet?" he demanded suddenly. "We have been lying down for ages." He sat up and began to put on his boots.

"I think it might be, but we have to stay in the wagon until father comes back," Jane reminded him. "I don't think we shall have Sunday school today, though."

Once Harry had put on his boots he joined Jane on the box at the front of the wagon, peering inquisitively through the gap in the tent door. Disappointingly, there was nothing to see.

Isabelle and James woke up shortly afterwards and both were cross when they were told that they had to stay where they were for the time being.

All four of them were thirsty and longing for a drink so it was a relief when Henry finally appeared.

The children immediately appealed to father for release and were allowed to go into the store for some milk and biscuits where they were joined, much to Harry's delight, by the Moffat children. They listened in fascinated silence to father's brief description of what had happened and the explanation that now he and Thomas were going to accompany Franz to try to see the king.

The men all agreed that there was some urgency in the appeal to the king, but they also knew that no one could demand to see the king and there was no guarantee that their asking for an audience was likely to be successful.

The guns had been unloaded as soon as Henry had made his appearance and assured them that the matter was under control, but every one of them was aware of the fragile truce between the newcomers and the natives. The Matabele lived by war and killing, they had taken this land by force and they guarded it jealously. Anyone other than their own tribe was treated with suspicion, as if they planned to take from the Matabele what they had so recently stolen.

The storekeepers were often threatened, as were the missionaries and they knew that they had to avoid any confrontation. They usually ignored hostile behaviour or made a joke to set the offender laughing, which persuaded him to forget his antipathy. They also made a point of keeping in the king's favour, offering him coffee and food whenever he came to the stores, mending guns for him, looking after the wagon he had been given, doctoring his horses and other animals and generally making themselves as indispensable as possible. The missionaries, who had usually had some medical training, were more able to cope with the king's health and that of his important advisers, but the storekeepers were willing to help in emergencies by pulling a tooth or putting splints on a fracture. Doing some simple doctoring was an essential part of living and working in these isolated parts and they thought nothing of it.

Having informed the others of his intentions, Henry made his departure and as there was nothing else to be done the gathering broke up.

Charles looked at the children sitting solemnly on their bench and smiled at them, "You know," he said kindly, "I have some presents in my store. I think there are enough for all of you. Would you like to come along now and choose something you would like?" The children gazed at him wide-eyed and Jane spoke for them all, "Oh yes, please. That would be very kind of you, Mr Charles."

No one knew if Charles had a surname or not. If he did, then he had never disclosed it. Everyone called him Charles and the children were allowed to call him 'Mr Charles'. He never volunteered any information about his past and, in a country where men were entitled to their own secrets, no one ever queried his silence, although there was always speculation about a man's past. The other storekeepers suspected that perhaps he had been a sailor who had jumped ship at Cape Town. Certainly he was a man who knew how to handle ropes and knots and he was always asked to ensure that loads were safely tied down, because his knots never came undone accidentally. Somehow he had learned about trading in the interior, possibly by working as an assistant and eventually he had arrived in Matabeleland where he was content to settle. Like early pioneers anywhere he could turn his hand to anything.

Somewhere along the line he had learned to ride and although he was competent enough on a horse he wasn't quite as at home in the saddle as were many of his contemporaries.

Charles was well liked amongst the traders, though he struck a hard bargain and like all of them kept his suppliers a secret, but he would drink and gamble with them when asked to join a party, would entertain them from time to time and was a fount of good solid common sense.

In his spare time Charles whittled away at pieces of wood. He chose his wood with care and created animals or people so beautifully proportioned that they were greatly admired by anyone lucky enough to see them.

His fellow storekeepers had suggested that he should send them to Cape Town for sale in the shops there and had at different times offered to buy them from him, sensing an opportunity to make a profit. Charles ignored these offers and suggestions and kept his carvings in a large wooden box at the back of his store.

Now he was about to give some of them away for the pleasure of seeing the faces of the recipients. He knew that the missionary children had few toys or belongings and whilst they didn't miss what they had never known they would certainly treasure his small gifts much more than the rich people in Cape Town.

Charles, at thirty-two, a year older than Henry, was the oldest of the storekeepers, though not the wealthiest.

It was George Lawson who had that honour and now as he walked towards his own store in company with Charles, George confided his plans to make this his last trading season in Matabeleland. He had saved enough money to buy himself a farm in the Cape and he considered that at nearly thirty years old he was ready to settle down and start a family of his own.

The feeling of adventure and the freedom he had enjoyed wandering through the bush for more than thirteen years had been stifled by the necessity of spending hours and days at the store for the past eighteen months. Since the age of fifteen he had travelled and hunted as far north as the Zambezi, facing danger, experiencing fever and sharing the comradeship of men whose lives revolved around hunting. Seeking out wild animals and challenging their instinctive methods of survival against human skills.

George thought that he might put a man into his store to run it as a manager for a few more years as he had with his store at Shoshong. This he said had proved profitable, though there were often serious worries about the transport of goods and other difficulties cropped up from time to time. The alternative of selling out completely was an attractive possibility if he could find someone who wanted to take over.

"Now is a good time to pass the word about," agreed Charles. "That will give you five months or so to make all the necessary arrangements. Henry can carry letters to Cape Town for you and he'll be happy to mention the value of your trading enterprise to people on the road or anyone else he meets. There are always men on the lookout for prospects of making a good living. I don't think you'll have any problem finding someone to buy both your stores." "I hope you're right. I have been feeling restless for weeks now and can't wait to be on the road south. How do you feel about staying on here, Charles?"

Charles laughed good-naturedly, "I think I shall stay here until I die. I don't want to farm and I don't need to see the sea again. Here I am free to do as I want with every day my own and no one to worry about or to worry me. I have everything I need, my own roof, enough food and companionship when I need it and I can make a living with only a little effort on my part. Why should I change it?"

By this time they had reached Charles' store and George asked if he could see the carvings that Charles was about to show the children.

"Yes, by all means, but remember, they are not for sale."

Jane had been walking quietly behind the men holding the hands of Mary Moffat and two year old Bruce Moffat. James had declared his independence and insisted on walking by himself close to his brother Harry, who in turn was with his friend Livingstone.

Isabelle, feeling left out of both groups, pretended not to care and lagged behind, humming a little tune. She was indeed feeling great excitement at the idea of receiving a present and was trying to think what it might be. Would it be something to eat, something to wear like a new hat or would it be a toy of some sort? Whichever one it was, she would be happy to have it.

As they reached Mr Charles' store, Jane gathered the children together. There was no need to remind them of their manners. The solemn day of Sunday always impressed an air of self-discipline on the missionary families and by long force of habit they remained subdued. Shouts of joy or signs of exuberance had to be contained and expressed in other places and on other days. Now they all walked demurely into the store, with Jane following.

Jane felt more at home here for there was a proper table with six proper carved wooden chairs round it at the right-hand side of the room. The store itself occupied all the left-hand side and it was much better stocked than Mr Wood's store. There were many more guns hanging on pegs and quite a number of rolls of brightly coloured cloth on the shelves.

Charles had made strong shelves with planed wood and attached them to the wall with brackets. Jane could appreciate this handiwork because her father was a competent wood worker and had always explained to her that every piece of work must be done properly. Both she and her father had deeply deplored the necessity of treating wood to try to protect it from the termites and she had already seen that the legs of the table and chairs were standing in tins of water.

Charles now pulled four chairs into a line away from the table. "Now young lady, you can sit there with the older children. I'm sure the little ones wouldn't mind sitting on the floor for a short time," Charles suggested smilingly. "George, perhaps you would help me to carry this chest out here?" So saying, Charles went over to a second door in the far corner. Jane realised now that there was another room and that must be the bedroom, for there was no sign of a bed anywhere in the store.

The children sat quietly, but there was a noticeable air of expectancy about them all as they watched the two men carry a large chest into the store by its rope handles. The chest was deposited carefully in a space in front of the children and George brought himself a chair so that he could join the group. Charles, meanwhile, had produced a key and was unlocking the chest with great ceremony. Gently lifting the lid, with all eyes watching every movement, he revealed a layer of calico.

The waiting was becoming unbearable and Harry almost fell off his chair as he craned forward to get the first glimpse of the contents of the chest.

Charles made no attempt to pull back the cloth, but reached to each side of a tray and lifted it right out of the chest. He put the tray carefully on the floor. The calico, still hiding the treasure beneath, was wonderfully lumpy and bumpy with points and hollows to intrigue any observer.

A second tray similar to the first was then produced and placed alongside the first. Finally a third tray followed the first two. Charles then closed the chest and, picking up the first tray, he placed it on top of the chest. Jane felt that she had stopped breathing, such was her curiosity and she could feel Isabelle tensing herself as she too longed to see what Charles had to offer.

Smiling at his audience, Charles gently lifted up the cloth and the children gasped their delight. George, who had seen some of Charles' carvings before, knew what to expect, but even he was impressed by the quantity and quality of the models. Every one of the carvings in this first tray had been carved from light-coloured wood, some almost white and others pale yellow. Charles picked up a fine giraffe and named the wood as beechwood then put it down between a beautifully carved owl and a crane. There were lions, buck, oxen, birds and even butterflies.

Charles looked at the children and told them, "I don't want you to choose anything until you've seen all the others. Have a good look at these first and then I'll show you the next ones."

The second tray contained carvings in dark brown and red coloured wood with a large hippopotamus taking up a lot of space and a fearsome crocodile leering among the duikers and impala. Jane felt James lean forward when he saw the hippopotamus and she knew he would choose that if he could. She wondered if the crocodile would be Harry's choice. She herself was fascinated by them all and knew she would find it difficult to make a choice of only one.

The final tray was of carvings made with dark grey and black wood; snakes, lizards, warthogs and sable antelope. Best of all were the elephants carved in different shades of grey and black. Charles lifted one up, "Panga panga," he murmured. "This wood was given to me by a native who had come from near the east coast. These trees don't grow here, but it's a beautiful wood." He smiled round at all the children and then gave a happy chuckle. "But you haven't seen everything yet. Wait a little while yet before you choose."

With the three trays and their fascinating contents safely on the floor Charles lifted the lid of the chest once more and reached in towards the bottom.

First he lifted out a box and then another slightly larger one before closing the lid of the chest. Placing the boxes side by side on the chest he opened the first one.

"Ninepins," ejaculated George as he spied what was lying in the box. "Well, I never knew you had those Charles. Do you know how to play ninepins, young man?" he asked Harry.

Harry shook his head, "No sir."

"Then I'll show you if Charles doesn't mind," George offered.

Charles nodded in agreement and George set up the ninepins near the far wall of the store. There were three round wooden balls in the box as well and he rolled them one by one towards the standing pins. His aim was good and eight of the pins fell over. The children couldn't restrain themselves any longer and showed their appreciation of this feat by clapping excitedly, but they all knew that this was a game they would not be allowed to play on a Sunday and none of them asked to play.

Harry knew immediately that this would be his choice, but Mr Charles had said that the choices would be made in order of age, which meant that Jane would have the first choice followed by Isabelle and then Livingstone. Harry was in an agony of suspense, desperate for the toy and hoping that Livingstone would choose something else, but he couldn't see how anyone would choose anything other than the precious ninepins.

Charles was thoroughly enjoying the reactions of the children and he grinned across at George, who was putting the ninepins and balls back into the box.

"Now my young ladies and gentlemen here we have the last box and this one is really for the young ladies."

When he had opened the box he lifted out a wooden doll and then another and another until there were five dolls lying on the top of the chest.

Jane felt her heart beating fast. She was glad there were so many dolls. She knew that she had first choice, but if there had been only one doll she would have left it for Isabelle and she so desperately wanted one of these lovely toys. They were not baby dolls. They were like small children and the head and body had been carved in one piece. The arms and legs had been attached to the body by small tacks or rivets so that they could be moved. Some sort of hair had been attached to the head of each one with glue. Brightly coloured pieces of cloth had been wrapped round the dolls to act as a dress.

Jane and Isabelle both gasped with pleasure and Mary reached out towards them, "For me?" she asked Jane. Jane nodded, unable to speak.

Charles couldn't have been more delighted and he held up the dolls one by one for the girls to make their choice.

"Thank you, Mr Charles," whispered Jane, holding her prize with care.

"Thank you, Mr Charles," beamed Isabelle as she grasped her chosen doll in her hand.

"Thank you," lisped Mary, clutching her doll to her chest.

"Well young man have you decided what you would like?" Charles asked Livingstone.

"Yes sir, please may I have one of the oxen?" said Livingstone clearly. Harry, who had been holding his breath and was now red in the face, let it out in a rush of thankfulness as he watched Livingstone receive the shiny, beige-coloured ox carved in mukwa.

"Thank you, Mr Charles, now I can put it with my model wagon." Livingstone beamed with sheer pleasure.

Charles turned at last to Harry, "Well I expect you know what you want, don't you?" he remarked, trying not to show that he was fully aware of Harry's strong attraction to the ninepins.

Harry almost stammered out his request. He just couldn't believe that no one else wanted such a magnificent present. "Please may I have the ninepins, Mr Charles."

Charles handed him the box and was so warmly thanked he eventually held up his hand, "That's all right. I'm sure you'll have many happy games with your friends. I think I must make some more."

"Indeed you must," agreed George. "I think we could have a few games when we are bored with card games." Then he looked at the watch he had taken from his waistcoat pocket. "I expect Henry and Thomas will be back very soon for the evening service. I'll just help you to carry that box away and then we'll go and join them."

"You'll have to wait a moment longer old man. There are still two young men to be served. We can't miss out James and Bruce can we?" The two little boys had been waiting anxiously for their turn to choose and had been alarmed when George had suggested leaving. Relieved now, they quickly made their choices, the red teak hippopotamus for James and a grey elephant for Bruce.

Carefully Charles re-packed the chest and helped by George returned it to the bedroom.

Jane, helped by Isabelle, Livingstone and Harry, carried the chairs back to the table then led the way outside.

The late afternoon was grey and cold. The children shivered as they left the shelter of the store hugging their treasures and needed no urging to hurry for the comparative warmth of their family wagons, arriving there just as the men returned from their abortive trip to the king's kraal.

CHAPTER 12

Henry had admired the toys and carvings in an abstracted way. He was more aware of and interested in the service he was about to conduct and he ushered the children into the wagon to deposit their precious treasures before joining him in the store.
Joseph had agreed that this evening service could be held in his store, as it was unlikely that the congregation would amount to more than the storekeepers and the missionary families. None of the Matabele people would want to be outdoors on this cold evening, they would be more likely to be round their fires eating a hot meal or drinking beer.
As it happened the service was held in Greite's store. Franz had come hurrying along within a few minutes of arriving back and requested the missionaries to preach at his home so that his wife might be able to take part in the service.
Thomas also had a special request to make of Henry.
"I have just been along to give a dose of quinine to Emily and John," he explained. "They are no better, but certainly no worse and I think it might be a good idea if they had some hot meat soup. I know we don't usually do any cooking on a Sunday, so I hope that perhaps we can make an exception today. What do you think?"
Henry pondered the question seriously. The Lord's Day was holy. It was a day to concentrate on His Word and His Works, that was why the ordinary mundane tasks of everyday life were suspended and Christians concentrated on the Bible. He had been tempted by the thought of a hot meal earlier, but had thrust the thought aside as unworthy. This Sunday had already been disturbed by the incident with Franz and Henry had necessarily become involved in the affairs of men. However, he reasoned, two of God's workers needed to regain their health so that they could continue to carry on His work. Surely it was not God's will that they should suffer further when His missionaries could help them to regain their strength
Thomas was looking at him searchingly, almost following his thought processes. He smiled when Henry nodded, "That was a thoughtful idea of yours. There is some meat, but no bread left so we should all have had a meagre supper. I'll ask Jane to show Nomalanga what is required and then we'll all go along to Greite's store. The soup should be ready when we have finished the service."
Everyone welcomed the large pot of meat and onion soup thickened with flour and some maize meal and Jane was especially delighted. It had been

one of her worries that there was insufficient food for supper.

Mrs Greite was still recovering from childbirth, Mrs Moffat was still too ill with fever to cook for her family and the storekeepers who were willing to provide basic provisions were only too delighted to be able join in with the Hargreaves' meals. This made the burden on Jane greater than ever. She didn't mind too much as she was thoroughly at home with the need to provide a family with meals. Nevertheless, she did worry about her ability to provide sufficient food for everyone.

After supper the four storekeepers settled down with a bottle of Cape Brandy and a pack of cards. Thomas made himself comfortable by the fire with his pipe. Jane ushered the younger children through the door to make their way to their wagons and bed.

Henry, feeling unusually restless, wondered whether to sit by the fire and talk to Thomas or to go outside for a walk. The sound of convivial laughter from the card game decided for him and he too left the store.

Outside he was struck by the bitter chill of the night and as he put on his hat he was glad that he had already donned his heavy coat. There was the glow of a candle in his wagon and he could hear his children arguing. There was some sort of altercation going on and he paused to find out what the problem might be.

"I want to take my hippo to bed with me!"

That was James' loud high-pitched wail.

"And I want to take my doll to bed with me!" Isabelle's statement was a deliberate challenge to her older sister, very different from James' hopeful wish.

"Mama wouldn't let you have that hard lumpy hippo in bed." This was Harry's common sense response to his brother. "That doll is just as hard and it's also pointy," he added for good measure, looking at Isabelle.

James began to wail again, "I want mama. I want mama. She letted me keep my toys in bed."

Harry was upset now by James' unhappiness and he too began to cry for mama. Isabelle followed suit and poor Jane, who was as saddened as they were by mother's death, was also close to tears. It was with the greatest difficulty that she controlled her sobs. Somehow she recognized that her tears would be as much for herself as for the loss of their mother. She didn't want to be a mother all the time. She wanted time to be herself and to play make believe with her doll as Isabelle did. It just wasn't fair.

Outside, Henry was stricken by the children's sorrow and unsure how he might alleviate it or even if he could.

Eventually, Jane recovered sufficiently to regain charge. She controlled her own tears and brushed them away with her hand, trying hard not to shout at her brothers and sisters, though she was sorely tempted. Then she thought how mother might have dealt with this situation. "I know what we should do," she suggested in her brightest voice. "We should make a special bed for all our new toys on the floor here. The hippo and the dolls will make each other happy and Harry's ninepins will be safe beside them."

The crisis was past and the children happily made up the special bed before tumbling into their own.

As the candle was blown out, Henry thankfully made his way to the kraal behind the store where the horses and oxen were collected at night. They had been safe so far, but the threat posed by lions was ever present and he knew that he should really spend more time ensuring their safety. There ought to be a guard at night as had been arranged when they arrived, but there was no fire to indicate that a watch was being kept. Henry wondered if the guard had gone to sleep or had just decided that it was more comfortable to sleep in one of the huts in the town.

Oscar gave him a snickered greeting and came to the fence to be patted and stroked. Henry was fond of horses and Oscar had served him well. It was too dark for Henry to see far, but he was aware that there were blankets on Oscar's back, for which he was thankful. Horses needed protection from the cold night air and too often blankets had been stolen. The horse nudged his arm, hoping for a titbit, but Henry had nothing to give him except a consoling pat on the neck. Gazing up at the clear star-studded sky, Henry suddenly (and for no particular reason that he could fathom) felt bereft.

"Oh, Katherine, why did you have to go to our Lord so soon, leaving me to manage on my own? The children miss you as I do and the boys cannot understand what has happened. They believe you have deserted them. Lord why did you take her from us?" Henry felt shattered by this sudden feeling of grief that tested his faith in God's infinite mercy and the rightness of God's will.

In an action that mirrored that of his daughter only a few nights previously he took comfort from the presence of a loved animal and, resting his head on Oscar's neck, controlled his emotions by praying fervently. Weeping was for women, he told himself fiercely, men, and especially men of God, put their fate unreservedly into His hands. Drawing strength from this firm belief Henry continued to pray.

"It's horribly cold out here. Are you all right Henry?" Thomas' voice coming from the darkness behind interrupted the flow of Henry's searching thoughts and prayers but he had regained his composure and he was able to reply quite steadily.

"I'm freezing as it happens, but I thought I'd better have a look at the animals. There doesn't appear to be a guard and I was considering going to find one."

Thomas sounded worried as he answered Henry, for he could ill afford to lose his horse. "I heard some lions roaring earlier on. They sounded a long way away. I'm sure they will have found other prey by now, but you're right, there should be a guard. We'll arrange the matter tomorrow after we've been to see the king with Franz. It should be possible to sort out that business satisfactorily by lunchtime. I was hoping to leave for home by Tuesday, though I think I may have to wait longer if John and Emily still need treatment. Their health is really a cause for concern, but they both managed to eat a good helping of the meat soup this evening and that is a good sign. Perhaps after a good night's sleep they will soon be on the road to recovery. What are your plans now?"

Henry gave a deep sigh, "I don't think I can make definite arrangements at present. We certainly hadn't planned to spend so many days here. We knew we would have to wait for the king to give us permission to leave, but had expected to depart immediately he had agreed, probably within a few hours after that." He sighed again, "As you know, our ideas have had to be changed and there seems to be no immediate solution. Meanwhile, we are using up the supplies that should have lasted us at least to the borders of Matabeleland. Tomorrow I shall have to kill the last goat and that only leaves the hens and the pork we salted down."

Thomas shivered and stamped his feet, "Perhaps the king will send us some beef tomorrow. I will remind him how ill the Moffats have been and I'm sure he will ask how he can help them, but now I am going back into the store to warm up in front of the fire. I couldn't go to sleep whilst the card game was in progress, but I think I heard the guests leaving."

Henry had heard the store door open a few minutes previously and shouted 'goodnights' as the other three storekeepers hurried off to their own beds. He too was ready to seek the warmth of his blankets. The talk with Thomas had lightened his mood a little, though he still felt angry that he had been left alone to cope with four small children. It worried him that he should feel angry and even more so when he wasn't sure whether he was angry with Katherine for leaving him or with God for having taken her.

As he removed his shoes whilst sitting on the bed in the wagon he could hear the breathing and small sounds made by the sleeping children. He reflected on his own childhood when, living in the nursery at the top of the house as he and his siblings did, he had rarely seen his parents. He remembered being taken downstairs to the sitting room to take part in Bible readings or to say goodnight to the adults of the house, who seemed like strangers to him. It was true that 'mama' always gave them a kiss and seemed fond of them all in a distant way, but 'papa' had a habit of questioning them and frowning fiercely if they stuttered a reply that he felt was incorrect.

'Grandmama' and 'Grandpapa' Hargreaves were awesome in their black garments and with their other grandparents as well as a number of aunts and uncles the sitting room had been crowded. At the Bible readings the servants were often present, too, standing in line near the door behind the family.

Henry went to sleep envying the settled and peaceful routine enjoyed by his parents, but remembering that this was the life he had chosen for himself, knowing that it was God's will for him.

Fully rested despite his grief and worries, Henry faced the morning with the certainty that some problems would be resolved today. As he said his morning prayers whilst the children still slept he placed his full trust in the Lord and, feeling considerably more optimistic, went outside.

When Jane awoke about half an hour later she knew exactly what she had to do once breakfast was over. She had to bake the bread and arrange for Nomalanga to wash some clothes. Baking bread did not worry her, but the thought of coping with baking and the crowds of Matabele at the same time did. Previously she had had father and Mr Wood to help her and she hoped she might be able to persuade them that she needed them again, but she knew that father and the Reverend Thomas had to go to the king's kraal in order to help Mr Greite. Would Mr Wood be able to help her on his own?

James and Isabelle woke at the same time and their movements woke Harry. All at once the peace of the morning disappeared into chaos as the three tussled good-naturedly all over the bed and over Jane who joined in happily. She was relieved to find them all in a good mood and it was only when they were all exhausted that she urged them to get dressed.

Jane was slightly dismayed when Isabelle insisted on picking up her doll.

"My doll wants some breakfast," she said, cuddling the doll fiercely.

Then James demanded to take his hippo to breakfast too.

"Hippo's hungry. He wants food," stated James firmly.

Harry, reminded of his new game, looked thoughtful. He could take his ninepins into the store and play a game with Livingstone.

"The store is a good place to play ninepins. Livingstone will play with me and Isabelle can have a turn as well later," he added generously.

Jane knew that she had no time to play with her doll during the morning, but it wasn't jealousy that made her want to prevent any of the toys being taken out of the wagon.

"Isabelle, you know how soon the crowds appear don't you? It might be better if you leave your doll here where she is safe."

Despite the gentle suggestion, Jane could see a mutinous gleam in Isabelle's eyes, but before Isabelle could voice her defiance Jane looked at Harry.

"Do you remember how quickly Livingstone's wagon was taken from you? Well there are three wooden balls as well as the ninepins and someone will want to steal them. Even if they didn't all disappear your game would be spoilt."

Harry clutched his box of ninepins with the pride of ownership, but he was uncertain about taking them out of the wagon. "When will I be able to play with them?" he demanded.

Jane could think of no suitable time or place. From early morning until late afternoon, people surrounded them, wanting to touch them, to take their things or just to stare at them.

"We'll ask father now," she suggested, knowing that Harry wouldn't take his game with him until he could be assured of its safety.

Harry carefully returned his box to the special place under the bed and Isabelle followed suit. James, however, refused to leave his hippo and Jane had to allow him to keep it with him or put up with a temper tantrum.

As Henry left the wagon he had been surprised to find Joseph talking excitedly to a young Matabele and as he was very obviously looking around to see if he was being observed Henry waited in the lee of the wagon. He saw Joseph hand over some calico and he waited until the youth hurried away before showing himself.

"Morning Joseph," he called. "Your business has started early."

Joseph smiled weakly, "I'm afraid you caught me arranging to go out to meet one of the hunters. The young man came to tell me that the hunter is on the way in. In business, here as well as anywhere else, one has to be ahead of rivals. This hunter has had a lot of good luck and is bringing in a full wagonload of ivory, skins, horns and feathers. He might want to store most of it here until the end of the season, but more likely he will need to arrange to transport it southwards. Some of it he will sell here so that he can restock his powder chest and supply of lead and buy dry goods to keep him going for at least another three months."

Henry smiled his understanding, "If the other storekeepers knew about it they'd be racing out there to try to haggle the price down."

Joseph nodded, "They would certainly try to buy as much as was on offer. I'm expecting a wagonload of goods from the south sometime this week. When it arrives I'll be able to send my ivory and skins back to the Cape, but I haven't got a full load so I can also offer to carry some more and thereby benefit from the transport fees."

Henry laughed out loud, "You're an astute businessman, Joseph. You'd get on well with my father. You sell some of your goods to the hunter, for a profit, naturally, and obtain ivory, which you can also sell for a profit. In addition you use your transport that was travelling to the Cape anyway with your own goods and charge a fee for carrying a little extra. Three lots of profit! No wonder you didn't want any of the other traders to know about it."
Joseph looked sheepish, but maintained his business attitude. "Life here is pretty grim you know. We give up comforts and a normal social life to try to make not only a living, but enough over and above that to accumulate some savings in the hope that one day we might be able to live somewhere better. It isn't easy to make a profit. We only do what we have to do."
"You're right about the deprivations in this country, but you probably chose to come here, as I did." Henry stopped abruptly as he realised that he was about to compare the choice of a missionary whose purpose was to bring the Light of the Lord to a heathen people and improve their lives with the more selfish venal goals of a trader, some of whom were fugitives from justice. Luckily, before he could try to explain any further, the children joined them. Then a few moments later the Moffat children and the other traders arrived for breakfast.
Charles and George had both contributed some eggs to the meal and these were boiled until they were hard, giving the children great fun as they shelled them before eating them.
It was as the meal was nearing a close that there was the sound of hooves outside fast approaching the store and as they all turned to look at the door it was opened by a young man who was new to most of them, but was obviously recognized by George. George leapt to his feet with a smile of welcome and great pleasure on his face. He hurried across to the young man and gave him a warm hug.
"Edward. What on earth are you doing here? How did you find your way? Are you alone?"
The young man lifted a hand in mock horror, "Steady on there, I'll tell you all about it, but how about a mug of that coffee and perhaps a bowl of porridge? I'm starving."
"Of course, of course. And let me introduce you to the company. This is my younger brother Edward. Come and sit down at my place. I'm afraid there isn't much room, but we have just finished eating."
Edward was provided with a bowl of porridge and a mug of hot, sweet coffee and the others watched him doing full justice to the food. When he had finished eating he explained briefly, "Father was in Cape Town when your wagon arrived there and he managed to get a high price for the ivory

and he knows he will soon sell the skins. He then set about fulfilling your request for trade goods. That was a long order you sent and it took days to complete the buying. I was glad of that because I have been pestering him to allow me to come north and eventually I wore him down. Not only that, but he agreed to go into partnership with me and in addition to your wagon I have brought up a wagon load of goods to trade on my own behalf." As he made this assertion a cloud of uncertainty crossed his face. "You'll help me, won't you?"

George laughed teasingly. "If you're good enough to travel all this way with the wagons, you're good enough to do your own trading. You don't need me."

He laughed heartily as he saw Edward's look of dismay. Clapping him on the back he suggested that they head for the wagons that were still several miles away. "Are you coming, Joseph? One of the wagons is yours. Charles and Franz have some goods in the fourth one."

Charles was just as eager as George and Edward to ride back towards the wagons, so they were all surprised when Joseph declined to accompany them and even more surprised when he made no excuse for his decision but said he would await the arrival of the wagon at his store that afternoon.

After the men had departed, Joseph wasted no time, "I'm sorry to leave you now. I am going to close the store for the day. Can you leave the dirty pots and wash up later?" Giving them barely time to reply, he ushered them all outside and put a padlock on the door He had his horse saddled and set off northwards at a fast gallop.

"Why is he in such a hurry?" asked Thomas as he watched Joseph disappear in a cloud of dust.

"I'll tell you later," replied Henry. "We had better go and collect Franz and go and sort out his troubles with the king."

Henry turned to look at his daughter, "Jane, you should have time to do some lessons with the younger ones now."

Jane looked stricken, "Oh. Oh dear. Forgive me father, but I thought I should make the bread this morning. We have so little to eat, we really need the bread."

"Ah yes. I'm sorry, I had forgotten about that. There is no one to help you with the meals at present. We had better forget about lessons for the morning. I will do some Latin with the boys this afternoon and if there is enough time we can do some reading and Geography as well." Henry looked around and seemed to realize that the store behind him was locked. "You'll need somewhere to work undisturbed. I'll ask Franz if you can make the mix the dough in his store."

The permission to use the Greites' store was readily given and proved useful in more ways that one. As the store had been completely ransacked of goods there remained no attraction there for the Matabeles. This meant that Jane could work without fuss. It also meant that Harry and Livingstone were able to play with the ninepins there without interruption and the smaller children could play safely with their toys. With James happily playing with the group, Nomalanga was free to take the washing to the river.

Jane chatted to Mrs Greite as she measured out the flour, water and other ingredients, sharing stories of life at Inyati and comparing them with life in a store at the king's town. Mrs Greite was recovering quickly from the ordeal of childbirth and was already able to cope with meals for her own family. Now she promised to take over all the meals for the next few days. With the arrival of the transport riders the numbers for meals had swollen and Jane felt the greatest relief. The bread she was baking would just be for the Hargreaves family and the Rev Thomas. Mrs Greite would bake bread for the others.

CHAPTER 13

Henry, Thomas and Franz returned to the store late in the morning feeling reasonably pleased with their visit to the king. They had been kept waiting for nearly an hour, as the king was holding a meeting with his chief advisers, but eventually they had been allowed into the royal presence and had been greeted with Mzilikazi's usual consideration.

Franz had first explained exactly what had occurred and added that he had fired in anger and to protect his family. He had meant no harm to any Matabele and he was ready to apologize to the youth for any damage he had done. He begged the king's pardon and respectfully asked if his goods could be returned, as the people who had stolen everything were not in any way involved in the quarrel.

"You say you shot at the youth who threw stones at your family and hit him on the leg? That was not a very good shot." Mzilikazi laughed and his companions obediently laughed with him. "It's a good thing you were not hunting a lion."

There was more laughter and Franz looked very put out. "Sir, I did not deliberately aim at him. I was cross and wanted to teach him a lesson. I just fired through the window without taking aim."

"If you wanted to teach him a lesson you should have beaten him. I don't like it when you shoot at my people. No one must attack us, as we always fight back and we Zulus fight to kill." Mzilikazi was proud of his Zulu heritage and although his people were now known as the Matabele the Zulu name was not forgotten. "You should know that. You might have injured many more people and that would have meant war." Mzilikazi looked stern.

Henry felt that he should help Franz at this point, "Sir, we are all sorry for what has happened. It was a regrettable accident. We know that it is wrong to shoot at people."

Thomas added, "None of us wants to punish your people. You must know that we never retaliate and never beat any Matabele. We would rather that you made that wise decision. We know that you will wish to punish a wrongdoer. That is why we have come to you now and we await your verdict."

Mzilikazi looked at his advisers; "We will discuss this accident. You can wait outside and we will tell you our decision. You may have some beer and meat whilst you wait."

Nodding their heads in agreement, the three men crawled out through the door and sought a place to sit against the wall of the hut that was in the sunshine. It wasn't exactly warm there, just a little less cold than in the shade. The dogs were in evidence as usual, but seemed a little less aggressive today and were easily pushed aside. Perhaps someone had fed them.

"What do you think the king will decide?" Franz asked the others anxiously.

Thomas looked thoughtful, "He is not at all happy about the shooting and we all know that it was a bad mistake. Though we don't blame you," he added hastily as he saw Franz' worried expression deepen. "I'm sure you'll be forgiven though. He wants to make us suffer a little longer and that is why he has sent us outside to wait."

A jug of beer and a platter of meat were brought to them and they tucked in with a will despite the fact that they had all enjoyed a good breakfast earlier that morning.

"I think the king, through his advisers, will order the thieves to return your goods and then you will have to pay the youth and his parents some form of compensation for the injury you inflicted," Henry remarked thoughtfully. "The advisers might even want presents themselves as compensation for a supposed insult against the nation, knowing how they all love presents." Then he added a warning, "You must be very careful in future though, Franz, these people will bear you a grudge, especially those who will have to return your guns. They believe that they were justified in punishing you for the injury to their friend and that their actions were correct. Although it may be that they thought they had an excuse to acquire guns and a wonderful opportunity to steal from the despised white man. The fact that the guns were stolen will not weigh heavily with them. Theft is an accepted and acceptable occupation. They will resent having to return them and losing something so valuable. Every Matabele youth wants to own a gun. It is a status symbol to them."

Franz looked crestfallen, "You don't have to remind me of my stupidity. I had just had enough of that youth and I reacted hastily. I am just thankful that there wasn't a serious injury. I know that many young warriors are longing to wash their spears in our blood and they don't need much in the way of provocation. I'm sorry I have put all our lives in danger following my impetuous impulse."

Henry patted his arm, "We all make mistakes and what we have to do is to learn from them. All of us at Inyati have spent years coping with exactly the same sort of problems as you have; petty theft, rudeness, deliberate obstruction, ingratitude, threats and even physical assaults at times and frequently we have to restrain our natural reactions. We pray constantly for the strength to control automatic retaliations either by word or deed. It is very difficult."

Thomas, his mouth full of meat, nodded his head vigorously. "I sometimes take myself off to the workshop or the forge and spend time hammering a defenceless piece of metal or wood to ease my frustrations."

Franz looked relieved to hear that the missionaries, too, suffered from the behaviour of the natives.

It did not occur to any of the men that perhaps the Matabele had every right to resent their presence. As far as the missionaries were concerned, they were there to offer salvation to the heathen and offer a light in their darkness. These people needed to know about God and Jesus for their own salvation. No Christian wanted to condemn people to everlasting darkness through ignorance.

The traders considered that giving blankets, beads or guns in exchange for the trophies of the bush was a decided asset to people who had none of these benefits of civilisation. Besides, they all reasoned that Mzilikazi had no greater claim to this country than they had. After all, he had occupied it by force less than thirty years before and had indeed stolen it from the previous inhabitants who in turn had settled there and displaced the hunter-gatherers who roamed the land. Who was to judge who should own and occupy the land?

So it was argued whenever questions arose in discussions round campfires and now occupied the thoughts of the waiting men.

They were eventually rewarded for their wait and Mzilikazi himself told them what had been decided. He had sent a message to the headman of the town and ordered him to collect all the stolen goods. These would then be restored to Franz later today. Franz must then call the youth to his store and ask him to bring his parents with him. Franz must apologise for his attack on the youth and allow the father to choose a musket for himself. The mother must be given a handful of beads of her choosing and the youth was to be allowed to choose a blanket.

It was galling for Franz to have to reward someone who had produced little or no work, stolen from him and then attacked his family, but there was little choice and though the fine was expensive for him it was not nearly as disastrous as losing all his goods.

Thomas and Henry accepted the decision, knowing that in Matabele eyes they had got off lightly. They thanked the king and his counsellors for their wise deliberations and were then pleased to be offered two large pieces of meat.

"You must make sure that the son of Mshete grows strong again," the king advised. "It is not good for him to be sick."

Once again thanks were offered as the men made their departure, followed by two women bearing the meat.

* * * * * * *

Jane had had a pleasant morning. Much to her surprise Harry and Livingstone had played ninepins for hours with only a few minor altercations. Livingstone was as accurate as Harry was so the games were hotly contested. The strong competition appealed to Harry who usually won most contests with ease and he concentrated fiercely. Jane was surprised by his attitude and equally surprised when he allowed Isabelle to have a turn. Although Isabelle had asked to play when the scores were even neither of the boys resented her interruption. To their intense amusement she threw the balls so wildly that she was in danger of hitting the little ones playing with their toys nearby. Luckily she soon gave up the effort, declaring, "It's a stupid game for boys." A statement that seemed to satisfy her pride as the boys returned to battle with renewed vigour.

Jane's baking was successful and uninterrupted. Mrs Greite had bolted the door firmly once they were all inside and with all the stores closed there were no curious crowds outside to disturb them. Even when she was carrying the dough along to the oven there were no onlookers, which surprised and pleased her. She didn't even stop to ponder why there were so few people in evidence.

When father came back to the store with the others he immediately spoke to Jane and went with her to put the largest piece of meat into the oven to roast. Enough potatoes and hard skinned squashes were put round the meat to feed the whole camp that evening. The oven was still warm from the bread baking and they soon stoked up the fire. It would take all the afternoon to cook and wouldn't be ready until evening, however, as Thomas had pointed out, they could cut some slices off the smaller piece and grill them over the fire for their mid-day meal.

Mrs Greite quickly prepared some beans, potatoes and pumpkin to accompany the slices of meat being prepared for cooking on the fire, as she listened to Franz' account of the visit to the king. Like her husband, she was considerably relieved by the outcome, despite the loss entailed by the compensatory gifts.

Joseph returned from his trading trip not long after the others had finished lunch and his expression suggested that he had been successful. Henry and Thomas were sitting on the floor in front of the store talking idly and they waited for him to unsaddle his horse before standing up and walking with him to the kraal behind the store. Joseph began talking even as he found some grain and water for his tired mount.

"The hunters were just where I had calculated they would be from the messenger's description. They have had a very good season so far and needed to off-load some of their tusks so that they can travel further to the west, where they believe there are more large herds. I have arranged to buy all the tusks they were prepared to sell now and they have agreed to let me transport the rest of their load down south if I have room." He looked thoughtful. "The trouble is that I only have one wagon, the one arriving today, and I already have close to a full load in my storeroom. That means I won't have enough space for everything." He hesitated for a moment before adding thoughtfully, "I expect one of the others might be able to carry some."

He then looked speculatively at Henry, "I don't suppose you have room for some in your baggage wagon? I won't need much space, and you will be paid, of course."

"I might have," Henry replied cautiously, but pleased at the thought of earning a bonus. "In addition to some family goods I only have a few tusks of my own that have been given to me over the years. As you know, we are not allowed to trade, but we do receive gifts from grateful hunters and sportsmen as they pass through Inyati and receive our hospitality and often medical care too. I will have a look later this afternoon."

But Henry realised that it might have been advantageous had he acted sooner. Within two hours the area around the stores was a seething mass of people.

The arrival of wagons from the south could hardly go unnoticed and as always aroused great excitement.

There was often relief amongst the white residents as food supplies were replenished and the stores restocked with trade goods. For some the arrival of bottles of wine, Cape Brandy and other spirits was cause for celebration and there was always the chance that there would be long awaited mail as well as newspapers and magazines. The news from the outside world might be weeks or even months old, but it was received with the greatest anticipation and often shared, to become a basis for conversation and discussions for weeks to come.

Who knew what might have happened since they had last had any information about life outside Matabeleland: a war might have begun or ended, a great personage might have died or rulers changed. All these excitements really meant very little to people who were so isolated that shattering events elsewhere had no impact on them or their way of life. Nevertheless, they longed to know what was happening and to feel able to discuss at length what they had learned. Personal news was even more precious and these letters would be read and re-read many times over the following weeks. One of the greatest treats for the educated amongst them was to receive a parcel of books and this was one of Jane's dearest hopes whenever wagons appeared on her horizon.

For the Matabele people the arrival of wagons with their lengthy spans of oxen was an entertaining spectacle to liven up their day. News of the approaching wagon train would reach the king's town days before the wagons actually arrived, as the drivers had to seek permission to enter Matabeleland. They had to wait on the southern bank of the Ramaquaban River and send news of their arrival there, stating their business and at the same time requesting the king to allow them to proceed.

If there was a danger of the incoming oxen carrying disease or if the humans accompanying the wagons were ill, then permission was refused. As soon as the king had given his permission and the wagons crossed the river, news of their progress would be carried daily and then hourly to the king's town as the journey reached its end. Some white residents would ride out to meet the cavalcade and the more daring or inquisitive of the native population then walked or ran to meet the visitors.

Some of them might get a free ride if they were agile and determined enough. Avoiding the large plodding hooves of the oxen, the huge ironclad wheels of the wagons and the long lashing whips of the drivers was a sport greatly enjoyed by participants and spectators alike. Lithe and muscular, revelling in their successes, the young men would leap onto the wagons in their hordes, with jeers for failure and cheers for prowess egging them on.

Later, some of them might be asked to assist in manhandling the wagons closer to the stores once the oxen had been outspanned or in carrying goods into the stores in return for payment, but most of them abhorred labouring tasks…they were warriors and menial work was beneath them. Their greatest pleasure was the prospect of being able to acquire something for themselves, unseen and unnoticed, but the transport riders and the traders were a wary group and it wasn't easy to steal, making the challenge even more worthwhile.

Thomas, Henry and Joseph, still discussing hunting and trading, were overwhelmed by the rushing and pushing crowds and were thankful that the children were still inside their own wagons.

Charles and George rode up to Joseph's store, their horses cutting a path through the mass of humanity, and spoke to the men over the incessant chatter of excited voices.

"We'll unload your wagon first, Joseph, then the one that Charles and Franz have shared," George suggested. "We'll leave mine and Edward's until the last as I shall have to decide where to store Edward's goods. I couldn't plan beforehand as I had no idea that he and his loaded wagon were about to arrive."

"We have decided to leave the drivers to guard the wagons, with perhaps one of us on horseback as support, along with Edward and William, who is the other transport rider. You'll meet him soon. The rest of us will deal with the removal of the boxes and other goods from the wagons into the stores."

Aroused by the noise of the crowd and Joseph's wagon being pushed up to the door of the store, the Hargreaves children left their bed and crowded onto the driver's seat to gape at the spectacle around them.

"We shall have to stay here," Jane told them firmly as hands reached up to touch them and stroke their clothes. Harry and Isabelle were giggling at the remarks being made by various individuals in the crowd. Few people realised the children's deep understanding and knowledge of Sindebele and were happily discussing what they might steal from these weak and pale foreigners who were so ignorant and yet had so much in the way of desirable goods.

Joseph stood in the doorway to receive the merchandise with Henry and Thomas in the store behind him to carry it wherever ordered. Franz and Charles were on the wagon manipulating the sacks, boxes, chests and bolts of cloth towards the front, from where they could be heaved to Joseph.

George had gone on his horse to act as a guard for the other wagons.

The unloading went with a swing and with most things in boxes or bags the men felt that they could keep a check on everything.

The empty wagon was pushed to the side of the store where it would remain until Joseph was ready to load the goods he had traded and which were for sale in Cape Town, then they all moved on to the Greites' store, where the activity and precautions were repeated.

As the crowd surged after them, leaving only a few hopefuls searching the ground and the now empty wagon for any overlooked treasure, Jane deemed it possible for them to descend from their wagon. Joseph had locked and barred his store, but the children found a place in the sun and played happily. Jane had rarely had time to herself before and as she played with the doll she had named Elizabeth she planned to make some dresses for her. If only mother had been here with them she would have felt blissfully happy.

The children were given their supper early and for once Jane had to go to bed at the same time as her brothers and sister as the men planned a celebration to mark the safe arrival of their goods. Whilst Jane coped with James' unhappy longing for his mama in the wagon, inside the store their father tucked into a satisfying meal.

George lifted his tin mug filled with brandy, "Here's good health to you all and a successful season," he called across the now empty table. "May your journey south be an easy one," he added, looking at Henry.

Henry acknowledged the toast and in return wished them all good health and a good trading season.

"At least we managed to empty our wagons and get everything locked inside safely," Joseph stated thankfully.

"I didn't see anything being stolen," affirmed Franz. "We kept a close eye on everything. I shall check my goods tomorrow when it's light, but I'm sure nothing is missing."

"Well appearances can be deceptive. I'll recheck my goods tomorrow too, but now let us hear about your journey here," suggested Charles, looking at Edward and William.

The stories continued long into the night, bringing pleasure to tired men who felt relaxed, happily well fed and secure with friends. They were warmed inside by the liquor and outside by the blazing fire.

In the king's town the chief induna sat silent by the fire in his hut. He gazed reflectively at the flames, seeing in them some of the glories of his past. He waited patiently and expectantly. The scratching at his door was barely audible and his voice bidding the visitor enter was pitched to carry no further than the ear pressed to the wood. Quietly the door was lifted and pushed inwards and two children crawled up to the induna on their knees. Without speaking they handed him a gun and then equally quietly withdrew. During the next hour there were numerous more arrivals and the induna gravely accepted a small bag of sugar, another of flour, a small block of salt, a cup full of tea leaves and another of coffee beans, a block of lead and a bullet mould and finally some matches. He was pleased with the gifts, though he regretted the lack of gunpowder. He would have to trade for a pouch of that. It was a nuisance, but he had the king's permission to enter the store where the elephants' teeth were kept, so he should be able to arrange for the exchange.

Satisfied that all was well, the induna lay on his sleeping mat beside the fire and was soon deeply asleep.

CHAPTER 14

On the following day the storekeepers all had a feeling that the goods they had received didn't quite tally with the goods ordered and expected. There was nothing really obvious, just a suspicion that all was not as it should be. They checked again thoroughly and came to the conclusion that the losses were small: one missed some sugar, another some flour, the lead was surely a bar short in another store and yet another discovered that there was a musket short. The missing items were so few they might have been easily overlooked, except of course for the musket and none of the traders could account for the slight discrepancies. They each had a niggling thought that perhaps they hadn't been as careful as they might have been when they were unloading, however unlikely that seemed, but there was nothing to be done. After all, the goods had travelled for hundreds of miles and the losses could have occurred anywhere along the route.

The hunter, with whom Joseph had already negotiated, arrived mid-morning, which meant that Joseph could now make definite arrangements for the onward transport of all his bartered goods and those he had bought. First he would load up his own wagon early in the evening with his stock then fill up the remaining space with the hunter's goods that he had promised to transport. Any goods that wouldn't fit in his wagon would be carried in Henry's wagon. Earlier that morning, before anyone was astir, Henry had inspected his own baggage wagon and informed Joseph that he could accommodate the excess goods.

William wanted to return south as soon as the wagons could be loaded up again and hoped to start by the next day. His oxen had rested for several days at the Ramaquaban River on the way up and had had another day to rest and feed here at the king's town, so they were in good condition. He wanted to make the return trip whilst there was still water to be obtained along the road.

Edward planned to stay with his brother and dispose of the trading goods he had brought on his own behalf, but he offered to ride with William to the boundary of the Matabele territory if William felt that he needed help. They all knew that keeping watch on three laden wagons and guiding them safely through the bush was no easy task. So both of them were delighted when Henry asked if he and his family might travel southwards with the transport riders and they readily agreed to the suggestion.

Henry was relieved and pleased at the thought of being able to continue his journey. He had agonized for several days about leaving the Moffats and travelling on alone, but John had been insistent that Henry shouldn't wait any longer. Now there was a satisfactory solution to his problem, but he was still loath to leave the Moffats.

Fortunately, both John and Emily were showing signs of recovery and had been able to sit in the warm sunshine for almost an hour on the previous afternoon. They would do the same today, but it might be many more days before they were strong enough to leave the wagon.

Jane had been awake very early that day and had dressed quickly as her father left the wagon. Peering outside, she saw him go to their baggage wagon and she hurriedly joined him, pulling her bonnet firmly round her head and drawing her shawl tightly across her shoulders against the cold air. Henry was struggling to unlace the tarpaulin.

"What's brought you out here so early?" he demanded as he turned in astonishment at her sudden appearance.

"I'm sorry, father. I didn't mean to startle you. I just thought you might let me look in mother's box. There might be some material there that I could use to make dresses for our dolls."

Henry, whose mind had been on other things, stared at her uncomprehendingly. He had been thinking that the opportunity to earn a little extra money was timely, with the expense of travelling by ship and train still ahead of him.

"Mr Charles gave Isabelle and me a doll each. I would like to sew dresses for them, but I haven't any material." Jane's voice faltered as her father made no response. Perhaps she shouldn't have mentioned mother's name.

Henry continued to free the rope and brought his thoughts back to his daughter's request. "It would be a good idea for you and Isabelle to do some sewing again. There has been too much free time and idle play for far too long." Then, thinking that perhaps he had sounded a little harsh, he added more kindly, "Yes, you may look in the chest packed with your mother's belongings."

"Thank you father." Jane's relieved response was accompanied by a bright smile that transformed her face and for a moment Henry saw that there was a kind of beauty in this normally solemn little girl.

As Henry prepared to move the boxes around and clear a space in the middle of the wagon for the skins and tusks, Jane opened the oak linen chest her real mother had brought all the way from England more than five years ago. Now it was packed with the clothing and items belonging to her second mother. Mama's clothes had all been used over the intervening years and her books and pictures eaten by white ants. Jane found some material she could use for making dolls' dresses and she also found two little baby's bonnets.

She remembered how she and Isabelle had sat for hours making these bonnets for their expected new baby. She held them for a moment and felt she would burst into tears at the sadness of losing baby Joshua and mother.

"What are you doing?" father called. "Have you managed to find what you wanted?"

Jane gulped. "Yes father," she replied steadily, then added with a sudden inspiration, "I've found two little baby bonnets. Do you think we could give them to Mrs Greite?"

Henry was still fully occupied with his task, but managed to glance up and, seeing items of clothing which didn't concern him, he immediately consented.

Jane closed the oak chest, feeling cheered at the thought of being able to give the new baby a present. She hurried back to the comparative warmth of the wagon where Harry was already stirring, his movements waking both James and Isabelle.

After breakfast, Jane held a reading lesson and was pleased that her little pupils had managed to remember most of the words even though they had had few lessons since before mother died. The arithmetic lesson wasn't nearly so successful and Jane had the greatest difficulty in maintaining her temper with Isabelle, who had soon lost interest and begun to play.

It was at lunchtime that the children heard about the intention to leave the king's town by the next day. They also learned that the Moffats wouldn't be accompanying them.

Harry became very cross at the news. "Who will play with me if Livingstone stays here?" he demanded of the whole company.

Henry looked surprised at the question. "You have your sisters and brother, as you have always had. Livingstone must stay with his parents and they cannot travel to Kuruman yet, but we have to leave as soon as possible. We have already wasted too many days."

The storekeepers nodded in agreement.

"You'll find plenty to occupy you as you travel," smiled Joseph kindly.

"I'll make you some throwing sticks this afternoon if you like," Charles offered. "I have some suitable wood, hard but not too heavy. You'll be able to practise aiming at targets as you walk along."

Harry's eyes lit up. The sticks he had brought with him were ones he had picked up in the bush at Inyati. They were nice and smooth from regular handling but were not really well balanced and it was difficult to be accurate all the time. "Thank you, Mr Charles. Having properly balanced throwing sticks will make a lot of difference. I might be able to hit the target nearly every time."

Harry's obvious enthusiasm pleased Charles and he was generous enough to offer to make some for Livingstone too. Bruce and James, with Nomalanga and one of the nursemaids, joined the group in Charles' store after their rest period, leaving Jane free to go with Isabelle to present the bonnets to Mrs Greite.

Franz and his wife were very touched by the gifts from the two little girls. They received the bonnets with obvious pleasure and remarked favourably on the needlework so patently achieved over many painstaking hours by little hands. The bonnets were each tried on the baby's head and again admired with exclamations of joy and pride. Their compliments were gratifying to the two girls who seldom received praise now that mother was dead. Their lips quivered and both looked as if they might burst into tears.

Franz gave his wife a quick glance and she nodded her understanding. Kindly, she invited Jane and Isabelle to partake of afternoon tea as if they were adult callers in a civilised society and both graciously accepted the invitation as if they had received numerous such offers. Indeed it was like a game they had played from time to time with mother when she hadn't been too tired and when she was describing her life in Cape Town before she had married father. All the domestic work had been done by servants, which meant that mother and all her family had been able to enjoy visiting friends or relations and receive visitors in return. The life she had described was hard for Jane and Isabelle to understand: it was one of leisure and pleasure in total contrast to the life they experienced at Inyati. How could mother leave such a life in exchange for hardship, near starvation and with few friends to share the loneliness?

Jane's reverie was broken when Mrs Greite asked her, " Would you like to hold the baby?"

"Yes please. I would love to," Jane replied. She sat on the edge of the bed and the tiny creature was placed in her arms.

"We think we might call her Maria," Franz informed them proudly. "It is my mother's name."

"It's a lovely name," Jane agreed. "I'm sorry we shan't see more of her because we are leaving tomorrow. I don't know when we shall be able to come back. We are going to school in England."

"That is a long, long way away," added Isabelle solemnly. "Perhaps we shall never come back."

"I think we must come back if father is living here," Jane chided her gently.

Isabelle was allowed to hold the baby for a few moments, with Jane standing protectively beside her and both marvelled at the tiny fingers and the downy cap of hair peeping from underneath the bonnet.

The arrival of fresh supplies from the south had enabled Mrs Greite to do some baking that morning and she produced a fine selection of cakes, tarts and pies. Despite the shortage of chairs, there were sufficient boxes for them all to be seated around the table, which had been laid with a fresh white cloth. All the niceties were observed, making Jane feel very grown up and extremely happy with the visit. She was sad when it all came to an end and they had to leave.

Franz' store had remained closed that day so that the new goods could be checked and packed onto the shelves. Only George had opened his store for a few hours, hoping to attract customers and perhaps obtain additional stock to send to Cape Town whilst the opportunity was there. Even so, there were the usual crowds wandering around, shouting loudly to each other. Jane knew it was rude to whisper or talk quietly. Only people with secrets would whisper so that other people couldn't hear what was being said. People who shouted had nothing to hide.

"I think we had better go to Mr Charles' store and find out if the boys are still there," Jane suggested to Isabelle. Isabelle held tightly to her big sister and the two girls threaded their way through the throng, their faces hidden by their bonnets as they kept their eyes on the ground. They ignored the remarks about them as they hurried along, occasionally having to pull away from a grasping hand.

It was a great relief when they were able to knock on the door of the store and were admitted.

Charles looked up from the throwing stick he was whittling and smiled at the girls, "It won't be long now. This is the last one and then they'll have two each."

Isabelle went to stand beside Livingstone and Harry, who were watching Charles at work.

Jane walked across to where Nomalanga and the Moffats' nursemaid were sitting in a corner keeping watch on the younger ones who were playing with their toys. Nomalanga looked very downcast, as if she would burst into tears any moment.

"Are you all right, Nomalanga?" Jane asked quietly. "You don't look very happy."

Nomalanga looked at the floor. "I am not happy. I am sad."

Jane was surprised to hear this, as Nomalanga generally had a happy nature and she had been delighted to be adopted by the Hargreaves family when her own family and the whole village had chased her away. She had been accepted as part of the household and was kindly treated, well clothed and fed, even if she was a servant. The only sign of unhappiness she had shown previously, was when she described her rejection and the fear of death she had experienced. With no home, no food and no friends, life had been very precarious until she had found her way to the mission.

"Oh dear. I am sorry to hear that," said Jane softly as she sat on the floor close to the little Matabele girl. "Can you tell me what is troubling you?"

There was silence for a few moments before Nomalanga spoke, "You are leaving here tomorrow."

Jane was puzzled, "Yes we are, but you have known for a long time that we are going to Kuruman. Father sent a letter to the mother and father of the Reverend Moffat to ask them if you could stay there until he comes back. You will be very happy at Kuruman. People will look after you. You will be able to go to school and learn how to sew dresses. Father explained it to us all."

Nomalanga tried to tell Jane her fears. "When we were at Inyati I could sleep in the kitchen. It was warm. It was my home. I was happy there. Then we walked to the king's town and on the way these two people from Kuruman let me sleep near them. They did not send me away. We could eat together. Now they tell me that they are staying here at the king's town until the Reverend Moffat can travel. I will have to walk by myself. Where can I sleep if they are not there? Who will eat with me?"

The questions upset Jane. She hadn't thought about Nomalanga at all. They had all left Inyati with a feeling of excitement and living in the wagon had been an adventure, but of course she had father and Isabelle and Harry and James. Nomalanga had been with the two nursemaids and had seemed as content as any of them. Jane had heard them laughing together and it had pleased her, because Nomalanga had no friends amongst the Matabele, who shunned her. Now the two nursemaids would remain behind and poor Nomalanga would be on her own at night and at mealtimes. Jane could understand the problem.

"I'll speak to father as soon as we get back to Mr Wood's store. He will be able to decide what we can do. You mustn't worry, Nomalanga, you will not be left all by yourself."

Charles had finished his task and the children thanked him. Harry and Livingstone both expressed their great pleasure as they held their new sticks. Each one was about a foot in length with a knob at the end so that it looked like a miniature knobkerrie. The handles were tapered slightly and had been polished smooth so that they would slip easily through the hand when they were thrown. The wood was heavy enough to ensure a straight flight and the balance had been carefully assessed to make them accurate if they were thrown correctly.

"There you are, young gentlemen. You now have the best throwing sticks in the country. You will be able to play games with them, aiming at a target or you will be able to hunt small animals and birds when you have practised sufficiently. You may become skilful hunters one day." Charles smiled with pleasure as he watched the two boys examining their treasures. "You won't be able to use them here, unfortunately, but I'll ride out with the wagons for a short way tomorrow and perhaps you'll be able to show me what you can do with them."

True to her promise, Jane told father about Nomalanga's worries, but when she heard later what he had arranged she was extremely upset. It was after supper, just as Jane was preparing to take the younger children out to the wagon and put them to bed, when father came across to talk to her.

"Jane, you told me that Nomalanga would have no one to share her sleeping area on the journey from here to Kuruman now that the Moffats are staying here. I have been thinking about it and she is quite right. We cannot take a young girl all by herself and expect her to manage, especially as there are often wild animals on the road. It would be most unchristian. I have arranged for her to stay here and help Mrs Greite with the baby. If she wants to travel to Kuruman, which would undoubtedly be the best opportunity for her, she can accompany the Reverend Moffat when he is able to make the journey. Should she decide to stay in Matabeleland, the Greites will look after her."

It took Jane several minutes to fully absorb the information and she longed to be able to argue, to ask father to find another solution, but he had just nodded to her, bidden them all goodnight and returned to the group of men around the fire.

It was already dark and extremely cold outside as she ushered the younger ones into the bed. It was much too late to find Nomalanga to tell her about the new arrangements and Jane herself was shivering, so she took off her shoes and dress and found a place under the blankets, pulling them up over her head so that her breath would help her to get warm. She couldn't sleep immediately, her mind concentrating on the early start tomorrow morning and the awful fact that she would have absolutely no help. How was she ever going to manage?

CHAPTER 15

Jane lay awake despite her desire to sleep. She was so cold even with Isabelle's warm body beside her. She would have liked to rub her arms and feet but didn't want to move too much in case she disturbed the others, as both James and Harry had fallen asleep easily after they had said their prayers. They must have been tired, for neither of them had asked for mother or complained of the cold. Harry had put his throwing sticks beside his ninepins in the special place under the bed, beside James' hippo and his sisters' dolls. Jane wasn't sure whether Isabelle was asleep or awake as she was lying quite still, but Isabelle liked to live in a pretend world and Jane had no wish to share it with her just now. Her own world was much too real and filled with enormous problems.

Inyati had been home, a wonderfully safe place with mother and father, even if they all had to work so hard. It was mostly a happy home, although there were worries about food from time to time and they didn't always have shoes to wear. She hadn't been sorry to leave, because the house just wasn't the same without mother and the prospect of going to England had seemed exciting.

Jane forced herself to think of happy things. Mother always said it was easier to go to sleep if one's mind was happy.

The journey had been exciting and they had had the company of the Moffats and the Reverend Thomas. The days at the king's town had been filled with interest even though the crowds were sometimes almost unbearable and they still had their friends with them. It was sad that the Reverend John and Mrs Moffat had been so ill, but they were getting better now and there had been the excitement of the new baby for the Greites. All the storekeepers had been kind and helpful and the children had all been given new toys. Having a wooden doll with hair was a wonderful feeling, so Jane tried to concentrate on Elizabeth and the clothes she would make for her when she had time.

It was at this point that all Jane's fears came flooding in: tomorrow they would leave the king's town by themselves and would have to say goodbye to the Moffats and all the friendly traders. Nomalanga would no longer be with them and to add to all the farewells Jane would have to say goodbye to Sandy, her beloved cow. She wondered how she could face tomorrow and turned her face to the pillow to weep silently. Somehow and at sometime she fell asleep.

* * * * * * *

William had planned to leave before first light. It was nearly sixty miles to the Ramaquaban River and oxen could manage no more than three miles an hour even when the going was fairly flat. The road south was full of obstacles and there were many streams to cross, which slowed them down. If there was an accident or a wagon became stuck, many hours could be wasted. Oxen needed to rest and eat during the day, so they usually trekked early in the morning, rested during the day and trekked again during the late afternoon and evening. On a good day they would manage twelve or perhaps even fifteen miles. On the way up, the fully laden wagons had been hauled through the stream beds and rivers with the minimum delay and only a loose wheel had held them up.

William knew that the loads of ivory, skins and trophies would be considerably heavier and there would be more strain on the wagons. There were fewer ostrich feathers to transport now as ostrich farming had begun in the Cape and the market for wild ostrich feathers was falling. William didn't mind how his loads were made up. As long as he had enough to fill the wagons that belonged to him, he was happy. Supervising wagons for other hunters or traders was a bonus. Of course, it meant extra work because there were more oxen to feed and care for, but he had trained two Hottentots to spot the beginnings of problems in either a wagon or the span of oxen pulling it and he knew that he could rely on them. They had both become reliable transport riders. No doubt they would go into business on their own account as soon as they could buy their own spans and wagons, but that wouldn't be this year. William had spent the day checking the wagons, chains, riems, yokes and disselboom. He had thoroughly greased all the axles and made sure that the wheels were sound. He had supervised the loading and checked that the tarpaulins were secure. That evening he had ensured that Diamond, his stocky bay horse was well fed and watered and was bedded down comfortably. Now he was satisfied that all was ready. William slept soundly, wrapped in his blanket on the floor beside the fire in George's store, a few feet away from his friend Edward.

* * * * * * *

Henry had managed to purchase three goats that afternoon, which, with the hens, would keep them supplied with meat for most of the journey to the Ramaquaban.

It was a pity they had to leave the cow behind, but it should be possible to buy milk at the Matabele kraals along the road for the children to drink.

Henry and Thomas had spent the evening discussing the future of Inyati and how Henry should try to obtain more funds for the Mission. For a short time

John had joined them as he wished to hand over some letters to be delivered to Kuruman.

Henry had accompanied him back to his wagon and spoken briefly to Emily to wish her farewell and with God's help a speedy recovery to good health. They had then said prayers together for the success of the forthcoming journey. Henry would probably leave Kuruman for Cape Town before the Moffats arrived there, so this parting might be for a year. He felt saddened to be leaving the colleagues who had been his closest companions over the past five years, but pleased nevertheless at the prospect of resuming his journey. William seemed a pleasant young man and very capable as a transport rider. They should get on well together. Bidding everyone goodnight, Henry retired to bed.

* * * * * * *

In the canvas lean-to attached to the Moffat wagon, Nomalanga lay awake on her sleeping mat spread on a pile of straw. She and her two companions had cut fresh straw that afternoon and it had retained some of the warmth of the sun, so that it had been not quite as cold as the bare earth on that very cold night. Even so, Nomalanga thought with longing of the warm kitchen that had been her bedroom ever since she had thrown herself on the mercy of the missionaries.

She was feeling very unhappy and afraid. When she was small she had had her own Matabele family. All that had changed when she began to look different from other children of her age. There had been a lot of trouble then and some people thought she had been bewitched. Young and defenceless, not understanding the fear engendered by accusations of witchcraft, and totally bewildered, she was driven out of her home and away from the village. No one wanted her any more. If she returned, she would be stoned and beaten. Even with these threats she had stayed as close as she dared to her family, begging for food and help. Her cries had been ignored. Weak and starving, she wandered alone through the bush, miraculously unharmed by wild animals and would have died had she not found her way to the mission station. Nomalanga remembered those days with a shudder and marvelled daily at the kindness of her new family.

Nomalanga loved the Hargreaves family, especially James, whom she regarded as her own baby. Now she had a real problem. Only this afternoon, whilst everyone was resting, she had overheard a conversation between the drivers and had learned that her family was to travel southwards the next day, but that the Moffats were staying at the king's town until they were well enough to travel.

The Moffats' two nursemaids had been kind to Nomalanga and allowed her to share their meals and this sleeping tent. They all conversed in a mixture of Sechuana, Sindebele and English, depending on which word came first to mind.

Working together whilst washing clothes at the river, carrying water to the camp or watching over their little charges, they had become happy companions. The two young women were ecstatic about returning home to Kuruman and meeting up with their families again. They enthused about their own country so much that Nomalanga felt she might be happy there even when the Hargreaves family had left. She didn't want to be parted from either her new family or the two girls who had become her supporters. She could hear wolves howling out in the bush and further away there was a lion roaring, but here inside the fence around the store and close to the wagon with her two friends sleeping beside her, Nomalanga wasn't afraid. Still worrying about her future she finally went to sleep.

* * * * * * *

In their stores, where fires had taken the worst chill off the rooms, the resident traders of the king's town in Matabeleland slept peacefully. The beds were rough and ready, but the blankets comfortable and those who shared their room with visitors were undisturbed by the extra presence. The arrival of supplies from the south had made life easier for all of them and the opportunity to send out their ivory was always a relief. Thomas, wrapped in his blankets in a corner of Joseph's store, thought briefly of his family back in Inyati and decided that he must leave within a few days, too. He would ask the king if he could hire a youth to walk the cow slowly back to the mission station as soon as the Moffats were able to leave. He was sorry to see Henry go, as they had been good friends and willingly helped each other in times of stress. He fully approved of Henry's plan to put his children into school, but he also felt that the loss of one of the missionaries put a severe strain on those remaining. It was some time since he had been able to go down country and on to his native Wales. He preferred to be here in Africa, but he really did wish that the other missionary at Inyati wasn't there. His mind on his Bible now, he concentrated on St Matthew's exhortation, 'Take, therefore, no thought for the morrow: for the morrow shall take thought for the things of itself. Sufficient unto the day is the evil thereof.' There was a great deal of comfort to be had in The Bible. Thinking on these things, Thomas drifted into a deep sleep.

* * * * * * *

Lying in his blankets beside the fire in his brother's store, Edward watched the glimmer of light from the dying fire. A faint whorl of smoke curled its way up the chimney and the smell of wood smoke attached itself to his blankets and hair to mingle with the smell of horses, of oxen and the outdoor scents of the bush. Edward loved the African bush and hunting, but like his older brother he planned to own his own farm one day. He only hoped that he wouldn't have to be a trader for as long as George had been. This was his first trip as far north as Matabeleland and he had visions of selling all the goods he had brought with him, then hunting for ivory and filling the wagon for the return trip. If he managed to do that, he would make enough money to buy and stock a second wagon. Edward let his imagination roam freely to spread over a few years of heady success with all the joys of youth and freedom. He would be a noted elephant hunter during the dry season and a successful trader or farmer in the wetter months of the year. He would buy a farm close to his brother's and their parents could come and live in a cottage between the two.

A piece of falling wood in the fire sent a shower of sparks flaring out and Edward hastily thumped them out. It brought his idle dreaming to an abrupt close and he remembered that he would be away for nearly a week, riding alongside the wagons as far as the Ramaquaban. William would be able to manage after that with Henry to help. Besides, at Tati there were always men wanting to return south and it was probable that one or more would be willing to act as transport riders for a fee. Some might even pay for the protection of travelling with an organized trek.

The return journey by himself held no worries. At nineteen, Edward was confident of his own abilities. He was well built, healthy and strong and used to long hours in the saddle. He thought he would probably ride from Tati to Mangwe and stay the night with the Lees there. That would make the final leg perfectly possible in a day without too much strain on his horse. Contemplating this journey and how he could avoid some of the Matabele kraals he fell sound asleep.

*   *   *   *   *   *   *

Emily had been asleep for more than an hour and as he sat watching her, John realised that the fever had exhausted her this time. He felt that she should never return to Matabeleland if she was ever to regain her health. The children were all sound asleep too, fortunately free of the fever.

It might be more sensible to stay and work at Kuruman with his father. He had already written to the London Missionary Society suggesting such a step and now he must take this letter with others he had written over the past few days and hand them over to Henry. He left the wagon still feeling shaky, but pleased to be up and capable of walking.

He found Henry and Thomas in front of a warming fire in Joseph's store. Joseph was busy rearranging his new stores whilst his guests discussed Inyati and the lack of success in attracting Matabele converts. A box was dragged over for John to sit on and enjoy the warmth as he joined in their conversation. They all pretended optimism for the future and felt that the practice of medicine gave them the greatest chance of success.

Henry had written a list of medications to include Holloway's Pills, quinine, morphine, iodine and salicylic acid. Thomas had wanted much more, including surgical instruments, but his colleagues had pointed out that the Society would not be able to afford even a modest amount and Henry would have to rely on subscriptions to obtain a fraction of their requirements.

However keen he was to continue the debate, John tired quickly and Henry escorted him back to his wagon, taking the opportunity to bid farewell to both Moffats, as Emily had wakened at the sound of their voices. With Henry's prayers and good wishes filling his mind, John fell gratefully asleep.

* * * * * * *

In the king's town, the chief induna left the hut occupied by his newest, youngest wife, feeling gratified. It had been a worthwhile purchase and he was satisfied with his own abilities that would keep her occupied for many moons to come. She made an agreeable change from some of his other wives who had grown lazy and no longer gave him the pleasure he expected, but there were some things she still had to learn. He would recommend her to his chief wife tomorrow.

Back in his own hut, he relaxed contentedly on his sleeping mat. He hadn't been thinking of acquiring another wife until he saw Lomaqele. Her father had come to him with a problem as he recounted the fact that his wife had just given birth to her sixth daughter. Being a poor man, he couldn't afford to buy another wife and he was sure that his neighbour had put a curse on them so that they would never have a son. The neighbour also had a flock of goats and sheep that always flourished even when the rains were late.

The induna listened to this tale of woe and asked the man what he would give to be rid of this tiresome neighbour.

"Oh lord, I will give my eldest daughter and half the flock of sheep and goats," offered the man.

"I will find you a witchdoctor and you will tell him your story. He will need a goat as a sacrifice and he will need more goats or sheep as payment. I will come and see your daughter and judge whether or not she is worthy of a place as my wife."

The induna had inspected the young girl, who had almost reached marriageable age, and decided that he did indeed require another wife. The whole matter had been amicably settled, with the witchdoctor smelling out the neighbour and accusing him of placing a curse on the father. The sentence of death and the execution had followed almost immediately and the wronged man as compensation appropriated his goods.

The witchdoctor was duly paid and the induna bore off his new young bride, along with a number of sheep and goats. A good bargain, as he would normally have had to pay a bride price from his own flocks.

He chuckled happily to himself. The white men were stupid to insist on a single wife. How could any man live with only one wife? It was a foolish notion and even more foolish to try to persuade the Matabele nation to follow this custom. A warrior must have wives around him to tend to his every need when he was not away on battle. He needed food, drink, warmth and comfort. That's what women were for, to supply his needs.

Still chuckling at the odd habits of the white people, he heard a scratching at his door. "Enter," his voice commanded the visitor.

Pushing the door to one side, a young man crawled through the opening, dragging an elephant's tusk with him. He was followed by a second youth with the second of the pair. Still on their knees, they offered the tusks to the induna.

"Huh! Cow's teeth. Small, but I think they will buy enough of the powder for my guns. You are learning well, my sons. Now leave me and I will reward you later."

The induna fingered the ivory thoughtfully. All the ivory belonged to the king, unless he had given it as a concession to an elephant hunter and no Matabele could keep tusks for himself. He would bury these tusks in his special place and when the new moon showed would take them to one of the traders. No one watched to see what happened in the middle of the night and the traders were always ready to accept ivory. He had done it before. He would do it again. Completely satisfied with his life, the induna added another stick to his fire, turned on his side and fell asleep.

CHAPTER 16

The following morning was just as grim and upsetting as Jane had thought it would be. She had woken up as her father was dressing, his movements shaking the wagon slightly and now he was pulling on his boots. As soon as he had climbed down and gone to supervise moving his wagons towards the gate, where there was sufficient space for the oxen to be inspanned, she crawled quietly out of bed as the cold greyness of the morning seeped through the tent opening. Hastily she pulled on her dress and boots, then her bonnet and shawl, which added much needed extra warmth.

The morning was even colder outside with only the dimmest greyness showing the horizon as she left the shelter of the wagon and made her way towards the cattle kraal. The storekeepers began to appear, rubbing their hands and arms against the chill of the morning air and calling greetings to each other. With William, Edward, the drivers, leaders and extra servants, there were enough people to push the two wagons belonging to the Hargreaves' through the gate and out into the open bush, thus allowing enough room for the sixteen oxen each one required to be inspanned. As they set to work to manoeuvre the heavy vehicles forward and round, Jane hurried across the side of the store.

On the previous day father and Joseph had decided that all the Hargreaves' animals should be separated from the ones belonging to Joseph and the Moffats to avoid the chaos and confusion of trying to separate them in the semi-darkness of predawn. To this end they had divided the kraal into two with a thorn hedge. Fearlessly, Jane went through the gate and, treading carefully between the resting horses, goats and oxen, she pushed through the thorn fence where it touched the wall of the store. She had now reached the farther part of the kraal where Sandy lay peacefully, surrounded by more oxen, sheep, goats and horses. The smells of the animals mingled until it was difficult to pick out any individual one, but it was so much a part of Jane's life that she was happy even as she breathed the heavily scented air. The animals scarcely stirred at her presence as she went to sit beside Sandy, murmuring soothing words to the creature she knew so well.

"I don't know how long I'm going to be away, Sandy. It may be quite a long time. I hope you'll be at Inyati when I come back. The Reverend and Mrs Thomas will look after you until father arrives back from England. He will come back long before I can come because I have to go to school. You mustn't get the lung sickness or any other illnesses because I shan't be here to help to look after you, but the Reverend Thomas knows all about sick cows and can make you better again if you do get sick. I wish you could come with us a bit further, but I know you have already walked far enough and you still have to walk all the way back to Inyati. I am going to miss you because there won't be cows like you at grandfather's house, only lots of horses. Perhaps father will keep one of your calves for me. Goodbye, dear Sandy. Father says it is better to say 'au revoir' which is French and means 'til we meet again.'" She planted a kiss on Sandy's forehead and gave her a hug before stumbling to her feet and making her way back to the place where she had pushed through the fence.

Wiping the tears from her face, she hurried quickly through the second part of the kraal and out of the gate. Now she had to say goodbye to Nomalanga. Jane went to peep into the tent at the side of the Moffat wagon, but there was no sign of her there. She hurried over to the store where there was a faint light seeping through the cracks around the door.

Nomalanga had already made a fire and was putting the kettle on to heat some water. The candlelight and the flickering flames made her look like some extraordinary character from one of Jane's fairy stories.

"I wanted you all to have a hot drink of tea before you left," she explained as she saw Jane come through the door.

"That was very kind and thoughtful of you," Jane responded, gently touched by the thoughtfulness of this Matabele outcast who had become part of her family.

"I'm sure a hot drink will be very much appreciated by everyone. It is cold outside and we shall keep trekking until eight or nine o'clock, which means breakfast will be later than that. I think I'd better see if Isabelle is awake. She is always thirsty when she gets up."

The Hargreaves' wagons were now outside the gate and the oxen were being led from the kraal. Despite the shaking, the thumping and bumping, the shouting, the rattling of chains and the lowing of the oxen, Jane found her siblings still sound asleep and decided to leave them to their slumbers, so she made her way back to the store. There she found Mrs Greite, who had kindly provided some food for them all and there was sufficient for Jane to put into a small box to give to the little ones when they awoke. 'How kind people are!' she thought. 'This food with milk to drink will keep the little ones happy until it is time to stop for breakfast.' She thanked Mrs Greite and said a tearful goodbye as she was given a warm hug.

The men were especially grateful for the hot, sweet, milky tea and a bite to eat before setting out on the journey, and wasted no time in consuming it.

Jane stayed beside Nomalanga, sharing the food and talking to her until the very last moment.

"If you go to Kuruman with the Reverend and Mrs Moffat you will be able to stay there and go to school like me. When I come back we can return to Inyati together. I'm sure we'll see each other again, even if we are both grown up by then," Jane concluded on a hopeful note, even though she wasn't certain of the future for either of them.

Nomalanga was nodding her head in agreement, "Yes. Oh yes. We shall meet again." She clasped Jane's hand between her own and tears trickled down her cheeks.

"Come along, Jane. We are going now and it would be best if you were inside the wagon with your brothers and sister," father urged impatiently.

Jane gave Nomalanga a quick hug and fled to the wagon. As the wagon moved off with its accompanying creaks, squeaks and rumbles Jane could hear the shouted farewells gradually fading into the distance.

Jane had never felt more alone. It was true that father was with her and she had Isabelle, Harry and James, but somehow there was no-one she could talk to any more. The circle of friends had diminished, leaving her vulnerable, but she didn't have long to dwell on this sad state of affairs as Isabelle woke and her stirrings disturbed the boys.

As she had hoped, the promise of pies and tarts had quelled the grumblings of Isabelle and her brothers a short time later as they dressed themselves in the growing light of the day. It wasn't easy trying to dress in the confined space when the wagon was lurching from hump to hollow and over ruts hardened now by the sun and wind, but somehow they had managed it and then crawled over father's bed to the front of the wagon where Jane produced the box of food and a bottle filled with milk. Contentedly they had munched at the delicious pieces of meat pie and then the jam tart with small sips of milk whenever they could manage it without spilling too much.

The four traders had stayed with the trek until full daylight, when they had bade everyone a cheery farewell before galloping off back to their stores to face the business of the day.

"We'll see you in about a week's time," they called loudly to Edward, who had waved happily back and then hurried off to the front of the wagons to be with William. Thomas decided to stay a little longer and perhaps breakfast with Henry. He had a great deal he felt needed to be discussed and most particularly he wanted Henry to put his point of view to the Governors of the Society.

The children who were still riding in the wagon shouted their goodbyes over and over, especially to Charles, who was also thanked profusely for the toys he had given them, their high-pitched voices echoing over the ever-expanding distance between them.

Jane was delighted when the trek finally came to a halt and she learned that Lukas, who was William's servant, was a competent cook and would be responsible for all the meals, which included the Hargreaves family. It was the greatest relief not to have to cope with that chore as well as looking after the children, trying to do some lessons with them and do the washing and ironing whenever they had sufficient water.

William, Edward and Henry had seen to the welfare of their animals whilst breakfast was being prepared. This task was of primary importance as their safety as well as their livelihood depended on fit, healthy oxen and horses. The oxen were out-spanned and then taken by their young leaders, who now acted as herders, to graze at a distance not too far from the camp. This task was an honour for the cattle-loving natives and they took sufficient food with them to last the day, which they would spend playing games or resting whilst guarding their charges. There were instances of the herders being so interested in resting that oxen strayed out of sight, then there was an acrimonious quarrel and recriminations as hours were squandered trying to recover the beasts.

The camp was always made near a river or pool so that men and beasts could drink and bathe. Once the oxen had been checked and safely dispersed the next task was to water and feed the horses before the men themselves could have a quick wash and go to breakfast. The horses were usually fed corn in nosebags and tethered near the wagons to avoid them straying, meeting up with wild animals or eating a noxious plant in the bush.

Thomas had already seen to his horse and washed in the stream and was sitting at the breakfast table before Henry and the two young men joined him. There was a smaller table for the children nearby and after Thomas had said prayers, they all enjoyed a bowl of hot porridge with milk and sugar.

Jane was then given some books so that she could take lessons with her siblings whilst the men went to ensure the safety of the wagons. Everything had to be inspected, including the yokes, chains and reims in case they had sustained any damage during the morning. It seemed unlikely because this first part of the journey was comparatively danger free, but safety precautions could never be stinted.

Thomas continued to talk to Henry by the wagons until he felt that he had exhausted all the topics that he wanted Henry to remember. When he was certain his ideas would be explained to the people with influence he saddled up his horse and, bidding everyone adieu, he left.

By mid-morning, lessons had been completed and the children were able to play with their toys. Jane was busy cutting out two doll's dresses from the material she had found. She didn't mind helping Isabelle with the cutting out, but Isabelle would have to do the sewing herself. As soon as she had finished the cutting out she called to her sister, who was happily taking her doll for a walk.

"You can come and do the sewing now." Jane put the two dresses side by side on the table and although they were identical she knew it would save a lot of argument if she let Isabelle choose the one she wanted.

James was sitting on the ground close to the wagon, happily moving his hippo around in a circle and making humming noises or muttering to himself. Harry was trying to make a smooth patch big enough for him to play a game of ninepins, but becoming increasingly frustrated as they kept falling over.

At lunchtime Edward noticed the ninepins and when he heard Harry's tale of woe he offered to help Harry to make a place where he could play properly. He had tools in his wagon intended for digging out the wagons when they got stuck in sand or mud, the spades and mattocks could just as well deal with the rough patches where Harry had chosen to play.

In fact Edward found a much better place for the ninepins with a longer path for rolling the balls. The ninepins were obviously a toy and rather small, but Edward kindly said he would like to play the game with Harry and challenged him to a match. This, it transpired, turned out to be a competition that lasted for the next five days and kept the whole party in good spirits.

At first it was Edward playing against Harry until William, who had watched at first with amusement and then with critical interest, decided to join in. Later the young men took time to show Jane and Isabelle how to aim the balls carefully and with some degree of accuracy so that they could join in and have some fun, too. Jane, who was precise and self-controlled, soon mastered the game. Isabelle, more volatile and with less concentration, remained erratic.

They all tried to persuade Henry to take part to make the teams even, but Henry was adamant that it wasn't his type of game.

In reality he had watched the players carefully and realised that Edward in particular was extremely accurate, so much so that he was never likely to be beaten and Henry had no intention of being a loser in front of his children. Henry was not a keen gamesman, though he had played cricket at school and shown some prowess with the bat as he had a good eye and powerful shoulders. On several occasions as a young man he had taken part in the town football match which entailed racing from the river near his home to the centre of the town near the library clock in a general melee during which the ball was rarely to be seen. Generally he was much happier riding and hunting.

Some people, he knew, counted hunting as a sport and competed for the biggest trophy or largest bag, whilst many hunters in Africa killed game as a livelihood. Henry had no quarrel with these ideas, but he himself hunted only for the pot and took the greatest pleasure in pitting his wits against a wild animal. He always took the trouble to ensure his shooting was as accurate as he could make it and nearly always made a clean kill. He would have enjoyed hunting elephants and selling the ivory if his calling hadn't precluded it. Elephant hunting was a tremendous challenge, Henry thought. This game of ninepins was childish and if Edward or William wanted a match he would challenge them to target shooting. At suppertime he made his suggestion and the challenge was accepted with alacrity.

Henry suggested that the following afternoon was the best time for the match.

"You realize that there are a number of native kraals between here and Lee's Castle, don't you?" William queried.

Henry had only been to the south once since he had first arrived in Matabeleland at the end of 1859 and that was in 1861 when he had taken his family to Cape Town after Harry's birth so that Katherine could show her young son to her parents. Now he thought about the African villages close to the road.

"Yes, I remember them quite well. There are four of them, I think. Two of them caused us no problems. The people were friendly and helpful and we managed to purchase food from them without any trouble. The other two were less than pleasant."

William and Edward both nodded.

"Yes, your memory is good. Nothing has changed since then," said Edward ruefully.

"Fortunately, we had been warned by the traders at Shoshong and were further reminded by some hunters we met at the Ramaquaban," explained William. "We made a plan to camp as far away from the Egokweni and the Monagobi villages as we possibly could. It meant having to trek earlier in the evenings each day and to trek longer so that we could pass them in the dark, but we felt it was worth it. We could do the same this time, if you're agreeable. The trouble is that if we held our shooting match, the shots would be heard and we would be surrounded by crowds almost immediately."

Henry gave it some thought. William was right, of course. It would be pointless to attract attention to themselves when they were doing their best to avoid it.

"Do you think it would be better if we waited until we reach Lee's Castle?" he asked.

"Either there or when we reach the Ramaquaban and before Edward leaves us," William replied.

There was general agreement to this suggestion and there the matter rested.

After the first day Isabelle withdrew from playing ninepins, saying that she preferred to watch or play with her doll. From then on Edward partnered Jane each day, whilst William and Harry made up the other team. The teams were singularly well matched and games frequently ended in a draw or occasionally with one team slightly ahead. Both William and Edward were delighted to have an opportunity to relax in such a pleasant way, for the morning and evening treks were exhausting.

It was whilst they were playing during the afternoon that Harry asked William about something that had been bothering him.

"Are we going to visit another king?"

William looked at Harry in surprise; "No. Whatever made you think that?"

"Well I heard you talking to father and you said that we would be going to Lee's Castle. I know that kings live in castles because we have learned about them in our History lessons."

"Oh, I see. Well, you are right of course, in England there are a lot of castles, and kings or rich lords did live in them. Lee's Castle is different. John Lee is a hunter and many other things beside. He is a great friend of Mzilikazi and was given a large area of land at Mangwe, where he built his house. We have to go past Mangwe to reach the Ramaquaban River."

"If Mr Lee has a house then why is it called Lee's castle? Is his house like a castle?"

"No, it is just an ordinary house, but there is a huge rocky outcrop near the house that looks like a castle and travellers see the high rocks before they see the house so they all say, 'Look there's Lee's Castle' and so that is name everyone uses now."

"I hope I'm the first one to spot Lee's Castle, then," said Harry. "When do you think we'll get there?"

William laughed, "You do ask a lot of questions, young man. It's about another forty miles, which will take us about three more days if we don't have any hold-ups."

The road was close to the watershed, but inevitably crossed innumerable small streams that frequently had steep-sided banks and every crossing required the greatest effort to keep the wagons upright and safe. At this time of the year many of them were dry, which sometimes meant driving the livestock to a suitable watering place downstream which might be a mile or more away from the outspan.

So far their plan of avoiding the Matabele kraals had succeeded and only once did they meet up with a crowd of villagers. As that was at the Mabukutwanin kraal, where the people were friendly, the encounter passed off easily. William purchased a sheep there so that the camp could have a change from goat meat and Edward said that he would rest his horse there on his return.

It was on the fourth morning that they were unexpectedly delayed. As it was Saturday Henry hoped they would reach Lee's that night so that they could rest there and celebrate God's Holy Day in civilised surroundings. William had made an early start and they were all in good spirits when just before daylight the cavalcade came to a halt. Henry, who had been riding in his usual place at the rear, had ridden forward until he was alongside his tented wagon so that he could discuss a possible hunting excursion that afternoon with Bokkis. As the driver neatly halted the oxen and muttered about the unexpected stop, Henry trotted forward to discover the reason.

It didn't take him long. The first two wagons were completely surrounded by a Matabele impi in full war dress, the ostrich plume headdresses standing two feet upwards from their heads making them seem huge in the pale grey light. Their ostrich feather cloaks, the shields and assegais added to their sinister and threatening appearance.

As Henry slowly approached, he became aware that some of the warriors had appeared behind him, so that he was surrounded as well. The atmosphere was hostile and the expressions on the faces of the warriors were as filled with malice as their gestures were menacing. Henry felt the hairs on the back of his head rise as his whole being recognized the enmity rising in waves from the belligerent warriors. It was obvious that they would attack and kill at the slightest provocation. Henry kept his face calm and continued to walk his horse forward until he was abreast of William and Edward. He was pleased to see that both of them appeared undisturbed as they waited for him, but remained alert. They were neither cringing nor threatening and their attitude kept them from immediate attack. Neither of them was fluent in Sindebele, so they were unable to discover the meaning of this sudden appearance, which held all the elements of danger for them. Their relief was palpable when Henry appeared seemingly relaxed and greeted the induna not only fluently, but also apparently with the respect that native custom demanded. There was a slight easing of tension as the warriors looked at their leader and awaited his response.

There followed a lengthy discussion that occasionally became vehement, the impi showing approval of their induna's words with an accompaniment of thuds as spears thumped on shields and feet stamped in unison on the ground.

"Wait here," Henry muttered quietly to the young men. "Stay exactly as you are. Show neither fear nor aggression whatever happens. Don't look them in the eye and try to look just a little bit bored if you can. I shan't be long, but I need proof that Mzilikazi has allowed us to leave Matabeleland. Something has upset them but I don't know what. These people want to keep us here or even make us go back to the king's town and I'm not sure that we should travel safely."

Wheeling his horse around, Henry trotted quickly to his wagon where he dismounted and began to search in the forward chest where he had stored all the letters he had been given. As he searched, he described the situation to Bokkis, whose indrawn breath indicated his appreciation of the possible outcome of the confrontation. The Matabele were no friends of the tribes from the south.

Finding the letter he was seeking, Henry mounted once more and returned to his place beside William and Edward. Thankfully, they had heeded his words and despite some provocation they had stolidly maintained their stance.

Henry now dismounted and, holding the letter towards the induna, he approached him with care. He knew quite well that none of the Matabele could read, but this man must surely have seen paper or books before. Talking persuasively, Henry presented the letter and, pointing to the words, he read them in the native language although the letter had actually been written in English.

He then pointed to the large cross at the bottom which was the signature of the king.

"You can see that the king has given us permission to travel this road. Some of the elephant's teeth in the wagons belong to the king and are a gift to Mshete. The king will praise you for making sure that his kingdom is safe from intruders, but he will be very angry if you stop travellers who have his permission to use the road."

The induna tapped the paper with his finger, "I can see the king, son of the great elephant, has given you the road. We shall let you pass this time. We are going, but we will not forget you." He gave a signal to his companions to resume their march.

With a frightening roar and a mock charge the impi then turned and disappeared into the forest within seconds.

"I'm glad you were with us," blurted out William. "I've never had an experience like that before."

"Nor I," added Edward. "I hope they don't bother me when I come back. I shouldn't stand much chance on my own and I know that those warriors can keep up with a horse for a short distance."

Henry nodded grimly, "We have had problems with warriors from time to time. They want the king to let them kill all white men and they count us as easy targets. Fortunately, the king is on our side and when we mention his name they restrain their natural impulse just to kill, sometimes contenting themselves with a blow heavy enough to knock a man down. Even when we are insulted in many different ways we have to keep calm, though, and not allow them to see our feelings. We try to pretend indifference as it's our best defence. It's a good idea to learn the language as soon as possible, though, and definitely try to get the king's approval by following Matabele customs and giving him presents when he asks for them. You'll be safe enough, especially if you tell them that George is your brother. George is well liked in this country."

Henry was particularly relieved that all the children had been sound asleep during the tense confrontation and he was adamant that they remain in ignorance of it. He requested the young men to avoid talking about the incident in the presence of his family and to discuss it fully now before they stopped for breakfast. This they did, for both had been considerably shaken by the ordeal. They had both been convinced that they were about to die and even Henry had to admit to having had a definite feeling of disquiet. He had never before been the centre of such wholesale animosity.

Speculation as to the reason for the appearance of the impi and excited recollection of the event kept Edward and William fully occupied during the period until they stopped for breakfast.

The journey continued that afternoon, but the delay in the morning meant that it was very late that night by the time that the Mangwe was reached and everyone was ready to fall asleep, relieved that there had been no other unforeseen occurrences.

It was dark long before they reached Lee's house, so Harry was unable to achieve his desire of being the first one to spot it, much to his frustration. William managed to calm him by offering to take him for a walk around the rocky kopje the following day and possibly even to climb up part of the way. With this promise, Harry went to sleep happily.

Jane, who had been awake that morning when the wagons were stopped, had heard her father explaining to Bokkis what was happening and was puzzled why no one mentioned it during the day. It obviously wasn't important, but she would try to remember to ask father about it tomorrow.

CHAPTER 17

Jane was to remember that Sunday as one of the happiest in her life. She was accustomed to a sedate Sunday walk, but never before had she had a picnic combined with a walk that entailed scrambling over rocks and later experiencing the pleasure of following a honey guide to a bees nest. At least she took part at the beginning of the trail, for she wasn't actually allowed to follow all the way to the nest, but even the first part was filled with excitement.

Father had taken the morning service early so that they could all explore the rocks around Lee's house. The Lees were away hunting, but were always pleased when travellers camped near their house, where there was abundant water and any ripe fruits or vegetables in the garden were made available to them. The children had never seen such a large house before and were intrigued by the wide veranda where the tables had been set up for their breakfast.

The large glass windows were bigger than the ones in their own house and they couldn't resist peering through them, only to be reprimanded by father, who accused them of being inquisitive. He didn't accept their explanation that Mrs Lee would have shown them the house if she had been there and they were sorry for upsetting him, but didn't think they had done anything wrong.

"I'll decide what is right and what is wrong. Curiosity can lead to meddling and snooping. I will not have you prying into other people's affairs. Now go along and pick some lemons."

Feeling troubled and slightly distressed by the rebuke, Jane led the others round to the garden, where they picked some lemons and took them to Lukas.

After breakfast, Lukas prepared a picnic for them with bread and cold meat and water flavoured with sugar and lemon juice to drink. This was put into a sack so that it could be carried easily.

Lee's Castle was an enormous rock, much too steep to climb, but there were other rocks nearby and these provided them with plenty of exercise. William, Edward and Henry could climb with ease and Harry had few troubles even with the steeper parts. Jane needed an occasional hand when there were loose stones to add to the difficulties, but Isabelle and James both needed to be lifted up frequently. Even so, they soon reached a fine vantage point where they could enjoy their picnic. There was a fine view from the top of one large boulder and Harry spotted some rock rabbits that had been sunning themselves on rocks close by and were now hastily disappearing into holes and cracks. There were lizards and insects and birds to detect, watch and discuss. Fortunately, as it was winter there were fewer insects to annoy them than was normal in the warmer weather, but the ants were present in large numbers.

It was on the way back to the wagons that the honey guide appeared. It was a small dark grey bird and was chattering away in great excitement.

"Why is that bird making all that noise?" asked Harry.

The others all looked in the direction Harry was pointing.

"It's a honey guide," explained Edward.

"So it is," agreed William. "It wants us to follow it to a bees nest."

"I have heard about these birds," Henry admitted, "but never seen one before. They like to eat the wax from the honeycomb and if they can't get into the nest by themselves they lead a man to it. The man opens the nest to get at the honey and leaves food for the bird, so they are both happy."

"Well, if we want to get some honey today we shall need an axe, possibly a hammer as well and a bucket for the honey. I'll go back to the wagons and get what we need." So saying, William hurried off, leaving the others to watch the bird, which continued to chatter impatiently.

When William returned, he was accompanied by Bokkis and Lukas who were both keen to have some of the honey and as they were neither of them afraid of being stung by the bees William had welcomed their presence.

After walking through dense bush for a few hundred yards, Edward suggested that Henry and the children might prefer to wait at that spot. Not only was the bush thorny and difficult to penetrate, but the bees might be dangerous if they attacked in large numbers.

"That is a sensible suggestion," Henry assented.

He had found it difficult enough already, even though he was following the four others and the children walking behind him had sustained numerous scratches.

Jane and Isabelle were quite relieved to be able to rest, but Harry was most disappointed to be deprived of the action. However, he knew better than to create a fuss and subsided with the barest mutter. James was tired and ready to go to sleep, as he was missing his regular afternoon nap. He sat on the ground with his head in Jane's lap and was soon sound asleep.

The honey gatherers returned nearly an hour later, delighted with their success. Both William and Edward had been stung, though not as much as Bokkis and Lukas and they were all delighted with the amount of honey that had been garnered. They displayed a bucket that was more than half full of the thick, dark, sweet brown honey and described the operation in detail before leading the way back to the wagons. Harry listened in awe as they told him how they had had to chop a large hole in the tree trunk around the crack where the bees were entering and leaving. The bees seemed to think that Lukas was their chief danger and had attacked him fiercely. Lukas laughed as he showed Harry where he had been stung on the neck and head. He appeared to be in no pain and was unworried by the attack. Bokkis had then continued the labour until the hole was large enough for William and Edward to scrape out the honey.

They had put a large piece of honeycomb on a branch for the honey guide and had thankfully left.

Some of the bees seem to have followed them, stinging both Harry and Henry on their hands as they tried to thrust the insects away from their faces. Luckily no one else was hurt as they hurried back through the bush.

Slices of bread spread with honey were served after the stew that evening, which was a great treat for everyone and left them feeling completely and happily satisfied.

Despite the grief that intruded itself in his quiet moments, Henry felt that God was with him and his service that evening was one of thanksgiving.

Crossing the Mangwe the following morning needed the combined efforts of every man. The river was sluggish, but still quite deep and the wagons became stuck in the deep sand all too often. There was no danger of a flash flood at this time of the year, but a constant watch had to be kept in case there were crocodiles or hippopotamuses and the efforts to free the wagons tired both men and animals.

The children had stayed in the wagon on this occasion, as Henry thought it was the safest place for them and they were fascinated by the swirling waters, lapping the bed of the wagon only inches below them. Harry hoped to see a crocodile and very nearly pretended to spot one in order to frighten his sisters, but father rode alongside at that moment and Harry wisely kept his mouth closed. He thought it very tame to ride in the wagon with his sisters and longed to be out in the river helping to urge on the oxen or pushing at a wheel. His appeals to father were ignored at first and then answered with a brusque, "It's too dangerous. We cannot risk having a serious accident. I don't want to see you getting drowned or crushed under a wagon."

To his delight, as the wagon in front of theirs lurched towards the bank, Edward asked (and received permission from Henry) if he could take Harry up behind him. So, in great glee, Harry sat behind Edward as they splashed through the water and up the steep sandy bank. Harry felt that he had arrived in style and ignored his damp clothing.

'Men don't mind a little discomfort,' he thought smugly.

It was such a relief to everyone when the last wagon was dragged up the far bank and an even greater relief to divest themselves of their sodden, muddy clothes, which were now draped on ropes near the fire. Now they could look forward to a hearty, hot breakfast and the bacon taken from Henry's saltbox was fully appreciated after a bowl of the all too common porridge.

The next two days followed the same pattern, trekking, crossing rivers and hunting for the pot. The men took it in turns to hunt, going out in pairs with the other left in charge of the outspan and the care of the children.

Henry was at ease with either of the young men, who were both excellent horsemen and successful hunters. Neither was quite as good a shot as Henry, but they proved their worth and the camp never went short of meat. They were lucky enough to come across a herd of eland shortly after leaving Lee's Castle and Henry killed a fine young bull after a long and weary stalk. William, meanwhile, had shot several guinea fowl to add to the larder. The following afternoon Edward killed two buffalo and the servants were in their element as they feasted on the meat, gorging themselves until they could manage no more and fell asleep where they dropped.

It was fortunate that they had such an abundance of meat, for twice they had been pestered by Matabele villagers and had been thankful on both occasions that an offering of meat had eventually, following prolonged negotiations, satisfied the demanding throng. It had been extremely difficult to avoid parting with any of their very precious trade goods to the numerous importuning Matabele whose persistence could last for a day or more and was extremely tiring. 'No' was a word they didn't seem to understand and they expected to acquire the coat off a man's back or his hat from his head if they didn't receive anything else. A white man was perceived as rich and a donor of never-ending gifts.

"Why they should think we are all a constant source of alms I shall never understand," remarked Edward. "I have the minimum of clothing and if I were to give away my coat I should suffer from cold until I could buy a new one in six months time. My hat protects me from sunstroke. I have to work hard in order to earn money so that I can buy clothes, yet I am expected to hand them over freely because they are desired by a man who never works!"

Edward's furious declamation set Henry laughing.

"You have obviously suffered from some resolute badgering today, Edward. Well, you had better get used to it if you are going to be in Matabeleland for any length of time because it is never-ending and you'll have to work out how to extricate yourself each time. Explaining that you have nothing to give is not acceptable, from the king down to the poorest slave and harsh rejections make enemies. These people never forget a grudge, so discover an acceptable ploy or carry large reserves of beads, snuff and cheap trinkets to satisfy them."

William had been listening to this, and now nodded his agreement, "That is sound advice, added to the warning of avoiding native kraals whenever possible in order to keep out of serious trouble."

"At least we were able to buy some milk and eggs today, which is a great benefit, and I'm really looking forward to eating eggs for a change," Edward acceded.

Unfortunately most of the eggs proved to be bad.

Their arrival at the Ramaquaban River was a cause for celebration, but also brought sadness, for now was the time for Edward to leave them and return to the king's town.

The river crossing presented the usual problems and this time there was an added complication when the disselboom of Henry's baggage wagon cracked as one of the hindmost oxen slipped on the steep slope down to the water. With the greatest of care the wagon was pulled across the river and up the farther bank, but the pole would have to be replaced, meaning a delay of at least a day there whilst a new one was fitted.

Jane hoped that perhaps Edward would stay with them for the whole day whilst repairs were carried out. However, sadly for her, that hope wasn't realised.

As the party outspanned on the open country beyond the crossing place they were approached by two obvious Englishmen who had been camping with their wagon nearby. These men immediately introduced themselves to the newcomers as army officers who had taken leave from their regiment, stationed in Natal, with the intention of visiting the famous Victoria Falls and possibly having an opportunity of doing some elephant or lion hunting on the way.

"Good day to you, sirs," called the older of the two. "Major Robert Butler of the Light Infantry at your service. This is Captain Andrew Scott."

Their moustaches and their conspicuous military bearing left no doubt of the authenticity of the introduction in the minds of the new arrivals, who now willingly introduced themselves.

The officers had a number of dogs with them and one little brown terrier immediately attached itself to William, who was supervising the outspanning of the oxen. Most of the others were of mixed breed and were yapping or barking in great excitement at the arrival of strangers. The children were not afraid of the dogs careering madly around them and were making a great fuss of any that stayed still long enough to be patted. Jane was particularly attracted to a black and white rough-haired terrier and eventually managed to calm him down so that she could stroke him. She learned that his name was Badger and when she called him that, he seemed to laugh. Harry was patting a large dog called Rover that was trying to lick his face. Isabelle had her arms round a russet-coloured dog that may have once had links with a setter and answered to the name of Bess, whilst James was squatting beside a large black dog that had rolled over beside him. James christened him Doggie.

"Come over and have coffee with us when you have seen to your horses," invited Major Butler. "We should like to have some different company and conversation as well as trying to obtain all the information we can about Matabeleland. I see your children are happy to play with the dogs."

Edward, who was already grooming his horse, was anxious to be on his way now, but he reluctantly agreed that an hour's rest with time for the animal to eat some grass might be a sensible move before recrossing the river.

"Now tell us a little about the road to the Victoria Falls," urged the major once they were seated in camp chairs under a tree and his soldier servant was busy preparing coffee for them.

The little terrier had immediately jumped up and made itself comfortable on William's knee and he didn't disturb it, but the rest of the dogs played happily with the children.

"None of us has actually been to the Falls," Henry explained, "but I have talked to men who have made the journey and I can pass on their descriptions, if you think that will help."

Andrew laughed, "I believe only a handful of men have made the journey and we haven't met any of them. It is only through hearsay and reading stories in the press that we have any idea about the famous landmark, but what we have heard has made us eager to verify the stories of a view that is more inspiring than even the Niagara Falls. If you can add to our knowledge it may prove useful."

William and Edward, whose knowledge of the Victoria Falls was limited to talk they had heard around the campfire, were happy to allow Henry to do the talking and they sat back to listen.

"Well," began Henry, "you will have to leave your wagon and horses at the king's town. There are some traders there who will look after them for you. You probably know that there is a fly belt all across northern Matabeleland and tsetse fly bites are fatal for cattle and horses, so you'll have to walk. The Falls are about three hundred miles northwest of the king's town. You'll need to hire carriers for your goods and you have to ask the king's advice on this. He will order some men to take you. The guides will pretend to know the road to the Zambezi, but you can't rely on that. You should follow your own compass, the sun or the stars and you can always check that you're on the right road from the inhabitants of the kraals you pass. There are a number of rivers including the Gwaai, the Deka and the Matetsi. If you remember those names you'll know you're heading in the right direction."

"Mmm, tell us more about the carriers. We'll have to pay them, no doubt. How many will we need?" asked Robert.

"I expect twenty might be enough for the two of you, but it depends on what goods you think are essential. Food, clothing, blankets, guns, ammunition and powder as well as calabashes for water, pots for cooking and axes for chopping wood. A medicine box with a good supply of quinine is fairly essential too, but I'm sure you will be able to decide for yourselves what you might need for five to six weeks in the bush. Once you've got everything together you'll need to divide it into loads of fairly equal size and weight. If you have some spare calico it can be sewn into large bags so that each load is kept secure and you don't lose some vital necessity. Yes, each carrier will have to be paid and you must make sure that payment is agreed definitely before you start or there will be trouble when you return. Offer a good blanket each. The induna can be offered a gun. Make this payment clear to them and stick to it because they will try by all means to get more out of you. They also fight over which load to carry, each one of them trying to find the smallest or lightest. You will have to feed them all and that means hunting every day. If you have an excess of meat they will abandon your goods so that they can carry the meat and don't expect them to make an early start in the mornings. They won't move until the sun is up, which is why fourteen to twenty miles a day is all you can expect to do."

Andrew gave a sharp laugh and spoke admiringly, "You may not have been to the Zambezi, but you certainly have learned a lot about the journey there. I suppose it's a good idea to carry some trade goods with us as well?"

"Indeed it is. The carriers have enormous appetites and whilst they will feast hugely on meat they need large quantities of meal too. Obviously they can't carry enough to feed themselves for the time that you'll be away, so it has to be purchased. The people to the north are not Matabeles and will be frightened of your carriers. They might even run away when they see you coming as they have been harassed by Matabele warriors for years. Mzilikazi claims them as his subjects and enforces his rule forcefully. I've no doubt you will sort it all out for yourselves. As to my being conversant with the journey, that is easily explained; the information came from a traveller such as yourselves. He was very ill with fever on the way back from the Zambezi and the bearers, thinking he might die before they were paid, brought him to Inyati. Although we aren't doctors, people throughout Matabeleland look to us for healing and it was possibly nearer than taking him on to the king's town. It took him many months to recover from the fever and the deprivations of the journey and during his recuperation he expanded on all the trials and tribulations. We had to feed and doctor all his carriers until he was able to sort out their payments and that is something I shall never forget. Eventually he had to go and seek the king's arbitration before he could be rid of them or he would have been beggared."

The coffee was hot, sweet and strong and it was whilst they were all enjoying this hour of relaxation that a Matabele messenger arrived bearing a note written on Mzilikazi's behalf by the Reverend Thomas, who was obviously still at the king's town. The letter gave written permission for the two men to enter the kingdom and was signed by the king's mark.

Major Butler and the captain were both relieved and delighted that their waiting was finally over. They immediately planned to ride forward without delay, carrying a few personal belongings and leaving their army servants to bring on their wagon.

"Would it be possible for us to ride with you?" they asked Edward.

"With the greatest of pleasure," beamed Edward. "It is about sixty miles and goodness knows how many rivers away so we shan't be there tonight, but we can overnight at Lees' Castle and sleep on a sheltered veranda there. If you have a kettle, some coffee and sugar, I will supply some meat for tonight and meal for breakfast."

"Don't worry about the meat, we'll do some hunting on the way," smiled Major Butler. "There's nothing better than a steak cooked over the fire or the smell of liver frying at breakfast time."

Edward laughed, delighted at the thought of having congenial company on what he had expected to be a lonely and not too pleasant a journey. It would now be a carefree ride with some hunting, too, which was exciting. He had previously felt desperately anxious to resume his journey in order to expedite his trading, but after weeks and months of trekking, the idea of a little relaxation was especially appealing. No doubt both these men had some good campaign stories to tell around the campfire and there was safety in numbers when wild animals and equally dangerous bands of unruly Matabele warriors roamed the countryside. He would be able to tell them about his encounter with the impi and what he had learned from Henry about how to deal with them to allay their ferocious instincts.

Robert looked across at William, still nursing the little terrier. " I see you like dogs so I'm surprised you haven't any with you."

William looked solemn. "Well I did have when I left Cape Town," he stated flatly. "There were four of them. Unfortunately sickness and accidents accounted for all of them. You know how easy it is for them to fall under the wagon wheels?"

Robert nodded in sympathy. "I do indeed. Well, Fox there seems to have adopted you. If you'd like to have him it will be one less for us to worry about," he added almost casually.

"If you're sure you can part with him I'd love to have him," William replied and they immediately shook hands on the agreement.

The two officers strode away to sort out their kit whilst their servants saddled their horses and put rolled up blankets behind the saddles.

Edward meanwhile said his farewells to the children. He gave each of the boys a firm handshake and patted the two girls on their heads, telling them how much he had enjoyed being with them.

His farewell to William was light-hearted despite their mutual regret at parting. They had shared months of close friendship and had been totally reliant on each other for company, safety and support during all that time, but it didn't do to show too much emotion. They both hoped to meet up again in the future and said as much, ignoring the lumps in their throats that thickened their voices.

Henry was thanked for accompanying them and especially for his lesson on how to handle Matabele warriors who were keen to wash their spears in blood.

Henry and William were sorry to say goodbye to Edward. They knew they would miss his energetic cheerfulness.

The children were close to tears, but knew that father would not tolerate a scene, so remained stony faced as they watched. Edward had been like a big brother to them, listening to their tales, telling them stories of his adventures in the bush and playing games with them. His departure would leave a big gap in their lives. Farewells over, Edward mounted his horse and was waiting for Robert and Andrew when they appeared.

Robert called to Badger and William lifted the little black and white dog up to sit in front of Robert.

"I'll take this little fellow with me. He enjoys hunting and knows not to bark when we're after game. The others can come on with the wagon. Goodbye then." With a hand lifted in farewell, Robert set his horse towards the water, followed by Andrew and Edward.

As they splashed through the river, the dogs left behind stared after them, restrained by the two servants and William. The large black dog had wandered along the bank and was twenty yards downstream when it decided to take a drink. James set off to follow it and Jane ran to catch up with him.

The sudden surge of a crocodile from the murky waters took her by surprise and with the briefest of yelps the dog was pulled into the depths. There wasn't even time for a struggle. The incident had happened so quickly and with no prior warning that Jane was convinced that she had imagined it.

James halted in mid stride looking puzzled. "Doggie gone," he said and looked at Jane for confirmation. "Where's Doggie gone?"

Jane grabbed her brother's hand and in a state of shock pulled him roughly back to the group who were all still staring at the retreating backs of the riders.

James continued to recite, "Doggie gone," over and over.

CHAPTER 18

Still in shock, and beginning to tremble, Jane, dragging James with her, returned hurriedly to the place where father, William and the two soldiers were standing. Harry and Isabelle, standing beside them, were waving energetically at the retreating figures; the three horsemen and the Matabele messenger, who, as the king's representative had to accompany them, was running alongside them.

"Father," stuttered Jane her voice preternaturally loud. "A crocodile has just eaten the big black dog."

"What did you say? Did I hear you say that a crocodile has taken a dog?" Father's astonished vehemence caused Jane to step backwards, afraid that he was angry with her, but his forceful words were due to his amazement that such an unbelievable occurrence had taken place whilst there were so many people close at hand. Not only that, it just seemed impossible that apparently none of them had noticed the drama. There must surely have been some noise, such as the sounds of a struggle.

All the men reacted immediately by racing to get their guns and demanding that Jane should point out where the attack had taken place. Unnerved, but determined to try to save the dog, Jane led them to the place along the bank where she had seen the dog disappear, though she stood several yards back from the water.

"Beauty! Beauty!" shouted one of the soldiers, leaning as far as he could out over the water. The men searched the bank for twenty yards in each direction, their guns at the ready hoping to see some movement or sign of life. There was nothing. The serenity of the river remained undisturbed and after half an hour of fruitless searching they realised the futility of continuing.

"We could come out later and see if we have better fortune," one soldier suggested hopefully to Henry. Then he added angrily, "I'd like to shoot that crocodile. Beauty was the mother of Ebony over there and a wonderfully gentle creature she was too. She was a fine gun dog in her younger days and still enjoyed going out hunting if the quarry was close at hand. She was a bit old for lengthy chases, though."

By now Henry's anger and sorrow at the loss of the dog and fear for his children had abated and he shook his head, " It isn't worth it. The Matabele strongly object to the shooting of crocodiles. You would be in very serious trouble if a report of crocodile killing reached the king and believe me he does know what goes on in every part of his kingdom. The creature's liver can be used in witchcraft, which is why there is such a taboo. I thank the Lord that none of us was attacked when we were in the water so close to this place. The consequences don't bear thinking about."

Once the furore of leave taking and the subsequent dramatic episode had passed, Henry brought his thoughts back to the important task that had to be completed before he could resume his journey. The pleasant interlude with refreshing coffee and an opportunity to talk to Robert and Andrew had been fully appreciated after the necessary strenuous efforts to cross the river, but now, with William's help, it was time to get back to work.

"The disselboom on my baggage wagon has cracked," he explained to the two army men. "We shall have to replace it immediately before we travel any further and the sooner we start on the repair the quicker we shall be able to continue our journey."

Both men immediately offered to help, saying that they were used to such carpentry and it wasn't necessary for them to take their wagon across the river absolutely at once. As long as they crossed sometime during the afternoon, their officers would be satisfied and they certainly were in no desperate hurry. One of them made a useful suggestion when Henry explained that he had two spare poles with him strapped alongside his wagons and he was intending to use one of these. It was suggested that he should keep the two spares for future use. The road south from Shoshong had few trees with trunks long enough and strong enough to provide a main wagon pole, but here by the river there were many suitable trees. It would be easy for them to go and chop one down and trim it to the right size, thus saving the spares for future use.

"Your idea is sensible," Henry acceded. "I have heard of men having to temporarily abandon a damaged wagon because they had no means of repairing it. Let us go and find a new pole, then we can fit it before we have our lunch."

The men collected axes and set off towards a wooded area about fifty yards away followed, by all the dogs. Henry lingered behind long enough to call out, "Jane, you must keep your brothers and sister away from the river. Stay near the wagons. Perhaps you should do some reading for a while, instead of playing. You have all had enough playtime this morning."

Dutifully, Jane accepted the order, though she sighed to herself she had no intention of going anywhere near the river after that horrible fright. She had been upset by the dog's death. 'Do animals go to heaven?' she wondered. 'No. That wasn't likely. Dogs didn't know about God and so they wouldn't know about heaven. She didn't think they would be able to go there if they didn't know about it. But God was kind sometimes and perhaps He loved

animals too. Yes He did love them for He had made them as well as people and other things on earth. God would look after animals when they were dead.' Jane smiled at that thought.
"Where Doggie gone?" pleaded James. "Jane, where?"
The constant tugging at her hand halted Jane and she looked at the upset face of her little brother. 'What was she to say to him? The word death would mean nothing and she couldn't say that the dog had gone to heaven.'
"Doggie has a proper name James. Her name is Beauty," explained Jane carefully as she tried hard to think of an answer that would satisfy James. "She is in the river now or perhaps she is on the other side of the river." Jane was as upset as he was and she was desperately trying to avoid telling a lie, but still uncertain of how she could explain the killing without upsetting him further.
Harry solved the problem for her. "A crocodile came out of the water and Doggie went with the crocodile James," he explained in a matter of fact way. Jane was pleased with Harry's account as it obviously sounded reasonable to James, who was nodding his head with satisfaction.
"That was well done Harry," smiled Jane. Then she whispered, "I just didn't know what to say and James is much happier now." Jane put her arm round Harry and gave him a grateful hug. Isabelle, trailing behind the others, felt neglected and jealous of the approval Harry was receiving. In a loud dismissive voice she chimed in, "We all know the crocodile ate Doggie. Crocodiles have big sharp teeth and they like to eat dogs."
James looked at Isabelle in horror and began to wail. Jane turned round to her sister, "That was a cruel thing to say, Isabelle. How could you upset James like that?" She spoke with unaccustomed harshness and when Isabelle muttered, "Well, it's true. The crocodile has eaten Doggie." Jane gave her a sharp slap and then another.
Isabelle's cries were added to James' howls and in fury she turned back towards the river. "I'm not coming with you. You're horrid," she cried angrily.
Jane would have been quite happy for her sister to remain by herself until she had regained her temper, but she knew how dangerous the riverbank could be. Jane had no intention of running after Isabelle, so she called in her sternest voice, "Come back here at once. Father will be extremely cross with you if you go anywhere near the river."
Isabelle ignored her sister and promptly sat down where she was, whereupon Jane marched over to her to haul her to her feet an action that proved far more difficult than she had imagined and Harry came across to give his help. Between them they managed to pull Isabelle into an upright position and

somehow as the tussle ensued they all ended up laughing and James ran over to join in the fun. Breathlessly and to keep the good spirits going, Jane called, "Who can reach the wagon first?"

Harry and Isabelle set off at a run, with Harry soon well in the lead. Jane stayed behind James, trying to maintain her dignity and pretending to be unable to pass him as his little legs kept up a stumbling run and he burbled laughingly. How difficult it was to keep the little ones amused and still behave in the correct manner, Jane mused. In one corner of her heart she would have loved to race about and take part in a rough and tumble, but the years of restraint forced upon her were impossible to cast aside. Ahead of her, Isabelle was touching the wagon, having been second to Harry and feeling very pleased with herself. She knew she couldn't beat Harry, but she hadn't been far behind and was a long way in front of Jane, who would be the last to arrive. She found that very satisfying. She had forgotten her anger by now and when Jane suggested that they should do some writing on their slates she and Harry agreed submissively.

Jane found a copybook and showed them the letters to practise whilst she counted numbers with James. James would be two years old in a few weeks' time and Jane knew that he should start more lessons soon. He could count a little already and he recognized the animals in the picture book he had. As well as beginning to learn the letters of the alphabet he would have to start learning to write some of them before they reached Kuruman. In some ways it would be easier to have him taking part in lessons rather than having to think up a different activity for him each time.

Jane could hear the chopping and hammering as her father and the other men worked on the baggage wagon and everything seemed so peaceful she could hardly believe that the sudden, frightful, horrible death of the dog had taken place. She could see the oxen and the horses all happily grazing in calm oblivion of the lurking danger in the water just beside them as they chewed their way along the riverbank. It was true that they were under the watchful eye of the herder, but if they wandered down to the river to drink would they be in danger too? They were such big strong animals, surely a crocodile wouldn't attack one of them. Just to be sure she began praying earnestly for their safety.

There was a tempting smell of cooking coming from the dining area, making her feel hungry and longing for lunchtime.

Lukas had taken some pork chops from the saltbox and cooked these on the grill over the fire. There were sufficient for the two soldiers as well, so they were invited to share in the repast with William and the Hargreaves family. It was a delicious meal with chops, pumpkin and beans accompanied by solidly thick mealie porridge as a replacement for potatoes in sufficient quantities to satisfy even their healthy appetites. To Jane's delight Lukas had also baked some bread in an antheap. It was greatly appreciated by everyone, especially those who had made strenuous efforts to complete the important task of fitting the disselboom.

There was satisfaction too for Henry in knowing that his wagon was now in good enough condition to resume the journey and that he still had two spare poles. There was also pleasure in knowing that the horses and oxen had found good grazing near at hand. Departures were all too easily delayed, often by hours if water or grazing could only be obtained several miles away and sometimes this led to the disappearance of oxen or horses either lost or killed.

The drivers and other servants had found friends amongst the major's servants and were delightedly sharing a klipspringer and a bush-pig with them that the major had shot in the early morning.

The two parties separated after lunch with the departure of the army contingent northwards across the river soon after. Jane was pleased to see all the dogs being carried across and was relieved that there were no untoward occurrences. The oxen had rested for many days and had no difficulty in pulling the wagon through the river. Jane joined in enthusiastically with the cheerful farewells, managing at the same time to keep the younger children away from the water.

With Edward gone and the departure of the two other men accompanied by the noisy, lively, frolicking dogs on their way to the king's town, the Hargreaves party seemed strangely solitary and silent. Jane felt that she had been abandoned. At first after leaving her home at Inyati the company of the Moffat family and Nomalanga had been a comfort for Jane. At the king's town in addition there had been the friendly storekeepers and the constant bustle of a busy town to fill each day with never-ending interest.

Now only William and her father remained and they would be busy for many hours each day, leaving Jane with only the younger ones for company. She wouldn't even be able to lose herself in one of her books, as she had to take good care of James who could disappear within minutes if she so much as looked the other way. How she missed Nomalanga! She should, of course, be doing some washing. Father liked to have a clean collar daily and all their clothes were dusty, but the thought of washing the family clothes in the river made her feel weak. As father said they would reach the Tati by tomorrow she hoped that it would be all right to do the washing there. Timidly she suggested this to him.

Henry fully understood his daughter's reluctance to approach too close to the river and she could hardly avoid doing that if she was to do the washing. Despite the fact that he would have enjoyed having some clean clothes to wear the next day as he found dusty, grubby clothes irksome, he agreed that it would be sensible to wait until they reached the river at Tati. Henry knew that there were crocodiles in every river and that they had been extremely lucky not to have seen any before. He would have to ensure a safe place for Jane tomorrow or get one of the servants to put water in the large pot. Perhaps it would be possible for her to wash the clothes in that.

The evening trek was begun in the late afternoon as William hoped to reach Tati the following day. It was a journey of nineteen miles, which should be possible to cover in three stages. It had been a warm day in the sheltered valley, but the sun was sinking and the cold soon struck as they made their way onwards. Shivering, the children were sitting in the wagon and Jane made a supper of bread with honey so that they could all go to bed early. They remained awake for a long time though and Jane had to tell four stories before one by one they fell asleep. For a time, as the wagon lurched and bumped over the rough veld on which the wagon tracks of previous travellers gave it the name of 'road,' she wondered how anyone could remain asleep in such conditions, but her siblings showed no signs of being wakened, even when the jolting almost flung them out of bed. As she remembered the days of their journey so far, she gently slipped into sleep.

The amount of game had been steadily increasing and just before dark William managed to shoot a tsessebe when it appeared suddenly in front of him. Not wanting to stop until they had travelled at least six miles, he sent three of the servants to skin the animal and to bring the meat as well as the skin and horns on to the outspan. It was satisfying to know that there was sufficient food now for supper. Supplying fresh meat for the servants meant hunting daily to cater for their enormous appetites, which was frequently a great worry, especially in areas where game was in short supply.

* * * * * * *

They came across their first herd of elephant the next morning, the great grey beasts appearing out of the morning mists, crossing the road and disappearing almost immediately, totally silently, amongst the rocks and trees as they headed westwards.

William, who was riding fifty yards ahead of the wagons, sat spellbound by the sight of more than twenty pachyderms looming up before him not more than thirty yards away. It was the sudden halting of his horse, combined with a low growling in Fox's throat, that had alerted him as he admitted to himself that he had been less diligent than he should have been. So astonished was he that he didn't even think of shooting any of them. No one else was aware of the sighting and the trek continued without pause, but William immediately rode back to tell Henry about the sighting.

"Elephants," he gasped out excitedly. "I've just seen a herd of elephants. It was rather like a ghostly dream," explained William. "There I was sitting happily on my horse just walking steadily along in front of the wagons with Fox trotting beside us. I know I should have been more alert despite the silence all around, but I suppose I was thinking of other things. Anyway I heard Fox's warning at the same time as Diamond suddenly stopped in his tracks. If he had been going at more than a walk I should have been off. As it was I was rudely brought to my senses. I don't know why I was so frozen. I suppose I should have taken a quick shot at them. I couldn't get a clear view of them for the mist and they were certainly going somewhere in a hurry, but I have a feeling that it was a herd of cows and calves. Do you think I should follow?"

Henry heard William's hurried description and explanation with a tolerant smile on his face. "No, I don't think you should go elephant hunting today, exciting as it might seem. Even as we speak, the herd will have travelled quite a distance and you would need a heavier gun than the one you're carrying, so you would waste another quarter of an hour searching one out with the relevant ammunition. It could be well over an hour, even more, before you caught up with them. You might be able to kill a cow or two and have a few more pounds of ivory, but the drivers and servants would want to stop and cut up the meat as well as cutting out the tusks, which would take several more hours. We really ought to try to reach Tati today."

William looked disappointed, "You're right, of course. It could be foolish for me to go racing off through the bush on my own and one of us has to stay by the wagons. Still it would be fun to shoot an elephant. It is a pity Edward is no longer with us, he would have enjoyed such an opportunity. He'll be furious when I tell him. The captain and the major have missed out too. They said they wanted a chance to do some elephant hunting. If only they had known there were elephants so close they could have stayed at their outspan for another day or two and not gone racing off to the king's town."

Henry nodded in agreement, "Yes, it is ironical that the hunters have all ridden northwards and some of the elephants at least are here in the south. I'm sure you'll get an opportunity to hunt elephants one day when you're not too busy organizing your transport and later on today you can be the one to go out and hunt for our supper."

Soberly, William accepted the offer and, turning his horse, he resumed his place at the head of the wagons. Nevertheless, he chided himself for having been so fascinated by the early morning scene that he hadn't grabbed a quick shot. Thinking about it in a more objective fashion he admitted that Henry was right and the rifle he was carrying wasn't heavy enough for elephant hunting. It would all have been a waste of energy. He would only have wounded an animal even if he had managed to hit one. For some reason this notion made him feel much better.

There was only one small stream on this part of the road and that was completely dry. Nevertheless, it was an obstacle that had to be crossed and William proposed to give the animals a short rest once they had traversed it successfully. There was time for them to have a mug of hot black coffee and a bite of bread with cold meat, which would serve as breakfast. The children were wakened before the wagons negotiated the steep banks and followed on after the last wagon had gone. The breakfast on offer was different from their usual fare, but they were all hungry and accepted the food from father with the expected expressions of gratitude after they had mumbled their way through the grace.

Fox stayed close beside William's chair, but Harry found that he could be tempted to abandon his place for a moment if food was offered and Harry was bent on attracting him. However, father soon became aware of the little activity taking place behind him and turned round.

With a frown on his face and censure in his voice he chided his son, "Harry, that is quite enough. Sit up properly and eat your food. William will feed Fox when he needs to be fed and you are not to interfere."

Harry mumbled an apology and concentrated all his attention on his bread and meat. Lukas had made them some more lemon water drink and there was also a slice of bread and honey each.

Harry was not looking forward to another long trek with the only alternatives of either riding in the wagon or walking along the dusty uneven ground. He hoped that perhaps father or William could be persuaded to take him up and give him a ride, being on a horse was the next best thing to hunting and he would need to be in their good books if his hopes were to be satisfied. William was kind, but he wasn't like Edward. He didn't laugh as much and he spent so much time caring for his oxen and his wagons that he didn't have time to play ninepins or think up fun games for Harry and Isabelle. Even so, Harry was hopeful that he might be persuaded to give him a ride. Harry sat up straighter on his chair and made a determined effort to appear good, which was difficult when he glanced at Isabelle who was making faces at him. She was trying to make him giggle or retaliate and that would annoy father. He was inclined to flick a piece of bread at her, especially as Jane was fully occupied in cutting up a piece of meat for James to eat with his spoon, but his attention was diverted by a single word in the conversation between the men. The word was 'lion'. Harry pricked up his ears and listened attentively.

"Did you hear the lions roaring last night?" William asked casually.

"I certainly did," replied Henry. "Oscar must have been worried by the sound and woke me up by tugging on his rope and shaking the wagon. I couldn't think what was happening at first and then I heard the roars. Thankfully, they were miles away and I knew there was no fear for the safety of the cattle or the horses, but I'm sure we'll have to make a strong kraal for them all tonight at the Tati. Where there is more game there will be lions and where there are baboons and rocks there are likely to be leopards."

"For the first few years when I began transport riding I only came as far as Shoshong. Then I had an opportunity to come to the Tati and that helped me to pay for my second wagon. This is the first time I've been into Matabeleland and that was because Edward had decided to join his brother there. The last time I came up old Piet van Rooyen had lost two of his beasts to lions and he was even more unfortunate during the rainy season when he lost four to a lightning strike. Anyway, he and I went on a lion hunt and managed to shoot three of the beasts that had been hanging round his kraal. Piet lives at his store at Tati and anyone who gets stranded stays there. He's only been there for about two years. No transport rider will travel in the wet season because the flooded rivers and the thick mud cause so many hold-ups it is economically ruinous, but hunters and travellers sometimes miscalculate the times when it is best to travel and find themselves in trouble. You have to know something about the country you're travelling in, don't you?"

"You do indeed and there are more and more people coming up, looking for adventure. The sportsmen are usually well equipped with sound wagons, a whole armoury of guns, a host of servants and enough supplies for a few months. Even so, they don't know how rough the journey is, just how long it takes to travel anywhere, the impossibility of finding water and grazing for their beasts over long stretches and so many other problems that beset the unwary. We have occasionally had hunters and travellers stuck at Inyati for months on end as they recover from the fever or try to obtain fresh horses or oxen." Henry enjoyed talking about his experiences at Inyati and could have continued the discussion for hours, but he realized that they had been stopped long enough. The animals had had a good rest so it was now time to continue. Accordingly, he stood up and called for the table and chairs to be packed away as William strode across to where his drivers were squatting round their own little fire still chewing on some mealie cobs.

Knowing that this was to be a short stop the oxen hadn't been out-spanned, but were lying comfortably in their places still yoked to the chain. The crack of the drivers' whips over their heads set them to scrambling to their feet.

Seeing the movements preparatory to resuming the trek, Harry helpfully untethered Oscar and led him towards father with an unusually submissive smile on his face.

"May I please have a ride?" he begged, as father turned to thank him.

Henry was in an expansive mood after the pleasant conversation and with good food inside him. He was also feeling the need to stretch his legs a little after several hours in the saddle and another sitting on a chair, "Yes, you may, just for a short time. You'd better have James in front of you for a while, too. He needs to get the feel of a saddle."

So Harry and James were lifted up and Henry led them forward as the wagons began to move.

CHAPTER 19

Everyone was weary by the time the Tati was reached. It was already late morning and the oxen had been walking more and more slowly. Despite the sunshine, it was still cold and a few gusts of wind blew the dust into their faces as they reached the more open expanse by the river. The Tati was wider than the rivers they had crossed previously and most of it was sand, but there was a wide ribbon of water moving slowly along on a winding course touching one bank and then the other. Later on in the dry season it would cease to flow altogether, leaving only a few large pools, or it might dry up completely, luckily at this time of the year there was enough water to keep moving and to provide a welcome supply for people and animals. William remembered from his northward journey the oxen's struggles to pull the heavy wagons through the soft deep sand. Now his spans were tired and it was the time of day when they usually had some water before being taken to their grazing, nevertheless he decided that it was better to cross straight away and give them a full day's rest tomorrow rather than outspanning where they were. He also decided that it would be wise to inspan extra oxen at the outset. It was much easier to keep a wagon moving slowly with added power rather than try to pull it out once it had stuck fast.
Accordingly, he consulted with Henry, who immediately offered his spare oxen, as they were comparatively fresh. There were only four of them, so William added four more taken from his third wagon.
It was hard work persuading the new animals to take up their positions, but with the whole workforce pushing and pulling them it was finally achieved. With shouts and whistles of encouragement and much cracking of the whip and with men rushing to push at the wheels if they showed signs of faltering, the wagon was coaxed to the other bank.
There was no respite. Once the oxen had dragged the wagon a hundred yards from the water's edge, eight were immediately taken back to help to haul the second wagon across, an action that had to be repeated another three times.
Waiting in their own wagon, the four children were restive and fretful. It was a long time since breakfast and the only thing they had had since then had been mugs of water from the canvas water bag kept hanging at the side of the wagon. Harry and Isabelle left the wagon for a time to go and watch the action at the drift, until father told them to return to the safety of the wagon. Grumbling and reluctant, they did as they had been bidden.
Jane felt hot, dusty and wearier than she had done for a long time. She was also very worried. James hadn't wanted to eat much at breakfast time even

though she had cut his meat into small pieces. When he had refused even bread and honey she knew that he was not well. He had been especially eager to drink, though, and she had had to give him some lemon water out of her own mug to satisfy his thirst. She prayed that he hadn't caught the fever. Despite feeling unwell, he hadn't wanted to miss out on the chance to ride on Oscar, but after half an hour he had been lifted down and had flatly refused to walk a step. Jane had carried him a little way until her arms ached and she had had to ask father if he could be put to bed in the wagon.

Initially Henry was impatient at the thought of making a stop less than an hour into the journey, but when he became aware of Jane's distress and saw that James' little face was bright red, he realised that all was not well. Accordingly, he called a halt for his own two wagons and Jane climbed up to receive James' hot little body as her father lifted him up to her.

"I'll make a draught for him when we reach the Tati," he promised. "I don't think it can be the fever, since we have had clean, fresh air ever since we left Inyati. Just keep him cool and let him drink as much water as he wants."

Isabelle and Harry, who had been watching, now decided that they had better take this opportunity to ride in the wagon and there all four had stayed.

Jane continually wiped James' face with a cool damp cloth and prayed to Jesus to help her little brother. It was upsetting for all of them, as they listened to his laboured breathing, to see his flushed features with his fair hair plastered to his forehead. Both Isabelle and Harry were subdued and took their toys to the front, where they sat and played quietly.

It was a great relief for all of them when finally their wagon was pulled through the river and they arrived on the farther bank with nothing worse than some slight bruises caused when the wagon lurched about in the sand.

Henry informed William of James' sickness and said that he needed to give him some medicine immediately, so William kindly offered to bring Henry's baggage wagon across.

Henry examined his son and could see, even without the use of a thermometer, that he had a high temperature, but there were no other symptoms that he could recognize. He decided that a potion made up with a weak solution of salicylic acid would help to bring the fever down.

He went to his medicine chest and prepared the medicine but when Jane tried to persuade James to drink it he steadfastly refused. Henry watched the struggle for a few moments, then, taking the measure from Jane, he commanded his son to drink. He would brook no refusal and James unwillingly drank it all, pulling a face and squirming as he did so.

"Right, another one tonight, my boy, and you'll be much better tomorrow."

James said nothing, but when father had left the wagon he began to weep, "Don't want medicine. Horrid medicine."

Jane cuddled him gently. "I know it tastes horrid James, but we have to make you better. You don't want to be sick in bed for days and days do you?"

James refused to be comforted. He was lost in his own little world of unhappiness. "Want mama. Mama make me better." He pushed Jane's arms away and sobbed himself to sleep.

Jane sat beside him all day and only left the wagon when she needed to do so, eating her food as quickly as she could without attracting disapproval or a reprimand, then returning to her vigil. Whenever James awoke, she would persuade him to have a drink of cold water and when he complained of the cold she tucked the blankets firmly round him.

Isabelle and Harry were delighted to have the freedom of the open air once again after the long hours in the confines of the wagon and they wandered happily round the outspan, hoping that Lukas would soon have some lunch ready for them. Once they had eaten, and with everyone else busy about their own affairs, they roamed around the outside of the store, and there they found children of their own age. Despite the fact that these pale brown children spoke a language quite different from English or Sindebele, they had somehow been able to play games together, especially Harry's favourite hide and seek, which kept them all happily occupied throughout the afternoon.

Henry and William also waited until they had eaten before heading towards the store. There they discovered that the van Rooyens were away hunting and had left the store in the care of a man called Stoffel. He and his Bechuana wife made the travellers welcome and offered to make them some coffee. Henry found it difficult to understand what Stoffel was saying. Although he had obviously learned some English words, they were few and far between and spoken with such a heavy accent they were almost unintelligible. His mother tongue seemed to be a form of Dutch, but after years of living with a Bechuana wife his sentences were interspersed with words in Sechuana. The result was fascinating and as William kept nodding his head wisely whilst saying 'Ja', Henry felt constrained to do the same. At one point William burst out laughing and after a moment of surprise the others followed suit.

"What was that all about?" Henry asked him as the laughter died away.

"I'm not quite sure, but it struck me as being very funny that we were all nodding our heads in agreement without having the slightest idea of what was being said. Anyway it's better to be happy, we certainly don't want an argument do we?"

Henry agreed, and when Stoffel mentioned mail he looked up hopefully, indicating that he would like to see the letters. Stoffel readily consented and led the way into the store, one corner of which acted as a post office. Henry looked through the accumulation of letters whilst the coffee was being prepared, but he was disappointed to discover that there were no letters for either himself or William.

After enjoying the coffee, which was dark and sweet with milk on offer if they wanted it and hearing the latest news from Stoffel, at least as much as they could understand, Henry and William were taken into the main part of the store to examine what goods there were. Stoffel was naturally hoping to make a sale, but at first they found nothing to tempt them, as they still had reasonable supplies of trade goods, powder and shot. They were, however, delighted to be offered some milk and eggs, which they were happy to purchase. Later, they were taken into a separate storeroom where they were shown some small elephant tusks weighing less than 20 lbs each. Stoffel was willing to sell them at 6s 6d per lb. William was considering the offer and also hoping to bargain for some lion skins, antelope skins and hippo teeth. Henry examined the ivory and skins thoughtfully, wondering how much he could sell them for when he reached Cape Town, but then agonised that this would be considered as trading, which was specifically banned by the missionary society.

"I don't think that I should break the rules of our society," he admitted ruefully and with obvious regret in his voice. "Trading is definitely not allowed and I must avoid such temptation." So saying, he left the store, leaving William haggling with Stoffel.

Some time later, William left the store to search for Henry, and found him by the wagons. He began to speak hurriedly as soon as he was in hearing distance, "I know you can't take part in trading Henry, but there is a tremendous opportunity for me here. I know we can find more room on the wagons for some ivory and skins and I discovered three fine leopard skins as well as the lion skins. There are lion and leopard claws, hippo teeth and some rhinoceros horns, in addition to ostrich feathers, but I have a problem. I've run out of funds. I know that this is an imposition and you can always say no, but if you could lend me some money I would repay you in Cape Town and give you half the profit. What do you say?"

Henry looked thoughtful and pondered the proposition. Would this be considered trading? He thought not, since he was doing neither the buying nor the selling. In fact he was in no way connected with the transaction. He would, however, be connected financially. He cast his mind to the Bible, remembering that in Ecclesiastes it was stated 'money answereth all things'. Did that mean that his conscience was clear if he agreed to William's suggestion? There were other references to money in the Bible and Henry well knew that people would pluck out such parts as suited their argument or purpose. Was he being unduly tempted because his annual salary was meagre in the extreme?

Katherine's parents had, as a dowry, put some money into a Cape Town account for them when they were married five years ago. Although they had of necessity used some on their last visit there four years ago, most of it still remained and Henry had planned that it should be used to provide for the boys' education and of course their keep whilst they were living with their grandparents. In law of course the money was all his and he was counting on a small portion of it to help to pay for the passage to England if he should need more than he could obtain from the sale of his own few trading goods. If he lent William a sum of money, it would be returned much increased and allow him to make the journey home more comfortably than he could on his own small income alone. But what if they were to lose some of the goods en route?

There were thieves everywhere and small items such as claws and horns were easily carried off. Accidents on the road or in a drift could ruin or destroy fine skins. It was a long way to Cape Town and even if the whole wagon full of trade goods arrived safely, there was no guarantee that they would sell for the hoped-for price. Henry would be dependent on William's ability to strike a good bargain here and achieve a much better bargain from the purchaser. As he thought about it, Henry became less and less sure of his answer.

William watched Henry's face expectantly and with some idea of the thoughts that were racing around in his head. He sought to reassure him,

"I have been trading long enough to know what goods are most likely to produce a profit. I also know what prices to offer here and what prices I can expect to receive in Cape Town. I started out five years ago with a borrowed wagon and span, now I own two of my own. It wasn't easy because I had a lot to learn and there are people just waiting to cheat a beginner. They will claim that a horse has been salted when it hasn't, they'll offer to pay later and then disappear. They'll palm you off with bad supplies and powder that doesn't explode. I'll be twenty-two next birthday and I want to retire from the transport business before I'm thirty. I know there is some risk on the road, but I wouldn't suggest this to you if I wasn't confident of the outcome."

As Henry still hesitated, William went on persuasively, "I'll strike a bargain with you. This is my offer; I will repay your money in full even if there is no profit or if some of the goods are lost. That is my guarantee if you don't want to risk losing money. If you want to have a share in the profits then you must share in the risks and possibly share a loss. You can decide now which one it is to be."

Henry fully understood that William was extremely keen to increase the profitability of this journey and he was impressed that William was so sure of his ability that he was prepared to make this proposal. Despite his doubts, which were really no more than a sensible appraisal of the situation, Henry had inherited some of his father's business acumen. He decided in favour of offering to share both the risks and the profit and said so.

"I can give you a note on my bank," Henry suggested. "Let's go and discuss it with Stoffel. It would also be a good idea for us to examine our loads and see just how much more we can take. There is no point in overloading the wagons and having to abandon them."

William looked at Henry with one eyebrow lifted and a quizzical expression on his face, and said without rancour, "Trying to teach me my business now, are you?" There was a laugh in his voice as he added, "You missionaries really do have to know everything about everything to survive in the wild!"

Henry looked puzzled for a moment, wondering what he had said amiss, then had the grace to apologise. "I'm sorry. I am so used to having to be the organiser and you look so young, or perhaps it is just that I feel so old, that my thoughts were put into words. Of course, you know how much weight a wagon can bear and how much the oxen can safely pull. You have had much more experience than I have. Let's go and sort it all out. I'll take your advice on how much more I can add to my wagon. We might even be able to put some of the lighter items in the tented wagon."

Inwardly, Henry was smiling, for the Hargreaves' family business in England was concerned with transport and he himself had been responsible for carts and horses and the transporting of goods from an early age. It was true that he had very little experience with ox wagons on long journeys, but he had travelled along this route before, so his apology to William had been made to mollify the young man and concede that he was in charge. After all, it was Henry who had asked to join William, not the other way round.

Having made the decision to finance the purchases, Henry felt that he should take every advantage of the opportunity made available to him. He and the children would all require new shoes and clothing by the time they reached Cape Town and he would find it extremely galling to have to rely on charity to provide their basic needs. The extra money was hardly going to make him a wealthy man, but it would make a great difference to him. He didn't mind the hardships here in Matabeleland, accepting his penurious calling as one of personal choice, but when he reached England he didn't wish to appear before his father as a penniless prodigal son.

The afternoon passed quickly as the two men continued their bargaining. Henry watched silently for the most part, occasionally nodding in agreement with William's bids until all the business was satisfactorily concluded. After that, Henry presented his note made out to Piet van Rooyen and the newly purchased items were loaded into the wagons.

Towards the end of the afternoon, Jane, who was feeling the strain of sitting still beside the bed for so many hours, felt that perhaps she could read her book for a short time, as she had noticed that James' breathing had eased. His rubescent colour had faded slightly and his skin looked almost normal. It was light enough for her to see if she sat on the box at the front of the wagon and she could still see and hear her little brother. She would be within call if he needed her.

On another occasion she would have wondered where Isabelle and Harry were, but she made no attempt to go and find them, knowing that she had to stay where she was. There was no point in fretting, she could only hope that Harry wasn't leading his sister into mischief.

Picking out her copy of 'Great Expectations', Jane settled herself on the chest and began to read. She still found some of the words difficult to understand, though mother had explained what they meant when she had first read the book last year. Since the book had first arrived, she had read it several times, as she had so few books, but she loved the exciting story, which still enthralled her despite her familiarity with it. She hoped she might find some more of Mr Dickens' books at her grandmother's house.

James woke up just before the evening meal and came to sit on her lap. It was too dark to read now and as she cuddled him Jane realised to her great relief that he was not raging hot any more and was in fact much better. Even so, with the chill of the evening increasing, she persuaded him to return to bed, where father gave him his second dose of medicine.

"I was right not to give him quinine," father remarked with some satisfaction. "Whatever it was that caused his high temperature, it wasn't the fever."

Jane was in agreement with father and had indeed always thought that he knew everything. She did, however, think that Jesus might have helped in the cure. After all, she had asked for His assistance.

Stoffel and his family brought a large dish full of mutton chops and some vegetables over to the outspan to share with their visitors and the children were allowed to stay up later than usual as a special treat. It was a celebratory meal, as both William and Stoffel were thoroughly pleased with their bargaining. They shared a bottle of brandy and even Henry, who rarely drank spirits, was persuaded to have a small amount in a mug.

With James asleep once more, Jane was able to join the party and meet the children who lived at the store. She tried hard to understand their speech, but it was a language she just didn't understand. She noticed, however, that Isabelle and Harry seemed to make themselves understood without too much difficulty and there was a great deal of giggling. One thing that did puzzle her was the colour of their skins. All the Matabele people were dark brown, some were almost black, but these children were pale yellowy brown and one little girl looked almost white.

Their mother was the same light brown as the Moffats' maids were, because they were Bechuanas too. So why were these children different?

When she asked William about it in a whisper, he just smiled and said that she would see many more people with pale brown skins at Shoshong, Kuruman and in towns all the way to the Cape.

"It is just the way some people are born," he told her, shrugging his shoulders as if it was nothing new or important.

The discussions during the evening ranged from trading to transport and hunting, all topics that were common to, and interesting for, the three men. Somehow the talk then led to speculations about prospecting and gold mining. Despite the difficulties of language and the constant use of gestures, Stoffel was able to inform them that there were some ancient workings not far from the store. They were indications that sometime in the past the people who were then living here had mined gold. He offered to show them the abandoned shafts and tunnels the following morning and they were both pleased to accept. They were not planning to leave until the afternoon when the oxen had had a full day of grazing and with good water nearby had been able to drink their fill. The journey to these abandoned workings, if indeed it was a short one, shouldn't tire the horses too much and the experience of seeing a prospective gold mine was too good an opportunity to miss.

Both Henry and William knew that prospectors were not allowed into Matabeleland. Mzilikazi had allowed the missionaries to settle only because of his remarkable friendship with Robert Moffat, and they were teachers. Since their arrival, they had offered medical services to the king and many of his counsellors, as well as to the ordinary population. This medical treatment was greatly needed, though not always as appreciated as it might be, and witchdoctors resented the missionaries' interference. The king also allowed carefully selected men to hunt, but they were not allowed to hunt in the land of the Mashonas and they were all closely watched, as were men wanting to visit the Victoria Falls. Any man seen looking for stones would be severely penalised.

Tati was an area in dispute. All the former inhabitants had been completely wiped out by the Matabele, leaving only the pathetic remains of long abandoned villages, but the land was claimed equally by the Bechuanas and the Matabele. William sometimes wondered if both kings would like Europeans to settle in the area and create a buffer zone between the two kingdoms.

Eventually, the children were sent off to bed and as they were happily tired by then and the cold was insidious despite all the fires there was no objection to the order. The adults continued their unusual conversation for a further hour, constantly adding logs to the fire before they, too, sought the comfort of bed. William first ensured that a ring of fires was kept burning around the whole outspan and that all the animals were safe.

CHAPTER 20

Jane had insisted on changing places with Isabelle in the bed for that night. Isabelle made a great fuss about having to sleep in the outside place and said that she would be too cold to sleep. Jane had patiently explained that James might be sick in the night and it would be easier for her to deal with that if she was sleeping next to him. Isabelle still wasn't happy with the arrangement, grumbling and muttering, determined to disturb her big sister in her form of retaliation by constantly fidgeting until she finally fell asleep.

Jane, unaccustomed to the new position, with bodies on both sides, also stayed awake for some time, but was fast asleep before their father came to bed. She awoke in the middle of the night to find that James was again hot and restless. Worried, she remained awake for several hours, wondering if she should disturb father or try to do something herself, finally falling asleep through sheer exhaustion.

"Come on Jane, wake up!" It was Isabelle who was shaking her awake.

Harry, too, added his urgings; "You really are slow today. We've been awake for hours, but father said we must stay here until you were ready to get up. Do get up now."

Wearily and with the greatest difficulty, Jane forced herself to get out of bed and dress herself with Harry and Isabelle also vying for space as they too shrugged on their clothes. There really wasn't enough room for all three of them to stand up and move their arms and legs about. In fact, Jane was becoming annoyed with them, when James woke up slowly, clear eyed and ready for food after his fasting of the previous day. Jane was relieved when he spoke, "Jane, me hungry. Breakfast."

Jane gave him a quick hug; "Come on. I'll dress you now and then we can go out for breakfast."

As they were eating the welcome hot porridge, Jane was reminded that there was some washing to be done and that today would be a good day to do it.

"William and I are going for a ride with Stoffel and will be away for the whole morning," father informed her. "Now that James is better, the little ones can play with their friends at the store and you will be free to wash the clothes, Jane. I know you weren't able to do it yesterday and tomorrow we won't have much water as we shall be many miles away from here. Lukas will bake some bread and possibly some meat pies for the journey, so you have only the washing to occupy you."

"Yes, father. I'll see to it whilst you are away. Where are you going?"

"Stoffel has told us that a long time ago an ancient race of people mined for gold not far from here. The shafts and tunnels can still be seen and as neither of us has been there before we would like to see these gold mines. We might be able to do some hunting as well."

"May I come with you, father," asked Harry hopefully.

"I'm afraid not, son. If we do have an opportunity for hunting, you might get hurt. In any case, old mine shafts are not very exciting to look at. It's much better for you if you stay and play with your friends. You could teach them how to play ninepins or get out your throwing sticks to practise and improve your aim."

Harry wasn't too disappointed. The excursion didn't sound as exciting as he had thought it would be and father was right, he could have fun with his friends at the store.

A short time later, the three men mounted their horses and rode off into the bush, leaving the four children to walk over to the store. Harry proudly carrying his special toys. Isabelle had insisted on bringing her doll and then James had demanded his precious hippo. As Jane could find no reason to refuse his request, children and toys processed across the dusty space between the wagons and the store.

Stoffel's wife had just finished her own pile of washing on the rocks at the edge of the river, helped by a friend, and they called out to the children, making them welcome. When Jane managed, by sign language, to convey her own need to have some clothes washed and staggered back with an extra large bundle, the two Bechuana women immediately took it from her, indicating that they would do it. As there was a larger amount than usual, Jane was a little embarrassed by this gesture, but the women were insistent and were soon pounding away at the Hargreaves clothes and blankets. Jane was still haunted by the death of the dog and the thought of a crocodile creeping up on her, so she had been dreading the ordeal of washing clothes in the river

Sitting in a warm sheltered spot with the rhythmic pounding on one side and the sounds of happy chatter on the other, Jane fell fast asleep, only waking when the women came to offer her something to eat and drink.

All the children were clutching little mealie cakes covered with honey and mugs of milk and Jane felt her eyes prickle with tears at the unexpected kindness of these people. She wished she had something to give them in return, but could think of nothing more than a bead necklace and matching bracelet she had once made from some of her father's trade goods. She immediately ran over to the wagon and found these little treasures.

"I want to thank you for helping me."

She tried both English and Sindebele as she handed the necklace to Stoffel's wife and the bracelet to her friend. The two women smiled and nodded, holding out two cupped hands to receive the gift and giving a little curtsey. Their faces were lit with smiles of happiness and in their own tongue they heaped praises upon Jane. She realised that they were overjoyed, even if the actual words weren't understood. The feeling of happiness and goodwill spread and soon they were all laughing together.

By the time the men returned, the washing was dry, neatly folded and put away in the wagon. Jane was feeling fully refreshed after her sleep and light refreshment. She was also deeply content and ready to face the onward journey, though it meant parting from these kind people.

Father had brought four pieces of quartz from the ancient workings, one for each of his children, and he showed them the tiny flecks of gold in the shiny white stones. They were all delighted and Jane knew that she would treasure hers all her life. Isabelle, too, swore never to part with hers and was immediately echoed by Harry.

There was no reason for them to linger once they had eaten a satisfying lunch of fresh waterbuck steaks with a green leafy vegetable and mealie porridge. The oxen had eaten and rested well during the twenty-four hour respite, the horses had been fed grain in addition to grazing the good grass by the river and a fine supply of water was available for all of them. Lukas and the servants had filled bottles and pots with water for the journey and packed the remaining meat away. The axles of the wagons had all been well greased, the wheels, the chains and the yokes thoroughly checked. Satisfied that all was in order, William gave the command for the oxen to be inspanned shortly after lunch and after brief farewells, including fervent good wishes to Stoffel and his family, the southward journey resumed. With more than a thousand miles of trekking still ahead, Henry knew that they should try to keep moving however pleasant and tempting the outspans might prove. Of course, the animals had to be treated with care and needed regular rests or they wouldn't survive the journey. The wellbeing of the trek oxen was paramount in every transport rider's mind. They were essential to his business and travellers too would come to grief if their oxen failed. Henry and William were both mindful of the fact that the worst part of the road still lay ahead between here at the Tati and Kuruman. They had been lucky so far, as the oxen were still in very good condition and there had only been one incident with a wagon, which had been a nuisance, but hadn't really held them up.

William rode in his usual place at the head of the column whilst Henry continually walked his horse up and down the flanks and kept an eye on the rear, where the four spare oxen were being driven. He let his mind drift to the experiences of the morning.

Visiting the ancient mines had been interesting though slightly disappointing, as the shafts were blocked with rubble and the tunnels so low that they had only been able to penetrate them for a few yards. The quartz veins in the granite rocks were dazzlingly white in the sunshine and the gold reefs had obviously dipped far underground, for there was no sign of visible gold on the surface. The men searched the area for some time, picking up likely stones, but it was in one of the tunnels that Henry had found the small stones with the flecks of gold visible to the eye.

Henry was glad he had seen these mysterious workings, comparing them unfavourably with the Yorkshire coalmines he had visited and like many men before him, he tried to imagine who the ancient miners had been. Henry couldn't understand why they had wanted gold or what purpose it had served in their lives. It wasn't an important commodity in the lives of the present day Matabele or other African tribes as far as he knew. None of them wore gold about their bodies or displayed gold ornaments in their huts. They didn't appear to have a god who needed gold, so why waste their energy digging into the earth for gold? Henry was aware that porcupine quills filled with gold had been traded from time to time. Did these ancients use it to trade for other things they valued more? If so, what was it? They had certainly known about the existence of gold but had obviously not had great knowledge of mining methods or advanced tools as far as he could judge from his examination of the sides of the shafts and tunnels. Fire had apparently been used to crack the rock and no metal tools had ever been discovered, according to Stoffel. Were these perhaps King Solomon's mines? It was indeed a mystery and there were no means of discovering the answer, as none of the people who inhabited this region had kept written records.

On the return journey to the store, Henry had providentially spotted a group of waterbuck standing in the trees by the river. Signalling to the others to stop, he dismounted and stealthily approached the animals on foot. He had reached within thirty yards of them when, without warning, they flipped up their tails and raced off along the bank, but Henry had been close enough to risk a shot and managed to bag a young male.

With a shouted hasty congratulation for the successful hunt, William rode hurriedly back to camp to call some of the servants. Gleefully, they had brought their knives and rapidly skinned the animal and cut up the meat. Joyfully, they roasted the offal over their fire whilst Lukas grilled the liver and steaks for William and the Hargreaves family. Henry had donated a haunch to Stoffel for his family, which was a welcome addition to their larder. He had also donated the skin to Stoffel as a present for his hospitality. The rest of the meat would keep the camp happy for the next two days.

All in all, Henry was content. It had been a happy time, his children were all well and he himself had an opportunity to improve his precarious financial position.

Although it was sad to leave friends behind, it felt good to be on the move once again. God willing, they would be in Shoshong in two weeks' time.

Henry rode forward to have a talk to William.

"It was providential seeing that group of waterbuck this morning," was William's greeting. "We need to keep moving all afternoon, so there is not time to go out hunting. As it is, we're all well fed and have enough for tomorrow as well."

"Indeed, we have to take every opportunity as it offers itself," Henry agreed. "I was just lucky to be able to get close enough. The game is becoming very shy these days. A man on a horse is now recognised as a danger and treated with as much caution as any predator."

"It's not surprising is it? The hunters and sportsmen take a terrible toll whilst traders, prospectors, transport riders like myself and travellers such as yourself all need food. Every expedition has many mouths to feed, so hunting is a necessity as well as a sport or a business."

Henry nodded his head in agreement, "Of course, you're right, the animals provide food, but most men get pleasure from hunting. It is a challenge to outwit and outrun a wild animal and another challenge to be able to hit a moving target. For English sportsmen there is the thrill of capturing a trophy to hang on the wall at home with stories to regale all and sundry of derring-do in a wild country infested with dangerous animals. Many of the animals we see are unknown in England and museums or zoos are willing purchasers of good specimens to display and attract the paying public. However, there is no pleasure for me in seeing a wounded animal, and far too many hunters just shrug their shoulders or are furious because their prey has escaped and they have failed to kill."

"You must be fair on that one, Henry. All the hunters I have known have followed up on a wounded animal and tried to affect a kill. I know that often it is because they have desperately wanted the meat or the ivory or hated being defeated and there is no sympathy for the pain of the animal. Is that so strange? An animal is just an animal, after all. It hasn't got a soul like a man and doesn't suffer the same pain. Not everyone can be the marksman that you are and you must get a good deal of satisfaction from the success of your skill. Which reminds me, we never did have that shooting competition, did we?"

"Do you know, I had forgotten all about it. It was Sunday when we were at Lee's Castle and our time was filled with more gentle pursuits, as was fitting. Then we were otherwise occupied right until Edward's departure. Do you still want to test your skill against mine?"

"More than ever, now that I have seen your ability. It would be a fine challenge."

Henry smiled, "Target shooting is different from hunting and I think your ability in that respect is as great as mine. It should be an interesting contest. Do you think we have sufficient powder and lead to waste like that?"

"We'll have a strict limit. We'll work it out together. We can have three rounds at three different distances. That's only nine bullets each. Surely we can spare that?"

Henry nodded, "I'll check on my supplies in the morning. At least we shan't need any powder for trading before we reach Shoshong!"

"No, we shan't. It may be a thirsty land between here and there, but at least there are no kraals and we shan't be troubled by hosts of beggars and thieves."

Henry laughed, "So, if you had to choose between the opportunity to trade and obtain food at a village or to face a wasteland you'd choose the latter."

"Without a doubt," was William's firm answer.

"I think you might qualify that by specifying Matabele villages, though," Henry added slyly.

William gave a loud guffaw, "Definitely 'yes' to that. The Matabele are proud and totally without shame. The world and all that is in it was meant just for them and no other people matter. They will kill or steal to get what they want or beg and wheedle if they think it will be more successful."

"It hasn't taken you long to come to that sweeping conclusion. Whilst it has taken me four and a half years to learn exactly the same, you have achieved the knowledge in one short visit."

"I know that personal knowledge and experience are best on most occasions but you don't have to visit a country to learn quite a lot about it. A great deal of knowledge comes from hearing other people's opinions and descriptions. The whole world knows about the Victoria Falls and how big they are simply because Livingstone has described them. They don't need to see them to know about them, but I know that I needed to visit Matabeleland for myself to verify if the stories I had heard were accurate, and I was prepared to disprove them because I have always enjoyed working with the natives. I felt I understood them.

The Matabele are different. They only respect their king because he holds their lives in his hands. If they offend him in any way it means instant death.

There is some appreciation of what it means to be Matabele too, they are pumped up with tribal pride, but no one outside the tribe has any value at all."

"There is one notable exception to that last statement of yours and that is the Reverend Robert Moffat," Henry reminded him. "I do, however, agree with you. It is precisely because the Matabele are so arrogant that they are unwilling to listen to us. They will take material goods from us whether they understand the uses of an object or not. They will eat our food, drink our drinks, wear our clothes and accept our medical skills, but when it comes to Christian principles they are deaf. An immediate benefit is desired; indeed it is all that matters....I could go on all day. I'm sorry, William, I shouldn't have said so much. I do tend to get carried away. I suppose it is the culmination of nearly five years of frustration. Five years and no converts after so much hope and enthusiasm, are we wasting our time?" Henry didn't wait for a reply. Wheeling his horse around, he set it into a canter, calling out, "I'll go and see how the wagons are coping."

The discussion with William had pleased Henry, who needed to be able to talk about his work and his aspirations. He found great relief in discourse with people who could understand his aims, even if they didn't necessarily share them. Oh, how he missed his wife, who was such a willing listener and could debate missionary policy with him. Gradually he slowed his horse's gait as he passed each wagon, noting en route that all was as it should be and calling a greeting to each leader and driver.

The afternoon was well on by now and the ground was becoming sandy, the heavier going slowing them down. William would soon have to find a suitable place for an outspan before it was too dark. In lion country it was essential to have time to build a strong kraal for the protection of the animals. Henry hoped that they might reach the Shashi before nightfall, but it seemed less likely now.

Reaching his own wagon, he was surprised to see that the three older children were still walking and obviously quite happy as they tossed a ball made up of rags from one to the other. He realised that none of them had had any lessons recently and he determined that he would set them some work on the very next day. James was sitting contentedly beside Bokkis and chattering away in his own language.

Harry spoke up cheerily as he saw his father approaching, "Father, will there be more friends for us to play with when we next stop?"

Henry drew to a halt and gazed down at the inquisitive face of his elder son. "I'm afraid not. It will take us at least two weeks to reach Shoshong and there are no other people living near the road for the whole of that distance.

Later on, there may be some cattle posts, but they are far from the road and the cattle herds there rarely leave their area. If we were desperately short of food we could always try to find such a place, I suppose, but unless we pass some other travellers going to Matabeleland we aren't likely to see anyone else for the whole of that time. You'll just have to amuse yourself and play with your sisters and brother, but remember that you will have to do some lessons every day. You have already missed too much school time."

Harry was disappointed, for he revelled in companionship. Perhaps William could be persuaded to play ninepins or set up a target for his throwing sticks. Lessons were not his favourite occupation, as he preferred a more active challenge, but he was an able scholar with an excellent memory and always tried to please father, thus making good headway in Latin and Arithmetic. Writing was just a chore, but Jane was always patient and willing to help him to complete his set tasks. She told him that reading was much more fun when you could read exciting stories, so he hoped that he would be able to read stories soon, as he didn't find reading at all exciting.

Harry no longer thought about Inyati; it was too far away and travelling was fun. He missed mother, of course, and often wished she could come back from heaven and look after them again. It must be a funny place, he thought, if people couldn't come back when you wanted them. Jane said that mother would stay there for ever and ever and Harry thought that Jane was quite wrong. Mother would come back for them. He just knew.

CHAPTER 21

William heaved a sigh of relief as he sat down in his chair beside the fire, rubbing his hands and holding them out towards the flames to warm them. Fox, ever faithful, flopped down beside him with a grunt of pleasure as he exposed his belly to the warmth. The morning trek had been cold and damp and whilst checking the wagon coverings after breakfast William's hands had become numb with cold. He felt the tingling in his fingers and palms as the warmth began to permeate his skin. He was relaxed, watching Henry teaching the children, who were sitting solemnly on their chairs busily writing on slates.
How lucky he had been to find such a solid, congenial companion for this return journey, he thought.
He still missed Edward's lively company, for they had become close friends. Edward had been a tremendous help on the journey north; full of energy, fun and laughter, yet reliable and hardworking. He had been willing to try his hand at any of the necessary tasks a transport rider faced and had proved to be a successful hunter. The two of them had made light of the setbacks and hardships that were inevitable on a lengthy trip into the interior. Edward had been younger by a few years, of course, and was willing to let William be the leader, so there was never any confusion about which of them made the decisions. Apart from the fact that Edward was fair-haired and blue-eyed and William had dark hair with eyes as brown as Henry's, they could easily have been related, so similar were they in build, temperament, attitudes and ambitions.
Henry, on the other hand, was much older and inclined to be solemn. He was not unlike William's elder brother in looks; tall, broad-shouldered and with thick dark hair, the Hargreaves nose was perhaps longer but the strong chin and heavy brows were similar to his own family's. Perhaps William's vision of the brother he admired was the reason why he got on so well with Henry. After more than three weeks of being in close contact, there had been no disagreement or feeling of resentment, no ill humour or even exasperation. Each man had taken responsibility for his own wagons and still been willing to help with the others, they had supported each other when there was a crisis and each had helped to supply the camp with meat. In one respect only did William find Henry's attitude restrictive and that was the fact that Henry could rarely be persuaded to enjoy a drink. All the men with whom he was acquainted had been prepared to share a brandy or a beer after a hard trek. It was true that some of them were inclined to over-indulge and became a

liability, but a drink around the fire with a juicy, sizzling steak and good cheerful company in the evening was William's great joy. Card games, anecdotes of personal adventures and music or singing with a bottle to share enhanced what was often a lonely life. William had a taste for wine, but was not averse to thirst-quenching beer when it was available, especially on the hottest summer days and when the winter's dust dried his throat. Cape brandy was something he drank only to be sociable.

William had agreed that they should not travel on Sundays, partly in deference to Henry's calling, but also because he knew that it was essential to rest the oxen at regular intervals. He was always hopeful of making a fast journey without aiming to break any records because oxen were valuable and in some areas irreplaceable. Profit could become loss if the needs of the draught animals were ignored. On other journeys he had passed abandoned wagons lying forlornly in the bush as a result of overworked or sick animals dying in the yoke. William was determined to avoid such a calamity if he could; he also felt that it was time he found a partner to share the stresses and strains of a long trek such as this and to provide companionship. If possible, he would choose someone like Edward who was honest, lively and hardworking, though he realized that such ideal partners were difficult to find and men like that were more likely to be in business for themselves. He had been lucky to have Henry to accompany him on the southbound trek, now he felt it was time to have a more permanent colleague.

Transport riders often teamed up to share the trials of the road on long journeys and William, who was a cheerful, friendly young man, never had any problem with these fellow travellers. He met some who were rather rough and careless and others who were downright disreputable and these he had happily abandoned at the earliest possible time, but never with any sense of ill feeling.

"Are you half asleep already or just daydreaming?" Henry sank abruptly into the chair beside William. William, who hadn't noticed Henry walking over to the fire, looked up sheepishly.

"I was just thinking that it would be a great help to me if I had a permanent partner or employed a good assistant. I shall soon be able to buy another wagon and intend to trade in the interior for a few more years, but more wagons means more drivers, leaders and servants and that means I shall have to provide more food. One man and his horse aren't enough. I just can't manage everything. If you hadn't lent me one of your spare oxen when one of mine could no longer cope and collapsed suddenly, I should have been in real trouble."

"Yes, well at least that poor worn-out ox provided us all with meat when none was available in the bush. Support works both ways and my servants would have gone hungry if it hadn't been for your ox. It is a relief to know that we shall be in Shoshong by tomorrow or the next day at the latest. These last two weeks have been much harder than I thought they would be."

William nodded his agreement. "I was surprised at how dry the bush has become in the few weeks since I was here. I knew that crossing the Shashi would be a problem, as it's a deep sandy drift, and I thought we might have had more trouble at the Macloutsie with lions. They are really a nuisance there now. We were lucky not to lose any of our animals."

Henry smiled wryly, "Well, they got most of that antelope you had shot. It's a pity it was so late in the evening and you couldn't bring in more than a few steaks. You lost practically the whole carcass overnight."

William grinned, "Yes, I should have taken Lukas out with me to carry in more of the meat. Well, at least the lions had left me the horns, so it wasn't a complete loss and we thoroughly enjoyed the steaks I had managed to cut out didn't we?"

Henry had to admit that William was right. "I expect some hunters will realise that there are a number of fine lion skins running around out there and deal with the predators before long. We really didn't have time to go out on a lion hunt on this occasion. I'm astonished, though, that the lions are still there, considering how many hunters travel along this road and every one has horses and oxen that are vulnerable. It is a benefit to us and other travellers that there are those strong thorn kraals already built near the river that only need to be kept in repair each time they are occupied. It certainly saves a lot of time and effort. Even so, they prove no barrier to determined lions."

"Well, if the lions are still in this area next year, I shall make a special effort to hunt them," William promised. "In any case, I should try to come up a bit earlier in the season. Finding the Seribe and the Seruli dry was a great trial, even though we got some at the Khokwi. The oxen were without water for nearly three days and I thought I would choke on the dust. If we hadn't found a good supply at the Palatchwi, I don't think we should have made it so far."

"It isn't an easy choice is it? Whether to travel when the road is dry and the going easier, but face being without water for long spells, or to travel soon after the rains have finished, and cope with the mud. Constantly being stuck in mud, sometimes up to the axles, takes up a lot of time and energy that is frustrating and wearying. The drifts are often more difficult, too, with the animals having to swim across. Then having to make long stops for the oxen to recover adds to the time taken for a journey. On the plus side, of course, is the fact that water is available and no one dies of thirst and the grass is greener for the animals," Henry reminded him.

William laughed delightedly. "You sound just like a seasoned transport rider, Henry, and I thought you were only a missionary."

"Only a missionary!" Henry exclaimed in mock indignation. "I'll have you know that we have to be doctors, nurses or midwives despite only the briefest medical training. We pull out teeth and act as animal doctors for our horses and cattle. We have to translate hymns and the Bible into Sindebele or whatever language the natives use. We have to build houses and churches and dams or irrigation channels for our gardens so that we can supply ourselves with vegetables and fruit. We act as peacemakers and advisers. We are carpenters, builders, wheelwrights, blacksmiths and gunsmiths, too. We also have to be successful hunters or we would starve. We do have to cope with wagon transport, but that is only a small proportion of our accomplishments," he added with a sly smile.

William held up his hands in surrender, " I had no idea that you had to be able to do so much. I don't suppose I had thought about your work seriously and I'm sure the majority of people just think you go and live amongst the heathen with a prayer book and the Bible in your hand. People living in civilised countries in towns or villages take it for granted that there is a doctor to assist them when they are ill and that there are craftsmen to cater for their needs. No one I know is sufficiently versatile to cope with every aspect of daily life as you do." William looked at Henry with marked respect. "In addition to all the attributes you have already mentioned, you forgot to add that you are a schoolmaster as well and here come your pupils with their work for you to assess."

The four children were waiting quietly for Henry to acknowledge their presence. They held their slates ready to display their work when asked.

Although he was the youngest, James was the first to approach when Henry beckoned them forward. He had drawn a number of squiggles and pointing to them said, "S S S". Henry wasn't quite sure whether the shapes were meant to represent a snake or whether Jane had meant James to copy a letter S so he asked him what it was. " 'nake," replied James proudly.

"Ah. I see. It's a snake. Say 'snake' properly James. 'Snake'."

James solemnly repeated the word rather separating the first letter from the following four at first until on the fifth attempt he was more or less successful. Jane gently moved him to one side so that she could present her own slate and after a quick glance Henry nodded his head.

Harry's work was equally accurate, but Isabelle's had a number of mistakes. Henry was inclined to be cross at her for making errors and told her to go and correct them, but when he noticed the trembling lip and sudden flush in the cheeks of this pretty daughter of his he ordered Jane to assist her.

Wisely, William said nothing, but he had noted before that Henry was inclined to treat Isabelle more gently than the others. He himself liked all four children equally: Jane for her solemn correct behaviour, Isabelle for her winsome ways (though he thought she might become very selfish and self-centred if she was over-indulged), Harry for his lively interest in everything about him and James because he was a happy and generally contented infant. How very different the four children were, he thought. He was aware that the two girls shared a mother and that the two boys were the sons of Henry's second wife, but even so, the differences were marked. Jane was self contained and her small, pale face could have seemed plain had it not been for the fine dark-brown eyes. Her straight brown hair could be dressed more attractively perhaps if she had a mother or servant to help her. That might make her seem prettier, but she had a kind and generous nature that would certainly attract some man who was looking for a wife to care for him and not just for a decorative woman to grace his home and show off to his friends.

Isabelle was the one with the greater appeal at first sight. She had a rounded face framed with dark curls and with expressive hazel eyes that could shine with delight when she was given a present or compliment, though they might just as easily become bright with anger and equally easily filled with tears if she was thwarted.

She used her wiles to gain approval, but she was far from being the fragile, pretty little sister, as William had observed on several occasions. Miss Isabelle wanted the world for herself and getting her own way was second nature to her.

She reminded him of a young woman who had once caught his attention in Cape Town. Fortunately for him she had set her sights a great deal higher than a transport rider, even one who came from a good family and who had a rich father. William had been greatly upset by her rejection at the time until he saw how she treated the man she did marry, almost ruining him with her excessive spending.

When he was rich enough to buy a property for himself and settle down, perhaps as a wine grower or a wine trader like his father, he would find a wife who would be obedient, kind and generous and a suitable mother for his children. He realised that he was thinking of his own mother as the perfect wife. She was attractive and intelligent, too, helping his father with his business by entertaining the wealthier denizens of the town. She was an excellent hostess and many were the lucrative contracts signed after a dinner at the Lodge.

Reluctantly, William brought his thoughts back to the present; it would be many months before he could enjoy the luxury of civilised living in Cape Town.

The mid-day meal was satisfyingly hot, but Lukas warned them that he had cooked the last of the meat and there was nothing for the evening meal for anyone. Henry and William looked at each other.

"Would you like to go out hunting, or shall I go?" William asked.

"I think we should both go," replied Henry thoughtfully. "We need the meat and if we both go in opposite directions there is more chance of success. I'll take Bokkis with me, but I'd like Lukas to stay in camp as a guard for the children, if that is acceptable."

"By all means. I'll take one of the other servants with me and provide him with a gun. In fact, I might take more than one, in case we need to carry large amounts of meat."

"Well I hope your optimism is rewarded. The more we can obtain now, the better it will be for all of us. We shall need to buy some meal in Shoshong, as our stocks are dwindling alarmingly quickly."

The two men saddled up and after agreeing to be back in the camp by five o'clock in order to start the evening trek, they galloped off, William with his attendants, including Fox, going downstream and Henry with Bokkis heading upstream. Both men intended to stay by the river for the first hour, then circle round and head back to camp, thus covering a wide area of ground.

Jane was content to be with the little ones for the afternoon. There was no washing to be done that day and she only had a small pile of mending to occupy her as she watched the three children playing. Harry had set up the ninepins on a space that William had helped him to clear and from time to time he persuaded Isabelle to have a turn, but he didn't mind practising by himself when she grew tired of his constant winning. James occupied himself with his hippo and a variety of sticks and stones he had collected.

Once the mending had been done, Jane gladly settled herself in her chair with one of her books. The weak sun offered a little warmth, but she was grateful for the comfort of a blanket she had brought from the wagon and wrapped round herself.

Perhaps it was because she was so enthralled with her story that the time seemed to pass quite quickly and before she had managed three chapters she heard her father returning, followed shortly afterwards by Mr William.

Their hunting plan had been successful and there was a rapturous reception for them all when they returned laden with meat; William proudly displaying a pair of tsessebe horn, followed by his servants staggering under the load of its carcass. Henry was holding aloft the horns of a reedbuck and Bokkis had bagged a bushpig which he was able to carry in. Immediately, he set off with two helpers back to the place where Henry's kill lay waiting to be cut up and transported. The camp would feast well for the next few days.

William straightaway gave the order for the oxen to be brought in and in-spanned so that they could travel as far as possible before stopping for the night. It would take some time for the message to reach the herd boys and for them to drive in the oxen, so Lukas was ordered to make coffee whilst some of the other servants began to skin and cut up the bush-pig and tsessebe.

It was whilst they were enjoying the steaming hot coffee that they became aware of excited chatter in the area where the carcasses were being butchered. Looking questioningly at each other, they both put down their mugs and reached for their guns.

The children, who had played contentedly during the afternoon and who had gone to see the animals the hunters had brought in, now came hurrying back, with Lukas following them.

"Well, what is all the noise about?" William questioned abruptly.

Lukas bent his head respectfully; he hated being the bearer of bad news, "The herders are bringing in the oxen, but they have sent a message to say that there are six missing."

"Is that the full message?" William queried angrily.

"Two of the boys are following the tracks. They say the animals were all there when they sat down to eat at mid-day, then when they began to round them up to drive them back into camp just now six of them had escaped."

William snorted, "They probably went to sleep all afternoon instead of watching the animals as they are supposed to do. Well, there is still an hour before dark. They had better find them."

Lukas hastily backed away before there were more recriminations and William turned to Henry.

"It doesn't look as if we shall be able to make a start tonight. Even if they find the animals soon, it will be dark before we get them back here."

Henry nodded, "We had better plan to stay here then. We shall need to make a kraal, so I'll go and organise that and then I think we should ride out and see if there is any sign of them. How is your horse? I had a short sharp gallop, but Oscar wasn't overstretched and can manage more miles if needed."

"I was lucky, too, and we ambled along for most of the time. We took the tsessebe by surprise and I got in a lucky shot before the troop disappeared from sight. My horse is fine. He's got many more miles in him if we take it slowly. I'll get the horses resaddled whilst you're busy, and find the messenger or one of the other boys to lead us to the place where the oxen were grazing today.

Within half an hour the two men were once more riding out of camp following one of the boys who was a leader for one of William's spans.

Jane went to find Lukas to arrange an evening meal for the children. There was a wide choice of meats and she chose some steaks from the tsessebe, which with beans and pumpkin would please everyone. She would read or tell a story until the meal was ready, then they could sing some hymns and rhymes until time for bed. If father hadn't returned by then she would be able to read her book again using firelight or a candle to light the pages.

All in all, it had been a happy day and Jane began to wish that this journey would never end. The family was together more often than it had been at Inyati when father was often out all day or away for days at a time. If only mother could have been here too, she would have thought that it was a perfect way to live. James sometimes cried for his mama when he was tired and ready to go to sleep, but Harry and Isabelle only seemed to remember her when they fell and hurt themselves. Although she had to take care of the little ones, do the mending and the washing, there were fewer chores than there had been at home and Lukas was always ready to help, so Jane found more time to enjoy her own pursuits. She hoped that the lost animals would be found soon, it was a horrible thought that they might have to spend the night out in the bush where there were so many dangerous wild creatures.

When they came to the place where the oxen had been grazing that day, William and Henry were shown the tracks of the six missing animals where they had left the grazing area and set off towards the west. A little further on they were shown the distinct outline of a human footprint in the dust and this trail continued with the footprint over the top of the ox hoof tracks. Fox sniffed busily around, making little forays to the left and right.

"It seems that someone drove the oxen away," William remarked.

"Yes, it is fairly obvious that the footprints are over the top of the tracks, as they would be if a man was following them, but we didn't see the footprints around the grazing area so I think that these animals had strayed away from the main herd. Perhaps someone thought they were completely lost and decided to appropriate them."

William snorted, "It's more likely that the man appropriated them; they can't have been far away from the others and as there are more than eighty beasts altogether it's not a number easy to overlook. Besides, the herd boys were there somewhere and if they weren't asleep they would be making a noise as they indulged in the rowdy games they play."

Henry looked abashed. "You're right, of course. Anyone coming across loose domestic animals in the bush would know that the owner couldn't be far away. I seem to remember that there is a cattle post a few miles in this direction. We can follow the track or head straight for the post and save some time."

William was decidedly angry at the theft of his animals and the unnecessary delay in their journey. With night fast approaching and the uncertainty of the fate of the oxen still worrying, him he was inclined to be terse. "You're right about the cattle post. I know a trader who keeps an extra span of oxen there and pays Khama for their keep. We'll go straight there." With that, he set his horse to a gallop, trusting Henry to keep up with him.

CHAPTER 22

They had covered not much more than a mile when they met two of the herdboys returning from their search for the lost animals. William reined in his horse and Henry came to a halt a few yards further back, patting Oscar to calm him.
"Hello there, Amos and Abdol. What news?" called William.
The two boys approached the horsemen, breathing hard as if they had been hurrying, although they were only jogging when William saw them. Abdol looked at Amos and nudged him to speak.
"We followed the tracks all the way to the cattle post. We got there but the ground had cattle prints in every place. We could not follow our animals any more because there were too many tracks there," responded Amos.
"We saw only one old woman in one of the houses. She told us that the people had all gone further away to find grazing and water for the herds. She didn't know when they would return. We asked her for our six missing oxen, but she pretended that she didn't know anything about them. She was lying to us. So we asked and asked many times her for an answer. She said that perhaps it was bushmen that had taken them. She said the bushmen were always stealing cattle from them. We couldn't find our cattle, so we came back."
Abdol nodded his head vigorously and Amos hung his head, wondering if the white man would be cross because they hadn't found the lost beasts and knowing that it was their fault that they were lost in the first place.
William gazed at the two boys, pondering the problem now facing them all. They couldn't continue their journey until the oxen had been found, but if the cattle herders and the lost oxen weren't at the cattle post then it might take several hours to find any of them and it was almost dark now.
Henry walked his horse alongside. "This is certainly a predicament," he commented.
"Yes, indeed. I don't think there is much point in our riding out to the cattle post now, as it's so close to sunset. We aren't equipped for a night away from camp anyway and have no food for the horses. We can't go looking for the cattle in the dark when we have no idea where they might be. But it's a great nuisance because that woman might take a message to the herders and if they are intent on stealing the animals they'll hide them where we'll never find them."
Henry nodded thoughtfully. "We could send one of our boys out there to keep watch tonight. If we leave camp before dawn tomorrow we could be at

the cattle post by sunrise and we could insist that the woman lead us to where the herds are being kept. Our horses will be fresh, well fed and watered and we will have the whole day ahead of us. We can take water and provisions with us in case we have a lengthy search. With determination and right on our side we are more likely to succeed."

"Agreed. I think your plan is a good one." William turned to Amos and Abdol and praised them for their efforts so far, "But," he went on, "it is necessary for you to keep watch on that cattle post. You must both go back there immediately and make sure that the woman is still there. If she has gone then you must follow her trail. You must stay awake. Take it in turns to sleep. Do you understand? We will bring you food and water early in the morning."

With looks of obedient resignation the two boys set off back to the cattle post.

"They may not look very happy at the prospect of staying awake out in the open all night, though they may be able to lie beside the cooking fire there if the woman is already asleep. Still, I'm fairly positive that they had a good sleep earlier today, so it is very little punishment for dereliction of duty."

Henry nodded approvingly, "I'm in full agreement. Most employers would have dealt much more harshly with them. It was a good idea to send two of them as they are so afraid of the dark and will appreciate the company. Besides it doubles the chance of success."

The two men turned their horses and set off back towards the wagons.

It was quite dark when they finally saw the welcoming light of several campfires beckoning to them in the distance on an evening already very cold. With all speed they hitched their mounts to Henry's wagon, unsaddled, rubbed them down, gave them nosebags of corn and covered them with blankets. Reaching the kitchen fire first, Henry ordered Lukas to bring them supper and a hot drink then sat down by his own fire where a windbreak had been made and there was some semblance of warmth. William joined him a few minutes later bearing a plate of food for Fox and a bottle of brandy. "It's not my favourite drink," he remarked, "but on a night like this it helps to keep out the chill. Why don't you have a little, Henry, and treat it as a medicinal dose?"

Henry was about to shake his head when a shiver ran through him. He held out the mug of coffee that Lukas had given him. "Just the smallest drop then. It wouldn't do for me to get the fever or a cold, but I don't really like it," he admitted.

William grinned and poured no more than a teaspoonful into Henry's mug.

"There you are, though it's not enough to warm you. Some of the hunters and traders swear that spirits ward off the fever, or cure it, though that is probably an excuse. Many of them don't need an excuse, of course, but it does help to enliven the evenings."

"That's as may be, but alcohol demeans the imbiber by removing his natural restraints. It leads to riotous behaviour, sometimes fisticuffs and in the case of the poor leads to wife beating and poverty."

"Only when it's taken in excess," protested William, but he was spared the lecture he had heard in different forms several times before, by the arrival of supper. There was a dish containing beans and pumpkin, a second one piled up with thick mealie meal and a plate with several sizzling steaks. Both men set to with a will and conversation was kept to a minimum. At their feet, Fox made short work of his supper.

Although William agreed with Henry about the adverse affects of alcohol and had seen some disgraceful scenes in the sea-front taverns in Cape Town, he felt that the judicial consumption of drink was beneficial. If drinking alcohol enlivened a party and kept men happy, then why not.

He remembered with pleasure some hilarious evenings spent in traders' stores and hunters' camps with music, gambling and tall stories or practical jokes. Somehow those celebrations rarely produced negative results and everything proceeded as normal the following morning. In addition, he knew of men who were sure that they would have died of the fever had they not enjoyed it, especially those who lived a lonely life in the wilderness, a bottle of whisky to hand. Anyway, he didn't intend to forego his comforts and he refilled his mug, revelling in the warmth as it found its way to his stomach. He was glad that Henry only offered a mild lecture now and again, which amused rather than annoyed him, and the conversation was considerably enlivened when William deliberately set out to be the devil's advocate.

"Those two boys of yours have very different names," ventured Henry after a long silence whilst they were both eating. "Are they both from Cape Town?"

"Yes, and both from the sort of poor background they were glad to leave behind. Amos actually ran away after his mother died and was lucky enough to be employed by a trader. He ended up at Kuruman, which is where he adopted the name 'Amos' and where he managed to learn a few words of Tswana, but he wasn't there long before he came to work for me. He seems to have an ear for languages and the fact that he can get by in a variety of local tongues is exceptionally useful. Abdol's father was a coolie on the docks. I expect you'll know that part of Cape Town."

Henry coughed discreetly, "Well, I'm not exactly familiar with it, but I do know that it isn't the most salubrious part of the town."

"That is an understatement. Anyway, he arrived at my father's depot looking for work just as I was preparing for this journey and as I was short of a leader I thought I could employ him. He offered to work just for his food, but of course I shall pay him. Apart from this lapse both of them have been reliable until now. Most travellers have to cope with missing oxen at some point on their journeys as it's notoriously difficult to keep them altogether when they are grazing, especially when there are several spans."

After some further desultory conversation they retired to bed knowing that they had to be up before dawn.

Whilst it was still dark, William was up and rekindling the dying fire. His breath hung in a white cloud and the chill bit into the exposed flesh of his face, hands and neck.

Henry arrived a few minutes later to find him filling the kettle and balancing it firmly on the crackling logs. Then William went to rouse Lukas, who made mugs of steaming coffee as soon as the water boiled. Fortunately, there was sufficient cooked meat from the evening meal to allow them to have a quick breakfast and there were several more slices to pack into bags to carry with them. After Lukas had made the coffee he fried slices of mealie cakes to add to the meat. He also produced a bag of food and a bottle of water for the two boys.

As soon as they had eaten, they collected their guns and saddled up, each man carrying extra cartridges, his bag of food, a canteen of water and a nosebag for his horse. They felt that the whole matter would be concluded within a few hours and in any case well before nightfall, so there was no need to carry a bedroll as well. William looked down at Fox, who was waiting expectantly beside him. "No Fox, you can't come this time. Stay."

"I think you'll have to tie him up," Henry advised, "otherwise he'll follow us."

William found a length of rope and, ignoring the reproachful look in the dog's eyes, he put a loop round his neck and tied the other end to the wheel of Henry's wagon. "There you are, you can go and lie beside the fire and the children will play with you when they get up."

Wasting no more words, they mounted and set off, following a path through the trees that would lead towards the cattle post. It was still too dark to see far ahead and William, who was leading, erred on the side of caution by walking his horse. "We'll ride faster when I can check the road ahead," he called over his shoulder. "There is little point in risking a fall just to save a few minutes."

Henry was in full agreement and was happy to let William lead the way.

"I value my horse, too. There is nothing to be gained by blundering about the bush in the dark. Already it is a little lighter. It won't be long before we will be able to see far enough ahead for a brisk trot."

As they were heading west the light was behind them and what had been a mere suggestion of light grey on the horizon had now spread upwards in a pale yellow band. Snorting and shaking their heads, the horses were ready to stretch their legs and warm their muscles, but the men held them in for a short time longer.

Jane had been only slightly disturbed by the movements of the wagon as her father dressed himself, but she was sufficiently awake to feel a chill along her side. Harry, at the other side of the bed, had rolled over and dragged the blankets with him, leaving her side exposed to the chill of the morning and this as much as the vibrations roused her from sleep. She heard father move to the front of the wagon and climb out and vaguely she heard him talking to William. Stealthily, she tried to pull the blankets back over to her side without disturbing the others, but Harry must have been sleeping on them, for they didn't move. She was tempted to give a hard pull and claim her share of the warmth, but knew to her cost what a riot that would start. She lay there miserably feeling the cold seep through her whole body. Eventually, she heard her father take his gun from the front of the wagon and then the men attending to their horses, putting on saddles and bridles. She heard Fox's name mentioned and it was many minutes later before she heard them mounting and riding away. Thankfully, she slipped quietly out of her own bed and climbed into father's bed. It was softer and warmer than the children's bed and within minutes she slipped into a deep sleep.

It was fully light when Jane was roused by an altercation between Isabelle and Harry. She listened to the quarrel and wished that she could ignore it, but there was no one else to intercede and from the sound of it James was being drawn into the fray. Harry and Isabelle were tugging at the blankets and both complaining that they were cold, whilst poor James was being knocked by both sides.

Jane roused herself and began to throw aside the covers when Isabelle gave a sharp scream. "He bit me. James bit me," she wailed. "Oh it hurts."

She turned immediately to give James a slap and he began to sob too.

"Stop it Isabelle." Jane reached over to pull James into her arms and gave him a cuddle.

"But he bit me. Just look." Isabelle pulled up her sleeve to display the red mark where James' teeth had indeed been embedded in her arm. Fortunately, the cloth had prevented the skin from breaking, but it was obviously a painful bite.

Jane tried to soothe her, "Oh dear. That is a horrid mark. Let me kiss it better." So saying, she took hold of Isabelle's arm and kissed the bite mark, then rubbed it gently with her finger. "It isn't bleeding, so it will soon feel better," she comforted her sister.

Turning now to James she looked sternly at him, ignoring his sobs. "You must never bite anyone. It is a horrid, horrid thing to do," she admonished him firmly but gently. "It isn't surprising that Isabelle smacked you when you hurt her like that. Now you can both say you are sorry to each other. I won't tell father of this bad behaviour, but I don't ever want to see you fighting again."

Harry, who had been equally to blame for the affray, said nothing but quietly got off the bed and started to dress himself, shivering in the chill air. He was beginning to find the days boring and was longing for friends to challenge and play games with him. Mr William would play with him sometimes when he had time, but Jane was always too busy, Isabelle was happier playing with her doll and would only play his games if he let her win sometimes, whilst James was too small. Perhaps he could persuade Bokkis to make him a bigger whip. If it was long enough he could make it snap and crack like a real grown-up one.

Once they were all warmly dressed, they climbed down from the wagon and were all delighted when they discovered Fox was with them. They hugged him exuberantly as they tried to keep warm whilst waiting for breakfast. Fox was equally delighted to have their company and sat close besides Harry's chair as he ate his porridge. Fox soon gobbled up his own food, amusing the children by licking his plate over and over and then looking underneath for more.

Harry's idea of spending the morning with Bokkis was, however, forestalled because Jane had decided during breakfast that they would all do some lessons that morning to keep them occupied. Harry's protestations were ignored, but when Isabelle suggested that they could work better if they were warmer Jane agreed that it was probably a good idea and that she would play some games with them before they started their reading and learning.

Isabelle glanced slyly at Harry with a little smirk on her face and he pulled a face at her in return. Luckily, Jane was busy helping James to eat the last of his porridge at that moment or she would have cancelled her permission for them to play first. As it was, they had some fun games of hide and seek, followed by some running and chasing games round the trees. Flushed and happy, their calls and laughter echoed around the camp and the drivers sitting around their own campfire nodded in approval. Fox barked and barked in his frustration and desire to join in the fun, but Jane insisted that he should stay tied up when Harry and Isabelle begged to be allowed to untie him.

"If we let him go he might stay and play with us, but he might run away and try to find Mr William. We would be in great trouble if he was lost," she explained carefully.

Reluctantly, they agreed and from time to time they left their games and went to pat and comfort the dog. When he was tired of running, Harry dared Isabelle to climb a tree and she gleefully accepted the challenge. James wanted to join them but he was too heavy for Jane to lift high enough.

When it came to climbing trees and swinging on the branches, Jane declined to participate and after watching Harry and Isabelle for a short time she insisted firmly that they were all warm enough now and could sit quietly with their reading books. She was uncomfortably aware that father would have been horrified to see Isabelle copying Harry and climbing trees. She knew that she should have stopped her and pointed out to her that such behaviour was unladylike, but keeping Isabelle happy was necessary for her own peace of mind. She comforted herself with the thought that father need never know and Isabelle wouldn't normally try to do such a hoydenish thing. She was just trying to show off to her younger brother and pretending that girls were as clever as boys, but as soon as she realised that she couldn't keep pace with his antics she retired and pretended that she wasn't interested any more.

Reluctantly leaving their games, they washed their hands and faces and sat down near the fire with the windbreak behind them. Jane began with a scripture lesson, as she knew her parents would have done, and then set them to do some sums on their slates.

She was busy working with Harry and Isabelle and engrossed in her explanations so she was unaware that James was undoing the rope that was tied round the dog's neck. It was only when Fox began jumping up and down and racing round the table where they were working that she realised that the rope was lying on the ground and no longer attached to him.

In her surprise, she called out suddenly, "Fox, come here. Come here at once."

It might have been the tone of her voice or it might have been the fact that she jumped up suddenly, trying to catch him, but the dog was immediately wary and backed off, barking.

Harry and Isabelle tried to entice him by pretending to offer food but Fox was having none of it. He turned quickly and raced off under the wagon and by the time the children had run round the end of the wagon he was disappearing into the bush.

Their first impulse was to run after him and this they did for about fifty yards before appreciating that they would never catch him. Jane stopped and told Harry and Isabelle to return to the wagon. James had hidden himself when he sensed the distress caused by the disappearance of the dog and Jane now had to try to find him. It didn't take long to discover him lying on the ground behind the windbreak and she didn't know whether to laugh or cry when he was found. It was all too much for her. The drama had occurred so quickly, one minute she had been quietly involved with a lesson, then the next minute the calmness was shattered. She was breathing heavily from the exertion of chasing after the dog and was very close to tears. She was the one who would be blamed for the loss of Fox. It wasn't right that it was always her fault, but when she looked at James' fearful expression she knew she couldn't berate him.

Brushing away her tears of self-pity, she stooped to help him up and held out her hand, "Come on, James. It will be all right. Fox will find Mr William and they'll all come back together."

In her mind she said a little prayer, asking God to make her words come true.

There was nothing more to be done, so in a subdued mood they resumed their lessons, all four with the underlying worry about how father and Mr William would react and if Fox would ever be found.

* * * * * * *

By the time the children had wakened and emerged from the wagon the men were miles away through the bush.

As they approached the cattle post they slowed their horses and took stock of the scene. A number of huts in poor repair stood in open ground with a cooking fire smouldering gently in front of one. As they dismounted, they saw a figure emerge from the nearest hut. It was Amos and he looked very relieved to see them. He walked quickly up to William and informed him that the woman had gone out very early that morning. Abdol had followed her and he had taken a stick with him so that he could mark the ground for them to follow.

"We stayed awake all night. No one came. The woman did not go out until very early," Amos assured them.

"You have done well," nodded William encouragingly. "Here is some food. You can eat as we go. Make sure you leave half of it for Abdol." Amos accepted the bag with customary politeness, a habit he had picked up during his travels and there was a sparkle in his eyes. He was ready for some food. He had noted which way the woman had taken and set off walking in a north-westerly direction. He reached into the bag as he went, cramming a handful of mealie porridge into his mouth.

Leisurely, the men remounted and set their horses to a gentle walk in Amos' wake. The sun had risen and gave a little welcome warmth, casting long shadows among the trees.

Henry thought they had travelled somewhere in the region of four miles when Amos stopped and slid behind a rock. Despite the leaves on the ground throughout this woodland, Abdol had obviously managed to follow his quarry without alerting her to his presence and his scratch marks in the dust weren't too difficult to find for keen eyes on the lookout for them. William and Henry halted too, aware of the sound of voices ahead of them. They dismounted, tethering their horses and walking forward slowly. There was a faint smell of cattle and wood smoke in the air that pleased William, for it meant they were downwind. He knew that the herders would surely have dogs with them eager to bark at the slightest indication of an approaching danger.

As they waited quietly behind the rock, planning the best course of action, Abdol materialised beside them and Henry smiled ruefully as he realised that their arrival hadn't gone completely unnoticed.

Abdol spoke in a voice little above a whisper. "I followed the woman as you told me. She came here. The woman spoke to the herders, telling that we came to look for our cattle. Our oxen were there. I could see them. There was also a bushman. He works for these people and they made him drive the oxen through the rock over there."

"That whole hill looks like a solid rock as far as I can see, but there is obviously a cleft in it that we can't see from here," William remarked. "Now that we know where our animals are, we can go and confront these people. I have no doubt they will pretend that they know nothing."

Henry agreed. "They will say the fault was not theirs and that the crime was committed by the bushman, even though they were the instigators and would be the ones to reap the greatest benefit."

William praised Abdol for his report and told him to stay with Amos and share the food. He would call for them if they were needed. As soon as they had located the oxen they would expect the boys to drive them back to the camp.

Once mounted, William looked at Henry, a gleam of mischief in his eyes,

"Shall we charge out at full gallop, yelling like demons?" he chuckled.

Henry was tempted to concur as he sympathised with William's idea of retribution, but common sense prevailed. "If we do, they'll take to their heels and disappear for the day at least, thinking we are devils. Much as I would like to share in the fun, I really think it would be better if we approached slowly, so as to reassure them and then we can really surprise them by discovering the animals they will say they've never seen."

William's eyebrows lifted comically as they did so often when he was amused. His suggestion had been a fun one, but serious Henry had taken it seriously as always. Laughing delightedly at his own idea of a joke, he accompanied Henry and together they broke cover.

In front of them there was a large grass covered area denuded of trees. The grass at this time of the year was brown and dry, but it was the only grazing available to the dozens of cattle scattered across it.

The herders, who were squatting round a fire eating their morning meal, leapt to their feet as their dogs began to bark frenetically. There were five men, their ages ranging in age from a boy of about eleven to an old man who might have been his grandfather or even a great- grandfather. The old woman was some distance away with another woman close by a cooking fire and eating their food away from the men.

As William and Henry reached the group, they remained mounted and in turn called out the customary greetings; their sole knowledge of the Tswana language. The responses were offered rather sullenly and the herders made no move to welcome their unexpected guests.

William tried to converse with them in Zulu and then Xhosa to no avail. The faces looking at them registered no understanding and showed blank hostility, which was unusual for people meeting in the bush. Henry tried Sindebele, but the effect was the same. In desperation, William called for Amos and Abdol whose immediate appearance caused as much surprise as had the arrival of William and Henry.

"Amos, I want you to talk to the old man over there. Tell him we have lost six oxen and we know that they came this way as we've followed their tracks. Don't let him know that we already know where they are. Just see what he has to say."

Amos grinned and nodded his head, then walked across to the old man. He greeted him and listened to the traditional replies followed by questions concerning their journey. It took almost half an hour for the courtesies to be complete, for these people never approached a subject immediately. William and Henry waited patiently. They knew just how important this polite approach was considered to be and there was little point in causing offence, even though they were anxious to have the matter concluded.

It seemed that the discussion was going well, as three of the herders resumed their squatting postures round the pot ready to continue their interrupted meal, but at this point a question from Amos was greeted by a loud verbal denial. Alerted, the men stood up again and joined the old man, all talking furiously. Arms were waving and voices raised.

William walked his horse forward and the herders turned to watch him.

"What is going on, Amos?"

"I asked him if he had seen six cattle. He says I am accusing him of stealing. I try to tell him I just want to know has he seen them. I didn't say he was a thief."

"He is angry because we have found our way here. He is worried that we will find our cattle and inform the chief. I think we must act now. We will go over to the large rocky hill and you two will come with us. I'm sure we shall find the missing oxen. The anger of this man is a sign of his guilt."

Without further words, William set off at a gallop with Henry close behind and the two boys running easily just behind them. They ignored the angry shouts of the herders and headed for the huge bulk of seemingly solid rock that dominated the landscape. Sure enough, as they came close to it they saw a large cleft partially hidden by a group of trees and bushes. William led the way through the gap along a narrow passage into an open area that was large enough to hold several dozen cattle. It had a pool of water at the far side and was a perfect enclosure for people or animals.

Henry reined in and gazed round in admiration. "No wonder they leave that cattle-post and come here, but where are our animals?"

William pointed to a screen of bushes over to the left; "Over there, I should think. Let's go and investigate, then we'll give our horses a drink before we set off back to camp."

The missing oxen were exactly where William had anticipated and appeared to have suffered no harm. The small, wizened figure of a bushman scuttled off as they came towards the animals and Henry stopped Amos and Abdol from pursuing him.

"We have our animals now and he will no doubt be in trouble from his masters. Let him go, poor creature."

The two boys began to drive the oxen out of the rocky enclosure at the start of their lengthy walk back to camp as William and Henry led their horses across to the pool.

"That was a satisfactory outcome," Henry said with some satisfaction.

William smiled. "I'm just waiting to see how the herders react when they see us with the oxen. Will they try to claim them as their own or will they deny ever having seen them before? Perhaps they will ask us if we saw a bushman with them. Let's go and find out."

The small group of animals with the two boys behind had nearly reached the place where the herders were standing by their fire. The herders looked at the oxen with complete indifference, and no sign of emotion appeared on any face.

"Tell the old man we have found our lost animals where he had hidden them," William called to Amos. He turned to look at Henry to see his reaction to this obviously accusatory statement, but Henry seemed to be intent on watching the response from the old man.

Amos addressed the old man and spoke quickly without the usual respectful tone and attitude a boy usually offered to his elders. There was a lengthy silence whilst the words and their full meaning were absorbed.

The old man turned away to avoid looking at these strangers and it was a younger man who replied. "Did you see a bushman anywhere? If you did you must know that he is the one who took your cattle. We have cattle of our own to care for, we do not need yours. You must take them back and keep them safe."

The blank expressions of the other herders didn't change, but with one accord they turned in unison and all five men then set off, without a backward glance, walking towards the large herd of cattle grazing in the bush all around.

"You should have known they would never admit the theft," Henry remarked, as they began to follow their oxen.

"I suppose I did, really," William admitted, "but I hoped there might be some sign of regret at losing their plunder. Still, as they never admit theft they cannot feel sorry, I expect."

CHAPTER 23

After a short stop, giving them time to sit on some rocks and enjoy their breakfast whilst their horses tried to find the occasional blade of dry grass to nibble, the two men continued on their journey, riding side by side in a relaxed leisurely fashion.

William was enjoying recalling and recounting their triumph at producing the oxen from the hiding place. "Those men didn't show their feelings, but I'm sure they were all astounded and absolutely furious that we had managed to discover their secret place. They pretended it didn't matter, behaving as if they weren't connected or involved at all. However, they knew the value of our beasts and must be annoyed at losing them. Gaining six cattle for nothing would appeal to any natives. It would make them rich if they kept them and would feed them for weeks if they slaughtered them. They must feel very irate," he concluded.

"I think they are possibly more philosophical about it than you would imagine. It is likely that they were delighted when they found the animals wandering unattended and thought it was a wonderful God-sent opportunity to enrich themselves, but once they knew the owners were looking for them and making enquiries it followed that their chief would inevitably learn of the incident and punish them. They are probably more relieved by now, since we didn't seek vengeance. Many men would have confiscated one or more of their beasts in retribution, out of fury at having to waste a whole day recovering their own beasts, or out of malice," Henry suggested.

"You may be right," William conceded. Then he gave an exclamation, "Hello. What's that?"

"What have you seen?" demanded Henry.

"I'm not sure. I just saw a movement. It must have been some small animal." Both men reached for their guns and held them ready as they noted a continued movement far ahead. It was obviously an animal.

William halted and dismounted, as he preferred to shoot across the saddle, which gave him a solid rest for his elbow and enabled a better shot. Henry was happy to shoot from the saddle as Oscar would stand without flinching and he felt the extra height was sometimes an advantage. He raised his rifle and sighted on the brown blur in the distance. He was on the point of firing when William yelled and made a grab for his arm pulling it downwards. The bullet hit the ground many yards in front of the racing creature, which then turned aside and disappeared into the bush.

"Henry was aghast and inclined to be furious. " What is wrong? Whatever were you doing? You made me miss."

William too was incensed," Couldn't you see? That was Fox you were aiming at and you very nearly killed him," he added accusingly.

Henry was appalled. "Fox? I thought he was tied up back in camp. The animal was moving so quickly he was just a brown blur and facing us head on he didn't look at all like a dog. Are you sure it was Fox?" It was a horrible shock to Henry, who was truly mortified. He could hardly believe that he had failed to identify the animal he had seen every day for weeks. He had sighted down the barrel of his rifle with his usual concentration and as he relived the moment he still failed to understand how he could have made such a mistake. What a mercy it was that William had noticed in time and ruined his aim.

Now that the danger to his beloved dog was past, William relaxed, "Yes, it was him. I expect he'll come if I whistle for him. He wasn't hit, just frightened when the bullet hit the ground in front of him, scattering leaves and sand around. He's probably waiting to see if he is really under attack."

William gave a piercing whistle and both men were relieved to see Fox emerge from under a small shrub. The dog came racing towards them at full tilt and leapt up at William, who grabbed him in his arms. Fox proceeded to lick his master's face with fervour until William firmly stopped him. "Right, that's enough." He held the wriggling dog under one arm. "How did you manage to escape, I wonder? I know you're very clever, but I was sure I'd made that knot secure. I think I'd better keep you with me until we get back to the wagons."

The children were waiting at the edge of the camp for the two men to arrive. Their obvious relief when they caught sight of the small dog sitting on the saddle in front of William was apparent to Henry, whose suspicions that Fox's escape wasn't entirely due to his own efforts were now confirmed. The servants, drivers and herd-boys soon crowded round to discover if the oxen had been located and they were assured that Amos and Abdol were already bringing them in. Their constant questions and excited chatter prevented Henry from questioning his children immediately and by the time they had seen to the horses it was time for the midday meal.

The oxen arrived shortly after the children had been sent into the wagon to rest, and were immediately taken to the river to drink their fill. Henry, still plagued by the thought that he had so nearly shot the dog, sat and stared moodily at the fire. He was startled out of his reverie by William's voice.

"If they are given three hours to rest, I think we should be able to start our evening trek by four o'clock," William advised when he returned from examining the recaptured animals. "We won't make it as far as Shoshong tonight, but we could possibly manage nine or ten miles. That will leave us about thirteen miles to do tomorrow."

Henry nodded in agreement. "If there are no more difficulties, such as the ones we have had today, we should be able to reach Shoshong by tomorrow afternoon and that is the next milestone to be completed on our journey. By the way, I have discovered how Fox managed to escape. Whilst you were looking at the oxen I spoke to the children. It seems that the three older ones were engrossed in their lessons and young James took it upon himself to rescue Fox. He thought the rope was choking the dog and pointed out in his own limited fashion that the dog had a sore spot where the rope had rubbed his neck. We all owe you an apology; the children for letting the dog go and myself for almost killing him. When the children leave the wagon after their rest they will come to you and offer their explanations and apologies."

"I'm sure it was an accident. Jane is always very responsible, but she cannot keep an eye on the three of them all the time. It was thoughtful of young James to want to help Fox." William showed Henry the raw patch under the dog's muzzle where he had been pulling against the rope. "I'll buy a proper collar for him when the opportunity presents itself. Although he can be with me most of the time there are going to be some occasions when he has to be left behind."

"It is kind of you to be so forgiving, but I shall have to talk to them about acting rashly and point out the disasters that can result from such actions. I know they hadn't been specifically told that the dog was to remain tied up, as they were asleep when we left. Nevertheless, they must learn not to take action without permission."

William and Henry were served tea after their lunch, which was unusual, and, when questioned, Lukas explained that the coffee was now very short and that there was still enough tea to last for a few more days. William thanked him and congratulated him on his forethought, an unusual trait in the natives, for whom the future was never considered.

"We shall need to buy more provisions at Shoshong," Henry remarked.

"Yes. It is lucky that Sechele and Sechomo aren't like Mzilikazi, who keeps travellers waiting at the border. If a few more days had been added to our journey our supplies would have run out before we reached a store. As it is we shall be all right if we keep going."

"The only reason that we haven't been kept waiting at the border is the fact that we are both known to the Bechuana chiefs," pointed out Henry. "The Reverend John Moffat sent word to the Reverend Mackenzie to warn him of our visit and he would have spoken to Sechomo, who has a kind regard for the missionaries and knows we pose no threat to his country or people. You were at Shoshong only a few weeks ago and both chiefs know that you trade in ivory and other animal goods. What they object to strongly is those who try to import alcohol. Selling liquor to the natives is banned here and one man who tried to bring some in by lying that he had none had his wagons confiscated and all the drink poured onto the veld."

"Yes, I remember hearing about that and, strangely enough, it didn't teach him a lesson at all, because a few months later he was seen with a full load of brandy and whisky up towards the Zambezi. He just has to make sure that he travels northwards by a different route and isn't caught again."

"I suppose there will always be sinful men," Henry conceded, "though why he persists with his foolish trade remains a mystery to me."

"He's certainly stubborn. To continue against all odds and risk losing another load seems foolhardy to me. I wouldn't run my business like that. Perhaps he feels that it is a challenge trying to outwit the tribes."

"There may be a challenge for him, but I am of the opinion that he wants to drag the natives down to his level. They all make slightly alcoholic drinks using grain and this native beer keeps them happy as well as being nutritional. It doesn't affect them so much as the European drinks do, at least they have to drink considerably more to get the same effect."

"Yes, you're right. I don't mind the native beer, at least I can drink it without pulling a face when it is passed around. Refusing it would cause offence, I know, but I have seen men drunk on it," With this parting shot, William retired to his wagon.

Henry kept his promise and later, when their rest period was over, four penitent children stood in line in front of William to make their heartfelt apologies. Henry then proceeded to explain to them in great detail how easy it was to set in train a series of events that can end in disaster. All four were frightened by the thought that Fox had almost died, though they were too young to fully appreciate how that catastrophe would have seriously affected their father. Both Harry and Isabelle were a little resentful that they had to accept part of the blame for Fox's escape. They had obeyed Jane's command not to free the dog and had been busy with their schoolwork when the rope was undone. They had indeed tried to catch the dog, but he was much too quick and clever for them. However, they were truly glad that he was safe and made a fuss of him whenever they had an opportunity. They fully approved of Mr William, who had accepted their apologies with gravity and exonerated them from all blame.

Jane felt guilty about the whole episode, for she fully understood how truly awful it would have been for all of them if Fox had died. She knew she should have watched James more carefully, but he was so quick now and she couldn't always give him her full attention. During the rest period she had sent fervent prayers to God, thanking Him for Fox's survival. She had also prayed for help to avoid sinning so often. She then remembered to pray for mother and baby Joshua and following that had added a thank you for Lukas, who had done all the family wash that morning. She didn't usually say prayers during the day, but she felt that this was a special occasion and she needed to express her gratitude.

After all her prayers, Jane was glad that there was still enough time for her to read one of her fairy stories and that made her feel much happier. She knew that she would have to say sorry to Mr William and then father had said they must do lessons for an hour before the oxen were in-spanned.

To everyone's relief, the remainder of the trek to Shoshong produced no other problems and they arrived at the town in the early afternoon of the next day.

As soon as William appeared close to the stores, the resident traders materialized as if by magic to welcome him and he was soon surrounded by a noisy laughing group. Henry was equally well received, as visiting Europeans were few in number and as a friend of William's he was particularly welcome. William had been to Shoshong several times before and of course had been there only a few weeks previously, so he knew all the resident Europeans. Henry was known to one or two of the men personally and by name to the others. The welcome was both pleasurable and vociferous, including the children as soon as they made their appearance.

Fox had rushed over to the stores with William and met up with the pack of resident dogs, setters, pointers, terriers and some larger but less identifiable ones. After some stiff-legged circling, sniffing and growling, with admonishments by the various owners, the dogs began to race and tear around as if they had been playmates for years. Gruff commands were eventually obeyed and the dogs lay down, panting.

Behind the stores, Harry discovered a group of pale-coloured children playing in the dust. He had been exploring, as he often did when grown-ups were talking and he was supposed to stand still and be well behaved.

These children reminded him of the children they had played with whilst they were at the Tati.

"Hello," he offered in English. Then he tried again in Sindebele before remembering the Sechuana greeting he had learned from the Moffat nursemaids and practised at the Tati store.

The children had been wide-eyed and uncomprehending initially, but now they burst into a torrent of speech that left Harry bewildered. However he soon squatted down and joined in their complicated game.

Isabelle, having missed her brother, soon discovered him and after watching the children for a while she started to play too. She discovered that they could understand some English words, though they were happier speaking their own language.

Meanwhile, the wagons were guided to an open space near the stores and when the oxen had been outspanned they were driven into a large kraal that had been built especially to accommodate visiting spans. It was too late for them to be taken out to graze, for there was no grazing near the town. Both William and Henry were aware of the fact that the greatest difficulty at Shoshong was the lack of water, so they requested that the animals should be taken to the water immediately. An urgent message was sent to the chief's representative, as Sechomo himself was away hunting.

The town had been built on a waterless plain close to a range of hills, so close that some huts were actually in the gorge in a rocky hill that led to the only water supply. Successive chiefs of the Bamangwata (one of the Bechuana tribes) wanted their capital to remain without water as a defensive measure and forbade any of the traders to dig a well. When enemies attacked the town, the whole population would escape into the gorge. From this refuge, which could be defended so easily, they could wait for their foes to leave or die of thirst.

Horses and cattle had to be driven to this water at certain times of the day and a constant stream of women carrying water pots on their heads could be seen throughout the daylight hours making the wearying journey to and from the town. All the traders employed water carriers, who had to be paid in beads for their labour and so the storekeepers had necessarily to manage on a small daily amount.

Jane could barely remember the town and as she looked at it now she thought that it might be as big as the king's town in Matabeleland but it wasn't nearly so neat. The huts were all higgledy-piggledy and crowded together inside a thick thorn hedge. They were so close together that she wondered how people could walk about between them. The walls of the huts were made of mud and the thatch of the roof overhung them by almost a yard making a sort of veranda all the way round. The doorways at least were large enough for people to enter or leave in an upright position, unlike the Matabele ones that were only about eighteen inches high.

The traders' stores were all built together in a group outside the town furthest from the water and the whole area was bleak, dry and dusty.

Jane looked around for Harry and Isabelle, who had disappeared. "Do you know where Harry and Isabelle have gone?" she asked James, who was sitting at her feet drawing in the dust.

"There," he said, pointing to the back of the store.

"Come. Let's find them," Jane urged, taking his hand.

It was a relief to Jane to discover that neither of her siblings was getting up to mischief and when she saw their playmates she was reminded that Mr William had told her at Tati that she would see many more children with these light yellow/brown skins.

Jane was pleased that the little ones had found some friends, but she thought that they should all talk to father first and she called them to come with her to the front of the store. Harry was most reluctant, but he obeyed his sister and, dusting his hands on his jacket, he followed her, with Isabelle bringing up the rear.

As soon as she could gain father's attention, Jane put into words the troubling thought that had occurred to her.

"Are we going to stay here long, father?" Jane asked anxiously. She had overheard that there was no water available until some could be paid for and carried to them.

"We shall be here tonight and tomorrow night certainly, possibly Monday night as well. We shall need to see how the oxen are before we face the next part of the journey," Henry answered. "Tomorrow is Sunday. You know that we keep the Lord's Day for His Service and we do not travel on Sundays. Besides, the Rev John Mackenzie lives here with his wife and we shall share our devotions with them. I will try to arrange for us all to go and visit the Mackenzies before it is dark." So saying, he strode back to rejoin the group of men lounging outside the stores talking avidly to William.

"It isn't going to be much fun here, is it?" asked Harry.

"Why do you say that? I thought you had just found some friends," Jane responded.

"Well, we shall have to sit and be quiet all evening when we are visiting and then tomorrow it is Sunday and we shan't be able to play either," Harry pointed out.

"I like the Reverend and Mrs Mackenzie," Isabelle interposed. "They were kind to us when they came to stay at Inyati last year and I am sure we can play with their children."

"Goodness, I thought you would have forgotten that," exclaimed Jane, who vividly remembered the death of the Mackenzie's baby daughter whilst they were at Inyati. "It is more than a year since we saw them."

"I'm not a baby any more," retorted Isabelle. "I can remember lots of things."

"I'm sure you can." Jane was interrupted by James clamouring for something to drink, which made Harry and Isabelle suddenly feel thirsty. The water bottles and containers were almost empty, but Jane managed to find enough to satisfy them and was even able to have a few sips herself. She was left wondering how they were all going to manage to wash themselves without water, when father appeared. He climbed into the wagon and reappeared several minutes later with his favourite rifle and a box of bullets and a bag of powder. In a matter of fact tone he explained to the children, "The men here were just about to have a shooting match and they have invited us to join them. William has been longing to challenge me to a contest even before we stopped at Lee's Castle, but somehow we never managed to arrange it. Now we have the ideal opportunity. You may come and watch as long as you sit quietly and do not disturb anyone by moving about."

Harry was thrilled at the idea of seeing a shooting competition, Isabelle wasn't so sure and Jane thought that James would soon become bored and his movements would distract the contestants. She elected to stay with James and play with him by the wagon. After considerable vacillation, Isabelle elected to go and she followed Harry, who was vainly trying to keep up with father's long stride.

Targets were set up; the first distance being fifty yards. The second set of targets would be at a hundred yards and the third at a hundred and fifty. After every man had had his three shots at the first distance, the totals were written down and the targets moved. Henry was selecting the most perfectly round bullets he could find and Harry watched intently, fascinated by the proceedings. Isabelle didn't like the noise very much and she was just a little afraid, but she wasn't going to let Harry know that, so she smiled and tried to look happy.

How glad she was when the competition ended and the men waited for the verdict. She hoped father had won.

Harry was more disappointed than was Henry when the competition was won by Mr Bennion, but they were both delighted when Henry was declared second and William third. The first prize was two bottles of whisky, the second two bottles of Cape Brandy and the third was two bottles of beer. Henry immediately handed his two bottles to William to be used for the party that was to be held that evening.

"Here you are, William. It's a good thing that the ban on liquor doesn't include Europeans. I shan't need them and I'm happy to contribute them to the party. I'm going to take the children to see the Mackenzies, though how I shall get them all there I don't know. James is a little too young to walk all that way."

William shook him by the hand and congratulated him on his win, admitting defeat 'but only just' and promising to beat him next time.

The winner of the competition, John Bennion, strode over to congratulate the two competitors who had so nearly beaten him and when he heard Henry's remark about walking over to the missionary's house he offered to drive the family round the town in his light cart. Henry accepted gratefully and returned to his wagon in good spirits to clean and replace his favourite rifle in its rack.

Half an hour later, John Bennion arrived at the Hargreaves' wagon. He was sitting in the driving seat of a two wheeled cart pulled by four donkeys.

"Whoa," he ordered sternly, pulling on the reins and the donkeys stopped beside the wagon. Harry, James and Isabelle were bouncing up and down with excitement and Jane, too, was filled with pleasure, especially as father was looking happy and relaxed. She had heard of his success at the shooting competition and she knew that he was pleased with his efforts. He was also pleased to be going to see his friend, the Reverend John Mackenzie.

"Well then. Climb aboard," ordered father gruffly.

Harry and Isabelle were jostling to climb up on the front so that they could sit beside father and of course it was Harry that gained the much-coveted position. Isabelle let out a wail of frustration, but when father glanced sternly at her she was careful to say no more.

Father was fully aware of the competition between these two and most frequently he approved of Harry's superiority, though occasionally, as he did now, he appeased his beautiful daughter. "Isabelle shall sit beside me on the way home. If we are offered a ride back that is," he ruled. Harry was happy enough to be in the best place immediately and wasn't worried about the future, whilst Isabelle was mollified by the decision, sitting down happily now in the back seat. Jane wondered why she was never considered for the honour, but accepted realistically that she was needed to look after James, who wouldn't be allowed to sit in the front.

When everyone was seated, James between Jane and Isabelle behind and Harry between father and the driver in front, John Bennion set the donkeys trotting, and the cart bowled along round the outside of the town. None of the children had ever seen a cart such as this before and the experience of riding in one was a mixture of sheer happiness and downright fear. There was no road, just cleared ground where people walked daily, so there were mounds and dips, small holes and the remains of tree roots poking up, hollows, lumps and bumps everywhere. The cart seemed to them to move extremely rapidly after their recent experiences; weeks of being accustomed to the pace of the ox-wagon. The unaccustomed speed took their breath away, making Harry laugh with glee, but there was nothing to hold on to as the vehicle lurched from one obstacle to another, and both Isabelle and Jane were less enthusiastic. They clung to each other, their arms locked behind James' head with their other hands clutching the seat in front.

It was the greatest relief for them when the cart finally stopped near the entrance to the gorge, leaving them a few hundred yards to walk uphill to the solid stone built house set on the hillside. Both Harry and James would have preferred the ride to continue and were disappointed to have to climb down and use their own legs to reach the house.

With many cheerful thanks and waves to the driver, who offered a return journey if they would send a message to him, the Hargreaves family walked over the rough ground and were soon being made warmly welcome by the Reverend John Mackenzie and his wife Ellen.

Ellen Mackenzie was all too familiar with the stresses of travel and she had made sure that there was sufficient water brought to the house, then heated so that a bath could be made available. After father had had his bath the children took turns and their hair was washed as well. The latter process appealed to Jane and Isabelle, who both preferred to feel clean, but was something to be suffered as far as Harry and James were concerned. They both endured the ordeal with a minimum of objections since this was not their own home.

Not anticipating the opportunity to bath, none of the Hargreaves family had brought clean clothes, so the clothes they were wearing were thoroughly shaken and brushed before being donned once more. The children were then given supper with the Mackenzie children.

Ellen and John insisted that they should all stay at the house for the two nights that they were to spend at Shoshong and bewailed the fact that the visit was to be so short. They did, however, understand Henry's urge to continue the journey and commiserated with him on the loss of his wife.

Harry's gloomy conjecture for the weekend proved to be less than accurate. It was true that The Lord's Day was celebrated as it was at Inyati with morning and evening services and a session of Sunday school after the morning service, but the walk along the gorge and scrambling over rocks gave the children ample opportunity to expend some surplus energy. It was a less exciting time for Jane who, as the eldest of the six children, felt her position was that of nursemaid, but there was the slight compensation in that Mrs Mackenzie did treat her almost as a grown up. The two were able to walk side by side and discuss the trials of journeying in Africa, the difficulties of providing enough food for families and some of the hardships endured by missionary families.

Ellen Mackenzie tactfully avoided talking about her friend Katherine's death, as she had noted earlier the distress of the Hargreaves children when their mother's name was mentioned. The Mackenzie children, in their innocence, had asked about the missing mother and been informed by Harry that she was visiting heaven and would soon come back to them. Isabelle had nodded her agreement, though she looked less certain and poor Jane had been obviously trying to hide her anguish. So Ellen Mackenzie talked to Jane as an equal and tried to make her feel happier by also discussing the future in England, telling Jane of her own experiences there. Jane in her turn discussed the books she loved to read and asked Mrs Mackenzie if England was really like Mr Dickens' books.

"Are there really dreadful people hurting poor people in workhouses? I know we are poor and sometimes have little food and our clothes are worn, so I'm afraid they might put us in the workhouse." Jane confided.

Ellen smiled gently and was quick to reassure this solemn little girl. "I don't think there is any need for you to worry about that. Your grandparents aren't poor and you'll be living with them. Your father chose to be a missionary because he knew that God had called him and unfortunately missionaries are not well paid." She sighed deeply. "However, we feel we are justly repaid when we save some of these poor heathen souls and we have been more fortunate in that than your father has. Come now; let us see if we can find any flowers by the fountain. There are not many at this time of the year, but we might find enough to brighten up the dining room."

CHAPTER 24

Henry and William had not intended to stay at Shoshong longer than just the Sunday, but John and Ellen were upset at the thought of their visitors leaving so soon and were gently persistent with their urgings for Henry to reconsider his plans. Eventually, on Sunday evening, Henry felt convinced that one more day would not go amiss.

After their supper, when the children were in bed, John and Henry had sat cosily by the fire and Ellen had withdrawn to the other side of the room to busy herself with her needlework. John had set about trying to convince Henry that he could and should rearrange his travel plan.

"We really need more than just one day to discuss missionary matters," he asserted. "Today we were much too concerned with the church services to enjoy discussions on other subjects. I have prepared a report for you to take with you to the committee, which I would very much like you to see and give your verdict on. I have included a letter requesting more money and medical supplies, but I would like you to use your persuasive powers on our behalf. You can describe our life here and explain in detail just what we experience and what we need."

"You sound just like Thomas. I have already promised him that I would stress our conditions in plain language. You need have no fear of that, but you're right to show me your report. It will be of great benefit if we are all in accord. I also need to be more aware of your life here so that I can have additional material to add to my arguments."

John nodded cheerfully, convinced now that Henry would stay another day, although he had not yet committed himself.

"There is one more thing. I'm sure you haven't forgotten how important it is to pay your respects to the chief, even though you had permission to enter the country and they are fully aware that you're here. Although Sechomo is away hunting he has left an important adviser in charge and this man would be insulted if you omit the courtesy visit. In fact, he would feel twice insulted: for himself and for the chief."

Henry smiled at the thought, "I appreciate that and I hadn't forgotten. I learned soon after we had arrived that the chief was away hunting, but other things occupied my mind on Saturday afternoon. I rather hoped that the counsellor might be attending our Sunday services and I could speak to him then. Unfortunately, he doesn't seem to be one of your converts. I shall go into the town and take suitable presents tomorrow."

John laughingly told Henry that Sechomo was supposed to be showing the more important Bechuana chief, Sechele, the best hunting grounds in the

Lake Ngami region where he sometimes hunted very successfully for ostrich feathers and ivory. John was fairly sure that Sechomo would take his rival many miles away in the wrong direction as he was extremely wily and would never share the secret of his lucrative source with anyone. He had done this before and Sechele was becoming suspicious as to how Sechomo could obtain so much ivory when he was out with his retinue, but rarely discovered the elephant herds when he, Sechele, accompanied him.

Henry appreciated the inference. "Businessmen of all nations have a talent for keeping the good things, meaning the profits, for themselves," he remarked. He then recounted the incident at the Matabele king's town when one trader rode out early in the morning to meet up with some hunters before any of his neighbours were aware of their proximity.

"Talking of traders, did you meet up with Sam Dyer yesterday?" John asked. "He is helping in one of the stores for a few weeks."

"Yes I did. He took part in the target shooting competition but was unplaced. I had met him before when he came to Inyati. You may remember the confrontation with Thomas. They went out hunting together and Dyer claimed all the feathers from an ostrich that Thomas asserted he had shot. There was a great deal of unpleasantness at the time, but I know Thomas still trades with Dyer."

Complacently, Ellen stitched the garment she was making for her younger child. How quickly children grew and how frequently they seemed to require new clothes. She was a practical woman, which was just as well for a missionary's wife, and she accepted the challenges as they came without sighs, complaints or apparent worry, though she did sometimes wish that life could be a little easier. Listening to the two men conversing equably, she smiled contentedly to herself, sharing their laughter and pleased to see Henry was still able to laugh despite his recent bereavement. She was well aware that men loved to gossip as much as women and she was sure, and serenely satisfied for both men, that they would now have more time to spend in each other's company. It would do them both good to speak openly and with great understanding on topics they shared. Living in isolation, as so many missionaries were forced to do, meant the lack of social intercourse necessary for complete happiness. Ellen knew of too many men wanting to escape their families and backgrounds who had become decidedly odd, even reclusive. She didn't consider that to be God's wish for the human race. As far as she was concerned, people were meant to be part of a large, caring group, preferably a family such as her own.

Ellen, too, was enjoying having company, although she missed Katherine dreadfully, and grieved for her young family. She found that she could talk easily to Jane, whose knowledge and wisdom belied her tender years. Surprisingly, despite her serious expression, Jane displayed a sense of humour that took Ellen by surprise. The child was disciplined and self-controlled, but she had a strong character and would make a delightful wife for a kind, considerate man. She did hope Henry and his family would share another day here, as much for her own pleasure as for her husband and children. Quietly, she added her gentle urgings to those of her husband.

Faced with such persistence, Henry felt obliged to acquiesce and promised to speak to William early next morning.

"I was lucky to find William as a travelling companion," he explained. "Once the Moffats realized that they couldn't continue the journey I had to decide whether to postpone my own journey for an unknown period or to try to find someone who was travelling in this direction. As it happened, William arrived at the king's town very conveniently and was delighted when I proposed to accompany him southwards. He is a congenial companion and he is not only kind to the children, he actually plays with them, which makes such a difference on a lengthy journey. Naturally, I shall have to discuss any suggested changes to our itinerary with him. He is the businessman and needs to be able to transport his goods with all speed. Besides, the lack of water and grazing near Shoshong means that the oxen don't get quite the rest that they might in other places, as they have to walk so far to reach either."

"Yes, your argument is a valid one. The lack of water and grazing here is the reason why the Batswana chief keeps his animals at cattle posts spread around the country. Still, we both hope you will be able to rearrange your schedule just a little and share one more day with us."

With a sudden look of consternation on his face John suddenly blurted out; "Oh dear. I'm sorry Henry. I was so pleased to see you on Saturday evening and we were entirely engrossed in catching up with each other's news that I didn't think of anything else. Then today we were preoccupied with the Sunday services, so I completely forgot. There are two letters for you in the bag that is to be sent to Matabeleland and Inyati. The messenger will be going tomorrow, if you should want to write a note to your colleagues. Meanwhile, I'll go and fetch your letters."

Ellen shook her head, "I'm sorry we have been so remiss Henry. I knew about those letters, as we sort through the bag when it arrives and remove all the letters addressed to Shoshong. I should have reminded John about them."

Henry smiled kindly, "I'm sure there is nothing urgent in them. I can read them now and nothing but a little time has been lost. We have had many other matters on our minds. There is also time to write short notes to my

friends at Inyati."
Relieved that their guest seemed unworried by their forgetfulness and kindly forgave them both, John handed over the two packets.
Henry looked at the stamps. The first one bore stamps from the Cape of Good Hope.
"A letter from Katherine's parents," Henry remarked with a tremor in his voice. "It is addressed to us both, so it must have been written before they had news of her passing."
He controlled his emotions with difficulty and quickly looked at the second letter. The stamps with the portrait of Queen Victoria were all too familiar and didn't need to state the country of origin. "This is a letter from my family in England. It will be full of family news. At least I shall be fairly well acquainted with their progress by the time I meet them again for the first time in more than six years. They, too, will still be unaware that Katherine is dead."
Henry tried to speak steadily, even with lightness in his voice, but the Mackenzies could see that it was an effort for him as he continued.
"I wrote to all our friends and relatives with the news about my wife on the day of her funeral and informed them of my intention to travel to England via Cape Town. I asked Katherine's parents if they would be prepared to look after the two boys and my own parents to care for the girls so that they could attend good schools. Those letters were sent many weeks ago. I only hope they receive the news of our arrival prior to our actual appearance, otherwise it might be embarrassing. I also hope they have heard of Katherine's passing before I see them, as it would be too disturbing if I have to break the news myself. If Katherine's parents have had several weeks to accept and grieve for her loss it will make our meeting bearable. Having the boys to stay with them might help them to recover a little, too. Thank you for these. I shall go and read them now."
Promising to do his best to persuade William to remain for another day, Henry picked up his candle and, bidding his hosts goodnight, he retired to the room he was to share with his sons. There he spent a long time engrossed in his mail before getting into bed, where he tossed and turned for many hours until sleep claimed him.
Henry was able to hand three letters to John next morning for onward transmission to Inyati. There was one each for his colleagues giving a brief description of the journey so far and he saw the missives placed in the bag that was to be collected shortly afterwards. The mail he had received had been happy and informative, which had worried Henry, making him feel uncomfortable, because it was intended for Katherine as well as himself and

this had upset his normally sound slumbers. However, he was able to put these sombre thoughts aside as he stood talking to John and discussing the problems of paying for a regular mail service when there were so few of them concerned.

He then had a pleasant surprise, for as they stood on the veranda before breakfast chatting idly and watching the stream of water carriers walk past, William rode up, leading Oscar.

"Good morning," he called out cheerfully. "It's rather cold at this hour, but there is nothing like a good gallop before breakfast to give one an appetite."

Henry gaped in astonishment and looked enquiringly at John, who laughed in delight. "I knew you needed to talk to William very early this morning so I took the liberty of sending him a message at first light inviting him to breakfast here."

Turning to William, who had now dismounted he held out his hand, "Welcome, young man. I speak for my wife as well as myself when I say we are pleased that you have been so kind as to accept our invitation. Had you not been otherwise engaged on Saturday and Sunday evenings we should have invited you here before, but we know how you young bachelors like to celebrate. Now, if you'll allow me to take your horses to my stable, I'll leave you two together." So saying, John took the reins of both animals and led them round to the back of the house.

"What's all this mystery? Why do you need to see me? I was quite happy to be offered breakfast and bring the horses over to give them the opportunity to drink before we left, but I was expecting to inspan the oxen about this time so that we can to make the most of the day. I didn't anticipate a conference, Henry."

Henry smiled wryly; "There's no mystery. The Mackenzies have been very kind to my family and their hospitality leaves me indebted to them. They are both most anxious that we should postpone our departure. I wonder if you would consider leaving on Tuesday morning instead of Monday as we originally planned?" he ventured carefully.

"Is there a particular reason for another day's delay?" asked William.

"Well, I would like more time to discuss Missionary matters with Reverend Mackenzie, as there are some important points he would like me to raise with the Society. In addition, you and I must go into the town to see Sechomo's representative sometime and I preferred to avoid that on Sunday. This courtesy cannot be avoided, as you know in fact we are already rather late and risk censure, but on a more personal level, I'm enjoying the rest from travelling."

William crowed with glee. "I'm delighted to hear you admit to a little weakness, my friend. I had supposed you were almost a saint and never suffered as we poor mortals do. The traders here have been extraordinarily hospitable and I'm equally happy. I appreciate some home comforts too, so I don't mind staying longer. Yes, let's decide to go on Tuesday."

To Henry's relief, the matter had been settled easily and amicably and the atmosphere at breakfast was almost jovial.

Afterwards, as William left to attend to the horses, they arranged to meet up with him an hour later and bear the necessary gifts to the chief's representative, John agreeing to accompany them as their interpreter.

They met mid-morning as planned and walked together through an opening in the protective hedge. At this point there was a path wide enough for them to walk side by side towards the centre of the town where the chief's huts were situated near the animal kraal.

"This must be one of the dirtiest towns there is," remarked William, screwing up his nose at the stench and gazing at the filthy, narrow passages between the crowded huts. One or two of the inhabitants had adopted European dress, but with the dire lack of water neither clothes nor bodies were ever washed. Human waste of every description was scattered everywhere and only the multitude of scrawny scavenging dogs kept the ground clear of bones and discarded waste food. The men had to pick their way carefully to avoid treading in the piles of animal and human ordure.

"I'm pleased to say I don't have to come here very often," commented John diplomatically. "Still, the king's town in Matabeleland isn't much better, is it Henry?"

Henry was even more diplomatic. "Cleanliness and sanitation are difficult in these crowded towns, especially when the people are ignorant of suitable methods of disposal and water is non-existent. The Matabele couldn't believe it when the Reverend Robert Moffat made a dam at Inyati to ensure a constant supply of water for the gardens and orchards. Our English idea of digging a deep trench for a lavatory amazes the local people and they have no desire to copy such an outlandish idea. But you must be aware that large towns and cities in England are faced with similar problems. In 1858 there was 'The Great Stink of London' if you remember, when even the Members of Parliament complained. Rich people always abandoned the capital to spend summertime in the Shires away from sewage problems in the cities. I believe Cape Town suffers from lack of water too, doesn't it William? There are some appalling districts there that are noted for squalor."

Shamefacedly, William nodded his head. "Droughts have occurred and there are definitely water problems in many areas. Parts of the town are really awful. The Shambles, where the butchers dispose of their leavings, smells horrible. Even the beach and the sea there look revolting."

The others nodded their understanding of the problems arising from the large congregations of human beings.

Arriving at the chief's enclosure, the men announced their presence in the accepted fashion and the meeting with the representative of Chief Sechomo, with John's guidance, went according to custom. Ritual greetings and answers were followed by platitudes and only when all avenues of the visitors' recent history had been explored were the gifts offered. They were accepted gravely but without enthusiasm. Ammunition was useful; guns were more desirable. The Batswana were not a warlike tribe and were easily defeated by the Matabele or the Boers, but they were learning to defend themselves against attack and in order to achieve success they needed to be well armed. Henry wondered if they should have bought a musket from one of the stores as a present, and he made a mental note to recommend such a course of action to William for a future visit. It was essential for a trader to be on good terms with the native chiefs. Besides, the Boers hated the missionaries for treating the natives as human beings and would attack them as they had threatened at Kuruman, so Henry believed it was his duty to help the defenders.

Jane had made herself useful around the house that early morning working under Ellen's instructions for bedmaking, sweeping and washing the dishes whilst Ellen prepared the midday meal. Isabelle had been charged with the care of James and was playing happily with all the children. She was revelling in the idea of being excused the domestic chores she hated and being allowed to play instead as long as she stayed with James.

After they had all enjoyed mid-morning cups of milk and biscuits, Ellen suggested that they might like to walk to the fountain. The horses and cattle had long since left the area and there was just the continuous file of women and girls along the road. She gave them each a small tin to fill with water, making them feel useful contributors to the household.

Despite the daily usage that had occurred for countless years, the road surface through the gorge was atrocious. Far from being worn smooth, it was uneven and rocky, with loose stones in many places and protruding ones in others, making the journey a precarious one. After a slow and careful walk, the children managed to reach the small pool without mishap and watched the water stream from the spring in the rocks as they stood awaiting their opportunity to fill their cans.

The return journey was necessarily taken even more slowly and carefully. Even so, there were spillages, especially as they had all filled their tins to the very top. Isabelle was being particularly careful in finding a safe place to put down a foot each time, and therefore holding up the others who were behind her. Harry had been determined to return with his can still full to the top and was also taking greater pains to tread safely, but he was becoming frustrated with the speed that Isabelle was moving in front of him.

"There is a dragon behind you," he called out suddenly, and was gratified when his sister gave a shriek, spilling some of her water as she glanced over her shoulder.

"Harry, you are horrid. Look, you made me spill some water," she complained.

"Well, I wish you would walk a little faster. We shall miss our lunch and perhaps only reach the house in time to go to bed," Harry declared jokingly.

"I'm going as fast as I can," Isabelle retorted. "My shoes slip on some of these rocks. I don't want to spill all the water."

"If I was in front I would have been back at the house by now," Harry goaded. "You had better let me pass."

Isabelle felt annoyed by her brother's jibes, but was equally determined not to let him lead the way. She felt aggrieved by the way he always assumed that he should be in the most important place, especially as she was older than he was. It was her right by age to be before him. Nevertheless, she attempted to quicken her pace to appease him and tried to ignore his taunts.

Jane, at the back of the line, was coping as best she could with one of James' tantrums. He couldn't understand why he didn't have a tin of water to carry like all the others and was demanding that Jane give him hers.

"Give me, Jane. Me want to carry water. Give me tin," he insisted plaintively.

Trying to carry her own container in one hand, hold James' hand with the other meanwhile keeping an eye on the uneven surface as well as trying to pacify her little brother was straining Jane's patience to the limit. She knew that he wouldn't even manage one step without stumbling, so bad was the road, then there would be tears of fury because the water would all be spilt.

"James. I'll give you the tin to carry when we are nearer the house. You can carry it inside and give it to Mrs Mackenzie. How does that sound?"

"No. Want tin now."

Jane knew that he was being unreasonable and there was little that would change his mind when he was in this sort of mood. It was because she was fully occupied with James that Jane failed to notice the mild altercation at the head of the column that quite suddenly erupted into chaos.

Due partly to the distraction of Harry's close proximity and his gentle hissing, and equally due to the fact that the sole of her right shoe was beginning to part company with the upper, Isabelle tripped over a protruding rock. Her left shoe slipped on the shiny granite as she stumbled, causing her to fly through the air, as did her can of water. She hit the rocks heavily though she had put out both hands to try to save herself. Her scream, followed by the shouts of all the other children, shocked Jane and, putting her can of water on the ground, she hurried towards Isabelle, who was lying on the ground.

James, who had been abruptly released, took this opportunity to obtain the object of his desire and somewhat gingerly, but in great triumph picked up the tin of water.

Harry had been so close to Isabelle when she tripped that he had almost fallen over her as she thudded to the ground and in stepping to one side half his water had spilled out. The cold water landed with a splash in the middle of Isabelle's back, the shock of it adding to her misery. She shrieked again, making no effort to stand up.

Harry and the other children remained still, frightened and awe-struck by the accident. The passing water carriers came to a halt, too, staring in fascination at the sight and sound of a young white girl prostrate upon the ground emitting piercing yells.

Kneeling beside her sister, Jane spoke urgently. "Isabelle, where are you hurt? Oh dear, your dress is wet, as well," she exclaimed as she touched her sister's back. "Come, dear. Try to stand up, and let me see where you are hurt."

At the sound of Jane's soothing voice and with her strong hands helping, Isabelle managed to push herself into a kneeling position, but she groaned aloud when she tried to put her hands on the ground to stand upright.

"I can't. I can't," she moaned pathetically.

Jane stood up and with her hands on Isabelle's waist she pulled her sister to her feet.

The watching crowd sighed with sympathy, "Ah. Aaah. Aieee," burst from many lips, followed by a babble of words.

Jane viewed her sister in dismay. Both hands were severely grazed and blood was oozing from the deep cuts masked by the dust and gravel on her palms. Her nose was bleeding too and there was a graze on it, but far more frightening was the large white lump on her forehead that looked like an emerging horn. Even Harry was struck dumb by the awful appearance and he felt a deep pang of guilt, knowing that he had been responsible for this disaster.

Jane tried to keep calm.

"Harry, you must go at once to the house and ask Mrs Mackenzie to come and help us. I cannot carry Isabelle and she cannot walk. We will wait here for her."

Eager to atone for his sin, Harry placed his tin carefully on the ground and set off at great speed towards the Mackenzies' house. On his own he was sure footed and Jane was amazed at the way he kept his balance as he charged up the hill, but pleased that help would soon be on the way.

Gently, Jane helped her sister to sit down on the ground and gave her a drink of water from the tin Harry had placed down carefully. She then pinched Isabelle's nose firmly to stop the bleeding. Mother had told her that it was the best thing to do. Isabelle made small noises of protest but she was too sore all over to mind one more hurt.

James provided a moment's welcome distraction by arriving at their side still carrying the tin she had abandoned. There was very little water left in it, but he was proud of his efforts and she was equally delighted that he hadn't fallen over. "Well done, James," she said approvingly. "How clever you are. You can sit down here now and talk to Isabelle because she is hurt and she needs us all to help her."

It was a great relief when Ellen Mackenzie arrived, and after commiserating with them, she picked Isabelle up and took her home, with Jane and the other children trailing disconsolately behind.

Of Harry there was no sign.

CHAPTER 25

By the time Henry was shown into the bedroom, the worst was over and Isabelle was lying in bed feeling sorry for herself. She had made a dreadful fuss as her grazes were cleaned and an even louder noise when the iodine was applied to her wounds, but since then a tranquillising draught prepared by Ellen had eased her pain.

A cloth, soaked in an infusion of leaves and roots, a restorative learned from the natives and used successfully many times by John, was placed on the lump on her forehead and added to the soothing effect of her treatment. This, as well as the fact that she was now the centre of attraction with everyone attempting to satisfy her needs, compensated somewhat for her suffering.

Nevertheless, she presented a sorry sight and Henry was stricken with guilt because he hadn't been at hand when the accident occurred. It was, however, fortunate that he had been absent whilst Ellen was treating the injuries and Isabelle was allowing her feelings full rein.

"Tell me how this happened," he commanded rather gruffly, trying to disguise his emotions.

Isabelle looked at him with a tremulous smile and tears in her eyes. She knew how to win father's sympathy. She also knew quite well that if she told father about Harry's behaviour, her brother would be severely punished. She was sorely tempted to blame him; to make him suffer as she was suffering. Then she remembered that Harry had been her chief friend and playmate on this journey and he would never forgive her if she told father about his taunts. She really needed his friendship and support. Besides, when Mrs Mackenzie had taken her shoes off, she had pointed out the broken sole. This dangerous fault, she suggested, was the cause of her downfall and Isabelle did remember catching her shoe against a rock.

"I tripped, father," she explained bravely. "The ground was very rough and my shoe hit a rock, then my other foot slipped and I fell. I put out my hands to try to stop myself from falling and hurt my hands and elbows, but I couldn't stop my head from hitting the rock."

"Well you must be very brave now and make no more fuss. You may have your lunch in bed then this afternoon I will make sure that you are provided with a clean dress. Mrs Mackenzie has told me that your other one will need mending and washing."

"Yes, father. Thank you, father," murmured Isabelle shakily. She was glad that she had not betrayed Harry, but she was determined to let her brother know of her generosity and forbearance. She would demand full recompense in the future.

Jane had cleaned her hands and face as best she could, although she could do nothing about the blood on her dress.

"Perhaps, Jane, you could obtain a clean dress at the same time," suggested Ellen kindly. "I will then have that one washed for you. The dresses might not dry properly this evening, but I can leave them by the fire and they should be ready for you by the time you leave tomorrow. Now it's time for lunch. Have you seen Harry anywhere?"

"I'll go and find him. I expect he's with the other children," offered Jane.

She went outside and saw the little ones still playing in the dust.

"It's nearly time for lunch," she told them. "You must go and wash yourselves. Please look after James for me. I must find Harry. Have you seen him?"

The children shook their heads solemnly and it took Jane another ten minutes to locate her brother, who was hiding behind the stable.

He was squatting on the ground with his jacket pulled over his ears to shut out the hostile world. Jane touched him gently on the shoulder. "Come, we are getting ready for lunch and you need to wash your hands and face. Your hair needs brushing too. Father will be cross if we are late. Why are you hiding here?"

Harry murmured something inaudible, but Jane had already guessed that he knew he was partly responsible for Isabelle's accident and was anticipating punishment. She had noticed his face when he had seen the blood and the frightening white lump on Isabelle's forehead. He had raced off as fast as he could to get help, ignoring the treacherous surface. She had marvelled at his speed and that he had managed to keep his footing, unaware that he was spurred on by guilt.

Jane did her best to reassure him that all was well and that no one blamed him.

"Isabelle looks much better now that Mrs Mackenzie has washed away the blood and tended her cuts. She made a lot of noise when her hands and knees were scrubbed to remove the dirt from the grazes and she hated the sting of the iodine almost as much. You may have heard her screams, but really she is perfectly all right and is beginning to enjoy being the centre of attention. She told your papa that she had tripped over her broken shoe and Mrs Mackenzie showed him the loose sole. Now he is cross with himself for not mending it earlier."

At last Harry looked at Jane as she offered this explanation. His tears had streaked the dust on his face and his expression was so forlorn that Jane pulled him to his feet and gave him a loving hug. Then she wiped his face a little on the hem of her dress.

"Come along quickly," she urged cheerfully.

Harry followed her, his courage and optimism returning with each step. To his great relief, no one mentioned his disappearance, although he had been missing for more than an hour, or even suggested his involvement with the accident, and he resolved to be especially nice to Isabelle when he saw her.

After lunch, Henry and John walked over to the wagons to collect clothes for both girls, taking Ellen with them. The children were left playing happily outside the house.

From time to time, Jane went inside to talk to Isabelle and even found time to read her a story. The Mackenzie children had some books that were new to Jane and to her delight she was able to indulge her passion for reading.

When the adults returned with the selected clothing, Isabelle was allowed to get up. She was looking much more cheerful, as the colour had returned to her cheeks and the lump had greatly subsided. Although it had taken on a bluish tinge, it didn't look quite as horrific as it had done originally.

With everyone treating her as if she were a fragile butterfly and eager to supply her every need, she was generous in a way that befitted her supposedly weak status and was particularly kind to Harry, who was obviously eager to please her.

John and Henry had retired to John's small study after their return from the town.

It was barely large enough to allow the two of them to sit comfortably and stretch out their long legs, but it had shelves for books and a worktable where John could write his sermons and reports. As at Inyati, all the furniture was homemade, in this case by John or one of the traders in the town. An occasional piece had been crafted by a passing visitor anxious to repay hospitality and the individuality of the items reflected the craftsmanship or otherwise of the maker.

The Mackenzies, like the other missionaries, had to guard their few treasures from the voracious appetites of the termites. Daily, it was essential to brush away the sandy tunnels creeping up from the floor along walls and furniture or down from the rafters. All the furniture legs stood in tins of water as further protection.

John handed his report to Henry, who read it carefully, commenting from time to time as he did so. He was pleased, and said as much, to find that John's account was similar to the ones from Inyati, saving only that he had been more successful than they had in making Christian converts.

They remained closeted in the study until dark, undisturbed by Ellen, who had decided that they would rather forego their afternoon tea than face an

interruption, since their day had already been disrupted by the necessity to walk all the way to the wagons. They had been able to discuss some of their missionary problems on that walk, as Ellen was fully aware, as she had heard them discussing tribal differences.
Undoubtedly, the Bechuana people were more able to accept Christian principles than the proud, warlike Matabele. John stated several times that he had no regrets at refusing the offer to stay at Matabeleland, knowing that the chances of success in that country were minimal.
During the evening an incident occurred that seemed curious to Henry. A poor, aged woman arrived at the house begging for help. John had immediately summoned one of his young male students from the schoolhouse and, giving him a handful of food, told him to take the woman a long way from the house before giving it to her.
Henry looked askance at the firm direction and the determined, but worried, look on his friend's face.
Seeing Henry's expression, John felt constrained to explain.
"The people here are always desperate for food and it is accepted that the workers and the children must be fed first. Once a person, especially a woman, becomes too old and weak to carry water, till the soil, or contribute to the food supply, then the community regards that person as an unnecessary drain on resources. The old are never cared for, they are left to die of starvation, thus easing the strain on the water carriers and food providers. It is awful for us, as you can imagine, seeing the desperate state of these abandoned people, but our own resources are frequently strained to the point of near starvation and we can do little to help. We do what we can to ease their lot, but we dare not encourage them to come here. We should be inundated if it became known that food could be obtained freely here."
Henry understood and empathised with both John's reasoning and his feeling of helplessness.
"I'm sure your decision is the right one," he agreed. "We, at Inyati, also know what it is like to be regarded as perennial providers of succour and sustenance, despite our all too frequent condition of near starvation. You must comfort yourself, though, with the thought that even in England, the old and destitute are sent to the workhouse, which is scarcely a less bleak existence. Large families might provide a blessed support in some cases, but only the rich can guarantee a comfortable old age. As missionaries living and practising God's word, we are frequently faced with unpleasant problems and, like Solomon, are expected to make wise decisions. We can only act according to our consciences and manage what is within our power. Don't spoil your own life, and that of your family, ruining your health by

worrying about your inability to provide for every sick or aged person you see. Give what practical help you can, extend your compassion and offer your prayers by all means, but keep a sense of proportion. Your family must come first"

John smiled gently. "You sound like my grandmother, Henry, but you are quite right, of course. Nevertheless, I cannot but wish there was more I could do."

The evening passed quickly and pleasantly for both families, leading to a night of untroubled sleep.

John Bennion greeted them with a broad smile and a cheery 'good morning' as his cart rattled up to the stopping place below the house on Tuesday morning.

The two families, who had been chatting quietly on the veranda as they waited, were dreading the moment of departure, but rose and walked down to meet him as soon as they were aware of his approach.

They had not seen him since the Sunday morning service, because John had been persuaded to join a convivial party at one of the stores with some of the other European residents, leaving the Mackenzies, Hargreaves' and the Bechuana converts to celebrate the evening service without them. A number of the partygoers felt guilty about their desertion, though they had no regrets about the party.

"We've had three days of revelling and few have suffered from a sore head," John proclaimed cheerfully. "Begging your pardon, Reverend. You'll have some rueful apologies later in the day no doubt, from those who feel they should have resisted temptation. Henry, you'll find young William has all in hand, horses fed and watered and the oxen inspanned. He was working hard when I left. You're lucky to have those two strong, salted horses. They'd fetch a good price here or anywhere else, I fancy."

Henry nodded equably. "Oscar, that's my horse, was expensive when I bought him, but I was given sound advice and I've never regretted my choice. He's served me well. He's fast and steady for hunting so I shall keep him as long as I may. William's horse, Diamond, suits him well and neither of us is likely to sell, however advantageous the offer might be."

John shrugged resignedly, "Ah well, there goes my opportunity to acquire a reliable horse for hunting."

He looked at Henry with such a doleful expression that everyone burst out laughing and the moment of parting was eased as handshakes all round were followed with warm hugs for the children.

"Do you still want to sit in front?" Henry asked Isabelle, kindly.

Isabelle was feeling stiff and sore, her bruises still painful, but she was

determined to have her moment of triumph, and nodded determinedly.
"Yes please, father," she replied.
Carefully, she was lifted up to sit beside John Bennion, and father climbed up beside her. Harry, James and Jane scrambled up behind and shouted happy farewells to the Mackenzie children.
With waving hands and fervent expressions of 'God be with you' to speed them on their way, the Hargreaves family was swept away in the swaying, clattering cart. The clopping hooves, jangling harness and ringing strikes of iron-clad wheels against rocks made speech impossible until they reached the dusty plain.
"Did you enjoy your stay with the Reverend?" enquired John, as soon as he could make himself heard.
"Most certainly," replied Henry positively. "We were just sad that our stay was such a short one and our hosts tried hard to persuade us to stay longer, even if it was only for one more day. Unfortunately, we were forced by circumstances to stay longer in the Matabele king's town than we had intended, which has lengthened our journey.
If we are to avoid travelling in the worst of the English winter, we really must try to reach Cape Town as quickly as possible, so we regretfully had to decline. It is a great pity, as there was much to discuss and I know how greatly visitors are welcomed in this isolated existence. No doubt the Reverend John Moffat and his wife will be able to stay longer, which will bring them all great pleasure."
Isabelle was rather squashed between these two large men, but she was pleased rather than otherwise, as her forward position was more frightening than she had anticipated. She had lifted her head and smiled in triumph at Harry being forced to concede the favourite seat as they had climbed up. Now she was feeling much less certain that it was an honour.
She tried not to gaze at the dusty ground whirling past, not far below her feet, as it made her feel dizzy. Instead she concentrated on the backs and ears of the donkeys as they raced round the town.
Harry, in his back seat, found this return journey even more exciting than the previous one, when he had been in the front. Somehow the rear end of the cart seemed to weave about in a more lively fashion, provoking him to laugh aloud. He could barely refrain from cheering. Only the sight of his papa's stiff back immediately in front of him forced him to try to restrain his exuberance. He was completely unaware of possible accidents and totally unworried that there might be any mishap.
Isabelle would have been furious had she known that Harry, far from envying her position in front, was thoroughly revelling in the excitement of

his present seat.

There were already people about at this hour and occasionally the donkeys swerved wildly to avoid a collision. Harry, waving cheerfully to all and sundry, was attracting jolly smiles and happy salutations followed their careering cart.

James copied his big brother, chuckling happily and waving his arms about whilst bouncing around.

Poor Jane had, perforce, to release her own tense grip of the seat in front, in order to restrain him. She, with her greater experience and imagination, understood how easily one of them might fall out of the cart and knew the damage such an occurrence might inflict. There was no one to notice her alarmed expression or to offer assistance and she hung on grimly, praying for the ordeal to cease.

When the donkeys finally came to a halt beside the wagons, her relief was matched in its intensity only by Harry's disappointment that the thrill was now over.

Thanking Mr Bennion profusely for the ride, the family climbed down and Jane was furious to discover that her legs were shaking. As father immediately handed her a large bag to carry, which had been presented to them by Ellen Mackenzie and was filled with vegetables, bread and other such luxuries, she was able to hide her weakness. Jane hastened to carry the food and the clean dresses that had also been parcelled up, to the Hargreaves' wagon.

There were still two wagons without their spans and whilst this was being attended to Henry told the children to wait in the nearest store, well away from the large animals and the scene of frantic activity.

The children were happy enough to have the opportunity to examine the goods in the store and they walked carefully into the cool gloom. The air was filled with a conglomeration of smells: of cloth and ironmongery, of blankets and hides, of oil, candles and soap, mixed with the strong tang of dried fish. Nearer the counter, the attractive smell of groceries was mixed with that of coffee, tea and tobacco.

They were welcomed by Mr Green, who immediately noticed Isabelle's damaged face and in sympathy hunted about for boiled sweets to offer his visitors. As he handed them out, he was rewarded with delighted smiles and expressions of gratitude.

Sucking happily on their sweets, the children wandered round the store.

Harry immediately went to look critically at the muskets and rifles, the powder, lead and ironmongery. Isabelle and James were fascinated by a musical box Mr Green showed them. Once she knew that her siblings were quietly absorbed, Jane moved across to examine the bolts of cloth and some ready-made clothing.

There was a pile of blankets and another of dried skins in one corner, with a shelf of tinned goods above them. Along another wall, a shelf of groceries and preserved meats stood above sacks of dry goods.

The children had never before seen such an intriguing variety of goods.

Mr Green explained to Jane that the younger Bechuana people now liked to wear cotton clothes like the Europeans and came regularly to trade for them. Guns, powder and lead appealed to the townspeople and travellers alike, so there was always a good profit made on them Tea, coffee, sugar, salt, rice and flour were valuable trading goods, too, as Shoshong was so far away from supplies of such goods. The stores here were the only ones on the road north where such essential stocks could be purchased.

Hunters, who needed to offer presents to a native chief in exchange for permission to hunt or to cross his land, bought trinkets such as the music box.

Brandy could only be sold to a European for his own personal use.

Jane listened attentively and asked about the cured animal skins.

"Oh those will be sent to Cape Town along with the horns, feathers, ivory and some gold dust I have in store whenever I have sufficient to make up a load. Sometimes all the traders here share a wagon or two, when we need to obtain fresh supplies from Cape Town."

Jane wished she could have one of the brightly coloured dresses, though she knew she wouldn't be allowed to wear colours whilst she was in mourning for mother.

Father would, no doubt, also point out that these very plain dresses would never do for a young lady such as herself. On closer examination, Jane realised that the style was very simple and, even worse than that, the workmanship was inferior.

The previous evening William and Henry had agreed that their food supplies needed to be augmented and Henry now came in with the list.

Bags of meal, rice, flour, sugar, salt, dried beans, tea, coffee, some dried meat, cheese, pickles and jam were taken across to the waiting wagons under strict supervision and packed away carefully. Every available container was filled with water and two gourds of goat's milk were purchased for a handful of beads.

Vegetables were a luxury in Shoshong because of the lack of water, but pumpkins were grown in the rainy season and they remained usable for many months once they were dried, so they were able to purchase several.

They were also fortunate enough to be able to buy some corn for the horses despite the fact that it was in short supply and was consequently very expensive. Once they had bought some powder and lead their list was complete, until Henry noticed a sheet of tanned leather.

He still felt responsible for Isabelle's accident as the loose sole on her shoe had been deemed to be the cause. His own boots and those of the other children were showing distinct signs of wear too and all were in need of repair. He had the necessary tools for cutting out and stitching leather so the hide was added to their purchases.

Charles Green was content to accept a note on Henry's Cape Town bank and William promised to repay Henry when he settled his previous debt.

With expressions of satisfaction and goodwill all round William and Henry bade the storekeeper goodbye.

To their surprise they discovered that John Mackenzie had ridden over to bid farewell yet again as he had wanted to see as much of his friends as possible and he had felt in need of a bracing gallop. He even proposed to ride out a little way with them and in this he was joined by some of the traders who were keen to spend more time with William.

The usual crowd of curious people had gathered, the children running alongside, jostling and shouting to the travellers as the little cavalcade with its escort of cheerful, noisy horsemen left Shoshong.

Harry was delighted when he was allowed to ride in front of William for a short way. Henry, less enthusiastically, had agreed to take up James. Jane and Isabelle were in the wagon.

"I wish we could have stayed there longer," sighed Isabelle who was already feeling put out at the thought of another extended journey and at having to ride because walking was still difficult for her. Her usually pretty face, marred as it was by the bruise on her forehead and the scar on her nose, was further spoiled by her look of discontent. "I liked sleeping in a proper bed again, just the two of us without the boys."

Jane, as always, tried to cheer her up by distracting her.

" Do you know it is James' birthday this month, I wonder if we should remind father that James will be two soon?"

Intrigued, Isabelle sat up." Can we have a celebration?" she asked hopefully.

" We didn't have a party for our birthdays in April did we?" she continued wistfully.

Jane looked at her in surprise. " No of course we didn't. Mother was very ill then and she had to stay in bed. At least we were given new bonnets and those pretty kerchiefs that Mrs Thomas made. I don't know what we can give James though. We shall have to think of something."

CHAPTER 26

Both Jane and Isabelle were feeling cold, as there was no sign of the sun that morning, and the early morning journey in the open cart had chilled them to the bone. It hadn't been much warmer even inside the store and the wagon temperature was almost freezing. Isabelle, on the bed, was able to pull a blanket over herself, though she was still shivering, whilst Jane, who was sitting on one of the side boxes behind the driver's box, had only her shawl as protection. She was shivering even more than her little sister, especially when the cold air swirled around her as the wagon was set in motion. She considered pulling the front curtain closed, then decided against travelling in the enclosed semi-dark vehicle.

"When we stop I'll ask father if I can get mother's woollen shawl out of the box in the baggage wagon. I can wear that and you can have mine, as well as your own. I think our capes are there as well."

Isabelle was still in an unhappy mood. "I don't know why you didn't think of that when we were at the king's town. I have been so cold," she remarked pettishly. "The only way I have been able to keep warm is by playing games with Harry. I didn't always want to run about with him, you know."

"I know," Jane replied soothingly. "I'm sure you were happy some of the time, though. It's always warm if you find a sheltered spot in the sun. You could have told me that you were cold and needed some more warm clothes," she added reasonably. "You know as well as I do that we have those warm capes mother made us."

Thinking of the clothes in the chest in the baggage wagon, Jane remembered seeing some scraps of material there too. "I know what we can make James for his birthday," she exclaimed with a sparkle in her voice.

"What?" asked Isabelle.

"We could each make him a ball. Father likes to see us practising our sewing, so he will be pleased and it will be easier than sewing our samplers. James will love having a ball to play with, he had so much fun with the pig's bladder before it burst, and he played with that rag ball too."

"How can we make a ball?" Isabelle questioned, sitting up and feeling intrigued by the idea.

Momentarily, Jane was lost in thought. "I don't really know. I don't have a pattern, but we can ask father. He will be sure to know."

Both girls were filled with a glow of well-being at the thought of being able to make James happy on his birthday.

"When is Harry's birthday?" Isabelle now asked, not to be outdone with being kind to their brothers. "We shall have to think of a present for him, too, shan't we?"

"Harry's birthday is next month. You must try to remember the family birthdays, Isabelle. Father's is in January; Mother had hers in March. Ours are in April, James' is June and Harry's is in July."

Isabelle nodded her eyes serious. "I'll try to remember. January, March, April, June and July. Will you read me a story now please Jane?" she added coaxingly.

Jane stopped to think before answering. Reading a story to Isabelle would be a good excuse to go and lie on the bed too and then she could cover herself with the blanket and feel much warmer. On the other hand, Isabelle needed to practise her reading and father was insistent that they should all do some lessons every day.

"I will read you a story when you have read one to me," she offered.

Isabelle groaned. "That means I shall have to sit up and get cold," she complained. "Besides, I can't hold the book very well with my sore hands." She hoped that Jane would feel sorry for her and relent when she heard this appeal.

"I am feeling cold as well," Jane reminded her, "and I can hold the book for you."

"All right," Isabelle conceded with reluctance. "Will you tell me the story about how you left England and came to Inyati when we've finished reading? It's my favourite story."

About an hour later the boys were lifted into the wagon when it halted briefly. They were both shivering, but delighted with their experiences.

There was chaos for a while as the two boys wanted to get warm and the two girls objected to having the two cold little bodies near them when they were beginning to feel warmer. However, they all eventually settled down and chattered happily until the first outspan was reached.

As they climbed down from the wagon, the mounted men who had escorted them so far were taking their leave, some of them challenging each other to a race back to the town. There were many loud and cheerful farewells and a cheer went up as three of the men set off at a fast gallop, the remainder betting on the probable winner, then setting off after them at a canter.

The children played happily as lunch was being prepared. They were pleased to be released from the confines of the wagon and equally glad to be able to get warm by running and jumping.

Isabelle, somewhat hampered by her aching body, went to sit by the roaring fire and Jane brought her a blanket. Later, after they had eaten and before lessons started, Jane explained to father the necessity for finding some warmer clothes for them all and he agreed to move the tarpaulin over the baggage wagon so that they could open the chest.

As he was doing this she reminded him of James' birthday and explained that she and Isabelle were hoping to sew some pieces of material together to make a ball for him. Tentatively she asked him if he could make a pattern for her.

"I know there are some spare pieces of material there, because mother planned to sew all the odd pieces together to make a bedcover. If I knew what shapes to cut out it would be possible to make a ball shape. Perhaps we could stuff it with feathers," she added earnestly.

Henry looked thoughtfully at the serious little face watching him and felt a little disconcerted. He had, of course, completely forgotten about birthdays. It was a woman's duty to think of such things and arrange any necessary celebrations or presents. His mother had always done it at home and his wives had taken over once he was married. Birthdays meant little to him, but he felt he should acknowledge his children's anniversaries and he should reassure her. He wasn't sure himself what shapes could be made into a ball, but he could no doubt find out.

"Thank you for reminding me of James' birthday. I suppose I have a note of it in my diary somewhere," he conceded. "I have so little time to write up my journal each day, I never have time to look back at last year's entries, but I do remember it's in June. You can talk to Lukas on the right day and perhaps he can make a special meal. Later, I'll think about the shapes needed to make a ball. It is a good idea of yours to make such a present for James."

He lifted her up beside the chest and watched as she extracted the things she needed; extra clothes for all of them, then a woollen shawl he recognized as one Katherine had worn. He was suddenly engulfed with grief and longing and was on the point of refusing to let it be taken out of the box, when he remembered how cold all the children had been that morning.

Controlling his intense yearning with an effort, he assisted Jane as she stacked capes, some woollen underwear and two jackets for the boys and then an accumulation of scrap material on top of the shawl. At last she was satisfied and when she had climbed to the ground he helped to carry the goods across to the wagon. Returning to close the chest and replace the tarpaulin he was glad to be alone to overcome his grief without anyone else being aware. Wrestling with the tarpaulin and heaving on the ropes helped. He would take a walk, he decided, before organising the children's lessons. Exercise always helped, especially a solitary walk in the bush. How was it that he could be completely self-controlled, even happy, on some days and then be overtaken by a desperate need to be with his wife again? He ached to have Katherine beside him again, listening, advising or sharing ideas and being always so warmly loving at night.

Later that afternoon, Henry mentioned James' approaching anniversary to William, who immediately became enthusiastic about celebrating the occasion.

This part of their journey was unbelievably harsh and unpleasant: mile upon mile of bushland, with occasional rocky outcrops, known as kopjes, large anthills and dusty vegetation with few trees and long periods without a source of water. They would have to spend many hours hunting each day and even then there was no guarantee of success. People could be hungry for meat and thirsty for days on end, and it was even worse for the poor oxen. Thankfully, they had managed to buy sufficient provisions in Shoshong to keep them supplied with basic food for most of the journey, at least as long as they were careful, but meat was always a problem. The servants could eat vast quantities of meat and became sullen or uncooperative if they had to manage without. Each of the five drivers could eat twice as much meat as William and Henry required. William had managed to obtain several sheep and goats in Shoshong, which had meant parting with one of the bottles of brandy Henry had given him and some of his trading goods. He hoped to make the meat from each of them last for two days so that would mean there was enough meat for the first two weeks, not including any meat they obtained from hunting. Having a celebration would help to enliven the dreary days spent battling the cold, the dust, the thirst and any other problems arising.

"So young James is going to be two years old?" William repeated. "Well I wonder what I can give him as a present? Perhaps I should try my hand at carving. I'll try to make him a little horse." William smiled at the thought.

Henry nodded his approval. "If you show me what size your horse is likely to be, I'll make a little cart to go with it. I have always enjoyed working with wood and there will be quite a few challenges there, but I mustn't forget that I've to mend all the family shoes, so time is of the essence."

"Have you decided how to make a pattern for the balls that the girls are going to make?" William asked suddenly.

"I've been giving it some thought," replied Henry. "I think the best thing to do is base it on one of the pumpkins we bought. There is one beautifully round one, which is just the right size for Jane to copy. If I cut the pumpkin into quarters and remove the rind from each piece I shall have the pattern. Lukas can cook the pumpkin for lunch and roast the seeds later."

William grinned appreciatively, "That sounds a fine idea. Somehow, I expected you to work it out mathematically. How will you manage a smaller one for Isabelle?"

"Oh that will be no problem. We'll just cut a quarter or half inch off all round, and it will be significantly smaller. Being a practical man as well as a man of letters, having a model to work from is quicker and easier. Besides, it is time the children had another lesson about fractions. I think we'll do it right away."

Once the pumpkin had been divided into halves and then the two halves split again Jane was able to see how father intended to make a pattern. He drew round one of the pumpkin skins, using charcoal from the fire.

Later, Jane was able to cut out four pieces of cloth, which looked like large leaves. She had found a number of felt squares amongst the cotton and linen ones from the chest and decided that this was the sort of material for a ball, soft but strong. She had chosen green and blue for her own ball and red and blue for the smaller one that Isabelle was to make.

Henry had expected them to do sums with fractions once they had seen the pumpkin cut into quarters, which was easy for Jane as she had done them before, but he had then cut the rinds down the centre, making eighths, which again Jane could understand, but Isabelle and Harry had found more difficult. Harry, eager to please, made a great effort and by repetition began to show some understanding. Father said he would keep the rinds for another day or two so that they could practise fractions until they understood them. He was a little irritated that Isabelle, especially, should have any difficulties.

"I suppose I shouldn't even try to teach you such things," he concluded. "It is well known that females aren't capable of comprehending the sciences and reasoning, but Jane has managed and it is easier to have you all together when we are doing lessons. Perhaps you should stick to drawing, reading and music."

At this censure from her beloved father, Isabelle burst into tears and was immediately banished to the wagon to compose herself. The lessons continued without her.

For the next ten days the times in camp were busy ones, with extra occupations added to the normal ones. Henry spent his time mending shoes, Jane and Isabelle were occupied with sewing and William busied himself with his knife and a chunk of wood. Only the two boys played in carefree abandon, totally unaware of the concentrated efforts being made for James' benefit.

As the small carved horse became a recognisable shape, Henry was able to judge the size of the cart he had planned to make and William took to doing his carving whilst the children were resting, so that the boys wouldn't guess what he was doing. This followed an incident one afternoon when James had questioned Jane.

"What is it?" he asked Jane as he left his game and came to gaze at her brightly coloured sewing. As she had almost joined three of the pieces by then Jane was nonplussed. She had been taught never to lie, but she didn't want James to know what she was making. Birthday presents had to be a surprise. Harry solved the problem for her, but also sowed the seeds for a reprimand from father.

He had followed James and was gazing at the object in Jane's lap. "I know what that is," he stated boldly. "It's a hat or a cap. Look, it will fit your head, James." So saying, he picked up the partly sewn ball and, taking off James' hat, he put the felt in its place, where it fitted quite neatly.

"You're very clever, Harry," Jane murmured. "Now please give me back my sewing and go back to your game."

Henry had, a short while previously, returned from an abortive hunting trip during which time he had seen no game at all. He was feeling tired, frustrated and dispirited. Through his weariness as he walked towards the wagon he heard James' question and Harry's response. Now he was suddenly confronted with the spectacle of James bouncing about with a ridiculous piece of nonsense on his head, looking for all the world like a court jester. Harry had been joined by Isabelle and they were dancing round him chanting, "You're a magic elf," over and over with great glee.

Henry recognised the object on James' head as the piece of sewing that had been Jane's. Suddenly feeling outraged he barked, "Harry and James. What are you doing? Do not disturb the girls at their sewing. As you don't seem to have anything to occupy yourselves with you had better go and collect wood for the fire. Go right now and stay within sight of the wagons." Henry's stern voice sent the boys scurrying away on their task, a particularly difficult one in this area with few trees, whilst Isabelle ran to sit down and Jane hastily recovered her sewing.

"Now miss," he went on, addressing Jane. "I thought you had learned from the cradle never to tell lies."

Jane looked up from her work and stared at her father with a puzzled expression. "Yes father."

"Then why have you transgressed?"

Jane remained staring at Henry, trying vainly to think of what had just occurred. 'How had she sinned?' After a horrible pause she spoke. "I have told no lie, father," she offered meekly.

Henry's face darkened. "There are sins of omission as well as sins of commission, miss, as you must be well aware." Then, noticing her puzzled expression, he went on. "Did James ask you a question?"

"Yes father"

"Did you give him a true answer?"
"Harry gave him an explanation."
"Was it the true answer?"
"No father."
"Did you tell the boys the truth?"
"No father."
"Then you let them believe a lie."
Jane hung her head. She had no answer.
"You omitted to tell the truth and you let the boys believe a lie. Do you think that that is the sort of behaviour a good Christian should accept?"
"No father." Jane felt close to tears, knowing that it was useless to explain that she had wanted to avoid spoiling James' birthday surprise by revealing the secret.
"You must learn to think more clearly Jane. I thought that you of all my children would have been more aware of your duty." Disappointed, Henry turned on his heel and sought refuge in the wagon and solace in cleaning a gun that hadn't actually been fired that afternoon.
Isabelle, her head bent, had concentrated on her own sewing during the reproof of her sister, forgetting to make her usual complaint about her poor sore hands that were in fact almost healed. Now she glanced sideways, feeling unaccountably sorry for her big sister who so often received the blame.
Jane tried hard to understand why she was so wicked. Why did she commit so many sins? She resolved to ask God's forgiveness in her prayers that evening and seek His help to avoid further transgressions.

CHAPTER 27

To Henry's dismay, within three days of leaving Shoshong, he noticed that one of the oxen in the span pulling his baggage wagon was beginning to flag. As soon as the next outspan was reached the beast was taken out of the span and was replaced by one of the three remaining loose ones. Unfortunately, the poor creature showed no signs of recovering, even after the mid-day rest and lay down where it had been led, refusing to rise despite extreme coercion from drivers and leaders. No amount of tail twisting, ear pulling or strikes with a whip could force it to its feet. Henry and William agreed that the only recourse was to put it out of its misery, which Henry did with a single bullet to the head.

"Well, we are now one ox less, but it isn't entirely a catastrophe as it will supply us with meat for a day or two and we can save the sheep for later," said Henry philosophically. "We still have two spare oxen and I hope they aren't needed for a long time."

William agreed, but had to admit that the journey wasn't going to get any easier. He called for Lukas to come and claim some of the better cuts from the carcass before letting Bokkis skin the animal and then, with the other drivers, take their share. Eventually Amos, Abdol and the other servants would be allowed to take meat for themselves.

"Listen to me," William called, as the drivers crowded round, slashing and slicing at the meat their hands, arms and faces covered in blood. "This meat has to last you three days. We haven't seen any game in this area and we have many weeks to travel before we reach Kuruman. There is no more meat for three days. You understand?"

Fifteen pairs of dark eyes stared back at him, but the nods and grunts meant nothing and William knew it. They would gorge themselves on the meat until it was finished, with no thought for the future.

"Well, you warned them. Not that it will make much difference. The idea of rationing themselves is totally foreign, and tomorrow will take care of itself," Henry remarked. "Just now though, I think you'd better watch out for young Fox."

William looked towards where Henry was pointing and spotted his dog yanking at the intestines only inches from a very sharp knife. Hastily, he grabbed the dog's tail and yanked him back out of harm's way. "All right, you greedy little beast, I'll get you something to eat right now." Holding the squirming dog under his arm, he took out his own knife and sliced off a portion of meat, which he handed to Fox. The dog being released made his way to the edge of the camp proudly bearing his trophy.

"He's satisfied now. It's a good thing you spotted him, Henry, the butchers wouldn't have worried about hitting or cutting him, they are much too concerned with grabbing all they can, before anyone else gets a turn," said William grimly.

The shortage of water at this time of the year was harsh for everyone. Washing clothes couldn't even be considered and only a mugful for each person was allowed for cleaning hands and faces twice a day. This water was then kept for the animals to drink, as it was too precious to be thrown away. Cooking and drinking water were the two essentials and even these were rationed. Cooking pots were rubbed clean by using dry sand. The horses were given a small amount but the oxen had to go for days without any water.

Another ox died within the space of the next four days, worn out by the lack of proper food and limited water whilst toiling each day to drag the heavy wagons through dry sand. This time it was one belonging to William. The consolation for William and Henry was that they still had replacements and the meat from the dead animal was in great demand in the camp. Hunting had remained sparse for several days and they had begun to despair of keeping the servants healthy and happy. The replacements were in much better condition, having had no strenuous work to do and both William and Henry were relieved that they still had one extra beast left from the four that Henry had brought from Inyati. Cutting down on the numbers in a span might have to be considered but would put a greater strain on the remaining ones and slow up their journey considerably.

"I suppose it isn't all bad news, "Henry commented tersely, as he looked grimly at the scene of carnage, a repetition of the one they had watched only a few days previously. Lukas had already chosen several cuts for their own consumption and now the drivers were finishing the task of removing the skin before helping themselves.

"I can't understand how they can tear off raw meat with their teeth almost as soon as the animal has stopped breathing and gobble the chunks with such glee or how they can bear to be covered from head to foot in blood," Henry remarked with a shudder.

"Well, I suppose it depends on how you were brought up, Henry," laughed William. "We are much too squeamish in their eyes, but we think we are civilised because we prefer our meat cooked and served properly. I'm sure our ancestors must have tasted raw meat. Anyway, it's a good job we all have strong teeth for I'm sure this meat will be even tougher than the last one was. I'll get Lukas to stew it all afternoon and it might become edible. I was sad to lose this one, he's been a steady brute and served me well over a number of years. It is a blessing you thought to bring the extra oxen and I think we'd better try to buy some more at Kuruman. Some of our present ones are in need of a long rest."

"I agree with you. We might even be able to exchange some with the Rev Moffat. He usually keeps a reasonable herd and is not averse to helping out by taking on the weary ones and keeping them until they've recovered their strength and exchanging them back on the return journey."

When a week later, June 13th in the year of Our Lord 1865, dawned clear and cold, James Bradford Hargreaves celebrated his second birthday.

The toys had been stored in William's wagon and brought out each day for completion only when the boys were otherwise engaged, thus ensuring that they remained a secret from them. Harry had only learned of the celebration planned and the existence of gifts by chance the day before and he was overcome by the fact that he alone would have nothing to offer his little brother.

The girls had been given a goodly supply of feathers when Bokkis had returned from a hunting foray four days ago bearing the carcass of an ostrich and the following day Henry had managed to bag two korhaan. The meat from these birds was very welcome and there were sufficient soft feathers for the girls to stuff the balls they had sewn. They were busily discussing these toys and the lovely model horse and cart made by William and father when Harry had suddenly materialised behind them demanding to be told what it was all about. As James was playing with Fox and was out of earshot Isabelle had gladly told him. "It's James' birthday tomorrow and we have a lovely surprise for him," she boasted. "We have each made him a ball to play with. William has carved a little wooden horse and father has made a cart to go with the horse. It even has wheels so that James can move the horse and the cart will follow."

Jane, not to be outdone added, "Lukas is going to bake some jam tarts and fresh bread and make a big meat pie as a special treat. It will be a lovely party."

Harry was filled with a mixture of pleasure and fury. Pleasure because it would be fun to have a celebration and he was happy that James' birthday would be remembered, but fury that he hadn't known anything about it and therefore had nothing to give his brother. He stormed away from his sisters and found a place where he could sit quietly by himself to think. His thoughts concentrated on his own special treasures, his ninepins, his throwing sticks and his secret tin containing buttons, coins and the quartz stone father had given him at Tati. Each thing was special and he could barely consider parting with any of them. Would he have to do so? James was too small to play ninepins or use the throwing sticks properly. Father had given the quartz stones to all the children, so he didn't need that and that left the coins and the buttons. Harry loved the shiny brass (which he privately considered were gold) and silver buttons from soldiers' uniforms that he had collected for as long as he could remember. The coins were mostly pennies received as gifts and were kept with the buttons in a tin bearing a picture of the queen, but there was one shiny silver sixpence. He didn't think James would appreciate any of these things.

Disconsolately, he stood up and sauntered over to the fire where the drivers were toasting a few miserable mealie cobs. The drivers spoke a mixture of languages, making it difficult to understand them, but Harry somehow managed to make himself understood and on this occasion he asked Bokkis if he had any baskets. All the drivers were adept at basket weaving and whenever they had time and there were the correct canes to be had they could be found chatting and weaving baskets to sell. They had all made purchases in Shoshong by exchanging a variety of baskets and bowls they had made.

Bokkis was sorry that he had nothing to offer, but fortunately one of the others had a basket about eighteen inches in diameter. It was rather shallow but it had a handle and was just perfect for what Harry had in mind. He negotiated with the Hottentot owner for its purchase. Many of the drivers and servants were familiar with coins as they had lived in Cape Town and Harry's offer of money was readily accepted.

Running back to the wagon, he opened his tin and gazed at the coins he had: four pennies and the silver sixpence. Clutching them in his hand, he returned to the group of drivers and showed them his fortune.

The owner of the basket handed it over and took the coins, whereupon a burst of irate language broke out amongst the others. It was clear that they were castigating the Hottentot and completely disagreeing with his action.

Resolutely, Bokkis stood up. He held out his hand and spoke sharply. Reluctantly, the Hottentot handed back the silver sixpence, which Bokkis solemnly returned to Harry saying, "That basket would sell for only a few pennies in Cape Town. He took too much because he knew you didn't know its value. Remember that some people will always try to cheat you, but some of us are your friends. When you grow to be a strong man you may learn the difference. One day you may be able to help us."

Harry was thrilled to have his precious silver sixpence back. He nodded vigorously, "Thank you, Bokkis. I shall always remember you. I will be your friend even when I am a man."

As everyone was still occupied with various tasks, Harry was able to return the sixpence to his secret tin and also hide the basket under the bed without anyone being aware of his actions. Now he felt happy, not only that but also extremely pleased with himself. He too had a present to give to James.

William had suggested that the gifts for James should be given at intervals so that he could appreciate each one and enjoy it for a while before being given the next one, rather than having them all at the same time. Henry and the girls thought that this was sensible and it was agreed that Isabelle would be to first to hand James a present after breakfast.

Jane had wakened her little brother, as the morning trek was well under way. "It's a very special day today James," she explained as she helped him to dress. "It's your birthday. Today you are two years old."

James looked at her wide eyed, "My burfday?"

"Yes, it is your birthday. You are now two years old."

Isabelle and Harry were both filled with excitement at the anticipation of the day's celebration and could barely conceal their joy.

"Happy birthday," shouted Isabelle, giving her little brother a hug.

"A happy birthday," growled Harry, trying to suppress his feelings.

"Come, let me brush your hair." Jane interrupted the greetings and fun huggings that were hampering her in that confined space. The sudden lurching of the wagon sent them all sprawling on the two beds amidst howls of dismay that soon turned to laughter.

Henry extended the morning grace to include special blessings for his son and the pious hope that he would enjoy a long and happy life. Breakfast was similar to most of their morning meals, but also included some piping hot liver and kidneys and chops from the sheep that had been slaughtered the evening before. James was wriggling about in excitement and anticipation as Isabelle, with father's permission, rose from the table to go and get her present from William's wagon.

"Here you are, James. I made this ball especially for you," she exclaimed prettily, as she handed him the bright red and blue ball.

"You must remember to thank your sister," father reminded James.

James, his eyes shining as he held this lovely toy mumbled, "Thankou, Isabelle."

Isabelle cast a look of triumph at Harry, hoping to see him look downcast. She knew that he hadn't had time to make a gift for James. She was puzzled to see him smiling secretively. They all watched James rolling the ball about and encouraged him to put it on the ground where he could try to kick it.

After about ten minutes father nodded to Jane, who then went to William's wagon to collect her own gift.

"Here you are, James. I have made you a bigger ball to play with." Jane handed over the larger green and blue ball.

With his father's stern eye on him, James chortled, "Thankou Jane. I like this ball, too. Two new toys to play with."

"Let me hold one for you, James," offered Harry and he took the smaller one so that James could play for a time with the bigger one. He was as delighted as James was with the presents as he loved to throw and catch a ball and he knew that he would have many opportunities to play with them. Gently, he tossed the ball upwards and caught it again. These two balls were soft and not too heavy, so he might not be able to throw them very far, but they wouldn't hurt anyone either.

Henry and William watched with interest as James ran around trying to kick the ball and frequently tripping over it. Finally, Henry urged William to bring out the model horse. "It's better if he has the horse first and then I'll bring out the cart to fasten onto it."

By this time, James was quite ready to come and sit by the others, having temporarily exhausted himself. He and Harry were sitting and admiring the two new toys when William appeared holding something behind his back.

"Well, master James. I wish you a very happy birthday. Here is a small present from me," and he suddenly produced the carved horse.

Tentatively, James reached out and gingerly picked up the small horse.

"Horsey. A horsey. For me?" He looked up at William.

"Yes, it's for you. Do you like it?"

"Thankou. Yes, thankou." James pranced the little model up and down, clicking his tongue and trying to make the sound of a horse's hooves. He showed it to Harry, who felt a small pang of envy. It was a lovely little thing and he wished he had one like it. "We ought to have a name for the horse," he suggested to James.

"Yes, oh yes," Jane averred. "Let's all try to think of a name."

"Fudge," suggested Isabelle. "He is the colour of the chocolate fudge mother used to make and it was so sweet we all loved it."

"Rusty," proposed Harry. "His colour is more like rust."

"Copper," proffered Jane. "It is very special and valuable."

"Those are three excellent suggestions," agreed their father. "James what would you like to call your new horse. Fudge, Rusty or Copper?"

"Crusty," replied James promptly.

Everyone laughed in delight. "Crusty," James reiterated.

"Well," said William. "I think you have made a good choice James. Crusty it is and your father has an extra special present for you now."

Henry went to William's wagon and came back with the little cart. He had made a leather harness to attach the cart to the horse and although the wheels were fixed solidly to the axle he had used leather brackets to hold the axle onto the base of the cart. Thus the whole axle moved round so that the wheels could move round too. Carefully, Henry attached the horse to the cart and put the completed model on the table. It was perfect and they all gazed at it in fascination.

James pushed and pulled his new toy backwards and forwards across the table top. "Thankou papa. Thankou." Carefully he said, "I am happy. I like it."

Jane beamed with pleasure. She had spent many long hours teaching him to say 'I' instead of 'me' and now at long last he appeared to have mastered it.

Both Henry and William realised that they had wasted enough time and went off to sort out their various tasks before lunchtime.

They had reached a dry riverbed that morning and made camp beside it. They had immediately set everyone digging for water in a likely spot in the middle of the riverbed.

Taking it in turn after breakfast, in between handing over James' gifts, and making sure that all the servants had time to sit and eat too, they each spent time digging and supervising the project. There was some ill feeling between the drivers, who felt that their superior position should excuse them from such menial labour, and the leaders, who felt they should be given an opportunity to rest after the morning walk. William had little patience with their bickering and pointed out harshly that finding water was absolutely essential and that they all had to assist because a small pool would be useless. There had to be enough water available to satisfy all the animals. He himself had a strenuous half hour session wielding the spade with vigour. He was thankful that he was still young and strong and that the weather was cool as he was soon sweating freely, but he revelled in the exercise. Infuriatingly, the others seemed to slow down and be more intent on watching him work, and he constantly had to nag them into continuing.

The oxen were straining to reach the water and wouldn't eat until their thirst had been satisfied, so they had been left in the yokes with two servants to each span holding them back. This cut down the number available for digging, but couldn't be avoided. On the plus side, it gave every man a change from digging.

Eventually, after all the water containers had been filled, the animals were led to the pool to drink.

CHAPTER 28

The children were happily playing with the new toys when the men returned after watching all the animals greedily slaking their thirst following the back breaking hours of digging in the heavy sand. Once they were sated they had been driven away to find some grazing. By late afternoon all the mud would have settled and baths would be possible for the first time in many days.

Everyone was feeling ready for a meal, having expended a great deal of energy in their various pursuits and there was the mouth watering expectation of a tasty mutton pie with gravy, pumpkin and sweet potato with rice, followed by jam tart. Lukas had excelled himself and the smell of the food wafting over from the cooking fire and the oven in the anthill set them all longing for the moment it would be served. Of course, there were hands and faces to be washed first now that there was plenty of water and then grace had to be said, so the meal wasn't imminent.

Isabelle chose this moment to boast to Harry about her own gift to James and by implication Harry's own failure to offer anything.

"James has been very lucky, hasn't he?" she goaded.

"Um," said Harry through the flannel he was using to wash his face.

"Well, he had a present from me and a present from Jane. Then he had 'Crusty' from Mr William and the lovely cart from father. That's four presents altogether." She looked at Harry and widened her eyes. "Didn't you want to give him a present?"

It was exactly the sort of opening Harry had been waiting for, as he had wanted everyone to be especially aware of his own gift.

"Isabelle." Father's gruff warning jolted her as she avidly watched Harry scrubbing his face dry. "Whether or not Harry has a gift for James is not your affair. We tried to keep the celebration a secret from the boys and now you are implying that Harry should have known all about it."

Isabelle blushed and hung her head. She still wanted to bait Harry, but she knew that she would be in trouble if she did. Quietly, she went to sit on her chair, but kept her eyes on Harry. To her amazement he was smiling broadly.

"I do have a present for James," he stated loudly and clearly. "I'll go and get it."

Harry's whole body was quivering with excitement now that the moment had arrived. He had wanted to offer his gift much earlier, but it hadn't been the right time, now everyone was watching him and would see that his present was as good as any of the previous gifts. Nimbly, he climbed into the family wagon and retrieved the basket from where he had hidden it beneath the bed. Proudly, he carried it outside and handed it to James.

"Here you are, James. This is my present for you."

James held the basket, his face puzzled. "Thankou, Harry."

Isabelle, who had felt piqued by Harry's claim to have a present after all, was ready to giggle at the thought of her baby brother having a basket as a present and even Jane was somewhat astonished at this idea of a suitable present. Henry wondered why Harry had chosen such a thing for a baby.

"Let me show you something James," Harry explained carefully. One by one, he picked up James' birthday toys. Each one fitted neatly into the basket. "There you are. Now you can carry all your toys together and keep them safe. There is even room for your hippo and a few other toys."

James was delighted. His toys were all quite light and he could carry the basket easily. He swung the basket to and fro and then carried it to his seat by the table so that he could keep all his precious gifts near him.

Henry coughed, embarrassed by his own lack of understanding, but feeling proud of his elder son. "That is a very thoughtful present, Harry. Yes, a very sensible gift. I commend you on your choice."

Harry beamed, his chest swelling with the feeling of having accomplished something worthwhile. The look he gave Isabelle seemed innocent enough but in his eyes was a smile of triumph. Harry liked to be a winner.

For three days, one of which was a Sunday, they camped beside the river. The presence of water made everyone happy and relaxed. The condition of all the animals improved with the rest and the opportunity to drink regularly, though the grazing was dry and sparse. The people were able to wash and even wash their clothes, which made them feel better as they changed their dust-charged garments for clean ones. It was necessary to dig out more sand from the pool morning and evening, which engendered more grumbling, but William and Henry ignored the protestations and both added their own labour to set an example.

The day of James' birthday celebration with the special food had boosted morale and Henry prayed fervently that the next three trying weeks would pass without any serious problems.

The forthcoming trek would be the hardest on the whole journey, with a scarcity of water, continued dry dusty vegetation and limited hunting. Despite this welcome break in their journey, the oxen would continue to lose condition. Limited opportunities to drink and a diet of hard dry grass that was little more than straw lacking any basic goodness would take its toll. There was nothing they could do except try to find a water hole as a goal at the end of each day. Food could become a problem if they were held up, so they would have to husband their resources. They would pass the small native villages of Molepolole and Kanye, then Molopo and Molito, where it might be possible to purchase a goat or some fowl, though villagers were naturally keen to keep their food supplies for themselves at this time of the year.

Fortunately, the presence of water had attracted some migratory animals. Bokkis came to tell Henry that he had seen some warthogs and a duiker, so on the second evening William, Henry and Bokkis lay in wait along the riverbank. They were taken by surprise when three giraffe appeared suddenly. Waiting and holding their fire, they watched as the wary animals approached the water. The large bull was unwilling to proceed and the two females stood uncertainly behind. Very slowly the larger of the females stepped forward and trod carefully along the sand. Knowing that he would never get a better opportunity then this, William fired. The bullet struck home and the stately beast fell kicking upon the sand. The other two disappeared with long loping strides.

"I know it might have been possible to shoot all three if I'd waited," William apologised to Henry, "but we don't really need all that meat and I knew I couldn't miss at this angle."

Henry was in full agreement, "It was a perfect shot and that one will provide us with enough meat for days. Do you think your baggage wagon can accommodate another skin?"

"It will be a tight squeeze, but I'm sure I'll manage it somehow."

Only Bokkis was unhappy with the result of their ambush. He hadn't been allowed to fire and if he had shot a giraffe he could have claimed the skin for himself. He resolved to come out later on his own and again at first light to see what he could kill. Even a warthog would provide him with a skin and tusks to sell.

To his delight, he shot not one but two warthogs the following morning and was especially pleased with his trophies. Henry was pleased for him as he had great respect for this driver and the extra meat was always welcome.

The next seventeen days were wearying for animals and people. The dust covered their clothes and when the gusts of wind caused little whirlwinds the dust got in their mouths and eyes.

Columns of dust rose in the air and whirled across the scrubby bush, fascinating the children and helping to break the monotony. These spirals of dust in the wind were known as 'dust devils'.

The days had an awful sameness about them, trekking, resting, doing lessons, walking, coping with the dust, managing without washing and facing the meals that were becoming more and more limited. There were no pumpkins left. Sometimes there was meat; sometimes it was just mealie porridge or rice with a few beans.

The children grew pale and developed coughs. William was troubled by boils and could no longer ride because of the pain. Henry was left to hunt with Bokkis, and the game remained scarce. The occasional duiker or steenbok with a few doves scarcely made a meal for the many hungry mouths and great was the rejoicing when Henry managed to bring down a kudu after a lengthy chase, but water, or rather the lack of it, was a persistent worry. The disturbing moaning of the oxen as they passed a second and third day without water was a constant upsetting irritant.

"When are we going to reach Kuruman, Father?" asked Isabelle as she sat toying with her food one lunch-time.

The others looked expectantly at Henry, waiting for his answer. Henry had been writing in his journal that morning as they were doing their lessons and he kept a record of the days. He looked at his younger daughter in surprise, "Finish your meal, Isabelle. I will answer your question when we have all finished eating."

Isabelle pouted. She didn't want to eat any more of the dry food, but she saw father watching her and forced herself to swallow another mouthful.

It was almost cold and totally unappetising. She wished Fox would come over to her side of the table so that she could slip some of it into his mouth, but he stayed resolutely beside William. Unhappily, she continued to put the smallest portions onto her spoon and then swallowed them quickly, pretending that she was eating something she really liked. Somehow, she managed to eat enough to satisfy Henry, who now picked up his journal.

"If the Lord continues to keep us in His care, we should be there in less than three days. There is no certainty about anything and we can only pray that we are able to do two or three treks each day. The oxen are very weary and we may have to travel more slowly, in which case it might take us a day or two longer. I expect us to be there before Harry's birthday, though," explained Henry.

Jane smiled and there was a great sigh of relief from William, who spoke for all of them, "I, for one, shall be relieved to reach Kuruman, where we can rest and recoup our energies. Perhaps the Rev Moffat will be able to cure these painful boils of mine. Life is very uncomfortable just now and I hate not being able to ride. Even walking is too much at times and I think Fox is in need of more exercise, but he insists on staying with me in the wagon."

Henry nodded in sympathy, "I hope you are continuing with the hot poultices. I was sure they would have encouraged the boils to burst by now. Perhaps they will this afternoon and then I have some soothing ointment you can apply."

William limped away and once again suffered the pain of a hot poultice across his thigh. To his great relief a short time later a mass of ugly, evil smelling pus oozed from each of the three bright red swellings and immediately there was an easing of the agony he had endured over the past days. Henry produced his soothing ointment and firmly bandaged the leg.

"There. It should heal properly very quickly. I'll put iodine on them this evening, but I think you need a rest from pain for this afternoon."

William smiled weakly, "Thank you, Henry. It's kind of you to give me a respite. It feels so much better already. I'll ride off now and see if I can discover some water for us. The oxen can't last much longer without and they won't eat until they can get something to drink."

Determinedly, and with only a fraction of the pain he had recently endured, William saddled his horse and with Fox eagerly trotting beside him he rode off. He took four of the servants with him so that they could cover the flanks and extend the area of search.

It was Amos on the right flank who discovered some brackish pools about three miles from their present camp. The water didn't look fit for people to drink, but it might satisfy the animals and it was the animals that were suffering most, as there was still a meagre supply of water in some of the containers for the people. William told Amos to remain where he was, saying that one of the other servants could lead his span for this trek. Then, wheeling his horse around, William galloped back to camp with the other searchers running easily alongside him. It was already late in the afternoon and it would take more than an hour to reach the water, but they might just reach it before dark.

William's return with the news was followed by the immediate bustle of striking camp. The oxen had remained yoked, lying down where they had been standing on arrival, with neither the energy nor the inclination to move, since there was no water nearby. Many of them were reluctant to rise, but the drivers and leaders shouted and cracked whips noisily and energetically until at last every ox was on its feet.

Slowly, agonisingly slowly, the great heavy wagons began to move. Henry prayed that the ground would remain firm and without too many ridges or deep, sandy riverbeds. The animals were struggling to keep the wagons moving and a patch of deep sand could prove an insurmountable obstacle whilst a dry riverbed would be even worse and bring them all to a standstill. If they could reach the pools this evening the animals' torment would be eased. Fortunately, Henry now had William to help him and one of them would always be in front to determine the best road, thus avoiding the worst pitfalls. The other could keep an eye on the following spans and ensure that a steady pace was maintained. Once the wagons were on the move, it was easier for the oxen to keep them moving at a regular speed and less of a strain on the animals.

During the days that William had been confined to his wagon, Henry had had to manage everything and the strain was beginning to tell on him. He had never been overweight, but now he was positively gaunt. Nevertheless, he disciplined himself to continue and took no rest from the constant supervision of servants and animals he deemed essential for the safety and wellbeing of them all.

Isabelle and James had decided to ride in the wagon on this occasion. Isabelle had been disgruntled at the thought of three more days trekking and hadn't been cheered by the news of water ahead, whilst James said he was too tired to walk. Isabelle hated the noise the cattle made and longed for it to stop, refusing to be comforted by Jane's explanation that the oxen would be happy once they had some water to drink. She cheered up a little when Jane offered her own doll, Elizabeth, for Isabelle to play with.

Jane and Harry thought it was much better to walk and try to keep warm. Because the air was cold, Jane had added her cloak over the shawl she had round her shoulders, but Harry didn't seem to feel the cold so much, although he was wearing a thick jacket over his warmest shirt. He was carrying his throwing sticks and from time to time would choose a target to aim at. Jane was impressed by his accuracy and with the speed of the sticks as they left his hand.

"I think it's going to be fun going to school in Cape Town," Harry confided, as they marched along behind the last of the wagons. "I shall have lots and lots of friends and we'll do exciting things."

"I hope you're right, Harry. I know you'll make a lot of friends, but you will have to be careful not to be too adventurous. You were always leading the Matabele herd-boys into mischief. I think you were fortunate that father never knew of most of your pranks."

"Oh, papa knows that boys have to have adventures. He wouldn't mind, I'm sure," Harry said nonchalantly.

"Well, you kept the escapades hidden from him. Shall I tell him about some of the things you did?" she added teasingly.

Harry looked at her in alarm. "No. That's not a good idea. I mean he really doesn't need to know about them now, he has other things on his mind. You don't mean it, do you?"

"No, of course not. Your secrets are safe with me. I was just trying to warn you that the masters at school might be just like father and you don't enjoy being beaten do you?"

"No," said Harry shortly. "You know, William told me that the boys at the schools in Cape Town play games. I shall enjoy those more than the lessons in the classroom."

"I expect you will, but you are good at lessons too. I wonder what a school in England will be like. Father said that there are a lot of children all in one room with a teacher and some monitors. Isabelle will come to school with me, I expect. I hope I can make some friends. I have never had a friend. Apart from Nomalanga, that is," she added hastily.

Just as Harry was preparing to throw one of his sticks again, a hare suddenly jumped up and set off through the scrub. Harry's reaction was automatic and his stick flew through the air, catching the hare a glancing blow on the back. It barely affected the animal's flight and it soon disappeared in the gathering dusk with Harry in hot pursuit.

"Harry. Stop. Come back here," Jane called urgently, but Harry was too excited to heed her warning. He stooped to pick up the stick he had thrown and then ran on.

Exasperated, Jane followed him and shouted again. This time there was a note of alarm in her voice because he was almost out of sight, the bush in parts being taller than he was. Jane continued to follow more slowly, "Harry. Harry," she called. Eventually she stopped, but continued to call, her heart thudding uncomfortably in her chest.

It was with the greatest relief that she finally spotted him moving, although he was heading in the wrong direction far over to her left. She walked forward to cut him off and berate him for his foolhardy action aware that the night was closing in and the cold was intensifying. When she reached him at last she grasped his arm roughly, "You really are very naughty," she scolded, shaking him hard as a relief for her own anxiety. "You know how easy it is to get lost in the bush. Some people get lost and are never found again."

She wasn't exactly sure of this last statement, but she thought she had heard someone say it perhaps to warn the children of the dangers of wandering too far from home.

"Come on now. We must hurry up and catch up with the others." Still clutching Harry's arm, she turned to see where the wagons were. Slowly, she looked first to the left and then to the right. Without being aware of it, night had taken them by surprise. She could see no further than a few feet in any direction and nowhere was there a sign of a wagon. Frightened now, she listened for the sound of the oxen moaning or the creaking of the wagon wheels. There was nothing.

"I'm sorry, Jane," mumbled Harry. "I just thought it would make papa happy if we gave him a hare for supper, but I don't think these sticks are heavy enough to kill a hare. I didn't miss though, did I?"

Distractedly, Jane agreed. "No, you didn't miss. Harry, can you see the wagons?"

Harry peered around; "No, it's too dark. We shall have to run to catch them up."

"Can you hear the wagons?" Jane asked fearfully.

"No, I can't. They are too far away, but we shall hear them when we run closer."

"Harry, I don't know which way to go. I followed you so that you wouldn't get lost. I walked away from the road and now I don't know where the road is."

Harry looked fearfully at his big sister, only now aware of their real problem. "Are we really lost?" Then he brightened. "Papa will find us. He won't let us be lost," he asserted confidently.

Jane knew that it would be difficult to find them at night. She didn't know how long it would be before father realised that they were missing. Even worse, she didn't know what to do.

CHAPTER 29

"What shall we do?" asked Harry, hopeful that Jane would be able to sort out the trouble they found themselves in.

Jane was trembling with fear, fully aware of the many dangers facing them. Trying to keep calm so that Harry wouldn't realise just how frightened she was, she said, "First, let us look all round and listen carefully. The wagons make a lot of noise or we might hear the sound of voices or the cracking whips." Solemnly, the two children turned round, straining their eyes and ears. There were no familiar sights or sounds, just the rustling of the bush that was never entirely silent. Night, with its clear, cold, star-studded sky above them, enfolded them. Soon the nocturnal creatures, such as the hare that had been the cause of their problem, would begin their hours of hunting. Jane shivered. She could hear Harry's teeth chattering.

"We shall have to keep ourselves warm," she advised him in her best grown-up voice. This decision helped her to control her mounting panic.

"If we jump up and down until we feel warm then we can wrap ourselves up in my shawl and cape. It will be hard lying on the ground and we need to be as close as we can to some bushes. The bushes will protect us a little from the cold weather." She rather hoped that wild animals wouldn't see them if they were close to a bush, but she didn't say this out loud.

They began to jump up and down.

"That's right. Swing your arms about too," Jane urged.

Harry began to laugh as he jumped and puffed.

"I can jump as high as you. Watch me."

They could hardly see each other as they continued to bounce about.

"I don't think I can do that any more," Jane confessed, at last feeling completely out of breath. "You are right. You can jump just as high as I can and I expect you can keep going much longer, but I think we'll wrap ourselves up and lie down now. I am feeling quite warm."

Jane took off her cape and shawl. She spread the shawl on the ground and when they were both lying on it she pulled it round them so that she was able to tie the ends together. It was mother's warm woollen shawl and easily wrapped around both children, though it only went as far as Jane's calf, leaving her feet exposed.

She pulled Harry's hat down as far over his head as it would go. It covered his ears and with his thick hair she knew that his head would be well protected. Then she made sure her own bonnet was firmly tied. The shawl was over their shoulders and would keep their necks warm, but she wished she had thought of giving Harry even warmer clothes. Finally she put her cloak over the top of them. The cape was much shorter than the shawl and Jane realized that her feet would soon become very cold. She curled up with her body surrounding Harry's and pulled the cape over their heads. She told him that their breath would help to keep them warm.

"I'm quite warm now," Harry complained and was about to put his head outside the cover when Jane stopped him.

"It's very important that we should be as warm as we can be now. It will get colder and colder all night."

"When will papa find us?"

"As soon as he knows that we are missing he will set off with Mr William and they will start to look for us," Jane assured him. She knew though that it would be almost impossible to find them in the dark and that it was most likely they would only be found the next day. A long silence followed this statement as Harry wondered whether or not they would be sleeping out here all night.

"I'm hungry and thirsty. We haven't got anything to eat have we?"

"No, we haven't. We'll just have to wait until father finds us. They will save some supper for us and we'll be able to tell them about our adventure." Jane tried to sound as if she was expecting father to arrive at any minute and that they were really playing a game of hide and seek. In reality, she knew that they were lying on the ground under a bush in the dark and couldn't possibly be seen unless the searcher tripped over them. She did know, however, that it would be dangerous for them to wander about and become even more lost by going further and further away from the road. They could easily fall in the dark and injuring themselves would only add to their problems. If they stood up and waited hopefully, they would just get colder and colder. Jane felt sure that lying down and trying to keep warm was the best thing to do.

It took Harry a long time to go to sleep. He was restless and kept wanting to throw off the cape, complaining bitterly about thirst.

Jane did her best to comfort him and after they had said their prayers she told him some of her favourite fairy stories so that his mind was occupied by more interesting thoughts. She succeeded in diverting him sufficiently to make him forget his thirst and hunger and his questions became less coherent as he slipped into sleep.

Eventually, he lay still and Jane felt a little relieved, although she felt more alone now that she had time to think of herself. Fervently, she prayed that God would look after them and that father would find them soon.

Telling the fairy stories and praying had kept her mind fully occupied, but now she became aware of the hard ground beneath them. The warmth created by their vigorous exercise had lasted throughout the story telling, but now Jane felt the cold seeping through the light covering and she knew that her feet were exposed, as they began to ache. She tried moving them and pulling her legs even higher up under the covers, but succeeded only in letting in the cold air. She was desperately uncomfortable and felt close to tears.

In her imagination the rustling sounds around them were magnified and she wondered if any of the big cats were around that night. She tried hard to remember what father had told her about lions and the other predators such as wolves. She thought she could hear feet padding towards them and the sound of snuffling as some creature came to sniff at this unusual bundle. She held her breath and tried to remain still. The sounds receded and presently, despite her fears and discomfort, she dozed.

* * * * * * *

It was with a feeling of great relief that William saw Amos waving to them. He wasn't much more than a shadowy figure in the dusk, but the oxen had already scented water. The speed of the wagons increased and the minute each driver came to a halt in line abreast the servants raced to release the oxen before they caused damage to themselves or the yokes and chains. There was no possibility of any human holding back the desperate animals as they lunged for the pools and stood knee deep in the dark-coloured liquid. Unconcerned with the smell, they slurped greedily until they had had their fill.

It was too late for them to be driven to seek grazing, so a kraal was hastily made with bushes uprooted and pushed together. It was a time-consuming task in the encroaching darkness. Meanwhile, Lukas had built a blazing fire and Isabelle, with James behind her, came to sit beside it to keep warm. Like Jane, she wore a cape over her shawl. She had wrapped James in a blanket, for he too was feeling the cold. Huddled together, they waited quietly for the evening meal.

Henry found them there when he returned from attending to the horses and helping William to supervise the fence round the kraal.

"Well, you two look nice and warm. Where are Jane and Harry?"

Isabelle looked round as though she hadn't noticed that the other two weren't there.

"I don't know, father. They weren't in the wagon with us because they wanted to walk. They said it was much warmer walking than sitting in the wagon. We haven't seen them for a long time."

Henry walked briskly round the wagons calling, "Jane. Harry. Where are you?"

He met William who, with Fox trotting beside him, was walking towards the fire ready to enjoy a warming brandy before eating his supper. William was feeling satisfied that the beasts were well watered as it was such a satisfactory ending to a day's trek and a wonderful time to relax.

"Have you seen Jane and Harry anywhere?" Henry demanded fearfully.

"No, not recently. I did ride all round the wagons soon after we set off to reach the water and saw them walking behind the last wagon. They were laughing and chatting and Harry had his throwing sticks with him. After that I stayed at the front."

He looked searchingly at Henry's worried frown, the firelight illuminating both faces.

"Oh, no!! They aren't missing are they?"

"I'm afraid they must be. I have searched all round the wagons and called them. There is no answer. I can't understand what has happened. Jane would never lose sight of the wagons and they are both capable of walking fast enough to keep up. I saw them after you had seen them as I was riding up and down each flank to make sure that all the oxen were pulling and that none was likely to collapse. I'm not sure how many times I saw them. It must have been at least four times." Henry paused, uncertain as to how to proceed.

William's leg was stiff and aching and he was feeling particularly weary after the lengthy ride following days of forced inactivity, but this was an emergency. All thoughts of resting quietly by the fire with a pre-prandial drink and revelling in a successful conclusion to the day's trek were forgotten. The most important task of all was to find the two missing children.

"I have two oil lanterns. I'll go and get them and my gun. We ought to fire off some shots as we always do if anyone fails to return to camp after dark. If the children hear the shots they can walk towards the sound. I'll get some of the servants to accompany us and we'll walk back along out tracks. They can't be far away. We only travelled about three miles altogether and if you saw them several times on the journey they must surely be within a mile, two at the most. Don't worry, Henry. They can't be far away." With these bracing words of encouragement, he walked off towards his own wagon to collect the lanterns and his gun.

Henry had lanterns of his own, but they only held candles and gave out less light than William's, nevertheless he went to light them and waited whilst William fired several shots into the air. The sound was sharp and clear. Henry prayed that the children could hear it, prayed that they would be able to follow the sound and would appear out of the bush.

"I'll tell Lukas to give the little ones something to eat and drink, shall I?" asked William, realising that Henry wasn't capable of making any decisions other than those concerning Jane and Harry.

"Oh. Yes. Yes, of course they must eat and then go to bed," Henry's reply was distracted as he gave his two lanterns to Bokkis.

William hurried over to the campfire. "Lukas, we are going to look for the other two children. It might take us many hours. I want you to make some food and drink for the two little ones here. Keep our stew warm and we'll eat later. Also, you must make another big fire back along the road we used when we came here. It will help us all to find our way back."

Walking over to the chairs where Isabelle and James were huddled, he smiled at them reassuringly. "Your father and I are going to find Jane and Harry. They seem to have got themselves lost somewhere and need our help to find their way back to the wagons. You will have to eat supper by yourselves. Isabelle, you must look after James and when you've had your supper you must go to bed."

Isabelle sat up straight. Mr William had spoken to her as if she was grown up and now she was responsible for James.

"I'll look after James and make sure that he eats his food. We'll remember to say our prayers, too. Should we say a prayer for Jane and Harry?"

William nodded gravely. "Yes, it would be a good idea to say a prayer for them. Goodnight."

"Goodnight Mr William," chorused two little voices.

It was with a heavy heart that William returned to the place where Henry and the drivers were waiting for him. The four lanterns seemed no more than minute specks of light, hardly illuminating the people who held them. The pitch black night and the rapidly dropping temperature caused his own spirits to drop. How could they possibly discover two small children in this endless bush? How could two small children survive this freezing weather, not to mention any other dangers? He had to avoid any suggestion of these depressing thoughts, however, so he increased his pace and spoke out cheerfully.

"Right. Isabelle and James will have supper and then go to bed. Lukas will make another large fire along this road just outside the camp so that we have a beacon to light our way home. I'll just fire another shot then we'll set off shall we?"

The four men set off in line abreast, each holding a lantern. There was no road, of course, so they had to constantly peer around ahead and to each side to discover the wagon trail. The ground was hard and only occasionally showed the wheel marks; broken bushes were a better indication, yet it was surprising how often these sprang up and resumed their previous shape unless they were actually snapped off.

It was slow and tedious work as they inched forward, stopping every few yards to fire another shot and to shout the children's names. More minutes would pass as they waited breathlessly for any response.

"Sounds travel a long way at night. Surely they can hear us?" Henry's fear caused him to sound irritable. "Where can they be? Why don't they reply?"

William didn't know how to reply to these desperate questions. None of them knew why the children were missing or didn't reply; they could only speculate. They might come up with numerous explanations, but none of them helpful to the present situation. Did it matter why they were lost or why they didn't reply? These were awful facts.

Would knowing the reason for them be helpful? William felt he was becoming more and more confused. The cold seeped through his clothing, his leg ached and he felt light-headed. He longed to be able to return to the camp, to the fire, to food, a warming drink and to his bed. From time to time he tried to persuade Fox to seek out the missing children, but the little animal stayed doggedly at his heels, just occasionally showing interest in noises only he could hear.

Henry had no intention of abandoning the search and constantly urged them forward, meanwhile shouting himself hoarse as they plodded step by step along the route they had taken so recently.

It was a shock for all of them when they reached their standing place of earlier that day. There was the burnt area where the fire had been. There was the cleared area where they had sat round the tables. Over beyond that was the place where the drivers had made their fire. Henry looked round in dismay. They had walked the whole three miles along the wagon trail and there had been no sign of the children. That could mean only one thing. The children had wandered away from the wagons and into the bush.

"There is no point in going any further, Henry. We must turn round and head back to camp." William's words were spoken quietly, but sounded loud in Henry's ears and he longed to deny them. Common sense prevailed as he stood there in the freezing darkness. Of course they must retrace their steps.

"Yes, all right," Henry mumbled as he rubbed his numb hands and arms, feeling the pain of the returning blood supply. "If we walk a little away from the road we might be able to find them," he suggested hopefully.

"I think we made enough noise to carry several hundred yards at least. If they had been within that distance they would have heard us and responded. We can shout and fire shots again on our return journey, but I think we must stay on the road and not wander off it. We really don't know which direction they have taken and we could spend hours getting ourselves further and further away from them."

Fox was sniffing all the remembered smells of people and food, but showed no sign of following any trail. William was disappointed, even though Fox had never been trained to follow a scent.

"Come on," he prompted Henry, who seemed to have become lost in a daze. "Let's move, before we all freeze."

"Will the children freeze to death?" Henry queried. "They have been out here for hours and are likely to be out all night. Can they survive?"

Once again William was being bombarded by unanswerable questions. He cast about in his mind for the most comforting words.

"They were both wearing warm clothes. Jane had on her cape as well as her shawl. They will find a sheltered place where they can keep warm. Don't worry, Henry, we'll find them as soon as it's light," he suggested. He wondered how truthful his last assertion had been and sighed at the frustration of being unable to do more.

The nightmare return journey was as fruitless as the outward one had been. The waving lights, the shouting voices, the fired shots produced no response. Totally defeated and downcast, they arrived back at camp. Lukas took one look at their slumped figures and grim looks and produced the hot food without making any comment. Henry was disinclined to eat, but William chivvied him into saying grace as usual and insisted that he should keep up his strength in order to conduct a lively search as soon as it was light. He added generous tots of brandy to their coffee, partly to help restore warmth to their frozen bodies and partly to help dull their sense of misery.

Neither man felt like conversing and both were exhausted, so they decided to retire as soon as the meal was finished. Henry was determined to pray for assistance in discovering the children safe and well, but he fell asleep after less than an hour, despite his best efforts.

On his way to his own wagon, William spoke to two of the young leaders, telling them that it was essential to maintain large fires all night and charging them with the task. They would have to find fuel and keep adding it to the fires surrounding the camp. Satisfied that he had done all that he could, he climbed into his wagon and was soon sound asleep, notwithstanding his aching leg.

CHAPTER 30

For several hours the two young leaders obeyed orders by staying awake and fulfilling their task of feeding fuel to the fires sited at various points round the camp. It was hard work chopping out small bushes and cutting them into pieces. Unfortunately, there were no large trees anywhere near that would provide heavy, slow-burning logs similar to the ones they had had in Matabeleland. These small, thin twigs with their dried leaves flared up with sudden bright flames and were consumed within minutes. By two o'clock in the morning the exhausted pair had wrapped themselves in their blankets and fallen sound asleep beside their friends. The flames of the fires diminished until there was nothing more than a pile of dry white ash overlying the red embers.

More than two miles away Jane awoke suddenly. A small creature, a shrew or a mouse perhaps, ran under the cape that was covering her and tried to thrust its way into the shawl that was wrapped about both children.

Some larger creature possibly hunting its supper came sniffing and scrabbling at the bundle lying on the ground where its prey had sought refuge.

Confused, Jane thought that it was Isabelle who had disturbed her and she mumbled her protest. "Oh stop it, Isabelle. Lie still and go to sleep." The little creature that had invaded their cover began to wriggle even further across her body and Jane was suddenly wide awake. Petrified, she lay motionless until the hunter moved away disturbed by her voice and the smell of humans. Jane listened to the retreating sounds and became aware of Harry lying still beside her. He was making a funny deep breathing sound and felt cold to her touch. She tried shaking him, but there was no response and her arm dislodged the mouse from its perch on top of her. The creature escaped by running the full length of her body and she could feel its tiny feet pressing down in its urgency to depart even through her thick clothing. She didn't know whether to laugh or cry, confused and worried as she was. Her feet were numb and her arms felt as if they belonged to someone else. Her mind began to wander and she could see mother working in the little room father had built for the Sunday school children beside the church. It doubled as a classroom during the week, but the pupils were nearly always just the children of the missionary families once the presents for attendance that had attracted the Matabele pupils had ceased.

Mother was trying to say something to her and it sounded very important. It was something about the birds. They had seen a lot of swallows that day wheeling and flocking around the mission buildings. Jane concentrated on her mother's voice, "You see, Jane, these birds don't like the cold weather. When we have our summer they come here to enjoy the warm sun, but when we have our winter they fly back to England so that they can have warm weather again. Little birds like that would freeze to death if they stayed here in winter. They cannot live in cold weather."

All was silent again and mother's voice faded from Jane's mind. 'Why was it important to listen? What was mother trying to tell her?' Perhaps if she went to sleep again she would remember when she woke up. She often remembered things more clearly in the morning. It didn't feel as cold now as it had done earlier, but she still couldn't feel her feet. Should she rub them? She really didn't have the energy. Harry was still making that funny sound and when she forced herself to touch him he didn't stir. She was surprised how cold he felt. She moved her hand towards his face and that was just as cold as the rest of him.

'Little birds cannot live in cold weather. They freeze to death.'

For some reason mother's voice echoed through her brain. "We're not birds," she cried out suddenly. "We're children, we won't freeze to death."

The sound of her own voice and the meaning of the words she had spoken aloud roused Jane from her stupor. Perhaps mother wanted to warn her that Harry was freezing to death just like a little swallow. What should she do? She was nine years old, almost grown up, she must save him.

Struggling against lethargy, the shawl, cape and her own frozen limbs, Jane rolled over. It took her several minutes to raise herself up into a sitting position and when her head broke out from underneath the cape she gasped at the rawness of the air. Her face felt torn by it and she had to inhale in tiny shallow breaths to avoid the tearing pain in her throat.

Trying to stand up was the most difficult task she had ever encountered. Her feet were numb and wouldn't obey her. She tried kneeling and began to rub her arms and legs briskly. Lying down again, she bent her legs and rubbed her ankles, moving her feet up and down. The pain of the returning feeling had her sobbing until her tears began to freeze and she used the shawl to wipe her face dry. Determinedly, she struggled to her feet and then stamped up and down, meanwhile calling to Harry.

As her own circulation was restored and she was able to move more easily, she bent over him and began to rub his arms and legs vigorously.

Despite the agony she felt in her own limbs, she rubbed and slapped and shouted at her little brother, pummelling him in desperation. Her actions became even more ferocious as her terror increased. He was alive. He was breathing. He just had to wake up. Jane became more and more convinced that she had to wake him up to save him. Rolling him over, she beat frantically on his back and then tried to lift him up onto his knees.

She was almost at the limit of her own strength when she noticed an easing in his breathing and a slight stirring of his arms as if he fought to push her off. Encouraged, she doubled her efforts and was finally rewarded by a furious exclamation, "Stop that."

Relieved, she staggered to her feet and, grabbing hold of Harry's right hand, she tugged hard. "Stand up, Harry. Stand up now. It's very important."

Harry responded by dragging his hand away. "Don't want to. Too tired. Leave me alone."

Having convinced herself that they needed to move and keep warm in order to stay alive, Jane refused to give up. "I shall smack you, Harry, until you do stand up. I told you it was important. STAND UP NOW."

It took many more threats and efforts at persuasion before Harry finally staggered to his feet and began to move his feet up and down as Jane was doing.

Once he was more fully awake, and with Jane dancing around him, Harry joined in with the game and as he gradually became more active so his actions were livelier. As they jumped and twirled, Jane scanned the night sky for signs of a fire and listened for sounds of a human presence. Sadly she could detect neither. They kept up their antics for almost half an hour, by which time they both felt warmer but also drained of energy.

"I think we should sit down now," Jane suggested. "We won't lie down because the shawl won't cover my feet and they get very cold. If we sit up and I pull my knees up I can wrap the shawl right round my legs and even over my feet. We can tell each other stories so that we will stay awake."

Jane's idea worked perfectly for nearly two hours before exhaustion overcame them both and once again they slept.

* * * * * * *

When Henry woke he realised that it was still very early, still dark. He knew instinctively that he would get no more sleep that night and as he had been too tired to undress the night before he immediately left the wagon, determined to resume the search for his children. He made his way towards the faint glow of the cooking fire, dismayed to see that it was no more than a heap of almost dead ashes. Turning full circle, he scanned the campsite and with no sign of firelight anywhere he realised that all the fires had been allowed to die back. Hurriedly, he grabbed some branches Lukas had left stacked ready for use and, breaking off the smallest twigs with some dried leaves attached, he thrust them gently into the centre of the warm mass, coaxing the red sparks to ignite by blowing lightly on them. The smoke caught in his throat and he coughed irritably, but he was encouraged by the glow spreading across the leaves.

"Keep going, Henry. You're doing a good job there."

William's voice startled him as Fox came snuffling at his heels.

"I left strict instructions for all the fires to be kept going all night. Those young varmints were supposed to take it in turns to supply fuel and feed the flames. I suppose they all fell asleep."

Henry's efforts were proving successful, as a small flame appeared and then another. By judiciously adding twigs, the flames were tempted to strengthen and soon it was possible to add one or two thicker ones until the fire readily took hold.

"It's almost light enough for us to set out," Henry announced hopefully, looking at the eastern horizon where there was just a slight tinge of grey.

"I want Lukas to have some hot water ready for when we bring the children back. They will need to be kept warm and to have hot sweet drinks. We need to set up a good windbreak here with two fires across the front so that there is a warmed space where they can sit. We'll get everything ready before we go to save time on our return."

William had the deepest sympathy for Henry in his present predicament and fully understood his desperate need to be positively active. Although understandably he himself wasn't as distraught as Henry was, nevertheless he, too, was deeply disturbed. The children had been part of his life for weeks now and had almost become members of his family. The thought of losing them was a thought too horrific to contemplate. He could only hope that the day wouldn't turn out to be one of tragedy, as he feared it might. He went to rouse the servants and with some of them to help him he began to erect the windbreak by piling bushes together as a thick, high fence curved into a tight arc and with two fires laid ready at the open end.

'It looks a bit like a horseshoe, let's hope it's a lucky one,' he thought inconsequentially.

Then he spoke to Henry, "I think it might be a good idea to make two beds here. It will be warmer for the children than just sitting in chairs and this area can be made warmer than the wagon," he suggested. "I'll bring some of my blankets and pillows. I think I'll bring the tarpaulin off one of the baggage wagons, too, to make sure this windbreak really does keep the warmth in."

As the cold night faded and damp, chill greyness surrounded them, Lukas supplied everyone with hot coffee then lit the two fires in front of the windbreak, taking care to keep the flames well away from the interlaced twigs making up the hedge. The tarpaulin, thrown over the thick hedge inside the arc, covered the back third, and the two beds, consisting of piles of blankets on two straw mattresses, were prepared immediately in front of it. It would never be really warm in this little cell, but the chill was taken from the air and the fires gave it a semblance of cheerfulness.

Amos was detailed to stay behind and keep the fires well supplied with fuel as the others crowded round waiting for instructions. William went to saddle the horses. He picked up two warm blankets and, rolling them up, gave one to Henry. "They'll need to be kept warm on the ride back," he advised cheerfully, determined to remain optimistic.

Henry took charge and instructed Abdol to carry a long stick with a cloth attached to the end rather like a flag. He was to walk along the wagon tracks so that everyone could keep line abreast with him and not wander off course. He and William would be on horseback at the end of each line, one to the east of the road and one to the west, with five or six men spread out between them and Abdol. From the height of the horses' backs they should be able to see all the way along the line to the flag in the centre. With a space of three yards between each man they would be able to cover more than twenty yards.

When they were all ready, but before the order to move had been given, William rode up to Henry. "I think we must spread out even further. I'm sure they will have wandered more than twenty yards off the road. If they had been as close to the road as that they would have heard us last night. We shall just be wasting our time if we cover such a small area."

Henry looked at him speculatively then glanced at the lines. With something like resignation, he nodded.

"Yes, you're right. I'm sure they are much further away from the road. Perhaps we should have just one long line instead of two smaller ones, but I had hoped to cover both sides of the road, as we don't know which side they might have taken. What do you suggest?"

"Well, if you ride parallel to Abdol, perhaps twenty to thirty yards away or even more if you can still see him and then we spread out all the others beyond that with me at the far end, we should be able to cover at least a hundred yards. We will walk for two miles and then return on a parallel course another hundred yards further east. If we have been unlucky, we'll do the same on the western side."

Henry agreed readily, impatient now to make a start. At his signal, Abdol began to walk along the wagon track that was rather more easily seen in the emerging day, holding his flag aloft.

Henry kept station almost forty yards away, with the next searcher several yards to his right. He couldn't see William. As they all began the walk northwards, the drivers began to chant. It was a repetitive sound and the sonorous rhythm carried through the chill air as they took regular stamping steps forward, their eyes searching the bush on either side, as well as the ground beneath their feet, for any signs of a human presence. Henry would have preferred an uplifting hymn to cheer his spirits but he recognised the need of the servants to express their own feelings. He began to pray as he scanned the bush all around.

William's heart was heavy as the minutes wore on. The longer it took to find the children the colder they would be and the less likely they would be to survive. If they were still alive. No one had even dared to suggest the possibility of predatory animals discovering a very easy meal. It was true that they hadn't heard lions roaring for the past few nights and their own lack of success when out hunting indicated that game was scarce in the area. Big herds would have sought out places where they could find water and grazing and the predators followed the herds. William wondered if his reasoning was nothing more than wishful thinking, there were always lone animals excluded from the pride. When he had persuaded Henry to have one extended line had he made a mistake? He had been guessing that the children would be further from the road. It had seemed to make sense when he suggested it but now he began to have doubts. What if they were really on the western side of the road and the searchers were wasting valuable time?

It was Fox that made the discovery. Half an hour after they had left camp and almost at the point where they were considering turning round, Fox left his place alongside Diamond and raced headlong through the bush to the front and then to the right.

He disappeared from sight and William wondered if he should follow when he heard the dog's excited barking some distance away.

"He's found something. I wonder what it is?"

Fox was an excellent rat catcher, but he had been trained to stand by his master and not interfere with the hunting when they were out with the guns, although he would put up game when ordered to. He would happily chase anything that moved if he was allowed to do so.

William carefully rounded a particularly thorny bush and headed towards the sound of Fox's continuous yelps that were coming from a distant area.

When William finally found him, Fox was underneath a bush out of sight, but readily heard. William dismounted, approaching the bush with caution in case there was a creature at bay. He forced up the lower branches slowly, peering into the gloom beyond. What he saw caused him to yell with sheer joy and thankfulness.

"It's them. It's the children. Thank God. Oh Fox, you wonderful dog." William backed out and yelled at the top of his voice, "Here. They're here. Everybody, come."

The cry was taken up, and resounded through the chill morning air until Henry understood what the shouting meant. Following the running figures, he urged his horse towards the end of the line and far beyond. Eventually, he reached the spot where the searchers crowded around, gabbling excitedly, and William was lifting Jane out from under the bush. Wrapping her in the blanket he had unrolled, he lifted her gently into Henry's arms.

"She's still asleep," he whispered. "I'll get Harry now."

Taking the blanket from Henry's saddle, he bent down once more and crawled under the bush. The other searchers flocked round, chattering delightedly and congratulating each other on the success of their mission, clapping their hands and executing celebratory jumps or stamps. They peered at Jane's face and noticed her breathing and their exclamations grew louder. All thoughts of hunger, tiredness and cold were forgotten as the success cheered them all.

Feeling the coldness of his daughter's body, Henry knew that this was no ordinary sleep. His worst fears that they might not be alive had thankfully proved to be unfounded, but this deep unnatural sleep was familiar to him and he was fully aware of the dangers it posed. Many times as he was growing up in Yorkshire, Henry had known, or heard of, people and animals caught out in the winter snows. Some froze to death, but occasionally a few were saved and even recovered from this sleep that was so close to death.

He had learned from wise old shepherds and experienced farmers that it was a mistake to try to heat up the cold creatures too quickly. They had learned from their forebears or sometimes discovered to their own sorrow that trying to warm up someone as cold as this too quickly was as fatal as leaving them in the cold.

They had to be kept warm and if they could be kept alive with steady warmth all the time they would eventually recover, though it might take hours or even days. The warm area back at the camp, protected from the cold but not hot, was ideal and as William emerged with Harry wrapped tightly in a blanket Henry congratulated him on his success.

"Thank you, William. There's no time to waste, though. I hope we're in time to save them, but it will be a close thing. They might still die. We have to keep them warm, but not too hot. They need to be kept in that windbreak at camp until they wake up."

William looked sharply at Henry, as he had not realised there was still danger for the children. He made no response, but showed his dismay as he handed Harry to Bokkis and remounted hurriedly. Then, reclaiming the child, he set the horse in motion. With hope in their hearts, but not daring to celebrate too soon, the two riders with their precious burdens hurried back to camp.

Fox, having been quickly patted and thanked by William, ran proudly beside Diamond holding his head and tail high.

The searchers on foot ran and raced each other through the bush, raising their voices in gleeful shouts, their spirits raised by the success of their venture and anticipating a reward for their diligence.

Bokkis trotted easily beside Henry and suggested that an ox be slaughtered to celebrate the safe return of the missing children. The drivers and leaders had gladly given their time not only last night, but this morning, too, even without breakfast.

Lost in his own thoughts and wrapped in anxiety, Henry felt some irritation that such a topic should be raised. With the knowledge that either or both of the children might still die he was not prepared to celebrate and order a feast. He was about to speak sharply to Bokkis and tell of the danger facing the children, but he found he couldn't speak. He nodded his head instead and rode grimly onward.

CHAPTER 31

When Isabelle woke up she was astonished to find that only she and James were in the wagon. She lay for a time, thinking about it. She remembered bringing James to bed and then remembered that father and Mr William had gone out to look for Jane and Harry because they were lost. They hadn't come back and father wasn't here either. It was very quiet outside. Perhaps everyone was lost. What if they were all alone in the world? She managed to frighten herself with this thought and turned to look at James, who was still sleeping peacefully. Because she needed to have someone to talk to and because she needed to find out what was going on, she shook James impatiently. James fought against the hands that were pinching his shoulders and muttered fretfully. Isabelle continued to push and shake her brother.
"Come on, we must get up," she commanded in a loud voice.
James was still only half-awake. "It's cold. Don't want to get up."
He pulled the blankets up over his head.
Isabelle took no notice of his protests. She pulled herself out of bed and began to dress hurriedly. Once she was dressed, she gave her hair a few strokes with the brush so that it was away from her face and put on her bonnet, then she dragged the covers away from James. He squealed with fury and tried to grab them back again, but Isabelle held them out of his reach.
"I told you it was time to get up, James. Jane and Harry are still lost. It is so quiet outside I think everyone must be looking for them. Come on, we had better see if we can help."
Subdued by the seriousness of Isabelle's voice and fearful of what it might mean if Jane and Harry weren't found, but not really understanding the gravity of the situation, James allowed himself to be dressed and have his hair brushed. The two children then climbed out of the wagon.
There was no one in sight. Lukas and Amos were away collecting more fuel for the fires and the searchers had not yet returned. Isabelle gazed around, bewildered, believing that her thoughts had become reality.
"Father," she called hesitantly.
"Papa," piped up James in a fearful voice, already affected by the strange stillness around the normally cheerful bustling camp.
Hand in hand, the two children moved cautiously towards the cooking fire.
They suddenly became aware of a strange phenomenon. It was the unexpected appearance of a tarpaulin-covered hedge, which had sprung up since they had eaten supper before going to bed the previous night.

Investigating this odd discovery, they found a warm area a bit like a room, produced by the protective windbreak, with two fires close by the opening and containing two blanket-covered beds. With no one around and nothing else to do, they began to play on the beds, jumping up and down and rolling about in the blankets, delighted to have a warm, sheltered place to play.

So engrossed were they in their game that they failed to hear the arrival of the search party, despite the joyful chattering and shouting as the servants headed for their own breakfast fires.

It was the appearance of father carrying Jane, followed by Mr William carrying Harry, at the opening of the windbreak that brought them to a halt, and silently they crept away from the beds. Wide-eyed, they watched as the two cold little bodies were laid gently on the beds. Father was too engrossed with his task to spare time for either of them and they remained quietly watching.

"Right. Now we must take off their cold damp shoes and rub their feet and legs," Henry instructed William, suiting the action to his words. "The temperature in here is about right, warm but not hot." He continued to rub Jane's feet and legs until he could feel that they were a little less icy. Covering her feet, he proceeded to rub her hands and arms.

"Now we must add some warmed blankets and then rub their feet again."

So saying, he took a blanket and held it in front of the fire until it was warm. Faithfully, William copied Henry's actions and once the warmer blankets had been added they began to rub the children's feet again.

Time seemed to cease as they worked, alternatively warming the blankets and rubbing arms or legs.

William could see no improvement in Harry's condition and began to despair. Henry did his best to encourage him. He felt Harry's feet and said he thought they were not as cold as they had been earlier.

"We cannot cease our efforts. I know our prayers will be answered. Both children are still alive and soon they will begin to feel warmer."

Noticing Isabelle and James still hovering apprehensively close by, he addressed his younger daughter, "Go and ask Lukas to make us some hot coffee. We shall be busy for a long time yet. You had better have your breakfast, too."

Isabelle looked up into her father's pale, strained face and nodded her head, then dared to ask in a frightened whisper, "Are they going to go to heaven, like mother?"

Henry was shocked into silence for several moments. He had a constant, nagging, subconscious fear that the children might not recover, but he refused to even contemplate the idea seriously, still less acknowledge it to others. He had to remain positive for all of them.

His reply was gruff and brusque, "No, of course they aren't. Now off you go."

Isabelle scuttled out, closely followed by James.

As the morning wore on a watery sun made its appearance. Though it had no real warmth to offer, the temperature rose a little. Henry and William took a short break from their gruelling task and ate the fried mealie cakes and beans Lukas brought for them, with some strong black coffee.

"We are close to Kuruman now," Henry remarked wearily. "We could ride there with the children when they wake. It is less than three days journey with the wagons but a horse could cover the distance in a few hours. It wouldn't be good for the children to be out here in the open all night and the temperature in the wagon isn't any better."

William nodded thoughtfully. "Do you think they will be well enough to face the ride?"

"There isn't a great deal of choice. They should be kept in a warm room so that the temperature remains stable and where they can be kept warm all the time. We cannot do that here and if the temperature falls as low as it did last night they would suffer a great deal. We'll wrap them up warmly and ride as quickly as we can, so that we'll be in Kuruman before dark. We might have to stay there the night unless you can find your way back here by starlight. This room might be warmer than the wagon, so Isabelle and James can sleep in here if Lukas and Amos keep the fires going."

With that decision made, the men resumed their efforts and were rewarded shortly after mid-day when both children appeared to be sleeping normally. The icy cold feeling of their limbs had disappeared to be replaced by a slightly chilled one.

Able to relax a little, William went round to check on the oxen and wagons. Whilst he was there the drivers again approached him and asked him to provide them with an ox for a celebration now that the children had been found. They were supported by the young leaders and other servants all eager to feast on meat.

William stopped to have a discussion with them. He agreed that a celebration was in order and that they all deserved a reward for their endeavours to find the missing children.

He then pointed out that they still had to journey several miles to reach Kuruman and that all the oxen were needed to pull the wagons.

When it was argued that there was still one extra beast and that could be slaughtered without diminishing any of the spans, William shook his head firmly.

"We need to keep all our oxen. It would be foolish to kill that one. Who knows what will happen on the next part of our journey?" he reasoned, but he could see that all the servants were disinclined to listen to him. They wanted meat and wouldn't be appeased. There was an unhappy muttering and he could distinguish some of the objections amongst the general grumbling.

"We can't work on children's food."

"We are men. Men need meat. We need meat now."

"We refuse to work if we don't get meat."

"We are hungry for meat."

Realising that there was real trouble brewing and knowing that he and Henry were going to be away for several hours, William had to find an immediate solution. It would be disastrous if an ox was slaughtered whilst they were away and these people were in the sort of reckless mood to do just that.

"All right. Listen to me," he called above the clamour.

"The best idea is for some of you to go out hunting," he interjected swiftly as he felt the anger rising. "Bokkis is a fine shot and I'm sure he will provide something for the larder. I will give him some lead bullets and powder. I will also give out two more muskets with powder and shot. You must decide who amongst you is a successful hunter. If you go out now you could have enough meat for a real celebration tonight. Furthermore, whatever animals you kill are yours, the meat, the skins, horns or tusks."

Bokkis fully supported William's suggestion for he was delighted at the opportunity to go out hunting with the prospect of obtaining trophies to sell as well as meat to eat. He expressed his wholehearted agreement of the plan in a loud voice, urging others to accept the offer. As he continued to assert his pleasure at the thought of a successful hunt, the grumbling subsided and Bokkis went to collect his weapon.

Somewhat mollified, the rest of the crowd followed William to his wagon and were handed the promised weapons with sufficient powder and shot. There was a slight altercation amongst several hopeful hunters, but common sense prevailed, for they all knew who was the best and most accurate shot. Lukas was one of the lucky ones.

Jubilant now in anticipation of a feast, they dispersed, a few carrying axes and knives were to accompany the hunters as bearers, one or two of the youngest were delegated to find fuel for the festive fires, whilst the others planned to while away the hours smoking or sleeping until the hunters returned

Relieved that the situation had calmed down and that everyone had accepted his decision, William returned to the windbreak, where he found Jane and

Harry sipping warm sweet tea.

Both children were very pale and needed to be helped by Henry and Isabelle to sit up a little, but they were fully conscious. The warm, sweet liquid was no doubt helping their recovery, but they were both shivering and William immediately took the top blankets to warm at the fire.

Once these had been wrapped around Jane and Harry and their shivering had eased, William recounted his confrontation with the servants.

"I knew we couldn't slaughter an ox, though it was impossible to explain it to them in a way that was acceptable. An animal is food as far as they are concerned and food is one of life's basic needs, so animals must die and no further thought is necessary. I suppose we all have those basic thoughts."

"Yes," agreed Henry. "If we were starving and there was no alternative, I would fully endorse that attitude. As it is we still have mealie meal and dried beans, so we won't starve. In any case, we should arrive at Kuruman in three days at the most and then there will be ample food for all of us. I suppose three days is too long for them to wait? They all know, though, that the wagons can only move with a full span of oxen and none can be sacrificed just to provide a celebration meal. How did you manage to resolve the impasse, or is there still a problem?"

"Well, of course, they pointed out that we still had one extra beast, so the spans wouldn't be affected, though they would be happy to abandon a wagon if it meant they could feast on meat. They were unwilling to accept that we might still need that ox in case of accidents. As we would have been without drivers or leaders if their demands had been ignored, I had to think of a solution immediately. I offered them guns and ammunition and told them to go and hunt for some meat.

Bokkis was delighted at the suggestion and his enthusiasm encouraged some of the others to think that they could provide the necessary meat. I can only pray that they are as successful as they expect to be."

Henry was filled with relief and immediately congratulated William.

"That was quick thinking and a most sensible solution. I'm glad you were there instead of me. I would have been much too engrossed with family affairs to even consider their importuning and yet I do try to understand this constant need for meat. I think I might have been less than sympathetic and ordered them to wait until tomorrow, when we can go out hunting. I do know that I wouldn't have satisfied them as you have. If you are ready now, I think we should all have something to eat, and then we will ride to Kuruman."

After they had been fed some hot sweet mealie porridge, into which a few raisins had been dropped, Jane was given her warm, dry boots and shawl and

Harry was helped into his warm, dry boots and jacket. Once fully dressed, they were wrapped up completely in warmed blankets. They were both quiet and listless, barely aware of their surroundings and content to be helped with every task.

Henry suddenly thought to tell Isabelle what was planned. "We are going to take Jane and Harry to Kuruman so that the Reverend Moffat and his wife can look after them. You and James are to stay and play in here. Amos will make sure that you are safe. After supper you may sleep on these beds until we return. Is that understood?"

"Yes father," Isabelle agreed solemnly. "I'll look after James. We'll stay here."

William had saddled both horses and now brought them as close to the windbreak as he could. Neither horse liked the fires, and shied away, but they were willing to halt several yards round the hedge, with the fires out of sight.

Lukas and Bokkis were both away hunting, so it was Amos who carried Harry out and handed him up to William, as Henry lifted Jane up to his own saddle and then mounted behind her.

Isabelle heard the horses gallop away and then she and James went to collect their toys and books from the wagon. She felt quite grown up as she helped her little brother to find his basket of toys, and then helped him to climb down to the ground, but as the hours passed by, she couldn't help wishing that there was a grown-up to help her. James kept asking for food and something to drink. She managed to find a water bottle with some water in the bottom, and that kept them both happy for a time.

"I could go and look near the cooking fire for some food," she suggested.

James thought this was a good idea and the two of them walked carefully round the fires in front of the windbreak across the bare earth to the cooking area.

There were pots, pans and the large kettle standing on the ground near the fire, which had died down to little more than a pile of ashes. The children bent to look hopefully in the pots, but they were empty. There was no food in sight. James looked up at Isabelle in dismay and unfortunately took a step backwards right into the fire. His little boot sent up a shower of sparks that landed on his dress.

Isabelle grabbed his arm and dragged him forward, but not before the red spot at the hem brightened and glowed, eating greedily at the material like a caterpillar.

Amos, returning with an armful of small branches, immediately dropped his burden and ran over to beat out the glowing cloth that was about to burst into flames. His quick action saved James from injury and his clothing from destruction, but both children were exceedingly frightened by Amos' sudden exclamation and shout of warning, as well as the way he beat so frantically at the cloth.

Subdued, with the smell of burning cloth in their nostrils, they returned to the windbreak and Isabelle did her best to try to disguise the brown singe mark with dust. She hoped the nasty little incident would remain a secret, terrified that father would learn about her disobedience.

"We'll have something to eat later," she promised James, and gave him a big hug. "If you sit quietly now, I'll read you a story."

CHAPTER 32

In his diary, Henry described the stressful journey from their camp by the brackish pools of water to Kuruman, as gruelling and wearisome. It had taken them more than four hours, including the two brief stops they had made in order to rest the horses.

On both occasions they had fortunately discovered some pools of water in otherwise dry riverbeds. Being able to halt by water was a profound relief, as it enabled the horses to slake their thirst. The two men had found the most sheltered spots close to the river banks. In the warming sunshine they sat holding the children whilst their mounts foraged hopefully amongst the dry, brown grass. Surprisingly, it was still light as they finally made the approach to Kuruman.

"Praise be to God," Henry exclaimed reverently, as the buildings of the Reverend Robert Moffat's famed missionary station appeared in the distance.

"Amen to that," William added fervently, his arms aching from holding onto Harry whilst keeping a firm hand on the reins. William was young and normally very fit, but he had recently been suffering from boils and this had weakened his strength, so that the early morning search, followed by hours of continuous caring, had fatigued him almost beyond endurance.

Added to this was the pain he suffered as a result of Harry's body pressing against his thigh. There was nothing he could do about this except accept it stoically. It would have been easier if Harry could have ridden behind him, but the boy was too weak and in any case it was essential to keep him warm and fully wrapped up in a blanket.

They were fortunate enough to find Robert and Mary both in residence and were welcomed with great hospitality, being ushered into the warmth of the house without ado by Mary whilst Robert arranged for the horses to receive attention. Their host and hostess looked anxiously at the two pale, blanket-wrapped children. They were obviously concerned for them and waited patiently for enlightenment. As soon as Henry had described the events of the previous twenty-four hours, Mary Moffat took over.

A large fire was made in the fireplace in one of the bedrooms and whilst that room was heating up the children were seated in the kitchen, the warmest room in the house, where they were pampered and cosseted with mugs of hot, sweet, milky tea before being fed some hot meat broth.

Neither Jane nor Harry had spoken much since their rescue and Henry had avoided asking questions, as he was mindful of their precarious condition.

Even now they spoke no more than the odd polite word, quietly thanking Mrs Moffat for the food, but they both looked considerably more alive than they had done throughout the day.

Once they had eaten, and with the sheets and blankets on their beds thoroughly warmed, the children were put to bed, where they promptly fell asleep.

Mary was in her element and immediately accepted the responsibility of caring for the children for as long as necessary, whilst Henry thankfully relaxed, feeling that he had done his duty. The children were now in the best place and would, God willing, make a full recovery.

He had no worries about the horses either, as they were being cared for by a Bechuana youth who had been well trained by Robert. They would be rubbed down, covered with horse blankets and well fed.

William and Henry had been given hot drinks almost as soon as they had arrived and stood drinking them whilst warming themselves by the fire as the Moffats busied themselves with the children. Robert, having given both children a careful examination, declared that they would soon recover from their ordeal if they rested quietly and ate well during the next few days. He didn't think they would need any tonic or other medicine.

Henry handed over the letter that John Moffat had given him to bring and explained that the family would soon be fully recovered and able to make the journey south. The Moffats were obviously disappointed to learn that their son and his family had been prevented from making the journey with Henry due to ill health, but were reassured that they were now recovering and would travel as soon as they felt able to face the journey.

Very soon the travellers were given an opportunity to bath in steaming hot water before everyone sat down to a substantial meal. Robert and Mary tactfully refrained from mentioning Henry's recent bereavement, knowing that this was to be a very brief visit and that the children's welfare was paramount in Henry's mind. They had no desire to add to his distress. The visitors were able to give a good account of the younger Moffats during the meal, which satisfied the parents, and once the meal was over they pronounced themselves fit to make the return journey, despite the fact that it was now fully dark.

William had feared that he would disgrace himself by falling asleep as he revelled in the wonderful luxury of a hot bath followed by a dinner that rivalled that of a fine hotel, but he had managed to concentrate on the conversation sufficiently to stay awake and agreed with Henry that they needed to return to their camp that evening.

If either of them was daunted by the thought of yet another long ride, neither of them admitted it and if there was just a hint of drowsiness it was dispelled the moment they stepped out of doors into the brisk chill of another very cold night.

Robert insisted on providing them with fresh horses.

"There is room in my stable for your two and they need a few days' rest with some good grain, by the look of them," he remarked, as he eyed them critically. "I have two that are suitable and I'll send one of my Bechuana friends to act as a guide. It would be unpleasant, not to say possibly disastrous, if you two were to be lost in the bush. I know how easily it is done however good you may be at navigating by the stars. God be with you," he added as the men mounted and rode away, their thanks and blessings carried back to him on frozen breath.

They rode, heads bent and in silence, for nearly an hour at a steady jog trot, following the running man who was leading the way.

"I'm glad we have a guide," William finally admitted. "We have been able to travel more quickly and surely than we would if we were trying to make our own way."

"Indeed," agreed Henry, repressing a shiver. "Do you think riding quickly makes one feel colder though, as the air rushes past faster than it would if we were travelling more slowly?"

"I expect you're right, and we probably feel it more because we are tired and have come from a warm house, but the greater the speed, the shorter the time it will take us to get back to camp. These horses are fresh and strong and they'll cover the distance in less than three hours without a stop and that means we shall be in the open air for a much shorter time than we were on our outward journey."

Henry was obliged to agree, although he felt that the cold night air was scouring his cheeks and worming its way into his clothes. He was thankful for the hat that covered his head and his full beard that was some protection for his lower face and neck.

To their joint relief, they saw the glow of fires in front of them much sooner than they had anticipated and immediately became aware of rhythmic singing, accompanied by drumbeats.

Henry had been offering a prayer of thankfulness for the happy outcome to the day that had dawned with such uncertainty and had been lost in his own thoughts as William had fallen silent. William in his turn had been concentrating on leaning forward and crouching low, to keep himself as warm as possible under the circumstances. The hot bath he had enjoyed had eased his painful leg and Robert Moffat had given him a special herbal unguent to assist the healing, which seemed to be working already.

The campfires were visible from almost a mile away and the sound of revelry carried nearly as far through the night, alerting the two riders to a celebration and the obvious aftermath of a successful hunt. They felt immediately cheered.

"I'm sure our guide will be welcome at the festivities. He is probably known to many of our servants," William remarked as they rapidly approached the camp.

"Yes, it will be a happy reward for him. I was wondering what we could give him to repay his services now he will be content to wait until tomorrow."

On reaching camp, Henry and William immediately attended to the needs of their horses. Then Henry went to check on his two youngest children, whom he found sleeping peacefully protected by the windbreak, before rejoining William, who had been to release Fox.

Fox had begun yapping long before their arriva,l as he had been aware of his master's approach, although he had quietened down when William gruffly spoke to him. He had been tied to William's wagon but with a rope long enough for him to lie beside the cooking fire. William knew it was better for the dog to stay at the camp rather than attempt the long journey and was determined to avoid a repetition of the occasion when Fox had almost been shot. Lukas had been given strict orders to feed the dog and to see that Fox remained tied up. The little dog leapt and twisted exuberantly around William as the two men walked across to the noisy, joyful party around the drivers' fire, where their guide was already feasting.

"Greetings everyone. You have been very successful, I see," called William as soon as they were close enough to be recognised. Numerous loud greetings were shouted or mumbled through meat-filled mouths in response. Beaming faces lit spasmodically by the leaping flames shone like grotesque masks greasy with fat and blood. Bones, skins and feathers were strewn around and Henry had no difficulty in recognizing two pairs of springbok horns amongst the ostrich feathers.

"Come and share our meat," invited Bokkis, waving a huge bone in the air. It had been stripped of meat and he carelessly threw it to Fox, ignoring the possibility of crushing it for the marrow or boiling it with others for soup.

The dog grabbed it happily and dragged it away to gnaw contentedly just outside the circle.

Although neither man was really hungry and they were both exhausted, they had no wish to offend the fortunate hunters. With courteous handclapping and offering loud praises, they accepted some pieces of well-roasted meat and as they savoured the venison they heartily congratulated the huntsmen on their success.

Bokkis was keen to recount his exploits and was soon joined by the other two who had been equally successful, though all three insisted on talking at the same time, making it impossible to distinguish who had gained which trophy. Smiling and nodding, Henry was at last able to slip away, continuing to express his thanks for the delicious meat. Quickly, William picked up Fox, who was still clinging firmly to his bone, and both men eagerly sought their beds.

Henry made a slight detour to check on Isabelle and James once more. He found the two fires burning low and had to add more fuel. The temperature inside the windbreak remained warmer than in the open air. James and Isabelle were sound asleep with only the tops of their heads visible above the blankets on the two beds made earlier in the day for Jane and Harry.

"God Bless you both. May the Lord keep you safe," intoned Henry, certain that the children would be warmer here than they would in the wagon.

During the next three days of the journey Isabelle had sole care of James and Henry was surprised at how well she adopted the role of 'little mother'. Previously, she had been dependent on Jane and avoided any responsibilities, now she was in charge and proved very capable not only dressing her little brother and making sure that he was clean, but also spending time teaching him or playing games with him.

Henry made his daughter particularly happy by telling her, "I am pleased with you, Isabelle. You are looking after James just as well as Jane does."

Praise from father was something to treasure and Isabelle hugged the words to her heart, repeating them several times during the day and preening herself as she did so. She was extremely careful to avoid any mention of James' scorched dress and Henry never learned of James' mishap by the fire, thus Isabelle was spared his reproaches or any punishment.

Luckily for Isabelle, Amos had no intention of mentioning the episode either lest he be blamed for allowing the children to get so near to the fire and James was blissfully unaware of the serious danger he had so fortuitously escaped. In any case, he had almost forgotten the incident. Isabelle was fully aware of the consequences that had been narrowly avoided, but had no wish to draw father's attention to her lack of supervision. She was thankful that the red dust from the ground successfully hid the scorch mark when James was wearing that particular dress.

"Look, there is Kuruman," called Henry on the afternoon of the third day. He lifted the children up to his saddle in turn to indicate the buildings that could just be seen ahead. They were suitably awe-struck.

"Is it a town, father?" asked Isabelle.

"Big house," declared James throwing his arms up to demonstrate his words. "Lots of houses," he added for good measure.

Henry smiled at them. "The big building is the church. The smaller ones are houses. It is a mission station like Inyati, but it has been here for a long, long time."

"Is it like heaven? Are Jane and Harry there? Will we see them?" Isabelle was full of questions now that she had Henry's attention.

"See Jane and Harry," echoed James, tugging at Henry's boot. "See mama?" he added hopefully, thinking of Isabelle's mention of heaven.

Henry looked down into his son's serious little face and his heart contracted painfully, but he kept his voice under control. "No, mama isn't there. Kuruman is a happy place but it isn't heaven, Isabelle. Jane and Harry are both there and safe and well. We shall see them very soon. I expect they'll be pleased to see us too."

"How long are we going to stay at Kuruman, father?" Isabelle hoped it would be for a long time. She thought it would be warmer and much more comfortable in a house. Besides, she was tired of walking. Perhaps they would be able to eat bread with butter again and have milk to drink.

"I can't answer that. We shall have to give the oxen time to recover from this part of the journey and grow strong again. Now back into the wagon you go. We need to start moving again."

At Kuruman, news arrived that the wagons had been sighted and Mary began to make preparations for the imminent arrival of her visitors.

"Jane and Harry, you must wait indoors. I know the sun is shining, but it is still cold outside and I think you must wait for a few more days before you venture outside."

Mary's calm, sympathetic care over the three days had elicited the full story of the children's night in the bush.

She felt she could understand Harry's desire to help the family and provide a meal for them, but she realised that Henry might not be so lenient when he learned of Harry's mad chase after the hare.

"You behaved with a great deal of sense," she pronounced in approval of Jane's actions when she learned of them. "Of course, you had to follow your brother and we all know how quickly one can become disorientated in this wild country. Keeping moving to warm yourselves and then wrapping yourselves up tightly afterwards kept you alive. You were very lucky."

Harry had remained silent, for he knew that his actions had caused all the trouble and he felt horribly guilty, even if he didn't completely appreciate how nearly they had both died. It would be many years before that knowledge was fully realised.

"I didn't think we could get lost," he explained. "We only ran a little way and I nearly got the hare, didn't I?" he asked, looking at Jane.

Jane gave him a hug by way of comfort. "Father will understand, I'm sure." She turned to Mrs Moffat, "Please may we watch through the window to see the wagons arriving?" she asked politely.

Mary looked at the anxious face beside her. Jane hadn't recovered as quickly as Harry, and remained thin and pale. Mary was worried that the little girl had developed a weak chest that might remain with her for the rest of her life. She had a hollow cough that persisted and was especially troublesome at night, despite being given doses of Robert's favourite linctus. She hid her worries, however, and smiled reassuringly at both children, "Of course you may. Now I must just go and check what is happening in the kitchen."

There was great rejoicing as the Hargreaves family was reunited, and Henry was considerably relieved to see that Jane and Harry appeared to be fully recovered from their ordeal, though Jane seemed to lack the determined attitude and bearing he associated with her. Perhaps he shouldn't be too surprised if she looked a little worn. His reception of their careful explanation for wandering away from the wagon was surprisingly mild. He had had three days to recover his equilibrium and realised that they had suffered as much, if not more, than he had and he only reiterated his lecture on stopping to think before rushing into action. If he was tempted to speak more vehemently, he held himself admirably in check.

William and Fox had been made equally welcome, though William had been invited and elected to accept an invitation to stay with one of the storekeepers who had become a friend as well as a business associate.

Once the greetings were over and initial welcome refreshments had been consumed, William made his excuses and hurried over to his friend's house.

The next three weeks were a wonderful respite for all of them.

It was true that the children had to attend more formal lessons than they had experienced since leaving Inyati, which kept them fully occupied in the schoolroom throughout each morning, but they were free to explore and play for many hours in the afternoons. The weather remained dry and sunny each day, though still very cold, and the orchard became a favourite place at first. There were still some apples and lemons on the trees that they were sometimes asked to pick, but mostly they could play chasing or hiding games. Harry and Isabelle enjoyed climbing some trees and swinging from branches.

Harry, with his usual ability to make and attract friends, gathered a number of the local children around him soon after they had begun to attend the school, and organised games for them all.

Occasionally, Jane would take a book into the garden to read if she could find a suitably sheltered spot. Mary made sure that she was well wrapped up with a scarf, gloves and sometimes even a blanket as well.

Jane sometimes felt guilty about the care and attention she received because she was really enjoying having such a wonderful holiday. Mrs Moffat always sent some of her young helpers to supervise the children so that Jane was free to be by herself and didn't have to run about after James.

Mary Moffat had gently refused her offer of help in the kitchen or laundry, where there were already sufficient helpers. Many Bechuana girls came to the mission to learn domestic skills, in addition to accepting the new faith, and always some of them wanted to remain in an environment where they were happy, the work was easier and their safety was guaranteed.

"It was thoughtful of you to offer to help, Jane, but our girls are remarkably quick to learn these new skills and are proud of them," Mary confided to Jane. "They would be disappointed if you were to take their work away. Most of them learn to read and write too. They are surprisingly adept in the classroom."

Mary had felt a great deal of sympathy for the motherless children and insisted upon providing them all with some new garments in addition to laundering and mending the clothes they had brought with them. They were still in mourning for their mother and so the new material had to be a dark colour, but all of them were delighted to have something new and different to wear.

A few days after their arrival, Henry had taken the girls to see their mama's grave and solemnly they knelt to pray whilst Henry intoned a prayer for the repose of her soul. They had picked some fresh leaves from a bush to lay on the grave as there were few flowers blooming at this time of the year. Jane tried in vain to remember what mama had looked like. All she could remember now was the dreadful day when Isabelle had been born. She had been left alone for a long time as the other missionary ladies kept vigil beside mama in the wagon. She played happily for a time then went to sit in the shade of the wagon, holding tightly to the wagon wheel for comfort as moans of distress struck her ears.

Frightened, she sucked her thumb, or the iron tyre of the wheel, a taste of rust and dust that would remain with her all her life. Above her head, the moans and grunts were interspersed by loud screams. Jane couldn't understand why mama was screaming and she wanted to run far away so that the sound would stop. It was in the late afternoon, a whole lifetime, that the noise stopped and then she heard the cry of a baby.

At last she was allowed to see mama, who was almost asleep, but she gave

Jane a quick hug before she showed off the new baby. Jane wanted to stay with mama, her own special loving mama, but she was taken to spend the night in Emily Moffat's wagon. She never saw her mama again but the baby, Isabelle, was there instead.

CHAPTER 33

Robert Moffat came to stand beside Henry in the little graveyard.
"We take good care of their resting places, as you see, but it is sad to see so many young people taking their eternal rest. There is my grandson's grave; baby Unwin, next to your Jane and next to her is the first Mrs Sykes with her baby. You knew them and they are just a few of those who have gone before us during the years we have been here. Of course there is a graveyard at Inyati, too, another bleak testimony to the hardships borne by missionaries in the Lord's name. We were so sorry to hear of Katherine's death along with your new baby son. A hunter gave us the news that he had heard at Shoshong. This is a harsh country, Henry."
"Indeed it is, though I remember many graves of children and young people in our churchyards back home in Yorkshire. Disease, poverty, accidents, ill treatment and the bleak winters are as unforgiving as the African fevers. We were sorry, too, to hear of the loss of your daughter, Mary. Two years ago, was it? She is not buried here, is she?"
"No, she is buried at Shupanga on the Zambezi where the Livingstones were exploring. She died in February 1862 but we only learned of her death many months later. Our son-in-law, David, was heartbroken and my wife took it very hard. Come now, we must not be gloomy on this bright day. We are about to hold a service in the church. We will pray especially for our loved ones, secure in the knowledge that they are safely with our Lord."
Jane shivered and swayed, feeling suddenly very cold and confused. Luckily, the Reverend Moffat noticed her weakness and immediately told Isabelle to take her sister back into the house, whilst suggesting to Henry that the girls should be excused church.
Timidly Jane asked, "Please allow me to attend the service, father. I would very much like to say some prayers for mama and sing some hymns for her."
Henry looked sharply at his elder daughter and before agreeing to her request looked askance at Robert, who was looking serious but who spoke to Jane gently.
"If you're sure you feel well enough you can bring the boys and we will have a short service, perhaps half an hour, for all the children, before we have a longer one for the grown-ups. I think that would be alright, don't you Henry?"
Jane, watching the men anxiously, saw her father nod his head and, taking Isabelle by the hand, she led her back to the house to collect the boys.
"I don't really understand about heaven," confided Isabelle as they threaded

their way along the path. "I asked father if Kuruman was the same as heaven and he said 'no'. We know that our own mama is in heaven so why is there that special little place with her name on it in the graveyard here?"

Jane was not feeling at her best and was certainly not able to think clearly on a subject that often troubled her, too.

"I don't think our mama can be here, because she's in heaven. We know that heaven is in the sky above and that's where Jesus lives with his Father," she explained. "Perhaps we can ask father some time when he has time to listen to us. Let's find the boys now."

The boys had been playing near the kitchen in the hope that they would be offered some of the fresh bread or cake that had just been taken from the oven and were not pleased to be taken away before their hopes, mouths and stomachs had been satisfied. However, they had little choice and Jane held each one firmly by the hand as she marched them across to the church.

The Hargreaves family was awed by the size of the church at Kuruman and truly felt that they were entering God's House each time they worshipped there. Henry often wondered if the Matabeleland Mission would ever warrant a church of this size, which could hold many hundreds. Judging by the lack of success over the past five years there seemed no possibility of that unless a miracle happened, and yet this church was filled from time to time.

Still holding Harry and James by their hands, Jane, with Isabelle following, led them to the front to stand beside the other children who were resident here at Kuruman. Although she had been to this church and the little graveyard four years ago, she couldn't remember it very well, although it seemed vaguely familiar.

Even with every person living at Kuruman attending this morning's service, the building was less than half full, but the enthusiasm of the congregation taking part in the prayers and the singing made up for the lack of numbers. In deference to the Hargreaves family, the Reverend Moffat conducted this part of the service in English, though most of the congregation were singing and praying in Sechuana.

Jane was glad that she had been allowed to attend and equally pleased when the Reverend Moffat bade the children leave.

Once outside the church, Harry and Isabelle went off cheerfully with some of their friends, but Jane took James back to the house, where he was immediately taken into the care of one of the Bechuana helpers.

With everyone else in church, Jane thankfully sat in a comfortable chair by the fire and dozed.

When Mary returned to the house in time for the mid-day meal, she suggested that Jane should go to bed once she had eaten and that she should remain there for the whole afternoon.

Later, as she was preparing, not unwillingly, for bed, Jane suddenly remembered something that had been troubling her for several days.

"It is Harry's birthday tomorrow," she confided to Mary. "I don't have anything to give him," she added despairingly. She was almost in tears at the thought. Mary Moffat patted her shoulder comfortingly.

"Don't you fret yourself. I'll have a look around and find something. If I give it to you then it will be yours and it is perfectly acceptable for you to give away your own things, isn't it?"

Reassured, Jane smiled thankfully at the kindly face above her and soon fell into a deep sleep.

"You'll have to have a care for that young maid," Robert warned Henry later. "That night out in the bush has weakened her chest and the bleak winters in Yorkshire could be dangerous for her. It would be a pity if she was to become an invalid after such a promising start. I've noticed her talent in the classroom and thought that if she'd been born a boy she'd have gone to university."

Henry accepted the warning with good grace and suppressed any signs of the irritation he felt. He wasn't pleased to be told what he must do with his own children, but he had a deep regard as well as respect for the Reverend Moffat, both as a man and a missionary. Besides, Robert was nearly forty years older than he was and must be accorded both courtesy and deference by a much younger colleague. It was his due and not one to be lightly tossed aside.

"I shall look after her, of course," ventured Henry cautiously, "but her life must be spent in either the cold dampness of England with her grandparents or the heat and dust of Africa with me. Neither is conducive to vigorous health and especially for someone with a delicate chest. I can only pray that she may grow out of it. At least in England with my parents she will receive good regular meals and any medical attention she might require, as well as an English education."

Later that afternoon, Mary Moffat showed Jane what she had found as a possible present for Harry. It was a kudu horn that had been hollowed out and fitted with a mouthpiece so that it was a musical instrument.

It was not an easy instrument to play as it required a strong pair of lungs to produce even a small sound and Mary was worried that it might prove unsuitable for a boy who was only five years old.

Jane was delighted. It was exactly the sort of present Harry would appreciate. She could polish it up so that it would look shiny and bright to become an attractive ornament to hang in a room when it wasn't being played.

"Oh, it is quite the sort of present Harry will like. It will be a challenge for him and he enjoys a challenge. It looks like a grown-up present, too, which will please him immensely. I'm sure he will be able to produce some sounds from it. It is big enough to be a present from all three of us. Isabelle and James will be so happy that they have something to give Harry too. Thank you, Mrs Moffat. Oh, thank you."

Mary Moffat smiled at the enthusiasm displayed by her young guest. The kudu horn instrument was one of several such presents they had received over the years and she was glad that it would be used at last.

The following morning had been planned as a normal day with school for the children as usual, but a picnic had been arranged for the middle of the day. A number of the Kuruman families would all bring their own contributions to the feast and everyone would walk along the water furrow to the dam built many years ago as a water supply for the houses.

Harry received all his presents before breakfast, to which meal William had also been invited.

First James, flanked by Isabelle and Jane, brought in the kudu horn. Harry's eyes gleamed with joy.

"Thank you Jane, Isabelle and you James. I have always wanted to play music on a pipe. Can I try it now?" he asked the adults. Receiving permission, he put the horn to his lips. It was so large that he had to balance the end on the back of a chair, but manfully he held on. His cheeks bulged and he exerted himself mightily before a low growl drifted from the end of the horn. There was merriment all round and Robert congratulated him on his efforts.

"Young man, you'll be able to play some good notes before too long. Most people cannot even extract a whisper from it at the first attempt. You did extremely well."

Harry beamed with pride and was persuaded to put the horn to one side as the Moffats gave him their gift. It was a beautifully produced book entitled, "David and Goliath".

Robert Moffat had brought a printing press to Kuruman thirty years before so that he could produce tracts and schoolbooks in the Sechuana language.
The Bible Society and well-wishers provided paper and ink.
He had printed Harry's book in simple English and Mary had added several water colour sketches.

"We heard that you like to challenge youths much larger than yourself and bring them to the ground, just like David in the Bible," smiled the Reverend

Moffat.

"We hope you'll always fight for truth and honesty with equal determination," added Mary.

"Oh thank you," whispered Harry. "I shall look after this book very carefully and try to do as you ask."

He placed the book gently down on a small table after looking at the pictures and showing them to his brother and sisters.

The final presents were from Henry and William. These were a cricket bat and ball. William had managed to carve a near perfect sphere from a hardwood and Henry had covered it in leather. Between them they had made the bat, taking it in turns to whittle away the excess wood whenever Harry was playing elsewhere or was in bed. It was rather large for Harry because they wanted him to be able to use it for a number of years. Of course, there was always the possibility that it might break before then, though it seemed unlikely.

"There you are, Harry. A cricket bat. William will help you to practise your skills during the next few weeks so that when you go to school you'll know how to hit a ball properly," asserted Henry.

"And here is the ball you will need for cricket," added William. "It's quite hard, so we won't use it for the first week or so until you can hit the ball nearly every time. Once you can hit a soft ball, we'll start using this."

Wide-eyed and filled with excitement, Harry could only stutter his thanks.

"I think it's time we all sat down to eat our breakfasts," Mary reminded them. "Time is passing all too quickly and these children will be late for school if we stand here talking any longer."

Her placid voice helped to calm the excited children enough for them to look solemn during prayers and the meal proceeded pleasurably, followed by a routine morning.

Harry's birthday, with its afternoon picnic attended by a large light-hearted crowd, was a memory that stayed with the Hargreaves children all their lives.

"We must have looked like the Great Trek," said Robert laughingly that evening, as they sat round the fire reminiscing on the day's events. The children had needed very little supper and were put to bed early, their own meal was to be a light one too, just bread and soup.

"There was certainly enough food for a Great Trek," agreed Henry.

"The ladies did us proud. I have never seen so many meat pies and fruit pies before. They must have used nearly a week's ration of flour and sugar as well as all the meat and other comestibles. I pray that you and they won't suffer a shortage due to the extravagance of today's feast."

"We are always very careful with our budgeting, Henry, to ensure that we never actually starve," explained Mary. "This means that very occasionally we can celebrate with a special meal, as we did today. We try to make sure that our guests are always given the best we can offer, even if we then have to be rather careful for the next few weeks."

"That does occasionally have its drawbacks," interjected Robert. "One of our guests, who had in a few days eaten most of our month's supplies, returned to Cape Town and informed everyone he met that the missionaries in the field lived like fighting cocks and were evidently being given too much money! He kept suggesting that our salaries should be cut. We resolved thereafter that official visitors should be kept on short commons and exist on our basic fare. Friends and fellow missionaries were not included in that, of course."

Henry laughed appreciatively. "An excellent idea on your part. We have to ration ourselves very carefully, too, and even then we sometimes go short. Our biggest problem lies not with the officials of our government but with the important officials of the Matabele people. Mzilikazi's wives can eat a month's supplies at one sitting. Our poor wives hardly dare do any baking, as the smell of food seems to attract a ravenous horde."

Robert nodded in agreement. "I well remember their gargantuan appetites, especially for cakes and biscuits, but they were all rather large ladies and needed to eat constantly."

"Changing the subject, Robert, or rather talking about animals eating instead of people, whilst we were out today William told me that the oxen are in good condition now. With water at hand all the time and with much better grazing than they have had over the past two months, they have put on weight."

"Does that mean that you are planning to leave us soon?" asked Mary anxiously.

"I know that some of your guests stay here for many months, Mary, which is no surprise, as you are both most hospitable. It is tempting to forget the rest of the world and just remain here in this oasis. However William has to transport his loads to Cape Town within a reasonable span of time and I have agreed to accompany him there. It is to the advantage of both of us, as you will appreciate. I have been particularly lucky to have William to share the journey and I understand his need to reach Cape Town at the earliest opportunity. Some of the hides deteriorate on long journeys, as you know. If I stayed longer and let him depart alone, I might have to wait for weeks before finding another traveller going to Cape Town and I want to reach England's shores before the worst of the winter gales make travelling unpleasant."

Sadly Mary nodded. "Of course you must leave when it is the right time for you to go, but I shall miss you all sorely. Your family has been a joy to me. It is sad that the girls will grow up separated from their brothers, but you are right to leave them in the care of their grandparents, who will be the best guardians for them."

Robert put a comforting hand on his wife's shoulder, "John will arrive before too long with our grandchildren and that will keep you fully occupied. Besides, Henry is right, travelling north in the winter months is hazardous. It will be September by the time they are in Cape Town, where they must no doubt stay for many days, possibly until the beginning of October. With nearly six weeks on the ship, it will be November before they land at Southampton, with several more days journeying to reach the wild country in the north where he lives." Robert turned to look at Henry with a merry twinkle in his eye. "Who knows, they could be held up by wild storms at sea or snowstorms on land?"

Henry laughed as he realised that Robert was teasing his wife.

"Oh, go away with you, Robert. I am as aware of the hazards of travel as you are. I just wanted Henry to know that we are not anxious for him to leave." And with that, she went to the kitchen to heat up the soup.

* * * * * * *

The following morning began as normal and whilst the children were in school Henry accompanied William on a tour of inspection. Every wagon and its equipment were examined, the metal tyres on the wheels tapped and tested to ensure that they had stayed firm. Robert had assisted them to shorten some of the tyres in his forge so that they would fit more snugly the wooden rims that had shrunk in the dry weather. Chain links were inspected and all the leather reims looked at for wear or weak spots.

The horses had been re-shod only a few days before and they were both looking in excellent condition, though probably in need of more exercise.

When every wagon had passed their scrutiny, they went on to look at the oxen and were equally pleased by what they saw. Every beast had put on weight and its appearance was sleek and shiny.

"I think we should leave as early as we can make it tomorrow morning," William suggested, looking hopefully at Henry.

"Yes, I agree with you. The cattle are fit enough to face the journey to Griqua Town, where they can have a short respite before crossing the Vaal and the Orange Rivers and moving on to Hopetown. The Karroo is fearsome and we can barely hope that all the beasts will survive. I think I must buy three more from Robert to add to the spare I already have and keep them in reserve. It will be another six weeks or so before we reach Cape Town. I think we ought to purchase some sheep and goats, too."

"I have an arrangement with the traders here," William volunteered. "I bring up supplies for them when I travel north and they supply me with my needs when I am returning south, offsetting the costs against what they owe me for transport. It's a useful arrangement. I shall be able to provide us with flour, sugar, meal, jams, tea, salt, coffee and tinned goods. I'll load up the stores this afternoon. If there is anything special you need for the children, you can come and choose it yourself. We shall, of course, need to buy extra meal and possibly meat, too, for the servants at some of the Boer farms. The farmers are always desperate for sugar and coffee, so we'll take enough of those to use as barter. You can show me your list of stores if you like and I'll make a start on it as well as my own whilst you negotiate for the livestock."

Henry produced a written list of his normal stores' requirements and handed it to William.

"We'll need provender for the horses as well," Henry reminded him.

The rest of the day was exceptionally stressful, including as it did two disturbing occurrences. The first was when they discovered almost by accident that three of William's and one of Henry's servants had decided to remain at Kuruman, refusing point blank and at almost the last possible moment to travel to Cape Town. This situation left the men little opportunity to procure the necessary help at a time when they were fully occupied ensuring that they had sufficient food supplies for several weeks. Provisioning required a nicety of judgement, entailing as it did the amount of space available in the wagons and the requisite amount of essential stores. To miss out an item, forget an article or confuse a detail meant untold misery for many days or weeks.

William didn't want his concentration disturbed and tried to ignore this sudden crisis, so it was left to Henry to cope with the emergency. He decided to seek Robert's help in solving their problem.

Robert was working in the carpentry room with some of his students. They were mending a broken board in his mule cart, but he put aside his work to listen attentively to Henry's woeful tale.

It was as Henry's story came to an end and as Robert was thoughtfully resuming his work, but before he had time to offer advice, that the second interruption occurred.

A breathless messenger came to seek the Reverend Moffat's assistance. He had heard news that the Boers were planning to attack his village. Once again Robert abandoned his task and turned a heedful ear to learn of impending disaster.

He turned to Henry, "It's many years since the Boers attacked Sechele and destroyed David's mission. His books were torn to shreds and his goods taken to sell at auction. We have forgiven them many times for their aggression but they can never forgive us. They accuse us of teaching the natives to read and write and to believe that we are all equal in God's love. They blame us for any deaths in their commandos when they attack native villages because the natives now have guns and are using them in self defence." He spoke calmly, without rancour, though he shook his head sadly, then stood, without speaking, for several minutes whilst he concentrated on the two problems suddenly thrust upon him.

"Go to my house and seek refreshment," he advised the messenger. "I will discuss this matter of a Boer attack with you later. Henry, come with me. We will spread the word that there is an opportunity for some young people to go to Cape Town. I should think it might be reasonably simple to find three youngsters to act as leaders. Finding a driver for William might be more difficult."

Henry, following Robert towards the stores, nodded his head in agreement, "Driving an ox wagon and wielding a long whip are skills not easily acquired and the best drivers have years of experience. It is a nuisance that this need has arisen only hours before our departure."

Robert turned to look at him and his eyes twinkled, "Life rarely runs smoothly, Henry. Just think how dull it would be if we had no challenges. Though there are times when I wonder if Mary and I might benefit from living in a less turbulent area," he added thoughtfully.

CHAPTER 34

It was whilst the children were sitting eating their lunch in the wonderfully warm, busy kitchen with its glorious aroma of baking, that they first became aware of their impending departure from Kuruman.
Mary, bustling in to check on the lunch for the adults in the dining room, spoke to the two Bechuana girls who were busy making meat pies.
"I should think that two of those large meat pies and two fruit ones, with three loaves of bread will provide enough food for their first day. Everyone can have a full breakfast at four o'clock tomorrow morning and be away from here before five. I'll pack some butter, cheese and cream for them, as well."
Jane looked up, her mind whirling at what she had just heard. To whom was Mrs Moffat referring, she wondered. There were no other travellers here at present. Mid-winter was too late for the hunters going northwards to Matabeleland, April or May were their chosen times and it was too early for them to be returning with their trophies. She wasn't left long in doubt, however.
Mary glanced at the children all solemnly eating their stew and eyeing the jam tart and cream that was to follow. She saw Jane looking at her with a question in her eyes.
"I shall be sorry to see you go, little miss. I have enjoyed having you all around, but your father and Mr William must get to Cape Town as soon as they can. You all have a long journey ahead of you."
Jane gulped and tried to hide the consternation the information had aroused in her. When her mouth was empty she spoke tremulously, "We didn't know that we are to leave tomorrow. I haven't been able to say goodbye to my friends."
Isabelle was more forthright; "I don't want to leave here. I'm happy at Kuruman."
"So am I," Harry added. "I have a lot of friends and we have fun games together."
Mary smiled at them, "I'm glad you have been happy here. You will have time to say goodbye to all your friends this afternoon and there will be a service in the church to pray for your safe journey, so you will see all the other people then."
When Mary had left there was an appalled silence amongst the children as they assimilated the awfulness of the news.
Kuruman had been such a haven for them, surrounded as they were with

warmth and kindness, good food and ordered days with warm beds on these cold winter nights.

To quell the complaints she could see from Isabelle's furious face were about to erupt into speech, Jane looked pointedly at her, "There is nothing to be said. Father and Mr William have made the arrangements. Finish your food. Whilst we are resting after lunch I'll read you all some of my favourite fairy stories."

Jane was just as upset as her siblings were, possibly more so, as she had always longed for a friend of her own age and here at last she had found one. Sarie Joubert was the daughter of one of the storekeepers who could speak two languages neither of which was English although she had picked up a few unconnected words in Jane's language. Nevertheless, the two had become firm friends.

Sarie was expected to do her share of the baking at her home and as Jane was equally adept with making bread and pastry the two girls shared happy, laughing moments in the Jouberts' kitchen whenever Sarie was involved with her chores. Jane tried to learn some of the words Sarie and her mother used and this usually provoked gales of laughter.

Best of all, Sarie was musical and loved to sing, as did Jane, and they often sang together. She could play the clavichord, not as well as her older sister Elma, but she could pick out several tunes and she had encouraged Jane to practise too. It was thrilling for Jane to sit in front of the instrument and produce recognisable sounds.

"Oh how I would love to be able to play properly," she whispered to herself. "I wonder if grandmama has a clavichord or a harmonium. I must ask father."

Remembering all the happy days filled with laughter, Jane knew that this goodbye would be one of the hardest yet. She wished fervently that they could stay longer at Kuruman.

By evening time a number of problems had been resolved.

After careful consideration, and, after a long discussion with the weary messenger from Sechele, Robert had decided that there was little he could do except to register a strong protest and appeal to the Christian nature of the Boers. Accordingly, he wrote two letters, one to the commander of the Boer commando intent upon attacking the village and the other to the Governor in Cape Town apprising him of the situation. He was saddened by the fact that there was little else he could do, but having other considerations to occupy his mind he sent off the messenger with one letter and knew that it would reach its destination by a number of devious means. The second letter could go with Henry to Cape Town.

Robert had managed to persuade William's driver to complete the journey to Cape Town, though the driver had demanded an extra payment before he would agree. That had made it difficult for William, who knew that the other drivers would now also want extra money. He had eventually accepted the inevitable: after all, smaller profits were better than no profit at all.

There had been no difficulty in finding three youngsters to act as leaders. Many young Bechuanas were keen to earn some payment and to visit Cape Town. William usually offered a contract that would bring them back to Kuruman within six months, so their families were pleased at the opportunity offered to their sons.

By mid afternoon, William had managed to purchase and pack all the stores they required and Henry had obtained six goats and two fat-tailed sheep.

He had hoped to purchase several more sheep as the fat from the sheep's tails was much appreciated by the children when butter wasn't available and of course was invaluable for cooking, but Robert could spare no more from his own little flock. Henry had approached some of the other residents who also kept livestock, but had again been unsuccessful. However, he was satisfied that they had enough meat to last them for a week, even if the servants would have to accept smaller portions than they preferred.

The children had each spent the afternoon with their respective friends before bidding them goodbye. Harry had waved cheerfully to his companions and run back to the house without a backward glance. Friends were everywhere and anywhere for Harry. It would be several years before he made the friends who would be his friends for life.

Isabelle, who had been playing with a group of girls and smaller children including James, was inclined to be both tearful and sulky when she was called in to the evening meal. She knew the others would soon forget her. They were all resident at Kuruman and were used to people coming and going, though few travellers had children with them. Isabelle had been of passing interest because of her doll, a doll that had real hair and with movable arms and legs. Although she tended to be possessive, she had occasionally let the others touch or even hold the doll and none of them had a doll like that, but once the Hargreaves departed they would play happily with their own rag dolls.

Jane spent a happy afternoon at the Jouberts' house. She and Sarie made some cakes, whilst Mrs Joubert and Elma made a mountain of rusks.

With six sons, four of them still in school, in addition to a well-built husband who was always hungry, baking was a necessary part of daily life for Elise Joubert and her daughters. As the time drew near for Jane to make her farewells, she became increasingly quiet.

"I shall miss you all," she burst out suddenly. "You have been so kind to me. I wish we weren't going so soon. I wish I could stay here longer."
If the Jouberts didn't understand every word of what Jane had said they clearly understood her meaning. They all smiled and muttered to themselves. Mrs Joubert found a bag and began to fill it with rusks, whilst Elma filled another with some sticks of biltong that were hanging from wires stretched across the kitchen beams. The bags were thrust into Jane's hands, accompanied by a torrent of words she couldn't understand.
Mrs Joubert and Elma gave Jane warm hugs, then Sarie accompanied her outside. There Sarie too hugged her and sadly whispered, "Tot siens."
As she walked sorrowfully away from the Jouberts' house, Jane wondered if she would spend her whole life making friends and then having to say goodbye. It was unlikely that she would ever see Sarie again. She had heard the Reverend Moffat say that the Jouberts really didn't belong to his church, but they were religious people and needed somewhere to worship, and as their children attended the school they all came to his services. 'It must be wonderful to be like Sarie,' thought Jane.
'To have a mother and a father and live with such a big family and to live in a place like Kuruman.'
Feeling tearful and downcast and clutching the two bags of very welcome food tightly, Jane decided to make one last visit to her mother's grave, where she could be alone for a time. Accordingly, she made her way to the cemetery close to the church and knelt beside the grave where the small stone headstone declared: Jane Hargreaves beloved wife of Henry 1837–1859. Sleeping where no shadows fall.
Jane put down her two bags so that she could pray and, closing her eyes, spoke quietly to her beloved mama. ' I wish you were here with us. Father said you were needed in heaven and I know God must be right, but we really need you here, too.' For a moment Jane felt engulfed in deep sorrow and almost began to sob, and then she took a deep breath, stiffened her shoulders and continued. 'I know you can't come to us and that it isn't your fault. I would like to be a doctor when I'm older so that I can stop people from dying and going to heaven, leaving their children here, but I know that only men can be doctors. I will look after Isabelle and the little boys when I can. I will work hard in school, too. You will be very proud of me, mama.' As she began to recite the Lord's Prayer, Jane felt as if gentle arms were enfolding her, bringing her peace.

* * * * * * *

Jane awoke suddenly, her eyes shocked and staring.

"It's all right, Jane dear." Mary spoke soothingly, the candlelight illuminating her gentle face. "It's four o'clock already and time for you and the other children to dress and come for breakfast."

Once she was sure that Jane was fully awake and wouldn't fall asleep again, Mary placed the candle on a chest of drawers and left the room.

Jane watched the orange yellow flame chasing shadows round the room and forced herself to contemplate stepping out of the warm comfortable bed into the very cold air of a room where the fire had long since died out.

It wasn't a happy prospect, as she knew just how fretful her siblings would be when she woke them. It would be an unenviable task getting them dressed as they shivered and objected to the disturbance.

Knowing that she would have to face father's wrath if she delayed too long, Jane steeled herself and flung back the blankets without uncovering Isabelle, who was sleeping peacefully beside her, and she gasped as the chill seeped up through her bare feet. Hastily, she pulled on her clothes, sitting on the still warm bed as much as she was able. The water in the ewer was so cold that Jane wondered why there was no ice. She poured some into the bowl and gasped again as she quickly rinsed her hands and face, reaching for the towel immediately and rubbing fiercely to bring back some warmth to her skin.

"Isabelle, wake up." Jane leaned over to shake her little sister.

"Go away," came the disgruntled reply.

Jane tried again. "Come on, Isabelle. We have to get up. Father is waiting for us. You will be able to go back to sleep in the wagon after we have had some breakfast."

It took a great deal of urging and persuasion to force Isabelle to vacate the bed and her petulant mutterings finally woke Harry, whose angry objections woke James. Somehow, with a great deal of tact and a few threats, Jane managed to cope and eventually led them all into the kitchen, where the warm fire was a most pleasurable sight. They welcomed the mugs of hot milk and tried valiantly to eat some of the sweet porridge and bread and butter, but were still barely awake. The adults were concentrating on their own food and conversation was fragmented.

Somehow, Jane coaxed them into eating the food they had been served, as she knew that the next meal would not be until lunch, although they might have a small snack when the wagons stopped mid-morning.

Silently, they collected their hats, cloaks and jackets before making their sad farewells with many expressions of gratitude for the hospitality they had so enjoyed. Eventually, the children climbed into the cold, dark wagon and thankfully fell into bed, still fully dressed and shivering now that they were out of the warm house.

Once they were mounted, William, clutching a shivering Fox on the saddle, gave the lead driver and his young leader the order to set off. With their goodbyes ringing through the cold air mingled with thanks from Henry and good wishes from the Moffats, the cavalcade left Kuruman just as the horizon appeared as a pencil line to the east.

Harry was soon asleep, but Isabelle tossed and turned and muttered, upsetting Jane, who was desperately trying not to weep. Jane felt and knew rather than heard that James was about to be sick. Hastily fighting off the bedclothes whilst pushing Isabelle roughly to one side and ignoring her furious protests, she fought her way off the bed, gripping James by the shoulders and heaving him after her. Putting her hand firmly over his mouth, she struggled over father's bed towards the drawn curtains at the front of the wagon. It was the fact that the flaps of the tent had been laced closed that defeated her intention to let her brother be sick over the side of the wagon. She needed both hands to undo the ties, whilst poor James, his full stomach disturbed by the motion of the vehicle and unaccustomed to food at this time of the day, when he was barely awake, couldn't keep back the flow.

Regurgitated milk and porridge hurtled against the tent flaps and dripped to the floor, splashing both of them and almost choking James.

It was too late really to open the flaps, but Jane, who was overcome with the futility of her actions, continued to wrestle with the cords. The sudden incursion of the icy air made her gasp and set her coughing.

James was already shivering and sobbing. "Sorry Jane. Sorry Jane."

Knowing that it really wasn't his fault, Jane held him close, their damp, stained clothing sticking together uncomfortably.

"It's all right, James. You'll feel better now. I'll find some clean clothes for you and you can go back to bed. You'll soon feel warm again." She gave his back a comforting rub and took him back over father's bed to their own.

It was no easy task finding clean clothes in the dark in a wagon that was constantly moving, bumping up and down or swaying from side to side. Undressing her little brother and dressing him again helped Jane to ignore the awfulness of the whole episode. Once he was back in bed and snuggling up to Harry he was soon quiet again, but Jane had to consider what to do. A feeling of total inadequacy swept over her as she removed her own damp clothes. There were two sets of clothing needing to be washed and a horrible mess at the front of the wagon to be cleaned. The smell of sickness would be replaced by the smell of sour milk, she was sure. 'Oh, why did this have to happen now?'

Crying wouldn't help matters, she knew. Although she longed to do just

that, she would just have to deal with it when the wagon stopped.
There was just one consolation, father wouldn't be coming back to bed now and she would have time to rectify the problems before he wanted to climb back into the wagon. As a further solace, Isabelle had turned and wrapped her arms around her older sister as, cold, shivering and unhappy, she had crawled into bed. "Poor James and poor Jane," she whispered, using her own warm little body to comfort her.
Gradually Jane's shivers subsided and she hugged Isabelle gratefully.

* * * * * * *

It was a hundred miles to Griquatown with very few waterholes on the way and Henry knew that they must keep the oxen moving well for the first three days whilst they were fit and strong from their three weeks respite. It was past ten o'clock when William called a halt and they made their out-span, by which time everyone was ready for a mug of hot coffee and some bread spread with butter. The butter wouldn't keep for more than a few days even in cold weather and by now the worst of the winter was past, with the sun warming the days pleasantly, so it was advisable to enjoy it with the fresh bread whilst they could.
"I should think we have covered more than a dozen miles already," Henry remarked cheerfully as he sat drinking the welcome mug of hot coffee and savouring the repast.
William nodded in agreement. "It is five hours since we left Kuruman and we've been able to move along at a good pace. This road is well used, but is slightly better than most. If we can manage to keep going like this we should be in Griquatown in a week, even if we stop for a whole day on Sunday.
William's prediction was a sound one and this part of their journey proved trouble free despite the necessity of discovering water each day. Even their hunting was blessed with success, so that their livestock remained alive and well. This was a secret joy for Jane, who visited the animals each day and spoke to them kindly.
Whenever William wasn't occupied with his essential chores, he spent time teaching Harry about cricket and when they were exhausted after hours spent chasing the ball they played ninepins, which was less strenuous.
Jane was delighted that Harry was able to expend his surplus energy without getting into more mischief, whilst his efforts to please his papa in the morning lessons made life considerably happier for everyone.
William had added some interest to the school sessions by telling them about his journeys from Cape Town to Matabeleland and drawing rough maps for

them to study. It wasn't Henry's idea of how geography should be taught, but he didn't object to his children learning a little about the places in Africa that were never mentioned in schoolbooks.

He was happier when they were given a list of the rivers to learn and name. William also taught them a little about the history of Cape Town from the time of its discovery in 1487 by Bartholomew Diaz until the present day.

Harry was most interested in the battles between the Dutch and the British and stories of the shipwrecks around the coast. Isabelle wanted to know what cargoes of spices and pretty materials were carried by the trading ships, but for Jane the Great Trek of only twenty years previously held the greatest fascination. The thought of hundreds of people setting out in their ox wagons to walk away into the unknown lands to the north was rather like one of her own fairy tales. On a more mundane level, she was surprised to learn that they were fleeing from the British. Jane was fiercely proud of being British, as were all the people at Inyati. Britain had brought civilisation and the Bible to the heathens, so why should anyone want to run away from them. It was totally beyond her comprehension.

Frequently, Jane considered the romance of the Great Trek as she walked alongside their wagon home in the morning as the rising sun presented the eastern hills with a golden halo or in the evening when an array of gloriously vivid colours painted the western sky. In her mind, she saw the five wagons of their own trek as part of a pattern designed by God to fill His world with people who would sing His praises. The splendid sunsets were his approval, but did he approve of the Boers who were trekking, or the British, who were her own people. She had heard that the Boers were religious people, too, and went to church regularly, but they didn't teach the black people about God and didn't want them in their own churches. There were so many odd things in the world and Jane wanted to find out the answers to the questions they posed. Sometimes she would ask father to explain, but he would often reply that there were matters beyond her concern, that young women should keep their minds on their family and domestic duties and leave such matters to men.

The children were all riding in the wagon when Griquatown first came into view in the distance. Henry, pleased to be completing another leg of the journey, rode alongside and whilst announcing the news to them, he pointed out the huddle of buildings just visible on the horizon.

At first none of them could see anything and it was only when the front three wagons began a slow curve to the right that they were able to see signs of human habitation in front of them. They were vastly disappointed.

"The church at Kuruman is bigger than any of those buildings," declared

Isabelle loudly, as she stared at the place Henry indicated.

"Quite right and so it should be. The House of God is of paramount importance," agreed Henry. "They do have a church here," he added, "but it isn't one of ours and is a little less grand."

"Griquatown doesn't look very big," said Jane tentatively. "I can't really remember it, but I thought it would be as big as Shoshong or the King's Town in Matabeleland."

"There are some stone houses and native houses all mixed up together," stated Harry, who was not to be outdone by his sisters and was eager to demonstrate his keen eyesight.

"Yes, well the people of this town are not quite the same as the natives. Some of them like stone houses as we do, but some of them are happier in native huts." With this explanation, Henry rode to the back of the column to check on the livestock.

Jane continued to gaze at the buildings rapidly increasing in size as the wagons approached. Altogether the town looked no bigger than Kuruman.

William, riding point with Fox trotting ahead, became aware of a number of dogs materialising from various quarters of the town and standing in the road on which they were travelling, watching and watchful they didn't appear to be a welcoming party.

Sensing trouble, William called urgently to the young native who was leading the oxen immediately behind him and then he spoke sharply to Fox. The little dog stopped in its tracks and turned towards him. The native boy ran up and hastily grabbed the dog before it could evade or snarl at him and then lifted it immediately into William's waiting arms.

CHAPTER 35

The dogs that had appeared from every area of the town as soon as the wagons came rumbling along the road from the west had within minutes become a single numberless pack running excitedly round the wagons, even before they arrived at the first houses. Their antics disturbed the oxen, which jibbed and balked at the cacophony of sound and the sight of whirling multicoloured bodies racing about them.

The children had at first been fascinated to see so many dogs of all shapes, sizes and colours. There must have been nearly twenty of them. However, the snarling, mangy, half starved curs with curiously pale malevolent eyes soon struck horror in them, especially as they would growl fiercely then suddenly leap upwards with snapping jaws. The oxen were so disturbed that the wagons swung from side to side alarmingly and goods inside came clattering down on to the bed of the wagon.

William, whose anticipation of danger for Fox had caused him to have the dog scooped up to sit in front of him on the saddle, realised all too soon that even this gesture might prove dangerous. The little terrier bared his teeth and barked furiously at the nondescript invaders, with every indication and intention of seeing them off. In retaliation, the native dogs, skinny, gaunt, neglected and vicious, surrounded Diamond, intent upon attacking this interloper. The horse was unused to such a noisy, motley set of attackers, and lashed out automatically, sending several of the curs hurtling backwards through the air with yelps of pain and fear. Two at least retired injured from the fray. The sudden movement, however, all but unseated William, who maintained his seat with grim determination as he held firmly onto Fox. Had he not been a superb and experienced rider, he would have been unseated and would then himself have been attacked by the frenzied pack.

The drivers of the nearest two wagons had come to the rescue by using their long whips judiciously and with great skill to beat away the dogs, giving William time to gallop far enough ahead to throw off pursuit for the moment. He would have to confine Fox to the wagon at night and possibly for part of the day, too, he thought, if this menace continued. He had never had such an experience before, not even when he and Edward had travelled through Griquatown only a few months previously.

The official out-span was on the south-easterly edge of the town with ample room for the wagons to stand, and a fenced kraal for the animals. The grazing area was to the north of the town where there were also some pools of water, but the distance wasn't great and the two days prospective stay here would give the beasts some rest and keep them in reasonable condition.

It took the combined efforts of all the servants to clear the unruly mongrels away from the immediate area around the wagons as the oxen were outspanned, though they remained as a suspicious, menacing threat, just out of reach of the curling whips.

Henry twice fired shots above the threatening pack, sending the less aggressive animals scurrying away with their tails between the their legs and even the more violent ones sensibly retreated a short distance, only to creep and crawl forward when they thought the danger past.

It was obvious that it would be unsafe to attempt to cook and eat food in the vicinity of the wagons under these conditions. At the first scent of meat the horde would undoubtedly advance relentlessly and would be impossible to repel. Henry had fears, too, for the sheep and goats he still had with him. In his five previous visits to Griquatown he had never before had such problems. There had always been large numbers of stray dogs here, as there were in most towns, but he decided that the numbers must have recently increased too rapidly for any sort of control. No one owned the dogs except for the few that were kept especially as hunting dogs and no one seemed to care about the strays.

William agreed with this conclusion when he rode into camp shortly afterwards and suggested that they should speak to the chiefs in the town with a view to shooting some of the fiercest dogs. They were all so obviously underfed that surely no one would object, and their presence round the out-span made life impossible for anyone who stayed there. He intended to confine Fox to his wagon until a solution had been effected.

With the idea of speaking to the authorities in mind, Henry immediately rode back into the town and sought out the predikant, Isaac de Kok, who was unfortunately not at home. By the time that Henry returned to the wagons he found that Bokkis had solved one of the problems for them.

The servants had wanted to cook their supper immediately, and when they found themselves threatened by the dogs as they started to cook the maize meal and the three chickens they had somehow obtained, Bokkis had picked up his gun and shot two of the invaders. The remainder had fled.

It was a great relief for all of them, as the remaining dogs would initially be leaderless and far less aggressive until a new leader took over. Nevertheless, they were likely to remain a nuisance unless several more were killed and Henry promised to speak to the predikant on the subject when he returned home.

The children had been excused lessons for the two days of their visit to the town and Harry had immediately found friends amongst the youngsters who had flocked to the out-span out of sheer curiosity to watch the strangers as soon as they had arrived.

The fact that none of them spoke his language made absolutely no difference and somehow Harry had made it clear that he would like to see them the following day to share his games. William, who was trying to control an angrily barking Fox, sent the piccannins back to town, and supper had finally been enjoyed in comparative peace.

When she had finished eating, Jane remarked to William that there were many children here who resembled the children they had met at the Tati River with pale brown, almost yellow skins. Some almost looked white, though they had noses like the natives, just like Stoffel's children.

"Were Stoffel and his family from Griquatown?" she asked, innocently.

William laughed as much as to give himself time to think as from amusement. He was embarrassed by the question, fully aware that Henry was listening and conscious that he could hardly explain that many of the occupants of Griquatown were coloured people who were the result of white men consorting with the Hottentots and other native women. Henry considered such behaviour as abhorrent and almost unnatural, whilst Jane was a naïve child, pure and unsophisticated, as was right and proper for children of her class.

How was it possible to explain the realities of the world to such people and describe that for many decades, centuries even, the shipwrecked sailors cast ashore and abandoned by their countries had of human necessity eased a lonely life by cohabiting with the natives?

Indeed, the African chiefs inland (for there were none at the Cape then) and near the East Coast, frequently insisted on sending their young girls to lie with any white man passing through their tribal areas. For the chief concerned it was equal to offering food, drink and shelter. A man had needs and women were there to satisfy them. It was an accepted custom and women were of no account. For some white men this was an admirable attitude and one of which they approved.

In addition, lusty young soldiers, priapic prospectors, virile hunters or sportsmen whose libido was enhanced by the excitement of the chase and rampant Boer commandos determined to demonstrate their dominance and contempt for the natives, added to the growing number of coloureds scattered around the continent.

Jane's artless, clear brown eyes were still fixed on William's face as she waited patiently for an answer.

William coughed and looked apologetically at Henry.

"No, I don't think Stoffel and his family are from Griquatown. Many of the people here are just different," William added lamely.

"Oh, a sort of in between people, perhaps half like the natives and half like us?" suggested Jane, ingenuously.

Poor William felt extreme discomfort at this guileless though accurate statement and although he was nodding, he was greatly relieved when Henry, who had become irritated by his elder daughter's persistent questions, peremptorily ordered the children back to the wagon for the night. Jane was still confused about the coloured people, though she felt sure that she had learned something that had been puzzling her for many weeks. There were half and half people. With that conclusion she slept untroubled by the chill night air.

Isabelle and James joined in with the Harry's games the following morning, but Jane was engrossed with domestic chores as she took advantage of the proximity of a water supply to wash clothes and sheets.

She also cleaned out the wagon, which still had a faint smell of sour milk, despite her best efforts to eliminate it, and aired the blankets in the welcome strengthening sunshine.

Henry spent some time negotiating with various storekeepers to replace foodstuffs used since they had left Kuruman and then enjoyed many hours with the predikant, Isaac de Kok, whom he had met on previous journeys and who had now returned from a visit to a farm. True to his promise, he discussed the feral dogs with Isaac and was assured that the townsfolk would not object, in fact they would definitely approve of the removal of some of the worst offenders.

The predikant's house was one of the better ones in the town and Henry found it both comfortable and stimulating in its differences from houses he had known. He was also inspired by the challenge of discussing and debating missionary principles with someone who had a totally different view of religion from his own. He had been invited to dine there that evening, an offer he had accepted gladly, especially as the predikant's wife, Martha, had also invited the children to join her own brood. He also knew that William was enjoying the hospitality of his own friends in the town.

It was during an early lunch the next day that William, who had joined them for the meal, mentioned that he had had an invitation to go on a baboon hunt with some of the Boers that afternoon.

"Have you ever met Oom Hendriks, Henry?" he asked.

When Henry shook his head saying, "The name doesn't come to mind." William continued, "Well, his homestead is a few miles to the south east, not far from the Vaal River, and he keeps sheep, mainly, but his wife keeps chickens and has a large vegetable garden that produces enough food for the family all the year round. They have a permanent fountain nearly as good as the one at Kuruman and she has developed the garden so successfully that there is sufficient excess produce each week for them to bring into the town to sell. Over the years they have frequently had their crops ruined or absolutely destroyed by wildlife, even though a raised platform has been built, giving Oom an all round view from fifteen feet above the ground. He sits on his tower all day, but the results are no different. The baboons squat in separate groups just out of range of his shot and gradually creep up. Once he has fired – and frequently missed -- they race in, grab a handful of vegetables or a chicken, and scurry away before he can reload. Buck, such as the little steenbok or impala, as well as porcupines and other vermin have been shot, but only once or twice has a baboon been bagged. Now the troop has become too large, there are more than fifty of them Oom Hendriks believes, so their food requirement is enormous and some of the big males are threatening people who venture near their territory. They wouldn't hesitate to attack and kill a child."

"What about predators? Are there no leopards to keep the numbers down?"

"It's a long time since there were any leopards seen around here. The farmers were afraid for their livestock when they first settled here, and organised shooting parties to eradicate them. I think they succeeded. You'll find leopard skin karosses in most homesteads. Now it's the baboons and jackals that take the newborn lambs and other livestock. Nature is cruel in Africa and not easily tamed."

Henry nodded. "It is a harsh and unforgiving land. A Godless land. We need many more missionaries to bring civilisation and order here."

William wasn't convinced by that argument, but he had no desire to begin a discussion on a subject that couldn't be resolved and might easily lead to disagreement.

"Well, Oom Hendriks has organised a hunt to take place this afternoon and he needs as many guns as are available. I have already accepted and you have an invitation to join us if you have a mind to do so. Everyone is meeting at the farm."

Henry was fully in favour. He needed some exercise and knew that he would enjoy the ride. He realised that the company of the Boers might not appeal to him, as he had heard a great deal about their appalling behaviour to the native tribes since his arrival on the continent and more recently during his stay at Kuruman, but he felt that the encounter might be instructive. People in England would be sure to ask him for his own impressions of these settlers.

William continued, "A strong fence has been necessary too, and they have had to employ an armed crop guard to protect the growing plants, but recently, with the lack of natural food in the bush, the depredations have not only begun to make an inroad into the profitability of the scheme but might also deprive the family of food for months to come. The jackals are frequently a problem round the chicken coops, but it is the baboons that are the greatest menace in the garden."

Henry smiled grimly. "I know all about jackals and baboons and their ability to destroy crops or livestock. We had problems with them in Inyati."

"Oh yes. Well the baboons are the greatest thieves and they show immense cunning. Apparently, they somehow manage to elude the guard."

Henry was unsure about how the Boers would treat him if once they became aware that he was a missionary who ministered to the Matabele. However, he really ought to know a little more about these people who rejected English law and order and felt that they were a superior race of people. He was not a man to miss out on such an opportunity.

In addition to all these considerations, he was a practical man. His father's carrier business in Yorkshire dealt a great deal with farmers and William was well aware of the necessity of controlling vermin and predators. Unlike many of his peers he might not approve of killing just for the sport, but he did accept that there were times when animals had to be killed for the benefit of the people who needed meat in their diet or to protect their own domestic animals.

As the meal was finished, Henry stood up resolutely and ready for action.

"I shall be pleased to join you. Oscar is in excellent shape and will benefit from an opportunity to have a good gallop. I'll go and saddle up now. I'll make arrangements for the children to stay at the predikant's house and I might also need to excuse myself from dinner there tonight if we are late returning. Jane, go and have a short rest before I take you to the predikant's house for the afternoon and evening."

William nodded. "Excellent. I shall be glad to have you with me as a trusted friend and fine shot. The Boers are first class shots, too, and live in the saddle, but I'm a stranger to most of them, so I'll be glad of a friendly face. I'll go and get my gun and extra bullets, then I'll join you at the kraal."

Isabelle and James raced off to the Hargreaves wagon, as they had been bidden, pushing to be first up and over the wheel. Jane and Harry were walking in the same direction when Jane spotted an animal entering the outspan area.

"Father, is that one of those dogs coming back to look for food?" she called out.

Henry paused at the gate to the kraal and looked in the direction Jane was pointing.

Initially, he couldn't see anything, but Harry's sharp gaze had pinpointed the place where the animal stood uncertainly in the shade.

"It's there, over there beside the bush," he shouted excitedly and turned to go towards it. As he moved he saw that there were several others behind it.

Henry's stern and peremptory command halted him immediately.

"Stop right now. Stand still, Harry. Turn round. Now go at once with Jane to the wagon. Don't run, but walk quietly. Jane, find my rifle and put it with the powder and shot on the driver's box."

Puzzled, Jane and Harry did as they were bidden, though the wagon was still twenty yards away. Standing in the wagon, Isabelle and James were watching curiously and suddenly called out. "The dogs are coming after you."

Henry looked towards the bush Harry had mentioned and saw the animals creeping forward into the sunshine and begin moving at a shambling run towards the children.

"You're right," he muttered.

As he appraised the situation, Henry's pulse beat faster. There was immediate danger. He was too far away to intervene.

"Run, Jane. Run, Harry, as fast as you can. You must get into the wagon and close the flaps."

Father's urgent shout unnerved Jane, who stumbled as she began to run the remaining few yards. Harry passed her and scrambled rapidly up over the front wheel into the wagon, tumbling headfirst in his haste and pushing Isabelle and James to one side.

Henry picked up a small stone, the only loose object he could discover and, running towards the dogs, he threw his missile whilst roaring injunctions at them to halt and disperse. The stone, little more than a pebble, struck the leading dog on the shoulder, but the animal didn't even falter or turn to see where the attack had originated. Its staring eyes fixed on the movement ahead, it ran on.

Henry knew that these cowardly creatures had sensed a fearful prey and he fully understood the danger to Jane, although he was already running to head off this small group of feral animals.

He shouted at the top of his voice, "Run faster, Jane."

His bellow was a primeval reaction aimed at releasing his own agony and tension, but also with the hope of temporarily distracting the savage animals, thus diverting their attention and slowing them sufficiently to enable Jane to reach safety.

Henry was so distraught at his own inability to race to his daughter's aid and with every sense concentrated on the drama unfolding ahead, that he had failed to hear or see William approaching from his own wagon, so the sudden roar of a gun took him by surprise.

It was fortunate that the dogs were still more than a yard behind the desperately racing, fearful child and that William was in a position to fire without in any way endangering her. Nevertheless, the bullet, entering the body of the leading beast just under its heart, didn't kill it immediately, merely halting it momentarily.

It was a large brute with a shaggy, unkempt, light yellow coat, and the impetus of its rush carried it forward.

As Jane reached the wagon, scrambling frantically for hand and footholds, the wounded, though still mobile and dangerous, dog reached her, jostled from behind by its followers.

Harry, trying desperately to pull his sister upwards away from the gaping jaws, and holding onto her arm, was in many ways more of a hindrance, as he prevented her from grasping the wooden side and pulling herself up.

The dog's jaws fastened onto the heel of her boot.

William's second shot had of necessity to be aimed downwards well away from Jane and hit not only the fiercest aggressor but two of the other dogs as well.

The dying animal was flung aside by the force of the bullet and the boot heel was wrenched away from the upper as Jane overbalanced into the wagon.

William immediately hurried over to put bullets into the still twitching bodies of the two injured animals whilst Henry raced across to examine Jane's damaged boot and foot.

The remaining dogs had fled.

"I thank God that you are not hurt," Henry exclaimed in relief as he saw that there were no marks on his daughter's leg or damage to the boot other than the missing heel. "I'll mend that tomorrow. Meanwhile you'll have to walk with it as it is."

The other children were white faced and still frightened by the fearsome event so recently enacted but were unaware of how nearly Jane had been to being savagely bitten, possibly even killed. Their fear had been engendered by Henry's obvious panic, his urgent exhortation, Jane's haunted face as she endured her desperate flight followed relentlessly by the fierce animals and then the brutal deaths of the animals right beside their wagon.

"All these dogs are a great danger to people and if their numbers increase any more the townspeople themselves will be in danger, in addition to visitors," declared William angrily. He was furious and shaken by the sudden fearful occurrence that had erupted in such a short time after a peaceful, happy, relaxed lunch. The violent and unexpected episode had upset both men.

Henry nodded silently, still out of breath after his hopeless but determined effort to reach Jane before the dogs.

Both he and William had had a severe shock. William at least had three consolations, one was the fact that Fox was still confined in his wagon and had therefore not become embroiled in the turmoil, the second was the fact that his cool action had saved the whole situation, whilst the third and most important was the fact that Jane had not been injured.

Henry turned to shake him by the hand. "Thank you, William. That was a fine bit of shooting. You saved my daughter from a severe mauling."

With the children still listening, he didn't add that William had almost certainly saved Jane's life.

William wasn't embarrassed by the accolade, he knew that he had aimed surely, even at such a tense and appalling moment when losing his nerve or misfiring would have resulted in devastating consequences. He knew, however, that his reactions had been purely instinctive and it was only after the event was over that he could view the outcome dispassionately and realise fully how close his bullets were to the little girl.

He spoke hurriedly to hide his emotions.

"We'll have to get these bodies buried. I know where most of the servants are. I'll go and ask Lukas to arrange it this afternoon whilst we are away and you can ask Bokkis to shoot any strays he sees."

"The danger is over, children." Henry was trying to sound reassuring, but he found himself trembling.

Jane, minus the heel of her shoe, was still ashen and breathing heavily. Her body was shaking as she tried to recover from the terrifying race and suddenly she began to cough.

"Could I please have a drink of water, father?" she begged, between spasms. She sat down, suddenly feeling very odd. Slowly, she sipped from the mug of water her father had handed to her.

"Why did the dogs want to attack us?" she asked, as she began to feel a little less sick and her coughing subsided.

Henry decided that there was little point in discussing the behaviour of animals whose hunting instincts were roused when they spotted a weaker prey running away. He spoke gently to his daughter, "Go and lie down. You need to rest after that race. I'll tell you more about these animals another time."

Not altogether reluctantly, Jane hobbled to father's bed in her ungainly boot and lay down. Despite the fact that she still felt funny and shaky, as she listened to Isabelle's monotonous voice reading a story to James in the welcome warmth of the sun-heated tent, she fell asleep.

CHAPTER 36

Jane woke abruptly when her siblings began clambering over father's bed, where she had been lying.

"Come on, Jane," Isabelle urged her. "Father is taking us to the predikant's house for the afternoon. He and Mr William are going to shoot baboons."

With James and Harry scrambling over her, Jane had little option but to lift herself off the bed and follow them, although she would have preferred to stay where she was. Father and Mr William were both mounted and waiting impatiently for the children to join them. As Jane climbed down from the wagon, she was relieved to see that there was no sign of the dogs' carcasses.

"Papa, please may I have a ride on Oscar?" begged Harry, hopefully.

"Papa, me. Me. Me ride Oscar," James demanded loudly, his arms raised in supplication.

"I think Jane had better ride with me this time," Henry decided, decisively.

"Her shoe is broken and she cannot walk easily until it's mended. Come Jane, give me your arm."

Jane was quickly lifted to sit side-saddle in front of Henry and there she sat, silently, hardly daring to breathe at this marvellous experience. It was almost worth suffering the nightmare of the dogs if this was the reward, even for such a short journey that she would normally have walked in five minutes.

William had decided against taking Fox with him on the hunt, but instead would leave him with his friends in the town, as he felt he couldn't leave the dog alone in the wagon for several hours. Accordingly, he set off with Fox trotting behind, and arranged to meet up with Henry later.

The predikant's wife met them at the door and, having learned about the mishap to Jane's shoe, she immediately promised to have the shoe mended that afternoon. Meanwhile, Jane could wear some slippers belonging to one of her children. Henry expressed his thanks and promised payment with store goods that were always acceptable.

Leaving the town behind, the two men spurred their horses forward, galloping away as fast as they could. It was a ride of several miles to the Hendriks' farm, which was much closer to the Vaal River.

As the cool wind rushed past him, Henry felt exhilarated and the tense fears engendered by the lunchtime affray were swept aside.

William, riding ahead, was equally unrestrained and the two men continued until their mounts began to slow, showing signs of fatigue.

Henry drew alongside William and smiled. "I needed that opportunity to blow the cobwebs away and enjoy the exercise without the strain of having to hunt or worry about the wagons."

William laughed. "Yes. Galloping like that is sheer pleasure. It makes a man feel like a king. You take life too seriously, Henry. You need to relax more often." He held up a hand, as Henry appeared about to object to this remark. "Oh, I know that you are a missionary, a man of God and a family man, but life does have more to offer, you know."

"We are all as God made us. I enjoy many things, perhaps not as you do or in a frivolous manner, though my life since arriving in Africa has been one of great responsibility. You are still single and free of the duties of a father. The care of four motherless children sometimes weighs heavily on me. Sometimes their lives seem so fragile that they may be whipped away when I'm not looking. I shall forever be in your debt for saving Jane's life. Your timely appearance, and the fact that you had your gun and ammunition ready, was fortuitous."

"Or God's will," William remarked seriously. "It would have been a great deal more dangerous if the dogs had arrived as we were eating. I'm surprised they didn't arrive earlier. Perhaps it was because we ate very early and were dining on cold meats rather than cooking, but there were no servants around to help today and the cowardly scavengers would have tried to get food from the two smallest people. We were fortunate to be spared having James and Harry as casualties. Bites from those stray dogs can become infected very easily."

"You're right, of course, but I shall not forget your opportune intervention. Is that the farm over there?"

"Yes, that is Lekkerwater and we seem to be the last to arrive, judging by the number of horses tied up in front of the house."

They tethered their own horses to a tree and off-saddled before going to get buckets of water for the animals. The hospitable farmer had also left out some grain and once the two horses had drained the buckets they were given a small feed. Then Henry and William walked through a small wooden gate into a walled garden from which the sound of noisy chatter and laughter emanated.

Oom Hendriks himself welcomed the two men and their names were shouted out to the large group of men crowding round a table, where dishes of steaming boerwors and lamb chops hot from the grills over the nearby fires were stacked alongside jugs of lemon drink and beer.

William and Henry joined the group, members of whom nodded at them and made way for them to reach the food, but continued talking to each other in their own guttural language. Although they had had lunch, the meat smelled so delicious to men who had just ridden several miles that both Henry and

William availed themselves of the food on offer.

Later, when Oom Hendricks had explained the plan of attack, the large group was split into two smaller parties. His son Jacobus led one group, first heading eastwards before turning northwards. Oom Hendriks rode off in the opposite direction, riding westwards for quarter of a mile before turning to the north. Henry and William had been selected to join this group and rode easily at the rear.

Numbers of hunting dogs accompanied both parties, eager to participate in the excitement, but like good hunting dogs they remained silent. Their baying and barking would begin when the action began.

"I wish I knew what is intended of us," confided Henry. "I didn't understand a single word of Oom Hendriks' speech. Whatever was he saying?"

"I'm not exactly fluent in Dutch," William apologised as they trailed behind. "I think the plan is for us to prevent the troop of baboons from reaching their regular sleeping places in the kopje about a mile away. There is a copse of trees between the farm and the kopje so if we can force them to seek safety in those trees we shall be able to surround and shoot them. If we waited until they reached the kopje we'd never succeed. Bullets ricocheting round the rocks would be dangerous and the animals would hide in the cracks and caves. Oom Hendriks and his friends have worked out the best way to accomplish their plan.

It's rather like Shaka's battle plan. He famously taught his warriors to fan out in two 'horns' from the 'head,' or centre, of his army and surround the enemy, taking them by surprise by the lightning pincer movement. Here we have two groups riding towards the horizon until we're out of sight of the baboons that are waiting near the Hendriks' garden hoping for some easy food after a fruitless search of the bush earlier in the day.

The Hendriks had scouts out watching where the baboons were foraging before they headed for the garden. That's why we were all waiting at the farm. Once we're out of sight, we'll ride round behind the kopje. When we meet up with the others some men will move slowly and carefully round to the sides and front of the kopje. I expect the baboons will have a lookout and no doubt the men will be seen, but the marauders will be too far away to reach the kopje before we have it surrounded. The baboons will be returning to their home just before sunset and it is hoped that if they find they cannot reach the rocks they will seek refuge in the trees."

"Well, for someone who claims not to understand the language you seem to have learned a great deal and it sounds like a well thought out plan. No wonder Oom Hendriks needed so many men. If the gaps between them are too wide as they spread out to circle the kopje the baboons will make a run for it and the men might end up shooting each other."

William grinned sheepishly.

"Whilst Oom Hendriks was telling everyone what was planned I was standing next to a man who spoke some English and he translated a few of the instructions for me, but I did understand most of it," he added defensively.

Henry laughed appreciatively. "You certainly make the most of your talents William. Oho! Now it looks as though we are turning east again. We must have passed the kopje on our north westerly ride, although we can't see it yet. It must be still too far away."

"Yes, we are probably in the right place, though it's probably nearer than you think. These Boers know the veld as well as they know their own home. Oom Hendricks is still travelling at a steady pace, but I fear the baboons will soon realise that we are closing up on them. They are intelligent brutes and always have their lookouts. I suspect there might even be a guard at the very top of the kopje and it will give the alert the minute it spots us on its horizon. Possibly even before, if it hears the horses."

The line of men had been following a dry streambed, which was not particularly deep, but the tall, thick, dry, brown grass that marked its course had kept them hidden from the kopje. As soon as the men at the front breasted the rise there came a sharp bark from the topmost rock of the kopje, which Henry was astonished to see was only a few hundred yards to the east. Oom Hendriks gave the order to gallop, since there was no longer any need for a stealthy approach and the foraging baboons were already alerted to the danger and could be seen heading with all speed towards their refuge. The plan to meet up behind the kopje had to be abandoned. The greatest urgency now was to form a line in front of the rocks before the baboons could reach safety.

With their horses at full stretch, they charged across the open ground, the dogs racing ahead and barking as they heard the calls of their quarry amongst the rocks. Excitement spread through the horsemen converging rapidly with those of Jacobus' group approaching equally swiftly from the east. Men were shouting and whooping with pleasure at the prospect of the forthcoming sport. The calls were also intended to disturb the animals that had abandoned their vigil by the garden many hundreds of yards away to the right and were bounding with great leaps for the safety of the rocks.

A few of the sprightly young males slipped between the rapidly converging forces, though the dogs attacked several of these and fierce skirmishes ensued. Watching the savage encounters, William was relieved that he had left Fox behind. He knew that baboons with their long, sharp canine teeth inflict terrible damage on an opponent and few dogs would escape without serious injury from such a battle.

In this sort of melee the game little terrier would have been torn to pieces. No one could risk shooting as dogs and baboons were a constantly moving mass, indistinguishable as they rolled around in a fury of snapping teeth.

The majority of the animals (upwards of thirty), by now thoroughly alarmed, headed for the perceived safety of the trees and climbed rapidly to the uppermost branches.

Exulting in the success of their strategy, the hunters surrounded the trees and moved inwards until they had formed a tight circle. Many of the men dismounted and moved their mounts away, but a number were happier shooting from the saddle.

With rifles aimed at a sharp upward angle, there was no danger to the men opposite them and the massacre began.

For almost half an hour the noise continued, with guns firing constantly, men shouting and cheering, animals chattering or screaming in fear, defiance, anger or pain and dogs barking and howling.

Henry ignored the noise and concentrated on achieving accuracy each time he fired, refusing to be hurried or distracted by others' shouts and reloading with painstaking care to avoid any mishaps.

When the baboons were finally disposed of men began to look for their dogs, a number of which were so badly injured that they had to be shot immediately. Many others would need careful nursing for days or weeks to recover from the tears and bites.

The men gathered together in the sudden silence and immediately began exchanging anecdotes about their dogs or their own shooting prowess. If anyone had cared to count up the numerous claims made that afternoon almost a hundred baboons had been killed instead of the actual number of just less than thirty.

The bodies littered the veld close to the trees and the men knew the vultures, jackals and other scavengers would revel in the unexpected feast for a day or two. Certainly within a week there would be nothing left, not even bones to show that so many pests had been slaughtered in one spot.

When it was all over, Oom Hendriks thanked them all for their help and invited them back to the farm for a celebration.

Although William and Henry were pleased to be included in the invitation, it was already very late and they knew that it would be dark before they could reach Griquatown. Besides, Isaac and Martha had made it clear that they would wait for Henry to return before eating supper.

Somewhat reluctantly, they made their apologetic explanations, hoping that they had been fully understood, and left the Boers with many words of goodwill shouted after them as they departed.

For a long time, neither man spoke as they headed back towards the town, each lost in his own thoughts. William was delighted with the outcome of the shoot.

He had exulted in his own ability to drop more than one of the baboons with a single fatal shot, not an easy accomplishment with targets that were constantly moving. The excitement generated by the hunters had been exhilarating. In fact, with so many men firing, he had been surprised at how long it had taken them to dispose of only thirty animals.

Henry was less pleased. His feelings were ambivalent and he said as much as they neared the town.

"When I was young I used to help some of the farmers kill the rats in the cornfields and barns at harvest time. We all considered it was great sport as well as giving us a feeling of righteousness for removing pests and would each try to kill more than anyone else. It was a great competition every time, but bloody, with heavy sticks, sickles and scythes to do the deeds. Somehow it seemed normal then and the right thing to do. We never considered the rats as anything more than a scourge and deserving of death. Then, as a young man, I studied theology and medicine in order to follow my calling as a missionary. My ideas changed somewhat and the more I tried to save lives the more I came to value all life.

When we lived in Inyati, I and my wife tried not to kill the rats if we could find other ways to discourage them, though that wasn't easy. Regretfully, we sometimes had to kill some animals to protect our crops, without which we would have died."

"Do you regret your participation in today's hunt, then? You sound unhappy about it," William queried.

"No. I don't regret helping to protect the Hendriks' crops. I know that it was necessary to remove some of the baboons. But I don't think I shall ever forget the sight of the piles of bodies underneath those trees. I know baboons are pests and ugly pests at that. I have never liked them, but some of the bodies looked almost human. The cries and screams sounded almost human, too, and I looked at the fierce exultation on the faces of the hunters and wondered if I looked like that. No. I have no regrets about helping Oom Hendriks to protect his crops, the product of his labour and source of his sustenance, but I hope never to participate in another such massacre."

"It's fortunate that your family didn't buy you into the army, Henry, where you would see worse massacres than we inflicted today," William remarked dryly. "After some battles there are hundreds or even thousands of bodies strewn over the battlefield. Men's bodies, not those ugly raiders there under the trees. I consider we were set a task and we performed that task to the best of our ability. Besides, animals were put on this earth to be used by men, they don't have feelings like us. I hope you don't think ill of me, but I enjoyed it. It was fine sport. In Africa there are always the hunters and the hunted. It is a circle of life and death that you cannot change.

You must accept that and set your mind at rest about the results today. I'll bid you goodnight now, as my friends' home is this way. I'll see you sometime tomorrow." So saying, William turned away with a cheery wave.

"Goodnight. God be with you," returned Henry, as he rode on towards the de Koks' house.

He off-saddled behind the house and tethered Oscar within reach of food and water before knocking at the door. He was in good time for the evening meal and was warmly welcomed. The children had had their meal earlier, but had awaited Henry's return because it was the de Koks' custom to have family prayers every evening.

"Was your hunt a good one?" queried Isaac as they sat at table.

"It was certainly successful as far as Oom Hendriks was concerned. The troublesome marauders have been considerably lessened in number. I should think that more than half the troop has been destroyed. It is possible that the rest of the baboons might well move off now, but even if they stayed they are not likely to be as much of a problem as they were before."

"You don't sound very excited by the event," Isaac probed gently.

"I didn't enjoy it as much as most of the men. As far as I was concerned we were there to help Oom Hendriks and we did. I don't think that wholesale slaughter of animals is particularly exciting and there is certainly no sport in exterminating trapped animals, except perhaps when men are desperate for meat. On this occasion it was necessary to destroy pests. Pleasure and excitement were not uppermost in my mind, but I did have an opportunity to meet some Boers for the first time and was impressed by their open hospitality. Unfortunately, I didn't have an opportunity to converse with anyone as very few of them understood English and I have no knowledge of Dutch. They seem to be hard men well suited to the hard life they lead."

"I lived in Cape Town when I was young, otherwise I would not be able to converse with you. Learning many languages is essential for a missionary. We cannot spread God's Word if we cannot communicate with the heathens."

"I have already discovered that truth," admitted Henry.

With the meal over and the prayers completed, Henry gathered his children together to offer their thanks to Isaac and Martha and gratefully added his own as they all made their farewells.

"I hope we may see you tomorrow," called Isaac.

The children waited patiently as Henry saddled Oscar, then Henry lifted a sleepy James onto Oscar's back in front of the saddle. Isabelle was allowed for the first time to sit decorously on the saddle itself and Harry was lifted up behind. Jane strode happily beside Henry, her mended boot comfortable once more, as they set off for the short walk back to the outspan.

The night was silent, with no sign of dogs or people on the dark road as they plodded along.

"Look stars. Lots of stars," called out James, suddenly pointing to the sky.

"I can see the Southern Cross," Harry claimed proudly.

"I can see it too. Right there," Isabelle added.

Henry had begun to teach them the names of the stars and planets after Jane and Harry's near fatal adventure, with a view to their learning how people need never get lost by day or night if they followed God's pointers: the stars and the sun.

It had been William's idea originally to include the movements of the sun in his Geography lessons. Henry hadn't been convinced, but as he watched the children facing east as the sun rose and west in the evening as it set, whilst using their arms to point north and south, chanting the directions over and over, he began to realise the value of this knowledge.

Daily on the trek from Kuruman, the children had been asked to point out the four compass directions and to decide which way the wagons were heading.

It was natural then to start teaching them of the value to travellers of the Southern Cross at night as a pointer to the south, from which they could work out a rough idea of the other directions.

"Every day when we set out you must notice which direction we take. Whenever we walk away from the wagons you must do the same. Always be aware of the direction you travel and you will never be lost again."

CHAPTER 37

The dog was chasing her. It didn't matter how hard she tried or how fast she ran, she simply couldn't get away and it was about to pounce on her. She could hear the scrabbling paws, the panting breath and a fearsome growling. As she tripped and fell she screamed in terror, her heart beating furiously, her body hot yet shivering in terror. Still gripped in the most horrible fear, Jane sat bolt upright in bed, her clothes sticking clammily to her skin, her breathing harsh and the chill night air rasping into her lungs.
Her shriek and sudden movement had startled Isabelle, who also sat up and began crying. This in turn wakened James, who was lying next to her.
The joint babble inevitably wakened Henry.
"What on earth is happening? Stop that noise at once."
Henry's tone of annoyance brought Jane back to reality more quickly and surely than her siblings crying.
"I'm sorry, father. I think I had a nasty dream," she mumbled apologetically. Her explanation faltered.
"Well, your nasty dream has disturbed everyone and spoilt a good night's sleep. Lie down immediately and go back to sleep, all of you. Don't let me hear another sound."
Obediently, the three children lay down again. Harry hadn't stirred and James was soon asleep once more. Isabelle, in one of her kindly, generous moods gave Jane a cuddle before she too was breathing quietly.
It took Jane much longer to settle, for her racing heart to resume its normal rhythm and her fears to subside. She concentrated on the gentle breathing of all her family, assuring herself that no harm would befall her whilst father slept there beside them. She said some fervent prayers, chief amongst them being that morning would soon come and that she wouldn't disturb father again. Thus comforted, she too fell asleep.
Drinking hot coffee at six o'clock in the morning, Henry and William sat in companionable silence. Fox sat happily beside William's chair. Birdsong and the noises of a camp coming to life around them were comforting in their normality.
By the early morning light they could see the servants drinking their undoubtedly oversweet tea and cooking their mealie porridge in a large black three-legged pot.
"It is a pleasure to be able to relax for a time without being disturbed," Henry remarked, eventually.
"Yes. We have helped the townspeople here considerably by removing some

of those dangerous dogs. I wonder how long it will be before there are just as many again?" William pondered.

He answered his own question by continuing, "Not very long, I suppose. Just about every traveller through here brings dogs, sometimes large numbers of them and some people are careless about leaving dogs behind when they move on. Not to mention natural increase."

"Now that you mention moving on, I have been wondering if we should move on today." Henry's expression suggested a question and William immediately replied.

"Let's go and look at the animals. If they are in good condition we could certainly leave today. We ought to spend the next hour greasing the axles on all the wagons, then we can breakfast before packing up."

As she and the other children arrived for breakfast an hour later, Jane was delighted to learn of the impending departure. Although the dogs had not harassed her since her appalling experience with them, she had heard them barking fiercely in and around the town. Fear of them had remained with her even during the day and the awful nightmare was still fresh in her mind. She would have no regrets when Griquatown was left behind.

"Where are we going to now, papa?" asked Harry eagerly when breakfast was over.

"We are heading first for the Vaal River then we'll cross the Orange River to reach Hopetown," Henry explained. "I think Mr William has told you about the two mighty rivers we have to cross."

The children nodded solemnly and their eyes sparkled at the thought of actually seeing the rivers MrWilliam had described.

By lunchtime William had led the caravan nearly twelve miles southeast of Griquatown.

"How long will it take us to reach Hopetown, father?" Jane queried after they had finished eating lunch.

"Griquatown to Hopetown is about seventy miles but it will take us about six days, as we won't be travelling on Sunday. The rivers are very wide, especially the Orange. Do you remember the rivers, Jane?"

"Yes, I think so. I remember seeing a lot of water and being afraid that we would never reach the other side, but mother was laughing and saying it was wonderful to be getting closer to Cape Town. I don't think she was quite so happy on the way home."

Henry gave a small smile as he too remembered that occasion.

"I had to remind her that Cape Town was still many hundreds of miles away and we still had the Karroo to cross, but she continued to be optimistic and happy about our progress. She loved Cape Town and you're right, she wasn't too happy about returning to the privations of Inyati. Only her spiritual strength kept her going. She never complained, though, knowing that we were both servants of the Lord."

Henry stopped abruptly. This was his daughter who was listening to his reminiscences. He had said quite enough. Quickly he changed the topic.

"In two days time we shall be crossing the Vaal and for this part of the journey the animals will have sufficient grazing and water."

Thoughtfully, he looked at his elder daughter and continued, "You missed your lessons this morning because we were travelling, so you must all go and rest now and we'll have time for some schoolwork before we trek again this evening."

Both Henry and William enjoyed successful hunts that afternoon and two fine roan antelopes provided some welcome venison for the camp. The horns and hides were added to the baggage wagons for sale in Cape Town.

For the next two days, the daily trek resumed its regular rather dull pattern through a dry bushy landscape with rocky hills dotted about and occasional ridges obscuring distant views, and so their first view of the Vaal River was greeted by excited exclamations.

Whilst they were still some distance away, William pointed out to children the line of green trees ahead and explained that the trees indicated the course of the river, as they flourished along its banks where there was also green grass. The trees could easily be seen above the low bushes that covered the area through which they were travelling, especially as there was a gentle downwards incline.

All the children were riding in the wagon, for the countryside was covered with wait-a-bit bushes whose thorns tore clothing and skin alike and none of them wanted to experience the unpleasant, indeed painful, barbed thorns again.

As they drew closer to the river, Harry and Isabelle, for whom this was a unique sight, were especially awe-struck at the amazing stretch of water. A short time later they experienced a closer view and could barely comprehend the size of this river. From where they stood, at the top of the steep stony bank staring over the fast moving brown water, the far bank appeared to be almost a day's trek away.

James too, clutching Jane's hand tightly, jumped up and down with delight.

"Is this the sea?" he asked, gazing up at her.

"No. Not yet. It is going to be a long time before we see the sea. This is a river. It is the Vaal River. Mr William and your papa have told us about it. I remember seeing it once before. It was when Harry was a baby."

"Will we see crocodiles?" There was anxiety in this question and Jane knew that he was remembering the time when he had seen a dog taken by a crocodile.

She smiled reassuringly, "I don't expect we shall see any today," she told him, praying that she was right, for she knew that there were crocodiles in every river.

"We might see some hippopotamuses though," she added encouragingly, seeking to distract him from the thought of crocodiles. You haven't seen a real live hippopotamus before. They like to live in deep water. They look just like your special toy, but they are very big animals."

Henry, who was still mounted on his horse, was just behind them listening to their chatter and now he spoke quietly to them, "If you look to your left, Jane, there, upriver, you'll see a whole school of hippopotamuses. They only appear now and then, so you'll have to keep your eyes on the spot. Can you see where there is a patch of sand on this bank further along to your left? The water isn't moving so fast at that spot because there is a deep pool. Hippos like to have a deep pool where they can go under water and they like to have a sloping beach so that they can come out at night to feed on the grass. They are interesting to watch, but they are very dangerous animals, so we don't go too close to them. Look, you can see four or five heads appearing now."

"I can see them," called Harry and within seconds the heads had disappeared.

"Yes, Harry, I expect you could, but your loud shout has frightened them. You must be much quieter next time. Use your eyes, not your mouth. Now, Mr William and I are going to find out how deep the river is before we try to take the wagons across. We shan't be too long. You will stay here until it is time for our wagon to move and then you will climb back into it."

William lifted Fox from the saddle and handed him to Harry.

"Harry, please hold onto Fox for me. The current is strong and fast in the middle of the river and I think it would be much safer for him to stay here. He can ride over in one of the wagons later."

Harry was delighted with the task and puffed out his chest. "I'll look after him," he asserted confidently and he lowered the dog to the ground whilst holding firmly onto the leather collar that Henry had made for Fox many weeks earlier.

Henry and William rode further along the bank and down to where there was a makeshift access route to the water. Over the past ten years the constant traffic of oxen, wagons and their owners across the most fordable part of the river had worn and cut a passage in the steep bank to make access to or from the river more possible. Twenty years ago the oxen and wagons had to cope with this untouched steep bank and weary beasts struggling out of the water could barely manage to haul the loads upwards.

The children watched the horses and their riders moving away from the safety of the land, forcing their way forward through the calmer waters into the fast moving current and into deeper parts, where the water rose over their stirrups.

They were almost swimming at one point until past halfway when they found shallower water. The men continued to the far bank before turning and retracing their path. Jane heaved a sigh of relief as she saw them moving slowly back towards the safety of the land.

Fox had whined anxiously as William moved further and further away, straining against his collar and testing Harry's strength to the utmost. Then, without warning, the little dog turned abruptly and gave several sharp barks, pulling Harry backward into the undergrowth. Harry hung onto the collar with grim determination, at the same time commanding Fox to sit and stay.

Isabelle hurried over to grab Fox at the other side, adding her exhortations to Harry's.

It was this noise and commotion that obviously disturbed a creature that had been lying unobserved in the undergrowth, for it appeared unexpectedly immediately behind them, racing hurriedly and noisily between them as it headed for the safety of the river. All four children screamed with fright as they were confronted by this horrifyingly fearsome-looking animal apparently intent upon attacking them.

Jane immediately lifted James up into her arms, hugging him close. Isabelle and Harry were dragged to the ground by an excited dog determined to give chase and even then to their credit they continued to restrain Fox.

As the children's screams reached their ears, William and Henry urged their steeds forward, but the horses couldn't move any quicker than they were doing already, owing to the drag of the water.

It was the greatest relief to everyone, the animal included, when it plunged down the bank and disappeared into the water with a rattle of displaced stones and a loud splash.

"Papa. Papa," shouted Harry with great glee as soon as he had picked himself up and recovered his composure. He stood sturdily facing the river, refusing to show or admit he had felt any fear. "There was an enormous crocodile. Fox wanted to chase it, but we never let him go." He glanced triumphantly at Isabelle, who was still trembling and brushing away the soil and leaves from her dress with her free hand.

It was William who replied, "That wasn't a crocodile, Harry. It was a monitor lizard. They prefer to be on land but always rush straight for the safety of water when they think they are in danger. It wasn't really large. I think it was only three or four feet long. Fox would probably have killed it, even though monitors have sharp teeth, but the monitor would have fought back furiously and no doubt caused a lot of damage. I'm glad you held onto him and made sure he was safe." He called Fox to him before riding back to his wagons.

Henry glanced at Jane. "Put James down, Jane," he ordered.

"There was no need for all that fuss. You weren't in any danger. That animal was much more frightened than you were. It was only trying to escape."

Jane hung her head. She felt that father's censure was unfair. After all, she had never seen a monitor lizard before and it did look like a crocodile. Besides, its sudden noisy rush for the river had startled them all and they had been unable to suppress their screams of fear. It had been an automatic reaction but now she felt ashamed at having been seen as a coward.

"Sorry, father. We didn't know what it was and we thought it was coming towards us."

Henry nodded curtly before going with William to organise the crossing.

Owing to the depth of the water in parts and the strength of the current in others they decided that the young leaders, who were small and likely to be swept away, should ride beside the drivers in the wagons and that they themselves would take it in turns to lead the teams across. Even Amos and Abdol were vulnerable, being light and skinny, though wiry and capable of handling the oxen.

Harry waited with growing impatience for papa to return so that the Hargreaves wagon could set off. He watched William's wagons reach the farther bank, papa was leading the second one with William now on his third journey across the Vaal leading the third one. Theirs would be next.

His excitement was great when at last the wagon rolled and bounced down into the river and the water rose up the sides of the wagon, threatening to sweep them downstream.

Jane forced herself to remain composed, despite her concern at the rising water. After all, she reminded herself, she had seen William's wagons cross safely, but as an extra precaution she murmured prayers to herself pleading with God to keep them all safe. She kept her eyes resolutely on the sturdy oxen ploughing strongly onwards, occasionally glancing at Henry's back as he rode confidently beside the lead oxen.

Isabelle, too, was filled with some trepidation but wouldn't allow Harry to see her fear and so she copied him by looking over the side at the water racing below.

James was dancing up and down laughing at the flood racing and gurgling just a few inches below them.

Jane had to speak to them quite sharply at one point as their antics almost caused them to overbalance. Hastily, she grabbed hold of James and pulled him to safety.

"Harry, you must not lean over the side like that. Isabelle, come away from Harry or you will fall into the water. This river is very dangerous." She leaned over and pulled Isabelle's arm to emphasise her order.

Annoyed at the interference, Isabelle tugged herself free and overbalanced. In doing so, she came very close to falling over the side, only saving herself by grabbing hold of Harry and almost pushing him into the water.

Harry was both furious and shaken, turning towards her and yelling, "Just be careful. You almost threw me into the river. If I hadn't been holding on tightly, I would have fallen."

Isabelle's face showed her distress. The incident had immediately sobered her. Alarmed by the narrow escape and the shouting, Jane glanced quickly forward to see if father had been aware of the mishap. Luckily, the noise of the rushing water and the fact that he was so far ahead of them had masked the slight sounds of the contretemps and he was forging resolutely onward.

"Sorry, Jane. We were so excited and it is fun watching the water." Isabelle muttered guiltily. Abruptly she sat down as the wagon lurched over a hidden rock.

Tensely, they all clung to the nearest part of the wagon and even Harry sat down for a time, but he was soon on his feet again.

Despite the shock he had experienced as he had so nearly been pushed into the water, Harry thought the crossing was a great adventure and he was sorry when the far bank was reached. The wagon was pulled safely ashore and a little further on the oxen were halted ready to be out-spanned. William led the Hargreaves baggage wagon up the bank behind them, delighted that the crossing had been accomplished so successfully.

They had found a pleasant camping place with ample water from the river for people and animals. It was obviously a place where other travellers had stopped. The undergrowth had been cleared, though it was rapidly re-growing, and logs for seating were arranged in the shelter of the trees. The children would have been happy to stay there for many days, with so much to see and enjoy.

Harry found trees to climb or birds and animals to watch. Isabelle was happy to sit on a log in the shade playing with her doll, whilst James pottered about digging in the sandy soil with sticks. They were all allowed to explore as long as they didn't go too far away. They were delighted with this idyllic spot, unaware, although the men knew, that mosquitoes made the evenings and nights here unbearable.

Jane took this opportunity to do some washing. It wasn't often that there was so much water available close at hand and Lukas was willing to carry the water for her. The weather was warm enough for the clothes to dry even though father had warned her they wouldn't be staying here overnight

The men, however, had no time to enjoy this respite. After their meal they spent a considerable time checking the condition of the wagons whilst the oxen grazed. The animals didn't stray far and barely needed herding so their young leaders fell fast asleep once they had eaten their meal, joined in this pastime by most of the other servants.

By late afternoon and with everyone in good spirits the trek set off once again towards the Orange River.

CHAPTER 38

Wanting to cover as many miles as possible, William kept going until very late that night and by the time they out-spanned Henry calculated that they must have travelled more than fifteen miles, despite the heavy going. The sandy soil was a drag on the wheels and the oxen strained to keep the wagons moving, but stopping at any time made starting again even worse. Everyone was exhausted by the time William ordered a halt.

"You certainly kept us all moving," muttered Henry gruffly. "I thought we would never stop."

William laughed. "This sand is terrible isn't it? But it's even worse for the oxen in the middle of the day with the sun beating down on them and the heat shimmering back from the ground. I wanted to get past this stretch in the cool of the night, but we haven't quite made it. There are another ten miles of this type of ground ahead of us. There are some pools not too far from here where the animals can drink early tomorrow morning. The water tastes horrible but it's alright for the beasts and our water casks are full enough to last us until we reach the Orange River."

Henry nodded. "You're quite right, of course. Even the horses don't like travelling in this sand." He broke off suddenly. "Now what does Bokkis want?" he asked as he became aware of his driver close by, just visible in the starlight.

Bokkis had helped settle the oxen for the night, leaving them tied in their places though removing the yokes so that they could rest easily but not stray. He approached the two men, who were still tending their horses now unsaddled, watered and tied to the wagon for the night.

"Well, Bokkis, what do you want to see me about?" asked Henry tiredly. He hoped there wasn't a problem.

"We have no meat," Bokkis stated baldly. "We finished the last goat before we left the river. Now we have nothing." It was a complaint and almost an accusation.

William could sense that Henry was about to reply angrily and intervened quickly before he provoked a quarrel. "Thank you Bokkis for telling us. We'll go hunting tomorrow."

Having made his point Bokkis turned away without speaking and left them, his burly form soon disappearing into the starlit night.

"I suppose I should have been more aware of the situation," apologised Henry, "But why is it that these people always tell me when there is nothing left? If they mentioned it before the larder was empty I could replenish the supplies and save the unpleasantness. They always feel aggrieved and rebellious when there is no meat."

"I know all about it," William agreed. "It happens all the time and we can't all be fortune tellers with a crystal ball. I, too, should have been aware that the meat was nearly finished. After all, most of the servants are mine, but we were involved with checking all the trekking gear whilst we were at the river and we had no intention of spending a night there to be plagued by insects. Bokkis could easily have gone hunting himself when we were camped by the river and the game wasn't too difficult to find. He preferred to sleep, as they all did. They will just have to make do with mealie porridge for breakfast. Anyway, the horses are fine now and it's time we went to bed. Goodnight, Henry. Sleep well."

"Goodnight, William. I'll try not to feel either angry or guilty for forgetting to keep up the meat supply."

William laughed merrily as they parted company, wondering how long Henry might pray for forgiveness before he fell asleep.

William knew of a salt pan a little to the northwest of their road and suggested to Henry that they might well find game there as they saddled up before dawn. They had managed to have five hours sleep and felt refreshed.

"All animals seek out a salt lick from time to time so there are usually some animals to be found there," he explained. "At one time some of the Boers collected salt there, too, until they found a much richer source."

Before leaving, they had ordered that the oxen should be watered immediately then in-spanned by sunrise and the drivers should continue to trek for four hours before out-spanning about ten miles further on where the men would find them. This would mean that the sandy stretch of road was completed in the cooler hours and the oxen could rest and graze until nightfall.

"Lukas, put Fox in the children's wagon when the drivers are ready to start. If we have good hunting we will return with meat for the mid-day meal," William promised. "If the game is scarce it might be evening before we return."

They set off at a quick canter across the dusty plain. During the rainy season this was a well grassed area with sturdy full-leafed bushes, but at this time of the year the sparse ground cover was dry and brown and the bushes looked shrivelled under their coating of dust. Rocky hills broke the skyline.

"The game is much scarcer these days," William informed Henry when they had slowed to a walk some time later. "There was a time when these plains and even parts of the karroo were teeming with vast herds of springbok, many, many thousands of them and wildebeest with eland, kudu, tsessebe and oryx plentiful. Every hunter could supply his camp with ease and sportsmen came in their dozens to shoot as many animals as they could, collecting vast mounds of horns and skins as proof of their prowess with a gun. Campfire stories described the slaughter of twenty springboks at a time and wounded animals were frequently left for the lions, jackals, hyenas and vultures."

"Yes, I have read about such hunters. A number of them wrote books that inspired like-minded sportsmen to follow and emulate or even surpass their claims. There seemed to be competition to see who could kill the largest number or the biggest or the best. It still goes on, but the hunters are now north of the Crocodile River and off up to the Zambezi. The resident Boers also killed large numbers of wild animals when they weren't busy hunting Bushmen."

William was in agreement, but he thought there were some mitigating circumstances. "The Boers mostly hunted to stay alive or to earn a living and came to hate the wild Bushmen because they stole their cattle, not to have herds for themselves but to slaughter and eat. If the farmers chased them and managed to prevent them from escaping with half a dozen cattle they would hamstring and mutilate the animals in revenge, leaving totally distressed beasts that had to be slaughtered immediately they were recovered. It is hardly surprising that there was hatred and constant warring between them. The farmers viewed the wild Bushmen as vermin."

Henry accepted that the Boers had some reason to hate the Bushmen but felt that there were times when the reprisals were excessive and unnecessary.

"Well there is no need to argue about that," William concluded, sensing a difference of opinion. "Most of it happened years ago and is really no concern of ours. Let's concentrate on finding some meat."

It was another hour before they spotted a small herd of springbok moving ahead of them but too far away to risk wasting a shot. The men followed slowly and when the group disappeared over a slight rise they urged their mounts quickly forward before stopping short of the crest. Tying the horses to one of the bushes, they crept forward, guns loaded, and ready for a quick shot. Unfortunately, the animals were very wary and continued to move rapidly away.

"We could try chasing them," suggested William quietly. "We might just get close enough to shoot. Shall we try?"

Henry nodded. "We might as well, since we haven't seen anything else so far."

Leaping onto their horses, they set off at full gallop in pursuit of the springbok. For a few moments they felt exhilarated as they considered that they were narrowing the gap, until the springbok spurted forward suddenly and, try as they might, they soon realised that their mounts would never be able to cope with the pace the buck were setting. As they slowed down by mutual consent and with some disappointment, a steenbok leapt up just in front of William.

Diamond was halted in his tracks as William pulled on the reins, jumped to the ground and fired as his feet touched the earth.

Oscar had stopped, too, at Henry's signal and stood waiting for the shot from his master. Henry, however, had no need to use one of his bullets, as the little buck was bowled over immediately.

"Well, it's rather small and certainly won't feed all our people, but it's a start," laughed William as he picked up the carcass, removing the guts with a few slashes from his knife and tying the buck behind his saddle.

"That was a good shot of yours, William. Right through the head. It was dead before it fell," Henry said approvingly as he examined the steenbok. "I never had a chance to fire and I thought my reactions were good. Yours are obviously much better."

William was feeling pleased at his success and accepted Henry's approbation with a nod.

"Thank you, Henry. I just happened to be looking at the right place when it popped up. I'm quite sure you would have done the same had you been in my place."

Before remounting, he picked up a handful of sand and let it sift slowly through his fingers, watching to see how it fell.

"I thought so," he remarked. "The wind has veered. We must take a detour and approach the saltpan from the northwest, or any animal will scent us long before we're aware of it's presence."

Henry agreed. "There isn't much of a breeze, but I thought it had changed since we set out."

He lifted his hat and wiped his face. "Let's go, then. We knew it wouldn't be easy to find game."

The hunt turned out to be a long one and occupied most of their day as they rode at an angle to their original approach and detoured round the saltpan that was still hidden from their sight.

Henry began to think that the day would prove to be fruitless until they spied a lone oryx bull almost hidden in the hollow where the saltpan was situated. Knowing that the oryx was not easy prey, William spoke quietly.

"If it senses danger the oryx will run and we will never catch it. Our horses are too tired to outrun such a magnificent bull. I will try to get round it. You stay here downwind and take a shot if it comes within range."

William tethered his horse where it could graze and set off carefully to stalk the animal.

Henry dismounted and lay in wait, watching the animal grazing unconcernedly about six hundred yards ahead.

As time passed, Henry was conscious of the sun beating down on his back and ants, beetles and other creatures crawling over his skin. He tried to wipe them away without disclosing his position. Their numbers and persistence, however, made him decide that he would just have to endure the discomfort. He constantly expected to hear a shot, but instead he saw the animal suddenly stand alert, looking fixedly at a spot to its right. It pawed the ground uncertainly and turned towards Henry.

There was no sign of William, though the animal's nervousness indicated that he must have reached the position he had chosen and that the oryx was now able to catch his scent or had heard a slight sound.

The oryx started to trot towards Henry and he held his breath, checking that his gun was ready.

Two hundred yards away the animal stopped. Its nostrils flared as it stared fixedly in his direction then began to turn. Henry knew that he had to take the opportunity offered and fired. The oryx continued to move and Henry felt that somehow he must have missed.

As he was preparing to take another shot the animal staggered and fell heavily to the ground.

William and Henry converged on the carcass.

"A heart shot," exclaimed William. "That's good. I thought we had lost him as he started away after you'd fired. Are you going to claim him as yours?"

Henry paused. "No," he said. "You were generous enough to give me the shot, but it was your stalking that sent him to me. We'll share. You can have the head and horns; I'll have the skin, if that suits you."

"Capital. These are certainly fine long horns. Someone will buy them to decorate a hall or sitting room."

Drawing out their knives, the two men severed the head and removed the guts, leaving them for the carrion eaters that would relish this unexpected meal. They lifted the carcass onto Oscar's back behind Henry's saddle.

"Well, that should satisfy the camp for a day or two," said Henry with some satisfaction.

"Yes, there is a lot of meat on an oryx and it tastes almost as good as eland," William affirmed. He looked critically at Oscar, now burdened with the heavy carcass.

"I think I must buy at least two more horses before I make my next trip," he continued. "On a hunt like this a pack pony would be useful and a spare horse would take away some of my worries. Diamond is strong and reliable but I keep wondering what I would do if he became sick or put his foot in a hole and fell when we are galloping after game."

"You would be very wise," Henry assented. "I really don't need more than one, although I should like to have two. Accidents and sickness are all too common and a man without a horse finds it very hard going in Africa. Some of the hunters and sportsmen I have met have half a dozen or more and they mount Hottentot servants, called after riders, to ride the game to a standstill or turn them towards the guns."

"Well, I turned that oryx towards your gun didn't I?" asked William slyly.

Henry had the grace to look ashamed, "Yes, but we weren't killing for sport. The meat is essential for feeding our camp and your stalk gave me the opportunity of a good clean shot. At least we haven't left wounded animals to face the predators."

William was delighted with Henry's defensive retort. "Not many people care about wounded animals, Henry. They are just annoyed with themselves for having missed a kill. I am inclined to agree with your point of view, though. Generally, that is. Now, shall we go back to camp? I'm ready for a cup of coffee"

Their water bottles were now empty and the few biscuits they had brought with them in the morning were finished.

Weary, hungry, thirsty and bloody, but content, they began the long walk back to camp, which they reached before the end of the afternoon.

"We'll eat as soon as we can," William said, as they drank mugs of welcome coffee. The horses had been rubbed down, given water and corn, and the men had cleaned off all traces of their hunt before relaxing in clean clothes by the wagons. They could hear the servants laughing and singing as they began to cook the meat of the oryx that had been quickly skinned by Bokkis. William had kept the steenbok for their own larder and had given Fox a shinbone. The dog had greeted him with great excitement and had only quietened down when his jaws were filled with the bone.

"We need to set off again before dark and I must spend some time on preparing that oryx head before then. Would you like the steenbok head, Henry?"

Henry gratefully accepted the offer, even though it was an extra task to be done as soon as possible and it would take some time to scrape the oryx skin ready for curing. Bokkis had experience with curing skins and preserving heads and would help once he had eaten his fill of the juicy meat already roasting on their fire.

****

The children had been as delighted as the dog to see the hunters arrive safely back and with the meat they had hoped for, especially Jane, who had had a wearisome day.

Somehow, the little ones were always thirsty when the water had to be used sparingly. Grazes and cuts had been numerous, too, and she had used some of the precious water to clean them.

Father had already left before the children were awake. It was the sound of the long whips and the shouts of the servants as they in-spanned the oxen that had awakened them. Before they could dress, however, the oxen were in-spanned and the wagons were on the move.

Jane realised to her dismay that there would be no breakfast until the wagon stopped and she had no idea how long that would be. The little ones would be thirsty and crying with hunger before then.

Once they were all fully clothed, Jane handed out mugs of water and biscuits, promising porridge as soon as possible after camp was made.

Having Fox in the wagon was a distraction for a time, especially as he eyed their biscuits and was occasionally given a small piece.

After the 'pretend' breakfast, they had all played happily with Fox for a while and then with their toys, until Jane had had to intervene when Isabelle and Harry began to bicker.

Travelling along this sandy road was less jolting than usual, though still far from comfortable. It was a relief for them all when the wagon came to a halt many hours later and they could all climb out.

Jane immediately organised a breakfast of porridge and sweet tea to be made and ordered Lukas to make bread after that so that they could have bread with jam as an afternoon snack in case father was late returning to camp.

Once they had eaten, Jane tried to interest them in lessons and insisted that they should read whilst she taught James his letters, numbers and colours.

Eventually, at the end of the morning, she agreed that it was too warm to concentrate and allowed them to explore the campsite or play whilst she did some mending.

Her hands were dry and sore from the washing she had done the day before and she wondered if perhaps father had a salve that would soothe the pain. Nevertheless, she got out mother's sewing box and plied herself to a task she never enjoyed, accepting only that it was a necessity and that she was the only one who could do it.

Isabelle and Harry soon began quarrelling again, this time over a game of ninepins, and a short time later James fell over, scraping his knee. He began to cry and make a fuss about a very small graze and when Jane was less sympathetic than usual he began to howl for mama.

Harry came over to discover the cause of the noise and within a short time he remembered the loss of mama and added his tears and wails to those of his little brother.

It took Jane and Isabelle some time to soothe the boys and Jane was relieved that the tears had ceased to flow by the time the hunters returned.

The boys' distress had once again reminded the girls of their motherless condition and they, too, were saddened.

Fortunately, the arrival of father and William helped to banish their grief, as everyone anticipated a tasty evening meal followed by another long trek and the intended arrival at the Orange River the following day.

CHAPTER 39

"It isn't orange at all."
"Not orange."
The loud despairing cry of disappointment and complaint came from Harry, who was gazing across a river twice as wide as the Vaal had been. The little echo of disillusionment was James' contribution as he followed his brother's lead and copied his wail.
Jane looked at the green-brown water close to the bank and almost motionless at their feet, and then across to where silver-white ripples edged with gold flickered in the sunshine as the current further out raced the water downstream over hidden rocks.
Undoubtedly, Harry was right, but she had realised that this was just another river some time ago when they had first observed tantalising glimpses of the silver-blue ribbon of water from a distance. Trees along the watercourse partially hid the river from sight as they approached it, offering only brief dazzling views until they were close enough to appreciate the vastness of this mighty river, with its fringe of willow trees.
She searched her memory for her five-year-old impressions, but somehow she never seemed to have questioned why a river should be called orange when it obviously wasn't, and yet she herself had never felt disappointed.
Isabelle, wanting to outshine her brothers, hid her own disappointment and pretended that she had never expected to see a river with orange water.
"I knew the water wasn't orange," she boasted. "It's just the name of the river, isn't it Mr William?" she averred brightly and turned to William for confirmation.
William felt slightly embarrassed, as he had never questioned the name of the river and didn't know how to reply. Hastily, he thought of a possible reason for the name.
"In the rainy season when the river floods it carries a lot of orange/red sand downstream. I expect the first person to see this river came at a time when it was in flood and the water looked orange to him, so he called it the Orange River."
The answer seemed to satisfy the children and they stood quietly watching as William and their father once again walked their horses across the river, testing the depth of the water and the strength of the current before leading the wagons across.
Neither crocodiles nor hippopotamuses were visible and Jane surreptitiously scanned the undergrowth all around them in case a monitor lizard was hiding, ready to pounce on them.

As at the Vaal River, the young leaders were ordered to ride on the box seats beside the drivers to avoid possible accidents. This was a wise precaution, since the drift proved to be a treacherous one with surprisingly strong currents in some places and sudden deep holes in others.

There were some rocks, too, from time to time that caused the wagons to rise up at a fearful angle, tilting alarmingly before the wheels dropped heavily down to the riverbed again.

The far bank was disturbingly steep, requiring the assistance of many men to supplement the pull of the span by pushing from behind or at each wheel. With only two extra pairs of hands, the first wagon couldn't overcome the rise, so Henry had to go all the way back to collect several of the drivers. They then clung to Oscar, like ticks on cattle, as they made their way on foot through the racing water to rescue the stranded wagon.

The extra pressure on the wheels and the strong push from behind by four large men eventually proved successful and the wagon rolled slowly upwards. They remained on that bank whilst the second and third wagons were driven across, then two of them, including Bokkis, had to brave the crossing again to drive Henry's wagons over.

Jane, who had watched anxiously as William's three wagons forged their way through the water, bouncing and rolling to such a degree that it seemed a miracle that they could cross in safety, told the children to lie on the beds to avoid injuries as their own wagon lurched down the bank. She herself proposed to pray earnestly that the wagon wouldn't be upset.

"I want to watch," declared Harry mutinously. " I can hold onto the side. I'll be quite safe." He pushed Jane's restraining hand aside.

Isabelle would have liked to have joined Harry in his rebellion, but wisely she lay on the bed and clung to the wagon side. Jane held firmly onto James, who was bouncing about beside her.

A sudden thump, as the back wheel mounted and then fell from a rock, jerked Harry unceremoniously onto his back, hitting his head on the side chest as he fell. He lay sore and semi-stunned, longing to cry at the pain in his body, but knowing he had deserved to be punished for his disobedience. Realising that he would get little sympathy from his big sister, he remained silent.

Eventually, and with difficulty, he crawled to papa's bed and pulled himself up onto it, where he lay trying to cope with the violent motion of the wagon whilst containing his frustration and tears.

When finally the far bank had been conquered, the wagon was pulled a short distance away from the river before it was halted and the animals outspanned.

Bruised and shaken from the frightening ordeal, but otherwise unharmed, the children climbed down to discover that there was a Boer farm close by.

The farmer here was in a prime position. He had a large flock of sheep and as many goats, a few cows to provide milk, cheese and butter for his own family with occasional excess to sell, an orchard with numerous trees of a wide variety of fruits and an immense garden for vegetables.

Once all the wagons were safely across the river, William and Henry immediately went to negotiate the purchase of some of this bounty, allowing the children to accompany them.

They found the farmer and his wife civil and quietly welcoming, though unable to speak English.

Much to their delight, the children were provided with lemonade to drink as the men indicated their needs and haggled over the price.

The time wore on and the children were offered milk and rusks by the smiling hausfrau. When Jane tried to make polite conversation the woman only shook her head and disappeared once more into the kitchen.

Henry was pleased to observe his children behaving properly and sitting quietly, waiting for him as the bartering was concluded. He and William had purchased some goats, two more fat-tailed sheep and a few available vegetables, as well as some dried vegetables, jam and dried fruit, in addition to some products from the dairy.

Henry was delighted. Not only would he be able to have milk in his tea and coffee again, but also the children would be able to drink milk for two days. The butter and cheese would last a little longer and be appreciated by them all.

In exchange, they had handed over a bolt of cloth, two muskets that William had kept for such a purpose, powder and shot, some coffee and sugar.

"We shall need to buy more sugar and coffee in Hopetown," William remarked, as they organised for their purchases to be taken to the wagons.

"It will take us more than two weeks after that to reach Beaufort West, with only a few Boer farms to be seen in that two hundred miles."

"I well remember that part of the trek," agreed Henry. "I shall pray that our animals remain well, for we shan't be able to rest on Sundays. It is fortunate that we still have extra beasts that can take turns in the yokes and give the weakest some respite. The strain of daily travel with very little water or grazing is a great trial for them. We lost nearly a whole span on our first journey northwards and one wagon had to remain on the road until oxen could be sent from Hopetown."

The afternoon rest at this outspan by the Orange River allowed all the animals an opportunity to graze on rich green grass and drink water, as they required. The people took this opportunity to bath and wash their clothes before filling every available water container to the brim, with stoppers secured and the containers packed so that they wouldn't spill. By evening it was time to move on.

It was the middle of the night when they reached Hopetown and the wagons halted for the rest of the night.

This settlement, with its few houses, some of them no more than shanties, and stores, was a lot smaller than Griquatown. As all the children of school age were occupied with lessons during the morning only a few babies and very small children were visible playing near their mothers. Generally, it was less exciting for the children, though it was an interesting stage on their journey and Jane was delighted to find that the dogs here were kept under the control of their owners and didn't roam around in packs.

It was true that dogs barked when they entered each store until a shout from the man inside quelled the noise, so that they could roam around the single room with its multifarious goods, absorbing the sights and smells.

The stores were similar to dozens of their kind in the interior and held nothing that the children hadn't already seen before at Griquatown, Kuruman or the King's Town in Matabeleland. Nevertheless, their inquisitive natures led them to investigate each one, to gently finger the materials, gaze at the guns, examine the jars and tins, smell the coffee or count the variety of pots, pans and implements.

William knew, and was known by, the traders, who greeted him warmly. They begged him to stay and share a celebration with them that night to brighten up their otherwise dull existence. Visitors here were not frequent and all too often stayed only long enough to purchase the necessary stores.

William made his excuses for moving on directly, promising to allow time for revelling on his next journey.

Once he had purchased extra dry goods, powder for hunting and barter and some more lead for bullets, he went to arrange some horse fodder.

Henry, too, obtained more coffee, sugar, powder and shot, as these were necessities for the Boers, isolated as they were in the wilderness that stretched before them. To his relief, he was lucky enough to find some corn for Oscar, enough to last almost the whole journey to Beaufort West.

They also bought some large water pots, so that there would be sufficient water for the servants, whose needs always seemed excessive. Unfortunately, the only ones they could acquire were native pottery ones and therefore all too easily broken.

"If we pack them carefully beside the skins they should be well protected," Henry suggested.

"That is a possibility, but I'm not too happy at the idea of water so close to skins that have been painstakingly cured. They would be ruined if any of those pots broke. You know how carefully we had to repack them so that they were well above the water line when we crossed the river. No, they will have to be in the wagons close to the drivers, I think."

Henry fully understood William's reasoning and this was agreed upon. Four were lifted into place, as there was no room in the Hargreaves' wagon. The children frequently sat beside Bokkis and their wagon was already overcrowded, leaving no space for a large water pot.

By nightfall, the wagons had set out on the dreariest and most testing part of their sixteen hundred mile journey, to cross the featureless Karoo.

Fifteen days of heat and dust lay before them: days of moaning, suffering, perhaps dying cattle, of anxious fears and fraying tempers, before they could enjoy the brief respite offered by the settlement of Beaufort West.

William was well acquainted with the route and was aware that they couldn't always rely on natural water sources. Pools and pans had been known to dry up overnight and even time-consuming digging in likely spots could be frustratingly fruitless. He sometimes regretted not having a Bushman as a servant. Those little people always knew how to find water, even in a desert.

There were, of course, some Boer farms along the route and these were always situated at perennial fountains, but not all the farmers were welcoming. William could well understand that the arrival of eighty to a hundred animals all desperate for water might be a strain on the water the farmer considered his own, but he felt that the animosity sometimes shown was out of place.

"I can never understand why some of these isolated farmers treat us with suspicion or occasionally downright hostility," he confided to Henry. "If I lived in this wilderness with only my family for company I should welcome visitors and an opportunity to talk to different people. Perhaps to learn the latest news or discuss ideas with them. Yet I have been almost pushed off the farm and treated with contempt by some of the farmers here."

Henry thought about it before remarking mildly, "Sometimes people who live alone begin to resent any person invading their solitude. They are content, I won't say 'happy', with their own relentless routine and possessive of their property. I have known some hill farmers who were exactly the same, disliking and distrustful of anyone daring to cross their land or approaching their house. In addition, you must remember that these farmers trekked here originally to escape the hated English. If you were a Scot you might receive better treatment. They perceive the Scots as victims of the English, too."

William was forced to laugh at that, but added resentfully, "Well, they might show a little kindness to desperate travellers. Most of us are willing to offer payment for any help offered. We don't approach them as beggars or thieves intent on taking some of their meagre food or goods. We are more likely to offer them much needed supplies in exchange for a little of anything they can spare."

It was obvious that he considered such surly, introverted attitudes as extremely selfish and they would remain a constant mystery to the gregarious William.

Both Henry and William knew that oxen were able to cope for two days and might even manage a third without water, though their condition would begin to deteriorate rapidly. After that, some would be too weak to pull the heavy wagons and others would die.

On the pencilled map he had in his wagon, William pointed out to Henry the places where he expected to find water. It might not always be fit for humans to drink, but it would keep the animals going, he explained. Although not a stranger to this road, Henry was content to acknowledge William's greater knowledge and to accept his leadership and for the first week all went according to plan. The weary days passed in tedious monotony. Trekking began before five o'clock in the morning and stopped briefly at around seven or eight for the people to have hot coffee and a biscuit or rusk.

The children dressed themselves quickly when the wagon stopped and climbed down to partake of a drink and some food. They then accompanied the wagons on foot for the next four or five miles, although James and Harry were usually taken up by the horsemen.

Inevitably, some of the oxen lay down to rest during this early break and had to be beaten before they would rise to continue the trek, until about nine o'clock when the oxen were out-spanned for the day. They were immediately led to the water, if water there was, but the grazing was almost non-existent and after listlessly nibbling at some of the dry stalks or leaves the animals would lie motionless until it was time for them to be in-spanned in the cool of the evening.

Lessons for the children continued for three hours each day, though their exercise books and diaries became grimy with dust and sweat. They were expected to read for a further spell during the afternoon rest and were only free to play for a brief time after the afternoon tea of water and a slice of bread and jam until the evening meal.

By the second week the condition of the oxen and the wagons showed signs of the terrible strain of the relentless, seemingly endless dry, dusty terrain.
When the wheels sank in the sand on occasions it required unremitting extra efforts from already weakened men and beasts to extricate them and keep the wagons moving. Once, the disselboom on the lead wagon broke from the strain put upon it by the struggling oxen as they wrestled the wagon free from sand.
William had a spare pole to hand, but it took a whole day to remove the broken one and fit the new one into place.
As the wooden wheels dried and shrank in the arid atmosphere the iron tyres became loose. There was no water to soak the wheels to make them swell so that the tyres fitted snugly once again nor was it possible for Henry to set up a forge and shorten the tyres. Instead, wedges were knocked into place to prevent the tyres falling off and the wheels disintegrating altogether. Annoyingly, the wedges were loosened all too often by the jolting of the vehicle and fell out to be replaced over and over.
"We'll just have to soak some of these wheels next time we find a pool deep enough," William said, as he once again hammered in some wedges.
"We won't have enough time to do all of them," cautioned Henry. "It takes hours for the water to have sufficient effect, but we can do one or two of the worst whilst we are stopped during the day or even whilst we sleep at night. That's if we are camped by water," he added gloomily.
It was a fearsome test of fortitude for men and animals.
Dust was everywhere and with only a damp cloth to wipe away the worst of the grime and dirt before eating, they began to feel unpleasantly and uncomfortably grubby.
Harry and James weren't worried about not washing, but Isabelle in particular objected to the constant dust on her body.
"Can't I just have a little more water to wash my face and hands?" she begged. Jane was sympathetic. She, too, hated wearing the same dusty clothes each day and her skin had begun to itch. However, she didn't know how long it would be before more water was available and their precious supplies must be kept for cooking and drinking.
"No, Isabelle. We cannot spare water for washing today. Mr William thinks there are some pools not far away and that means that the poor dear oxen may be able to drink. After that we may be allowed to have washing water, God willing."
Isabelle turned away crossly and stamped her foot in frustration.
That morning the first ox died.
There had been great difficulty in getting the wagons moving after the stop

for coffee. The spans were weary, starving and suffering from thirst, but William knew of a Boer farm only four and a half miles away.

It wasn't directly on their road and meant a detour, which added more weary hours to their journey. However, the animals were now distressed and Henry agreed that they must have water soon or they would die.

Slowly, slowly they continued, lagging behind William who had ridden ahead to seek permission for their animals to drink and to locate the fountain. After no more than a mile an ox in the span of the second wagon dropped heavily and without warning to the ground, creating chaos and confusion. Unable to stop immediately, the wagon struck the two nearest oxen heavily as they in turn stumbled over the next pair where the stricken beast was lying.

Abdol, who was leading, was thrown to the ground by the sudden stoppage and the wildly plunging animals, whilst the driver strove desperately to wind on the brake to prevent further damage. The disselboom had snapped like a dry twig and the wagon was being swung from side to side. The two heavy oxen, known as the wheelers, were in danger of being stabbed by the splintered end of the pole as they frantically twisted away from the pain of the prodding wagon behind them and in panic tried to escape their bonds.

Henry, galloping along the column as all the wagons came to a disordered unscheduled halt and trying to discover the cause of the chaos, became aware of the frantic movements of the wagon and its span. He roared loudly for all the servants to come and assist in extricating the frightened, bellowing oxen from the twisted chains and yokes.

This task resulted in numerous bruises and cuts from the sharp-pointed, vicious horns whirling in arcs through the air around the heads of the terrified beasts or their tough lethal hooves kicking aimlessly at a lower level. The air was soon filled with shouted curses, screams of anger and pain mixed with the bellows of the cattle and the crack of whips as drivers sought to achieve order from disorder.

The stricken animal refused to rise. Surrounded by fractured yokes, twisted chains and tangled ropes it lay on its side, scarcely breathing.

William, returning happily with news of lifesaving water to hand, discovered to his astonishment and dismay a scene of confusion. Every wagon was at a standstill and when he saw his second wagon he could hardly comprehend the mess and destruction.

There were people sitting or lying about hugging their various cuts and bruises whilst loudly bemoaning their fate, bleeding and disorientated oxen wandering untended in every direction and his wagon with its trek gear in total disarray.

"What on earth has happened?" he demanded of no-one and everyone.
Henry, who had immediately gathered what had caused the catastrophe, quickly explained the origin of the accident and pointed to the stricken beast William dismounted, holding his rifle with care as he did so, and walked across to the fallen ox. A close look assured him that it was close to death.
"Right, I'll shoot it," he decided. Many men would have saved the cost of the powder and shot on a beast that was so obviously close to death, but William wasn't one of them.
"Lukas. I'll have the liver, kidneys and the best steak you can find. The rest is to be shared out amongst yourselves. And give Fox a bone, will you?"
Aches and pains were forgotten as they all rushed off for knives and bowls to collect this bounty.
The children arrived in time to see the head and hooves chopped off, followed by the rapid removal of the hide. They had watched similar processes many times before on this journey and no longer identified with the dead animal. It was dead and a source of food for them all. It was just a carcass.
"It's almost like taking a jacket off," remarked Harry as the sharp knives made short work of the skinning.
"Keep well away from those knives," ordered William. "One serious accident is quite sufficient."
"Come and stand beside me," Henry called and was, as he expected, instantly obeyed.
Once the meat had been removed, William and Henry could assess the damage.
"I can see three broken yokes and their jukskies that will have to be replaced, as well as ropes for at least eight more. The chains appear to be sound but the disselboom is broken. It is going to take us many hours to repair everything, but it might have been much worse, I suppose."
Henry nodded, "We have sufficient replacements with us and we can begin work this afternoon as soon as we've eaten. Meanwhile, we must have the other wagons driven to the farm so that the oxen can drink."

CHAPTER 40

Jane was always to remember the two days they spent at the van Rooyens' homestead. 'An oasis in the desert', she had first described it in her diary, feeling proud of her description, then later added, 'but I wasn't sorry to leave a house where we had no friendship or conversation.'

The van Rooyens were an elderly couple, whose own children were now grown, only two remaining to work on the farm. These two young men were as reticent and uncommunicative as their parents, their reserved demeanour not intended to be rude or unsociable but born out of years of living with an immense, brooding silence until it was an ingrained habit.

None of them were able to articulate their thoughts and this was linked to an inability to understand or speak English.

Though they were somewhat aloof and introverted, they were generous in their own way and far from unkind to their child visitors. The vast, seemingly empty world around them and their isolation from others of their kind, made them reserved and because of this they were unable to make their visitors feel at ease.

They offered food and shelter, as they would for any passing travellers. In offering this hospitality they saw it as part of their moral duty to people less fortunate than themselves.

After the hardships of the previous seven days, it felt like heaven for Jane and the little ones to be given quantities of fresh cool milk to drink, and eggs to eat with fresh bread and butter. There was also the joy, for Jane and Isabelle in particular, of an opportunity to bath and put on clean clothes. Their shoes, unfortunately, were beyond repair, though Harry and James had already outgrown their boots and had been walking barefoot for several days.

"I hope we can stay here for a few days," said Harry appreciatively, as he tucked into a sweet honey pudding covered with cream. "There must be lots of things to see round the farm."

He didn't mind that their hostess couldn't converse with them and appeared taciturn "I would like to stay here a little while, too," agreed Isabelle. "I'm tired of walking."

"Me too," mumbled James through his food, nodding his head comically, so that Jane couldn't help laughing.

She was ready to agree with them, though she had some reservations, realising that their presence was tolerated rather than welcomed. She couldn't feel truly comfortable and knew that she would find it hard to

endure this silent atmosphere for any length of time.
She also knew that father would stay only long enough for the broken wagon to be repaired.
In this she was quite right.
It took the men longer than anticipated to ensure that the wagon and trek gear were in usable condition once more, yet they were ready to depart by the end of the following day.
Although the oxen now had sufficient water to satisfy their thirst, their previous suffering continued to take its toll and a second ox had had to be shot only a few hours after the first.
With an ample supply of meat already in the camp, William offered the carcass to the van Rooyens, who were pleased to accept the gift. Eating beef made a welcome change for them, as goat, mutton and venison made up their usual fare, with an occasional old hen that had ceased to lay and could not be wasted. This wasn't country for cattle, and although their few dairy cows were accustomed to the sour grass, they still had to be fed on the produce from the garden and a small cereal crop they somehow managed to grow.
With this whole ox to consider, they began work immediately, salting large chunks of meat and packing it away to preserve it. What remained would either be eaten fresh or cut into strips and made into biltong.
In the late afternoon, with their repair work completed and in readiness for their departure the next morning, William and Henry went to examine their spans. They discovered that most of the oxen were showing signs of recovery from the effects of the severe thirst they had endured, though they were still in a weakened state. Several of the animals were in poor condition but William knew that they wouldn't improve a great deal on this sour veld even if they stayed here for weeks.
Two of the beasts were so obviously unfit that they would not last more than a day on the march. Since they were extras, it was decided to offer them to the van Rooyens in exchange for some goats or sheep and whatever food they could spare.
Jane had learned from William, who had somehow been able to converse with their hosts, that the road to Beaufort West was as barren and wearisome as the road they had travelled from Hopetown. Her heart sank at the thought of more than another week of the uncomfortable, seemingly endless days under the burning sun, with the monotonous routine and the constant dust.
They would have to walk in bare feet until father could somehow provide them with suitable footwear and she would have to bear the burden of looking after desperately weary, unhappy children. However, she could do

nothing about the situation.
It had to be borne.
Although the oxen were inspanned before dawn, the children were wakened and taken to the house to say goodbye to the van Rooyen family.
Smiling firmly and with innate good manners, Jane bade a polite goodbye to the van Rooyens, thanking them gratefully and sincerely for their kindness. They nodded in acceptance as if they could understand the meaning of the words. Isabelle and the boys added their well-rehearsed tributes before they turned to follow the wagons once more.
The ground was cold under their feet and puffs of grey dust spurted up with each step taken, but they had slept well and were full of energy as they helped to drive the goats in the wake of the last wagon.
None of the children really minded too much about walking in bare feet. Harry preferred it and the soles of his feet were hardened almost as much as the native children's feet were, as he always removed his boots when he was out with his friends. Jane and Isabelle had worn boots more frequently. Mother said that civilised people always wore shoes and her children must do likewise whatever the cost, though she was unaware of Harry's transgressions. Consequently, the girls and James found it less comfortable to walk without them, wincing and hopping when they inadvertently trod on a hard projection.
"Jane, why are you looking so cross?" queried Isabelle.
"I'm not cross. I'm just sorry that we have so far to go before we can have a few more days rest and I'm worried that my feet will be sore."
"Is it far to Beaufort West?" asked Harry.
"It will take us about eight days to get there. That is, if the oxen stay well enough to keep going. If they slow down or some of them die it will take us longer," Jane informed them.
Harry didn't mind. There were always games to play when lessons were finished and sometimes he could persuade Mr William to play ninepins or teach him to play cricket. If he tired of walking he might be fortunate enough to ride with papa and that was tremendous fun. Poor Jane and Isabelle were never allowed to ride. He was glad he was a boy.
'It can be no fun being a girl,' he thought.
The backbreaking daily march endured by the children, interspersed by spells in the jolting wagon, was as nothing compared to the agony of the oxen on that journey. Sick and weak, they strove to drag the heavy vehicles over soft roads day after day, with the threatening crack of the whip to keep them moving.
The days when water wasn't available for them were especially harsh.

Jane listened to their tormented moaning and tried to close her ears to the distressful sound. She prayed with all the fervour she could muster that they would all survive.

Her prayers, alas, went unanswered.

Vultures appeared in the sky and began to follow them each day, circling high above the wagons in anticipation of a meal. They could sense death, and before long some of the oxen began to flag.

By the time that Beaufort West appeared on the horizon, four had succumbed and even the voracious appetites of the servants could no longer manage the surfeit of meat, much to their disgust, as they hated leaving any behind. The vultures landed to bicker and fight as they cleaned up the detritus, squabbling noisily over scraps. They were ably assisted by the hyenas and jackals that sneaked in and bore off the bones.

It was fascinating to watch them.

"I don't like hyenas or vultures," whispered Isabelle, gazing back at the mass of birds and animals clustered round the remains of the last ox to die.

"Not many people do," Henry assured her, "but they do clear up the remains left by the hunters. Just think of the diseases that would spread from the awful smell of decaying meat."

He paused to look critically at his children, noticing for the first time with dismay and not a little irritation how thin and pale they all were. 'Why haven't I seen it before?' he wondered.

The skin on their faces was dry and sallow, what was visible of their hair beneath their hats was dull, whilst their hands and bare feet thrusting out from filthy clothes were barely discernible under the layers of dust.

Their appearance reminded him suddenly and forcibly of the troublesome, grubby urchins who had been a nuisance to the carters in the meaner streets of Manchester and Leeds.

He had always felt revolted by the dull eyes pleading his charity, the sour smell of their unwashed bodies and their filthy hands reaching out for alms. Recoiling from the coarse language and penetrating, whining voices, he had sought to feel pity. His parents and his religion taught charity and he had tried to feel compassion for the creatures who seemed barely human.

Henry accepted that he had a duty to the poor and after more than five years at Inyati he had experienced poverty at firsthand. He knew exactly how difficult it was to manage on a small income. However, Katherine had ensured that the family should always maintain a high standard of cleanliness as well as Godliness, neatness of attire, good manners and correct attitudes to their fellow human beings, whatever their circumstances.

His family had never been, nor would ever be, he vowed, in any way similar to the tatterdemalions of the English towns.

Now, as he viewed his children looking like ragamuffins, their appearance was a scourge to his sensibilities.

How could Jane have let this happen? It was true that recently Jane had begun to cough again, a harsh, rasping cough that sometimes woke him in the night.

He had regularly given her doses of his special linctus, which brought her some temporary easement and she never complained, but the cough persisted. Was she too sick to care for her siblings properly?

Harry seemed to be the strongest of the four, though even he appeared less energetic over the past three days and James had been constantly fretful over minor problems. Henry had seen Jane carrying her little brother when he grew too tired to walk and managing until the wagon stopped so that they could all climb up to be bounced about unmercifully on the hard seats.

In bewilderment and anger mixed with sorrow, Henry walked his horse forward until he was beside William.

The pace of the wagons was slow now with two reduced to having spans of only fourteen oxen to pull them, every beast unable to manage more than a very laboured walk.

"I think we must spend at least a week here," Henry suggested, pointing to the small settlement ahead.

William, almost as weary as the animals, nodded his agreement.

"Yes, Henry. We are all fatigued. We shall have to purchase more cattle to replace those lost and every one of these is in dire need of rest, good food and water. A week might be enough."

* * * * * * *

It was in fact nine days before William led the wagons southwest from Beaufort West, by which time everyone was in considerably better health.

The English and Scottish inhabitants of the tiny village of Beaufort West had done their utmost to make the family welcome. They had shared their food and cosseted the children. They had helped to wash and repair clothing. They had even assisted Henry to fashion some sort of footwear for the children.

Their kindness and friendliness was a blessing to the jaded travellers and Henry was especially gratified to be asked to take the services on the two Sundays of their sojourn.

The oxen were watered daily and with some fodder added to their diet they slowly began to recover from their ordeal. Viewing them anxiously each day, William and Henry could only pray that they would be strong enough for the three hundred mile task that still lay ahead. There was still a portion of the Karroo to cross before the mountains were reached. After that they would have to tackle the steep mountain passes. Once they had conquered these there were the Cape Flats to cross before the town itself was reached.

Once they had left the Karroo behind there might be grass for the animals and water was certainly more plentiful in the mountains, but there was at least a week of the interminable dry, dusty plains to endure before then.

They had been fortunate enough to purchase a span of oxen from a recent settler in the town and these sixteen were now in-spanned in William's leading wagon. They were somewhat frisky, having been idle for several months and the driver was almost thrown from his seat as they set off at cracking pace, moving erratically first to the left and then to the right, with the wagon swaying precariously behind them. It was a comical sight for all but the struggling driver and the children were delighted, laughing and clapping at the spectacle.

The grown-ups, however, more aware of a possible tragedy, could only gape and put their trust in the skills of the driver. There was certainly no possibility of anyone being able to intervene.

Fortunately for William and his wagon, the driver proved equal to the task and eventually managed to bring order from the chaos.

It had been decided that twelve of the weakest beasts were to be left in the care of a farmer close to the village who would see to their needs until William returned when he would be reimbursed for his trouble. The remaining oxen had been carefully sorted and allotted positions in spans in each of the other four wagons so that the more robust animals were placed beside a weaker one.

It was, however, essential that each beast was in its correct position with its usual partner whenever possible, otherwise there would be more trouble as the oxen refused to co-operate.

In good spirits, and light of heart, they parted from the kindly people of Beaufort West to begin the final leg of their journey. Knowing that they would, God willing, soon leave the Karroo behind, they remained cheerful for several days.

Inevitably, their clothes and persons were covered in dust within an hour of leaving the village behind, but in their present mood the discomfort was less burdensome than it had seemed ten days previously, and when the mountains finally appeared on the horizon there was a distinct feeling of satisfaction and anticipation. It was true that the oxen were becoming weary once more and though their speed had slowed considerably it did not worry

William greatly.

The greatest problem each day was to find water and with so many riverbeds dry William's task often took him many hours as he sought out known pools. Somehow, he always managed to discover a source and the thirsty animals were kept alive.

"We are making steady progress and I'm sure the beasts will manage the mountain passes if we let them walk at their own pace," he confided to Henry. "Shall we go out hunting this afternoon? Diamond is still full of vigour and I shall enjoy a good gallop."

Henry was delighted at the suggestion. "Oscar is in good shape, too. He needs to be stretched a bit. Besides, we could do with some fresh venison as a change from this continual goat and mutton."

William laughed, "Tired of goat and mutton already? You are lucky that you have never lived in the Karroo, where people have to live on goat or mutton for years unless they go hunting. It is because you dined too well at the village. We were really indulged in Beaufort West weren't we? The people there are always so generous and welcoming."

Just before dark the men, dusty and weary, but triumphant, rode into camp, Henry with Oscar bearing with the carcass of the rhebok he had shot, and William proudly carrying a steenbok behind his saddle.

Both were welcome additions to the larder and supper that evening was a particularly happy meal.

"Why do the mountains keep moving away from us?" Isabelle suddenly asked William. He looked at her in surprise.

"The mountains don't move and we are getting closer to them every day. The mountains here are very high and can be seen from a long distance away."

"Well, we first saw them two days ago and I thought they would be nearer and bigger by now, but they aren't," Isabelle went on doggedly.

"It does seem that way, Isabelle. We were a long way away from them when we first saw them and we still have some miles to travel, but you'll see tomorrow that we are getting closer."

William was right and to their surprise two days later they had left the Karroo and were approaching the mountains.

"This is wonderful scenery," Jane remarked to Isabelle as the wagons wound their way up Mitchell's Pass. "Our own mama could draw beautiful pictures and in her diary there were many pictures of the mountains."

"I have never seen those pictures," accused Isabelle. "Why haven't you shown them to me? She was my mama as well. I need to know about mama too," she demanded furiously.

Jane gave her little sister a hug and then explained. "I can't show them to you. I wish I could. Mama's diary and many of her things were in a chest at Inyati. I only saw the diary once when our second mother was sorting out some of the clothes to make dresses for us. The chest was moved into our room then and when it was opened many months later the white ants had destroyed the books and pictures. I wasn't very old and I cried because we had lost mama's things."

Isabelle pulled away from her sister, feeling aggrieved that Jane knew so much about mama and she knew nothing.

"I shall draw my own pictures of the mountains for my diary and I shall show them to grandmama in England," she pronounced defiantly.

"That's a very good idea," Jane agreed soothingly. "You are much better at sketching than I am. We'll ask father if drawing can be one of our lessons this afternoon. Isn't this mountain air so wonderfully clear? Have you noticed that there is no dust in the wind?"

Jane was feeling much happier now that the heat and the dust of the Karroo were behind them. Her cough had disappeared too.

Yesterday they had all been able to bathe in a mountain stream where the water was clean, cool and fresh.

There was only one concern that caused her some disquiet, however much she tried not to think about it.

Although the anticipation of their holiday in Cape Town was pleasant and it would be agreeable to have a bed of her own, or at the very least one she would share only with Isabelle, the day would come all too soon when she would have to say goodbye to Harry and James. The very thought of leaving the two little boys on their own without their papa or their sisters to care for them distressed her greatly.

She had tried to curb these unhappy thoughts and this she did by remaining vigilant for their welfare as the wagons drove through rocky streams and alongside precipitous roads above those same streams.

She washed clothes and mended tears in them; she tended cuts, scrapes and bruises too. Whenever she wasn't telling stories to the younger ones she would try to lose herself in her own special books.

Inexorably, they came closer to Cape Town.

CHAPTER 41

Harry had delighted in the journey through the mountains.
Their sheer size was initially daunting, but as he listened to the echoes of the sharp cracking of the whips that sounded so like gunshots and the rumbling clatter of the ironclad wheels against the rocks he suddenly felt a surge of excitement.
William told the children about echoes and how sounds bounced back from the rocks, then he demonstrated the effect by shouting; 'Hoy.' Back came the eerie sound...Hoy..oy...oy.
Harry immediately copied him shouting; "Hello. I'm Harry" and heard with awe the words reverberate Hello..ello...ello. I'm..m.....Harry..arry..arry.
Isabelle and James in turn also tested the echo and even Jane self-consciously called her name.
There was pleasure for all of them when their disembodied voices returned to them only slightly distorted. Disappointingly, they soon passed the place where the phenomenon occurred and their shouts were reduced to normality.
There were times when the road was balanced precariously on the mountainside, suspended above a tiny stream glittering in the sunlight many feet below. Jane was afraid that the oxen or wagons might suddenly be pitched into the abyss and she walked with James and Isabelle as close to the mountainside as possible.
Harry would stand as close to the edge of the road above such a steep valley as Mr William or papa would let him, daring himself to defy the fear that mingled with his joy. He had just learned the word 'precipice' and now he would repeat it over and over.
Once he and Mr William had thrown stones outward as far as they could, watching and listening to see if they would reach the river. They never did. Although the slope was almost vertical in places and the river seemed to be directly below them it was obviously further away than their eyes suggested.
Occasionally, he would scramble up the mountainside, hoping to get a better view of the road in front or even the long awaited sight of Cape Town. Once Jane had been rather cross with him as he had been followed over some rough rocks by Isabelle and James who had returned to their big sister with scraped hands and knees and muddied clothes.
Not only that, but there were some small tears in their dresses and the material was so worn that Jane had the greatest difficulty in repairing them. She was almost in tears as she strove to make the dresses look tidy again.
It was on the first part of the journey through the mountains that Harry,

Isabelle and James saw a bridge for the first time; a construction that fascinated them and they watched in awe as the wagons safely negotiated this unusual feature.

"Why isn't there a bridge over every river, papa?" asked Harry, who was curious as always. "This bridge makes it so easy for the wagons to cross over the river here."

"Because bridges cost a great deal of money and take a long time to build. Special people called engineers are needed to build bridges. They are built only where they are needed. When there are a lot of people using a road, sometimes every day, a drift becomes a miserable nuisance to them all, so they decide that a bridge is needed. It is easy to build a bridge over a small stream like this by using a few trees and planks. It would be very difficult to build a bridge over big rivers like the Vaal and the Orange. Just think how long and how high each one would have to be. You'll see many more bridges before we reach Cape Town and they will be properly built ones using stone and cement. Of course, in England, where there are more people, better roads and even railways, there are many bridges and they are made of iron, bricks or stone, not wood like this one. There have been bridges in England for many hundreds of years, ever since the Roman times, because the people there needed and wanted them and knew how to build them."

The reply made sense to Harry, though he didn't understand what 'Roman times' were and as Henry rode forward over the bridge after the last wagon had clattered satisfyingly across Harry listened admiringly to the echoing sound made by the horse's hooves on the planks.

In imitation, he stamped his way across the planks, listening with pleasure to the hollow sound made by his feet, 'It would be even better if I had some boots to wear,' he thought. 'much more satisfying'.

James and Isabelle copied his actions, whilst Jane was happy to watch them, although she was pleased that father had now ridden away and was unaware of their game, especially as they repeated it several times until she chivvied them forward.

"That's enough now. We mustn't get too far behind the wagons. We don't want to get lost," she admonished them.

Reluctantly, but obediently, they scampered along the dusty track, still full of energy and in good spirits.

Exciting as the bridge had been, undoubtedly the greatest thrill that morning was the sight of a train. Even Jane was transfixed with astonishment as, without warning, it came roaring along behind them within view of the road. Fortunately, it wasn't too close, though the noise and appearance of the huge unknown black object belching smoke and hurtling past their vision, assailing their ears with an unaccustomed loud sound, disturbed the oxen and the drivers had difficulty in controlling the frightened beasts as they danced out of control.

The servants who had joined them at Kuruman took to their heels and disappeared into the comparative safety of the bush until the more seasoned drivers yelled and shouted at them to return.

Whilst the melee occupied his master, Fox was barking frenziedly, first at the intrusion of an unknown object into his familiar world and then at the equally astounding commotion taking place around him.

Henry was astonished at the hasty desertion and added his voice to the cacophony, but it was almost half an hour before the frightened youngsters could be persuaded that their lives were in no danger and they came creeping furtively back.

Jane had seen a train before, but she too was startled, as she had been unaware of the railway lines running alongside, since they were hidden by the long grass, and the abrupt approach of the engine made her jump and cower in fright.

James and Isabelle immediately ran crying to cling to Jane, shocked by the sudden unnerving vision and loud unaccustomed noise rattling and puffing past before disappearing from sight. Even Harry had been stunned by the apparition and he stood uncertainly, seeking reassurance from someone, anyone, whilst refusing to outwardly admit his dismay.

William had come galloping back down the line of wagons in order to help quieten the agitated animals and as he reached the children he was assailed by a babble of questions and remarks.

"What was that, Mr William?"

"What made that noise, Mr William?"

"That thing frightened me."

"I think it was a train wasn't it, Mr William?"

William spoke soothingly as he had to the oxen.

"Yes, Jane, it was a train. I'm not surprised that it frightened you all. It must have been travelling at almost thirty miles an hour. The train came from Wellington and was taking people to Cape Town to work, to shop or just to visit. I don't suppose we shall see another one, at least not for some time, but by then you'll know what it is and won't be frightened."

Eventually, order was restored, but the excited chattering continued for most of the morning and remained a topic of discussion for days as descriptions and reactions were mulled over.

When at last they came within sight of Cape Town there was great excitement for everyone.

There was a strong south-easterly wind blowing that day, whipping up the dust in the streets and open spaces and this hung like a pall over the dwellings. The mid-morning sun shone onto and through the dusty air, making it seem to the children like some of the fairy tale pictures they had seen. Gleaming white houses with an orange halo.

There was also a glimpse of the sea sparkling blue and gold in the sunshine, a reflection that was dazzling to the eyes.

"It looks just like heaven," Isabelle confided to Jane as they sat in the wagon.

"Heaven," shouted Harry picking up on the word. "Is mama here? Are we going to see mama at last?"

"Mama. Mama. I want to see mama," chanted James.

Jane controlled her momentary annoyance with Isabelle for having unwittingly reminding the boys of their loss. She had to agree that Cape Town this morning looked exactly like some of the pictures in her book of fairy tales and could easily match their idea of heaven.

It took all her patience to convince Harry and James that they wouldn't see their mama here, that this was Cape Town where their grandmama and grandpapa lived and just a large town, not like heaven at all. At least not like Jane's idea of heaven.

Their thoughts were eventually diverted when Jane pointed out the ships that could be seen and offered a promise that father would probably take them all to see the ships. They might see some trains, too, and a castle. The thought of all these wonders distracted the boys sufficiently for them to cease their clamour and even Isabelle became animated at seeing so many new exciting things.

William was pleased, as well as relieved, to be safely at the end of an extended, lengthy journey, although it would be many days before he could completely relax and enjoy a holiday. His business would keep him fully occupied for perhaps a week or more.

He would first unpack and store the numerous goods he had carted so far.

The servants must then be paid and dismissed with the promise that if they wished he might be able to employ them again on his next journey. Then the welfare of the oxen had to be arranged, after which he would have to organise the sale of the goods he had transported, both his own and those belonging to others.

Advantageous selling was as important as the actual purchase and carriage of the items that belonged to him, perhaps even more so, as he had to make a worthwhile profit. If he had paid too much initially or had not calculated market prices correctly he knew he would soon be out of business. He wouldn't lose on the items he transported for his customers as his carriage fees were calculated to a nicety and he would take the money from the sales immediately. Cash in hand was the basis of his trade.

After that, all the finances must be carefully assessed, not forgetting his debts to Henry. He had dealings with banks and many traders to consider and at some point he knew he should put the word around that he sought an assistant. If he was lucky, there might be opportunities to make some profitable shorter journeys to the farming areas around Cape Town in the coming months.

Eventually, when he was preparing his next trip northwards in a few months time, he would buy at least one more horse in addition to more oxen, but there was no hurry for that since he had no wish to care for extra animals until they were needed.

Once his business was temporarily concluded he would spend time with his family and wallow briefly in the excitements and pleasures enjoyed by the young men of his home town.

When that palled, he would set off once more into the vast heartland with no regrets, indeed with a light heart and soaring spirits to pit his youth, health, strength and knowledge against nature, a pitiless, unforgiving adversary.

The bush had its own excitements and a part of him preferred the wildness, the space where he could be himself without having to consider other people or the niceties of social behaviour. There was the thrill of hunting, an element of fear in the danger of camping amongst wild beasts and the satisfaction in honing his many skills with horse and gun.

William never forgot that there were also the people of that land who were equally demanding. They could be unscrupulous and devious or extraordinarily kind. It took hard won percipience to differentiate between the two. William felt that he was learning. He was certainly becoming known as a reliable and honest transport rider, which was a reputation he cherished.

Knowing that they would be at their journey's end later that day, Henry felt some trepidation at the thought of meeting Katherine's parents. He prayed that his letter describing her death had been received, hopefully many weeks ago, so that the wounds wouldn't be too fresh, their grief too horribly apparent.

If somehow his missive had gone astray he would be faced with the appalling task of breaking the news himself.

The arrival of Harry and James might in some measure ease their grief, he thought, or at least their presence in the house would provide some distraction. From his own experience, there was little or nothing to assuage the soul-destroying sorrow experienced on the loss of a loved one. Hard work or concentrating on other interests merely forced the mind temporarily away from introspection, but grief had a habit of intruding unexpectedly. It wasn't easily controlled, even with fervent prayer and the knowledge that one would be reunited with the dear departed in God's Kingdom.

He knew that the Bradfords had been worried by his hasty marriage to their youngest daughter at a time when he should have been in deep mourning for his first wife, and considered it unseemly. Only their deep religious beliefs, the fact that they had known Henry and his family previously when they had lived in the same town in England and their understanding of his desperate need of a loving helpmeet and companion had swayed their verdict in Henry's favour.

Katherine's pleading to be allowed to dedicate her life to God's service and to share Henry's life hadn't been ignored either. The wedding had been arranged with all the propriety expected and the happy couple had left Cape Town soon after.

Now he was leaving Katherine's sons in her stead whilst he proposed, God willing, to leave Cape Town within two weeks.

He would need to book a passage for the three of them immediately on the steamer going to Southampton and the sailing date would depend on available berths, but as it was already mid September he didn't want to wait longer. It would be early November by the time they reached Europe and the autumn winds might easily be gales by then. He had no desire to experience a storm in the Bay of Biscay.

"Time we called a halt, Henry."

William's shout interrupted Henry's thoughts and immediately he told Bokkis to stop the wagon. William was right, it was much later in the day than their usual time for making their outspan and resting the oxen.

Dismounting, Henry walked his horse to the stream where William was already standing beside Diamond as the horse drank.

"Initially, I thought we could travel all the way into the town during this morning trek, but we still have several miles to go and I'm sure everyone is hungry," explained William.

Henry was in full agreement.

"This is a good place to stop and you are quite right, it is better for the oxen to have a rest and the opportunity to drink and graze now. Even if we were to continue it would be the middle of the afternoon before we reached our destinations, weary and hungry. Besides, we need to bath and make ourselves look reasonably civilised before we meet Katherine's family."

"My family are familiar with my dusty, unkempt appearance when I return from my journeys, though I do try to make myself look clean and fairly tidy. I often stop here, but by the time I have travelled the remaining few miles I'm covered in dust again," laughed William. Then he continued, "There is plenty of water for the animals, reasonable grazing and if we walk a little way upstream where the water is clear and fresh there are one or two deeper pools where we can bathe."

"Right, we'll show the children where to go and then find a place for ourselves whilst Lukas is preparing the meal. There isn't much food left, but tonight we should be offered a full dinner in very civilised surroundings."

"I'm looking forward to some fresh fish. My mother has an excellent cook and the fish is bought as soon as it's landed. It is the one thing I anticipate savouring after many months of meat."

There were no crocodiles in the mountain streams and the children thoroughly enjoyed the opportunity to play. Jane was happy to let them splash about laughing and calling to each other whilst she concentrated on washing her hair and trying to scrub the dust from her fingernails. The sun was warm on her shift, but the water was icy and she shivered as she lowered herself in. It was always difficult removing the damp clothing that hid their bodies from prying eyes when the time came to dry themselves and dress in their clean clothes, but with a struggle they managed it. Then Jane brushed their hair as they wriggled and protested at the painful tugging, especially Isabelle, whose curls always seemed to be in a tangle.

James would never stand still until she became really cross with him, but she always gave him a hug when the ordeal was over.

Jane had searched out the least worn pieces of clothing for all of them and as they approached the camp again they all looked neat. Unfortunately, they no longer had any boots or shoes and all were barefoot.

Seeing his children without shoes made Henry feel very uncomfortable. How could he possibly introduce them to Katherine's family dressed like this? He sought some way of rectifying the problem but was forced to concede that there was nothing he could do until he had been to the bank and obtained enough money to shop for clothes and shoes.

Gruffly he ordered, "Come to the table now. We are ready for prayers."

The children did as they were bidden then sat quietly to eat. Lukas had prepared an odd meal as he seemed to think that he should use up all the available stores. There were dishes of porridge with jam or pickles and some overcooked beans with a stew made from dried beef.

Everyone coped valiantly and Jane was kept occupied encouraging James to eat, though she tried to listen to some of the conversation between father and

Mr William, who were making arrangements for future meetings.

"I will drive my baggage wagon round to your warehouse tomorrow morning," Henry stated, "so that we can unload all the goods that aren't mine."

"Yes, that would be most suitable. I will be there all day and probably for the rest of the week. I shall certainly be too busy unpacking my own wares today to deal with any extra merchandise. I have to separate my own goods from the ones I have merely transported and keep strict accounts of them. Then I must count out the feathers and store them safely where they won't be damaged. After that I must make sure that the hides have been dried properly and stored correctly so that they remain in a saleable condition. The ivory has to be weighed and all the small items counted into boxes. Even before all this I must immediately ascertain the current market prices before some alert rascally buyer tries to make a quick profit and cheat me out of mine. The predators are always waiting when they think they can make a dishonest shilling."

Henry concurred, "I am fully aware of people like that they are to be met everywhere." William continued, "If you need any help to sell your wares I will find time to assist you. I can introduce you to some of the overseas agents and the local exporters or if you prefer it you can make a list of all your wares and leave them with me to sell for you. I shall, of course, have to charge you a fee as this is my business and there will be a lot of extra work involved. However, you know me well enough to know that my charges won't be excessive and will save you a great deal of time."

Henry immediately responded, "That is most kind of you and I accept your offer. I am not over eager to be drawn into meetings with agents. I am not a trader and shouldn't really be trading at all. The goods I have are all presents that I cannot keep myself and they mustn't go to waste. Besides, I need to clothe my children and I have the boys' education to consider. If you could arrange the sale then I will most happily reimburse you for your trouble."

They shook hands on the deal.

"I shall need to see you at the bank within the week as I have to repay my debts to you and ensure you receive payment for the carriage of goods from Matabeleland. We shall need to work out the value of your sale goods, too. If you agree to the valuation, I'll deduct a percentage for my trouble and do all the selling for you so that you needn't be directly involved in trading."

Henry wasn't too sure that the arrangement would leave him with an entirely free conscience, but it was decidedly better than actually dealing with the agents himself. Perhaps he should give the money to the Missionary Society, even though many of the items were gifts to himself personally. He considered this for a time and was almost persuaded that this was the right thing to do when his reverie was interrupted by a shout of anguish from Isabelle. She had inadvertently trodden on an insect or other small creature (for no one saw it) that had stung her and her howls of pain, accompanied by her flailing arms as she tried to pull herself away from the table and scene of her discomfiture, considerably upset the other children.

"It hurts. Oh, it hurts," cried his younger daughter, as Henry immediately rose to investigate the reason for this annoying disturbance.

He was inclined to be brusque as he bade her to cease her lamentations and show him the source of her pain.

As he viewed the white pinpoint spot in the centre of a rapidly red and swelling area, he was reminded forcefully of his own failings as a father to provide his children with suitable footwear and guiltily he felt he could hardly blame Isabelle for his own shortcomings.

Instantly, he assisted her to hop over to the stream to sit with her foot in the cold water, which gave her immediate relief from the sharp sting. He then went to search in his medical box for the white alkaline powder he used on such occasions.

Having received the attentions of her father and the commiseration of Mr William as well as her siblings, Isabelle felt satisfied. Even Fox had come across to lick her hand in a gesture of support.

Then, as the servants began to clear away the tables and chairs and to in-span the oxen, Isabelle, clutching Jane's arm fiercely, hopped back to the wagon with the exaggerated appearance of someone bravely bearing the agony of severe discomfort calculated to induce the utmost sympathy from everyone.

Satisfied with the response, Isabelle accepted William's offer to lift her up into the wagon, where she sat looking woebegone as everyone was occupied with preparations to leave the out-span.

As William would soon be leaving them to head for his father's warehouse in Burg Street near The Strand, not far from the customs house, he took this opportunity to say a brief farewell to the children as they took their places in the wagon.

It was a cheery parting, for they knew that they would all meet up again, possible several times during the next two weeks.

CHAPTER 42

The strong wind blew constantly and loudly from the mountains toward the sea, taking the children's breath away and making conversation a trial except for someone close by.

Despite this and the thick dust in the wind, the journey through the town streets to the Bradfords' house was an enthralling one for all the children who, with the exception of Jane, had never seen anything like it before.

The immensity of the sea had them gasping, though from a distance they had difficulty in believing that it was indeed water. It looked solid.

Every time he caught a glimpse of the shimmering sea, James crowed with glee. "See see sea. I see sea," he chanted happily.

"Look at all those white houses," said Jane, eventually, pointing them out to her little brother to distract him slightly and stem the ceaseless singsong repetition.

"There are thousands of them," Harry declared. "But they don't have roofs. Where are the straw roofs, papa?" He had to shout against the wind to make himself heard.

Henry, who was walking his horse alongside, explained, his stronger voice carrying more easily as the wind was in his favour. "They all have flat roofs, Harry, thatching is never used here because of the danger of fire. A fire raging in thatched roofs could wipe out a whole town, especially with a wind like this to spread it along."

"These houses are very big," remarked Isabelle shrilly, determined to be in on the conversation and pointing to a large terraced building on the left of the road. "Why are the windows so high up?"

Henry looked at the row of terraced houses they were passing and smiled to himself. His children had seen so little of life that everything was new to them, whilst he himself hadn't even thought to question a double storey terrace. "There are many houses in Cape Town all built together like this Isabelle, so that several families can share one building, but each family has a separate part of it and they have rooms upstairs as well as downstairs."

"How can a house have rooms up there? How do the people reach them? Isabelle persisted, with a puzzled look.

"Papa told you that it was upstairs," said Harry scornfully, not knowing what 'upstairs' might be, but wanting to show his superiority.

Jane knew all about stairs.

When they had visited Cape Town all those years ago Mother would urge her brightly, 'up the wooden hill to dreamland now' when it was bedtime.

The steep flight leading up to darkness had frightened her and she longed for a comforting hand as assistance and reassurance
Mother was carrying baby Harry and a candle, Aunt Janet was carrying Isabelle, who was still a baby too, and there was no-one to hold her hand.
She had had to stifle her fears and follow them.
The wooden steps had sounded hollow and she thought they might collapse, but somehow they had all reached the top safely and she had slept with only one nightmare to waken her.
On the very first morning, as she was coming down these frightening stairs, she had slipped and fallen almost halfway. It was a painful memory. Now she heard father's description with renewed disquiet.
For once, Henry was patient with the questioning and took pains to explain the necessity of a staircase.
"Inside every one of those houses there are stairs, just like those steps there, leading up to the doors, only longer. People walk up the stairs to bed. When you stay in Grandpapa's house you will have to go upstairs to bed."
This novel idea appealed to the three little ones and for a time they were silent as they pondered the thought of sleeping up in the air and having to climb steps to reach there.
The terraced houses and the numerous white houses with flat roofs were certainly different from anything the children had seen before.
"That is the New Market over there," Henry pointed out, and as they gazed across to where father was pointing, Harry spotted the Castle ahead.
"That is not a house," called Harry suddenly, pointing to the building close to the sea on their right hand side. "It is huge and it is a funny shape," he added.
"It is the Castle of Good Hope and it has five sides, that is why it looks so odd. Most buildings have four sides," explained Henry carefully, delighted to be able to impress his family with his knowledge of Cape Town.
"Oh, a hexagon," proclaimed Isabelle nonchalantly.
"You mean a pentagon, Isabelle." Harry was quick to correct his sister. "A hexagon has six sides, hasn't it, Jane?"
Isabelle looked pleadingly at her big sister, "I'm right, aren't I? You always think you know everything, Harry, but you don't."
Jane hated to point out to Isabelle that she was wrong and thereby disappoint her little sister, so she tried to diffuse the situation, though she knew she had to be fair.
"Let's try to count the walls of the castle and see if it has five sides. We might see some soldiers there, too, as it is a castle," she suggested. Without directly confirming Harry's assertion, she subtly added, "If the Castle has

five sides it is a pentagon, Harry. If there are six sides then Isabelle is right."
They couldn't actually see all the sides so it wasn't possible for them to be sure how many there were, but father had stated there were five and father was always right.

Jane was fully aware that Harry would remember the conversation. Father had somehow missed out on this interaction since the children were facing the wrong way and he couldn't hear their remarks, but Harry would no doubt ask father about the castle later and point out Isabelle's mistake whilst parading his own knowledge. For the moment, however, a noisy disagreement had been avoided and as there were so many fascinating sights to occupy their attention a pointless altercation was temporarily forgotten.

The wide, dusty streets were crowded with people of different nationalities walking or striding along or standing and gossiping with friends. Almost all were wearing a variety of brightly coloured clothes and equally fascinating hats. Soldiers, sailors and policemen were amongst them in their distinctive uniforms as yet unknown to the children.

Harry had noticed that there were many people wearing conical hats and such a novelty aroused his curiosity.

"Papa, can I have a hat like that one that pointed one over there?" he asked loudly.

Henry didn't need to look to understand what his son meant by a pointed hat. The Cape Malays' distinctive headgear was a common enough sight.

"Those people are Malays," he said shortly. "Muslims. No, you can't have a hat like that."

The subject was abruptly closed.

Harry was bewildered. Neither the word Malays nor Muslims meant anything to him, but he had admired the hat. It would be fun to have a hat like that.

Jane hadn't heard of Muslims either but she had often heard father use the term malaise when he was referring to sickness and especially mother's illness. Now she looked carefully at the people in the pointed hats to see if they looked ill, but it was too difficult to tell if people here were ill or whether their complexion was their natural skin colour.

Some people were carrying bundles of goods on their heads or baskets of wares in their hands and a few had buckets of water carried on wooden poles across their shoulders. Others seemed to be on errands of importance, judging by their speed and determination.

There were dogs, too. Dogs everywhere, of all shapes and sizes, trotting about singly or in small groups, but they didn't seem to be in frightening packs such as those the children had seen in other towns.

They could see more ox wagons with their equally long spans on the street ahead or sometimes in the streets at each side, whilst everywhere there were carriages pulled by horses. These, as well as a number of horsemen, were dashing past at great speed, heedless of dogs, people or other vehicles, which excited Harry, and he bounced about on his seat as if he were one of the riders.

There was one carriage that he found particularly fascinating. Pulled by four horses, there were more than ten people sitting on benches along each side.

"Look at that carriage," he shouted excitedly. "That must be for a big family. I should like to ride like that."

Jane remembered the strange word she had almost forgotten. "It's an omnibus, Harry. People who want to travel, but don't own a carriage, pay money to travel on an omnibus. Where is the omnibus going to, papa?" she asked loudly.

"It's the Wynberg omnibus," Henry informed them. "Wynberg is a village where many people like to go and live away from the smells, dust and noise of Cape Town. It is a long way away and it takes many hours to reach there, even though the omnibus can travel at eight miles an hour. That is three times faster than we usually travel."

The carriages, the streets, the people, and the houses with their multiplicity of shining windows, were an unbelievable sight to the four pairs of eyes drinking in the scene, despite the wind and the dust that sometimes made visibility difficult and occasionally got into their eyes. Jane thought that it would be easy to get lost in this town where there were so many streets and they seemed to go on forever.

"I hope we shan't get lost," she said tentatively to Bokkis.

He laughed. "I know my way round Cape Town, little missy, don't you fret. I have lived here many years."

He could certainly turn the corners with great skill, thought Jane admiringly.

Bokkis gave a great laugh and then a sigh of happiness.

"I shall see my family tonight," he told Jane confidingly, though in fact he had to speak rather loudly.

Actually, Bokkis had several families. As a transport driver of many years who spent nearly half of the year travelling, his need for a woman's comfort couldn't be denied. He solved it easily by taking a wife whenever it suited him and he visited each of his families regularly, if infrequently, bringing great happiness to each. Of course, he kept all this knowledge to himself. He didn't like to boast.

Henry felt that truly God was with him during the next two weeks. The Bradfords had welcomed the family warmly, despite the underlying sadness for all of them and once they had recovered from their first shock at the appearance of the shabby, dusty, travel-weary and barefoot children, they did their utmost to make their stay comfortable.

The girls were instructed immediately to call Katherine's parents Grandmama and Grandpapa and her sister Janet as Aunt Janet, even though they were not related, so that they could feel as much part of the family as were the boys.

Once the family had been settled into their rooms, the children were given a good wash and tidied up and then taken directly into the town on a shopping expedition to remedy their lack of footwear whilst Henry attended to the unpacking of their personal goods.

The following morning, as he had planned, Henry took his sale goods to William's warehouse in Long Street near its junction with the Strand.

The street was narrower than Henry remembered and the smells assailed his nostrils unpleasantly. He was glad that Bokkis had been able to manage with a span of only twelve oxen, since the wagon was considerably lightened by the removal of his trunks and boxes, as manoeuvring the shorter span was considerably easier in the narrower street. It would take only a short time to unload, then the wagon could be driven away to the farm owned by his father-in-law.

Inside the warehouse he found William unhappily presiding over his books in the office, surrounded by piles of his own merchandise.

"This is the worst part of my business, Henry," William confessed. "I cannot afford to employ a clerk to work for only a few weeks each year and my father's man of business is too busy to assist me at present, but it is a pleasure to see you. I trust your family is well?"

After exchanging pleasantries for a further five minutes they organised a space in the warehouse to accommodate Henry's merchandise, separate from the goods that he had transported for Joseph from the King's Town.

Together they spent the morning unloading then cataloguing Henry's commodities before setting out to share some much-needed refreshment.

William had to laugh at Henry's expression of disgust as the heat, smells and dust assaulted their noses and lungs when they stepped out into the street.

"I think you must have forgotten what Cape Town is like at this time of the year," he remarked. "Perhaps you haven't visited this part of the town before. There is the smell of the gasworks all the time and when the wind is in the other direction there is a distinct aura of fish from the fish market not too far away, in addition to the revolting miasma from the grachts, that is canals in your language, Henry. I have been trying to persuade my father to find a better site for our warehouse, but the grachts and smells are everywhere in this town, that is why the south-easterly is called the Cape Doctor, as it blows the smells and their consequent sickness out to sea."

Henry was trying not to breathe too deeply as he battled the wind hurtling down the street and only responded when they were indoors and sitting down to lunch.

"I have noticed that the canals are full of the vilest filth imaginable and that there is a desperate shortage of water, as well as lack of sanitation in Cape Town, but that is a problem experienced by most large settlements in England as well as here. Now, if you don't mind, perhaps we should discuss brighter topics as we eat."

Smilingly, William addressed himself seriously to the beefsteak pie he had chosen and ate with the single-minded enthusiasm of a hungry young man. Henry, carving into his beefsteak more slowly, but with equal pleasure, disdained the wine chosen by his companion and drank water instead. Both chose to eat fruit after their large repast.

"So tell me, Henry, are you still serious about leaving the boys here in Cape Town? Most people prefer to send their children to school in England. I know that the education here is improving, with teachers arriving from Britain and new schools being built, but customs die hard and you have the choice of taking them to England with you now."

"The boys will do well here, William. They will live with Katherine's parents and her sister. Their Aunt Janet was engaged to a Captain stationed at the castle many years ago. Unfortunately, he was sent to India with his regiment and died there. She vowed never to marry and has accepted her state as a spinster destined to comfort her parents in their old age. She will look after the boys as if they were her own, and they couldn't do better. The Bradfords are comfortably situated and the boys will lack for nothing. Besides, my life is here in Africa. From the day I arrived in Matabeleland, I knew that I was destined to spend my life there. I cannot like the Matabele. They are immoral and godless. I abhor their attitudes, their behaviour and their customs, but for Jesus' sake I must love them. They are God's children, too, whatever I may think of them. I know that God has chosen me to bring a light into their darkness."

Henry spoke with such fervour that William could only marvel at the sacrifices he was prepared to make by devoting his life to caring for and ministering to a tribe of people who were indifferent to his efforts.

Henry would be faced with deprivation, sometimes amounting to starvation, as well as danger, isolated from all that made life worth living, William thought, for a cause in which he believed so wholeheartedly that nothing else mattered; that of saving the souls of the heathen.

But Henry showed that he was also human when he added. "Of course, I shall be able to see more of the boys if they are in Cape Town than if they were to go and live in Yorkshire. I shall be able to take leave regularly and perhaps even take a sabbatical, which will allow me to observe their progress. Communications between Cape Town and Matabeleland are still slow but they are improving and are much quicker than the mail service from England."

Accepting Henry's arguments, but still unconvinced that Harry's education would be better in Cape Town, William could only nod his assent.

Their meal being finished, they parted company, William to return to his accounts, Henry to visit the Union Steamship Company Offices and arrange for a passage at the earliest possible date. In this, he was fortunate, as he was able to book berths for the three of them sailing two weeks hence on Thursday 28th of September.

Satisfied with his endeavours, Henry rode back to the Bradfords' house in Hope Street in a light-hearted mood.

With his father-in-law to advise him, Henry visited a tailor that afternoon, where his measurements were taken and he was promised half a dozen shirts and two suits within the week. Three pairs of boots were procured during the same afternoon and with most of his pressing requirements fulfilled, Henry had only his finances requiring his attention. These could safely be left until William was available to conclude their arrangements the following week.

With the children safe in the care of their aunt and their grandmama, Henry was pleased to spend several days with his father-in-law.

Andrew Bradford had been a highly successful farmer and businessman in Yorkshire in the past. When his wife's health and that of his youngest child became so precarious as to be deemed dire, he had sought professional help. Doctors and friends had suggested that he should take Ellen and Simeon to the Cape of Good Hope, which was noted for its healthy climate and the only possible cure.

Andrew had immediately decided to retire, and left his two eldest sons to manage the family farms, whilst his two younger ones took charge of the textile firm he had founded. With his own fortune and a regular guaranteed income, Andrew and his wife with Janet, Katherine and Simeon, the three youngest of their twelve children, set sail for the Cape of Good Hope in 1857.

The sea journey was beneficial for Ellen, who began to thrive, and with the purchase of a fine house in Hope Street, Andrew was positive that he had made the right decision. The Bradford family adapted quickly to the new life.

Unfortunately, the town wasn't as healthy as people supposed and Simeon's life may well have been shortened when he contracted a gastric illness within a few months of their arrival. Despite the attendance of the foremost doctors, twelve-year-old Simeon died.

Andrew sought to ease his grief by searching for an occupation to fill his empty hours. He had soon realised the need for good horses in a town where horses were used by the military and by the transport companies. The army in India also required mounts for their many campaigns and there was a growing interest in horse racing in the town itself.

Andrew bought a farm on the outskirts of Cape Town and imported good sound stock from England and Montevideo.

Within a few years, what had begun almost as a hobby, a means of alleviating pain, had developed into a thriving business. Even now, when there was a severe depression in trade in the town, there was a constant demand for horses.

Henry was more than happy to leave the town behind and spend his days with Andrew on the farm.

Ellen had the comfort of her garden. Observing the growing plants was her solace and the time-consuming daily planning was a satisfactory fulfilment.

In a town where gardens were a symbol of wealth and success, Ellen's was a model envied by many. The house was situated close by a mountain stream that provided ample water for both the house and the garden. Ellen's gardener had diverted the stream to run through the garden itself, winding and trickling between the flowerbeds into a small pond, before overflowing and continuing down to houses further along the street.

When she wasn't actually gardening, Ellen busied herself painting exquisite watercolours of the flowers she grew. Gradually, she extended this to include some of the glorious wildflowers she discovered on her walks.

Jane's knowledge of gardens was limited to the purely practical ones she had known in Matabeleland or seen on the journey south. All were dedicated to producing food.

The missionaries and traders were, of necessity, pragmatic people. Time, labour, water and effort could never be wasted on the purely aesthetic.

Now, to see a large garden filled with shady trees, unusually shaped beds of colourful and sweet scented flowers with a stream and a lawn of smooth green grass, was like stepping into a wonderland. It was an oasis of peace where brightly coloured butterflies fluttered peacefully and the clear sounds of birdsong delighted the ear.

It was true that the shouts of vendors could be heard from time to time as they called their wares but for the most part there was comparative silence.

Grandmama had allowed the children to play on her lawn that seemed to them surprisingly green, but the hot weather sapped their energy and curtailed their games after no more than half an hour. Then, overhot, they lay in the cooler shade, hoping for a cooling, thirst-quenching drink.

On the first afternoon they had all been delighted and excited at the thought of riding in a carriage into the town.

The actual experience had been less than happy.

The carriage was hot, dusty and stuffy and once they had all been fitted with new boots, Grandmama had taken them to a store where they could be provided with a set of clothing suitable for attending church on Sunday.

This proved to be a lengthy procedure and even Jane had difficulty in standing and waiting quietly until Grandmama was satisfied.

Although these shops were large and filled with so many goods that the children had much to occupy their eyes and their minds, trying to keep the younger ones controlled was a great trial and Jane sighed with relief when they finally entered the coach once more. That, however, was not the end of the day's purchases.

Grandmama believed that ready-made clothes were inferior ones and she strongly maintained that her grandchildren deserved better. She determined, therefore, to obtain suitable lengths of cloth that very afternoon from which at least two outfits could be made for each child. With this in mind, she ordered the coachman to drive to Stuttafords the drapers.

The children were instructed to remain in the coach whilst Aunt Janet and Grandmama spent the next three-quarters of an hour in the shop.

The children had never known such torture. In addition to the stifling heat the new boots were beginning to feel very uncomfortable indeed.

After weeks of wearing soft home-made shoes followed by more weeks of walking barefoot, the well-fitting leather boots pinched horribly. The dust and the sweat made them all feel itchy and fractious.

Jane did her best to keep them occupied by playing counting games and guessing games, but their unhappiness only increased.

Finally, James went to sleep lying across Jane's knees and though she was pleased to be relieved of his wailing, grumbling, squirming and crying, his weight pinning her legs to the seat with the added warmth of his body was distinctly unpleasant. Even worse, she daren't move, in case she should disturb him and provoke a tantrum.

Relief was a long time in coming.

CHAPTER 43

The next day, Jane learned that they had just two weeks to spend in Cape Town.

From that moment onwards, she tried to hold onto every minute, to keep the memories of her own small family forever in her mind. She prayed ardently and often that somehow they could all remain together, either that the boys would be allowed to come to England with them or that father might consent to Isabelle and herself remaining in Cape Town.

Inexorably, the days slipped past far too quickly however hard she clung to them by rising early, spending every minute she possibly could with the boys and sitting beside James' bed long after he had subsided in sleep.

Gently, but firmly, Aunt Janet attempted to loosen the bond by distracting Jane, encouraging her to consider her own desires occasionally and leading her thoughts to the pleasures of the Cape whilst she herself became an indispensable, caring friend to the boys.

She made these efforts partly because of the love she had shared with her younger sister, with whom she had been close, and partly because of her own deep compassion and understanding of the almost unbearable sorrow Jane would face within the space of a week or so as the ship bore her away.

Janet Bradford knew only too well the lifelong strain imposed on female children who were forced to become 'little mothers' at an early age, and never had time to be themselves.

There were many days of joy.

After church, on the two Sundays they spent together in Cape Town, the children were taken for walks in the magnificent Botanic Gardens.

By this time, their feet had adjusted and become accustomed to formal footwear, so that the gentle strolls along the tree-lined paths were pleasurable, rather than the painful experience of the preceding days.

Jane and Isabelle tried not to stare or display their amazement at the crowds of people.

There were ladies in flowing, beautifully ornate crinoline dresses and neat attractive hats, accompanied by smartly dressed men in their top hats walking proudly beside their families.

In the centre of the gardens they could gaze at the fountain and marvel at the constantly falling water whilst watching the swirling fish in the pool below.

They were also taken to listen to the regimental band playing stirring tunes. Surrounded by a crowd of people all dressed in their Sunday best, they were engulfed in the emotional patriotic fervour and Jane was proud once more to be English.

Most of the tunes were new to the children, but they soon came to recognise 'Rule Britannia' and other patriotic songs.

Aunt Janet took them to an auction market one Saturday, where they could see hundreds of goods being sold and they were excited by the noise engendered by sellers and bidders alike.

Father took them to the seashore one morning to see the boats, but they found the smells there appalling. The fish offal, along with rubbish of all kinds, was scattered along the sea edge, whilst the people engaged in the trade of selling the fish were noisy and unattractive.

On one morning, they were taken to the Parade Ground where the soldiers were marching and Harry decided that one day he would be a soldier with a smart uniform and a musket. For the next few days he marched round the garden with a stick held at his shoulder, calling commands to James, who tried hard to march behind him, but succeeded only in stepping onto and tripping over his stick.

Jane was entranced, amused or anxious in turn, but they came to no harm.

Perhaps their most memorable day was when they were taken to Green Point to see the menagerie.

The people of Cape Town and visitors from abroad flocked here to see the strange collection of wild animals and the little ones were enthralled to see them close up. For Jane, who loved animals, the sight of the caged beasts and birds was unsettling and she was glad when the visit was over, but she was delighted by the boys' enjoyment.

On another day, they were all bundled into the coach and driven out to the farm, where Grandmama had arranged for them to have a picnic.

Despite the wind, there was almost no dust here and the day was a perfect one for all of them. Harry was allowed to ride and even James was taken up to be trotted a short distance away and back. He wanted more, but accepted papa's refusal with good grace and Jane felt proud of him.

She was awed by the proximity of the huge mountain they called Table Mountain and the view they had over the town from this place on the slopes. She fixed this day in her mind and knew she would remember it for the rest of her life.

Twice, William came calling, and he played cricket or skittles with the children on the lawn.

He was pleased to make the acquaintance of the Bradfords, as he regarded the meeting as beneficial. One day, he would need to buy a good horse and knowing a sound horse breeder could only be an advantage.

Henry and William had met at the bank in Adderley Street and satisfactorily concluded their business.

Despite the depression, Henry's goods had fetched an attractive price and his bank balance, whilst not large, was certainly comforting.

The calendar that Jane studied each day indicated that the remaining days were rapidly disappearing.

Neither Harry nor James was fully aware that this glorious holiday was about to come to an end and that they would all too soon be abandoned by papa and their sisters, their real family.

They had been told that Jane and Isabelle were going to school in England and that papa would take them to England in a ship, but the concept was beyond them until the day of departure dawned.

Early on the morning of Thursday 28th September, with the trunks and boxes packed, locked and carried out to the carriage, Henry called his children together.

"Today, we shall be going on board the ship that is in Table Bay. You will say goodbye to each other now and I want no unnecessary fuss. Harry and James, you will be allowed to travel with us to the jetty, but only if I have your promise that you will not cry or shout as we leave. You may say 'Farewell' and wave to us but that is all. If you cannot behave like English gentlemen then you will stay here. Do you understand?"

Two pairs of blue eyes stared up at him. Harry and James were shocked and unbelieving. Mutely they nodded their heads. Jane, gazing down on the bobbing golden hair, felt as if her heart was about to stop. She held Harry close for a long moment and felt his controlled sorrow before he pulled himself abruptly away to share a quick hug with Isabelle

James clung to his big sister who had been his 'little mother' for almost as long as he could remember. It was Jane who had to let him go and give him a gentle little push to one side as she gulped back the tears she dare not shed.

Aunt Janet came briskly into the room as if she had been waiting for just this moment, dispersing the tension that threatened to overspill into tears and wails.

"Come along now, girls, you must say goodbye to Grandmama and then let's check that you have all the things you need. Harry and James, you can wait here for a few minutes, then I'll be back to collect you."

Her calm, no-nonsense approach dispelled the gloom and like automatons the girls let themselves be ushered from the room to say goodbye to Grandmama, who had no intention of sitting in a hot dusty carriage then going to stand on a windy jetty just to wave to rapidly diminishing figures in a lighter.

Grandmama had been kind to them and it was sad to say goodbye to her, knowing they were leaving behind the comfortable existence they had so enjoyed. Surreptitiously, Ellen Bradford wiped away a tear as she gave the children a gentle embrace and bade them a safe journey.

Shortly afterwards, they were squeezed into the overcrowded carriage, though Grandpapa was accompanying them on his horse, and driven down Hope Street, through the neat blocks of streets until they entered Adderley Street.

Jane stared through eyes that were no longer wide with amazement at the flat-roofed houses they passed at a trot, the street lights on the corners, the wandering dogs and the shops with their large glass fronts. The crowds with their multicoloured clothes, the carriages and the busyness of it all that had appealed to her only fourteen days ago, had lost their charm.

Jane could only stare dully. Everything passed by in a blur.

Her only feeling was an ache that encompassed her whole being.

Isabelle was in a state of fearful excitement, fearful of going out in a boat on that unstable enormous stretch of water, fearful of being on a ship going into the unknown but excited because she was going to do something that Harry couldn't.

The boys still couldn't believe that they were to be left here whilst their family set off without them.

Silently, they all stood on the jetty as their baggage was lowered into the boat. With only one last quick hug for her brothers and Aunt Janet as a comfort, Jane felt herself being lifted into the boat with Isabelle, to be followed by father.

Isabelle, unnerved by the sensation of rocking up and down, clutched frantically at Jane. Jane felt the hand holding hard onto her arm but couldn't take her gaze away from the little party on the jetty.

Grandpapa stood straight and still, whilst Aunt Janet held tightly to the hands of the two boys as the lighter pushed off, and urged them to wave, whilst calling adieu.

Her eyes still glued to the small figures being buffeted by the wind but waving bravely and forlornly, Jane let the tears slide silently down her cheeks.

If father should notice, she could excuse her weakness by explaining that the tears were due to the dust in the wind.

ACKNOWLEDGEMENTS

Ted Davison, for supplying information on South Africa.
Western Cape Provincial Archives and Records Service.
Melanie Geustyn, of the National Library at Cape Town, for information.
Gabriel Athiros, of Cape Odessey, for information about Cape Town.
Douglas House for his time, efforts and technical help.
Jillian May, who kindly read the first draft and gently criticised.
John House and Diane Rasteiro for their support and encouragement.
James Openshaw for kindly searching out essential maps.
John Troughear of Sable Publishing House for proofreading and tidying up the draft.

* * * * * * *

BIBLIOGRAPHY

'Victorian Life at the Cape' by Catherine Knox
'Cape Town The Making Of A City' by Nigel Worden and others
'The Cape of Good Hope, 1806 – 1872' by Graham Viney and Phillida Brooke Simons
'Gold From The Quartz' by Rev Elliot
'Missionary Travels' by David Livingstone
'Eleven Years In Central South Africa' by Rev TM Thomas
'First Steps In Civilizing Rhodesia' by Jeannie M Boggie

* * * * * * *